The Sign of the Dragon

MARY SOON LEE

JABberwocky Literary Agency, Inc.

Praise for *The Sign of the Dragon*

"It's as close to perfect as a book can get... I already know this will be one of my favorites for the year. A favorite book, period."
— Beth Cato, two-time Rhysling Award winner

"What an utterly beautiful, impressive, & occasionally heartbreaking reading experience!"
— Ann K. Schwader, SFPA Grand Master

"This is an absolutely stunning work that I will read and reread."
— T. Frohock, author of the Los Nefilim series

Praise for *How To Navigate Our Universe*

"Mary Soon Lee's remarkable collection of poetry traces this journey, capturing the wonder of the celestial bodies that comprise our universe, the elegance of the rules that guide its evolution and the humanity of those who search to better our understanding."
— Andy Connolly, Professor of Astronomy, University of Washington

"Ranging from witty to elegantly serious, apolitical to frankly feminist, this collection celebrates astronomy and space exploration — but never limits itself to those topics."
— Ann K. Schwader, SFPA Grand Master

"With eloquent celestial-themed verse, Mary Soon Lee educates, delights, and surprises."
— Beth Cato, two-time Rhysling Award winner

"Mary Soon Lee's extraordinary poetry brings [that sense of wonder] rushing back, rekindling the visceral awe in even the most rigorously sophisticated contemporary models of the universe. Combining a whimsical and graceful voice with a deeply probing mind, she reminds us that at heart, science remains a human endeavor."
— Jake Yeston, Editor, *Science Magazine*

Praise for *Elemental Haiku*

"*Elemental Haiku* is a special alchemy of poetry and science that demonstrates something that's easily forgotten: that these chemical elements are more than just symbols in squares on a table."
— *The Sciku Project*

"Lee is a master alchemist of words."
— Salik Shah, *Strange Horizons*

Books by Mary Soon Lee

Elemental Haiku
The Sign of the Dragon
How to Navigate Our Universe

To Lucy, William, and Andrew,
who were there during the writing,
and in memory of my parents,
who gave me Xau and Donal,
though I didn't realize it at the time.

Table of Contents

Crown

INTERREGNUM

Sixteen years old, fourth son,
still they sent him to the mountain

together with his brothers
before their father's body stiffened,

the kingdom suspended without a king:
four princes, one crown

(a crown he had no use for,
a crown of war, alliances, duty).

He slept on straw near his horse,
displacing the stableboy,

waited for his eldest brother to return
triumphant, ready for the throne—

then brother after brother vanished
into rock and ice and cloud.

The steward took his sword,
his shield, sent him out at dusk:

no torch, no guide, no horse,
no servant, no food, no water.

Snow deepened under his boots;
he waded through drifts,

fell once, twice. The wind mocked him;
he thought of the warm stable,

the bed of straw, his horse,
sleep—but sleep meant death,

so he stumbled on. The wind
called his brothers' names.

He shouted back his own name;
the wind laughed. Snow fell.

He walked half-blind; sleet kissed
his forehead. The wind said sleep.

He sang to drown it, sang hymns,
nursery songs, drinking songs,

dirges, ballads, marching tunes,
the love songs his mother had favored

(she who was bartered for peace
to a man she'd never met).

He fell, pushed himself upright,
saw a black cloud speed against the wind.

She landed beside him, her breath ash,
snow steaming from her wings.

He knelt, but did not beg,
and asked after his brothers.

"One slept. One fought. One pissed
himself. They didn't taste like kings."

She laughed. "And you? What will you
pay for a crown, little princeling?"

"Nothing. I don't want it."
She flamed, and he saw himself reflected

in her scales, a kneeling, shivering boy.
"Then why," she asked, "are you here?"

"Because they sent me." He stopped. "No."
He was so tired, he couldn't think—

"Because the kingdom needs a king."
He struggled to his feet.

"And what will you pay for the crown,
little princeling? Gold? Men? A song?"

"My freedom!" he shouted at her.
"Well," she said, "that's a start."

*

Years later, on a spring morning,
his queen asked, greatly daring,

about the woman whose name he cried
in his sleep. "Not a woman," he said,

his heart on the mountain
where he entered his kingship.

GUARDED

Waking, that first morning,
in the king's bed—*his* bed—
dawn brightening the paper windows,
Xau saw the guard, Gan,
standing in the same position
he had been in when Xau fell asleep.
(Had he stood there all night?
Or silently paced the room?
What if he'd needed to piss?)
Xau didn't know what to say,
but he would not say nothing.
Xau got out of bed, bowed to Gan,
poured a cup of water:
"Thank you. Are you thirsty?"

Gan stared at the boy, the king,
standing there in his pajamas
holding out a cup of water
to him, the guard.
A small thing,
but the boy's father
had never done it.
"Thank you, Your Majesty."
Gan bowed back,
took the cup, drank.

TRAINING: WEIGHTS

Tsung, used to masking
his reactions so opponents
did not anticipate his moves,
showed none of his disappointment
as he assessed the boy
who would be both his charge
and his student:
sixteen years old,
close to full height,
but the boy could not even lift
the medium-weight bar.

Clear then to Tsung that the boy
was not his father's equal,

was not his brothers' equal.
Un-muscled, overlooked
fourth son.
Now king.

The boy, Xau,
struggled to hold the lightest bar,
sheened in sweat,
arms trembling,
but at least he held it,
didn't use his newfound rank
to demand a rest.

Small consolation
to carry away
when training was done,
when Tsung instructed the guards
who would protect the boy
for the rest of the day,
when Tsung himself returned
to his darkened room
and burned incense
for Xau's father,
the weight of that loss
hard to lift.

SUCCESSION

One king dead, a new one crowned.
The royal court seething with rumors,
fibs, fears, fancies, phantasms, fictions.

Gossip for innkeepers, beer drinkers,
wine merchants, vintners, sots, soldiers,
servants, slatterns, strumpets.

Mothers name their sons for the new king;
little girls name toys after him;
little boys crown themselves with twigs.

The royal bees in the royal hives
huddle in clusters, shivering,
waiting for spring, ignorant of kings.

GRIEF

The new king to his steward:
    Is it required that we visit
    our father's grave?
    Then we choose not to.

To the guild master:
    We may be young,
    but we are old enough to count.
    Where are the missing barrels?

To his tailor:
    Take it in an inch.

To the palace barber:
    For such little stubble as we have,
    we prefer to shave ourself.

To the captain of his guard late at night:
    Secure the stables.
    Let Khyert—the boy who sleeps there—
    let him be.
    Thank you.

To Khyert the stableboy:
    It's all right. Stay.
    We are no different than we were
    a month ago when you helped us
    muck out Micha's stall.

To his generals:
    How many cavalry at that outpost?

To his senior advisor:
    We will fight for them,
    if necessary, die for them,
    but we will not weep for their approval.

To the captain of his guard, another night:
    Check the stables. Let Khyert stay.
    Thank you.

To Khyert the stableboy:
    You're welcome. Your old blankets
    were more holes than blanket.
    Good.

Her near front fetlock?
Micha likes the snow.

To his generals:
If they attack, what options remain?

To his senior advisor:
We will fight for them, die for them.
It appears we will even consider
marrying for them.

On being shown the portraits of his dead brothers:
Give them to our sister.

To Khyert the stableboy:
Let us help you with that.

To a visiting envoy:
Perhaps. We are of an age to marry.

To his tutor:
War looms. Lessons are done.

To Khyert the stableboy:
We are angry, not sad—
our father should have warned them.
No.
We are fine. We will be fine.
No.
We... miss our brothers.

To his tailor:
Take it in again. We were too fat before.

To Khyert, four years later:
We never thanked you for your kindness.
Thank you.

MAP

Vast forests here
diminished to a
handful of trees.
Above the name
of every city:
three tiny houses.

Down the eastern edge
ink horses gallop
over ink rivers.
Beyond their hooves
a reddened swath
of hostile lands.

To the west,
lines of arrowheads
mark the kingdom's
mountain border,
flecked by flame
where dragons dwell.

The northern seas
a wash of blue,
dotted by islands
where stirs an evil
unguessed by those
who drew the map.

NOT SO

An hour till dawn,
Princess Mei sat on her bed,
zither on her lap,
playing her tangled thoughts
into the notes.

Two months since her father died,
since the steward took away her brothers
to select the new king.
Mei, not considered—

A knock on the door: "Come in."

—Xau, her fourth brother, now king.
"We heard you playing. Are you well?"

Mei nodded. "Are you?"

"Well enough."
Xau sat on the floor
as his guards searched her rooms.
He looked tired, rumpled, thinner,
more boy than king.

In public, Xau so assured.
Now, not so.

Mei hesitated, then blurted out,
"Will you really marry her?"

"Yes."

"But you've never even met her!"

"Shazia has never met us either.
We need to secure peace with at least one
of the countries threatening us."

Mei wanted to ask
whether she, too, would be married
to someone she'd never met;
two months ago
she would have asked.
Now, not so.

Instead she sat opposite Xau
and they played cards
as if nothing had changed,
as if their brothers were still alive,
as if Xau were not king.

Only at the end,
day brightening the paper window,
Xau said to the floor
so that Mei could barely hear him,
"Sometimes we cannot breathe
for men looking at us."

Then he got to his feet,
composed, the king again,
bowed and left.

Xau had found his path.
Mei unsure what hers would be
or whether any part of it
would be of her own choosing.

TRAINING: STANCES

Two months since the boy Xau
came to the throne,

two months in which Tsung—
captain of the king's guards—
had watched the boy
for the better part of every day,
but something awry, that afternoon
in the innermost courtyard of the palace,
that Tsung could not identify.

Xau's shift from Leaning Horse
off-form, stiff, his stance in Snake
rigid rather than solid,
and before the training session
the boy had been scathingly sarcastic
when the Finance Minister
tried to manipulate him.

The boy unimpressive as a warrior,
yet a natural ruler:
considered but decisive,
impartial, measured.
Except today.
The minister had been shaking by the end,
just as the boy shook now
when Tsung touched his shoulder
to correct his position.

A crane flew into the courtyard,
landed near the boy,
who held motionless in Snake
as the bird stepped delicately
right up to him
and tilted its head
inquiringly.

The boy's face opened, gentled,
and it came to Tsung then
that what he'd seen before was a mask,
measured and deliberate
as a training stance.

The boy crouched down,
laid his fingers on the crane's
feathered softness.
A long stillness,
Tsung aware of something passing
between crane and boy,
something that hurt to watch.

Then the crane flew away.
The boy's face closed.
The boy returned to Snake position,
completed his exercises.

It wasn't until next morning
that Tsung remembered how Prince Keng
used to call the boy Little Crane,
Keng the only one of the older princes
who had paid attention to the boy,
Keng who would have turned twenty-four
the day before.

THE HORSE LORD

Three months into his kingship,
the young king rode to claim fealty
from the horse lords.

They bowed to King Xau,
their braided hair swinging
like so many horse tails,
their gold armbands glinting.
Though their leader bowed with the others,
Xau read in his eyes a mocking amusement.

"Such a great king," said the horse lord,
"such fine armor, such a large army.
They must think you too young
to look after yourself."
He raised a hand. "Fetch a cup
of mare's milk to help the king
grow into a man."

The counselor beside Xau
made the finger motion for death:
he had advised Xau again and again
to assert authority early.

Xau had but to order his archers
to shoot the horse lord,
a word, a gesture, quickly over,
but Xau said instead, "Save the milk
for your many and excellent children.
Let the two of us walk to the hills—"

"Sire!" said the counselor.

"It is their custom, is it not?"
said the king. "You taught us that."

"It is our custom," said the horse lord.
"Yet your father never honored it."

"Sire!" said his counselor.
"You are the ruler of these men,
not one of them.
Their ways are not our ways!"

The king said to the horse lord,
"Before we take your horses for our wars,
we will honor your custom."

The horse lord bowed,
and this time the king saw no sign of mockery.
They set aside their weapons, their armor,
left the king's entourage
gabbling behind them.

They walked to the hills,
drinking from each other's water bottles.
The king knew they might meet bears... or dragons,
that even wolves could kill them both.
He didn't care.
He was fed up with prudence, politics, protocol,
people prostrating themselves.

A clear, cold night.
Trees silhouetted by the half moon.
No wolves howled. No bears prowled.
No dragons threatened.
But sometime after midnight
the wild horses came:
first a pounding of hooves,
then the smell, heat, breath of them:
forty, fifty, too many to count.

The horse lord knelt
while Xau went from horse to horse,
speaking to them,
laying his hands on them.
At his touch, the horses
lowered their heads.
All night, more horses came.

At dawn, the two men saw below them
the hillside covered in horses.

Eighteen hundred horses followed them back
to the other horse lords (who prostrated themselves)
and the king's soldiers (who cheered)
and his counselors (who looked peeved).
In front of all these people
the horse lord bowed so low
that his braid brushed the dirt.

"Your horses are in our heart,"
said the king. "We will ride them to war,
but we will not squander their lives."

And Xau gave one of the horses,
a black stallion,
to the horse lord,
who rode it and none other
for the rest of his life.

TUTOR

"That turned out rather well,"
said King Xau, triumphant,
happy as I'd ever seen him.

The other counselors
studied the patterned rug
on the floor of his tent.
Even Artoch, who had shouted
at the king two days ago,
had nothing left to say since
the king's rashness had led,
all too conspicuously,
to success.

"Good outcomes are not proof
of good decisions," I said.

"So you think our decision was poor?"

"Very."

"What should we have done then?"
King Xau directed the full beaming force
of his pleasure upon me—

the lowest of his counselors,
there only as a courtesy
for having taught him
the rudiments of algebra
when he was the least and youngest
of four princes.
"Should we have killed him as Artoch wished?"

"Yes," I said, "or ridiculed him:
cut off his braid, or spanked his bottom,
or merely laughed at him."

"So we could make an enemy rather than a friend?"
He looked decidedly less pleased.
"So we could take his horses by force,
rather than having them come to us?"

"So you could live."

All trace of pleasure left him.
I imagined what he would have said
had the two of us been alone—
that it wasn't a life he wanted,
neither prudence nor diplomacy nor war.
He wore power well, but he wasn't one
who craved it, not like his eldest brother.
In another world, he might have been
a farrier or a groom.
In this world, he stalked out of the tent.

"That turned out rather poorly," I offered.

"Perhaps," said Artoch, "but what you said
needed to be said."

"Perhaps," I said, "but he's unlikely
to thank me for it."

"Where do you think he went?" said Artoch.

"To his horses."

When the king returned, a long while later,
I saw by the quietness in his face
that I had guessed correctly.

"There are lessons we do not like to learn."
He nodded first to me, then to Artoch.

"We will... strive to be more cautious,
but we will not hide.
We will not watch from a hilltop
while our soldiers fight our battles below."
He sat down cross-legged on the rug.
"Sit with us. Eat with us. But no more advice.
Not tonight."

It is hard not to admire him,
but I do my best not to show it.

HORSES

They do not call him king.
They say nothing.
They smell of grass, hills, sweat.

    Men call him king.
    Men sing about him.
    Men will die for him.

The horses say nothing,
but they came (unasked),
willing to die for him.

    He has a wart on his toe.
    He has shouted at men
    who could not shout back.

But on horseback,
he is almost the man
he needs to be.

TRAINING: HORSE

Tsung's duty clear,
but yet he hesitated,
watching from his hilltop vantage
as the boy—King Xau—sat ahorse,
five soldiers mounted to his left,
five to his right.

The reins trembled in the boy's grip:
only the second time Tsung had seen
Xau's nerves show.

Tsung did not wish to be the one
to disillusion him,
but unless he did so
the boy would likely lead them to disaster.

Tsung gave the signal
and the boy started forward,
accompanied by the ten soldiers,
the horses in good formation.
The boy called out, signaled left,
and all the horses swerved
in perfect unison.

Well enough,
but no test of what the boy
would face in war—
Xau insistent that he would command
his cavalry in person:
seventeen years old,
untried in battle.
The kind of courage
that led to the loss of armies.
Or kingdoms.

Tsung gave another signal.
Trumpets blared, drums boomed.
Guards ran toward the horses:
flapping long red banners,
tossing clods of dirt
at the king and his men.

Who rode as if they were alone,
as if they were eleven shadows
of a single faultless form,
the horses turning to Xau's command
almost before Tsung saw the boy
giving the hand signals.

Tsung on the hilltop, stunned,
signaled a third time.

From a stand of trees
a troop of lightly-armored cavalry
charged full at the king.

Xau turned his men to meet them,
galloped headlong at his mock-enemy,

the two lines of horses
thundering toward each other.
Two hundred yards apart,
the cavalry troop stopped, mid-charge,
one man thrown from his horse,
so sudden their halt.
(Unplanned, unbidden, unaccountable.)

For a moment,
Xau and his ten men rode on in perfect order,
toward the baffled, confounded cavalry.

And then Xau called out,
gave the signal to end the exercise.
The boy dismounted clumsily,
sprinted over to the thrown man,
took off the man's armor,
ran his hands along the man's limbs
before helping him to his feet.

Tsung on the hilltop,
clapping and crying,
looking down at his king.

SHAZIA

This is not a discussion.
You will marry him.

Her father's words haunted Shazia
as the covered chariot sped her
further and further from home.
What had she thought?
That her life would be different
than her sisters'?

The royal guards rode escort
without once speaking to her;
her brother drove the chariot
as if she were not there,
as if the wicker bench
behind him were empty.

She slept in fragments,
dreamt of warrior kings:
crowned, armored, their swords red.

Awake, she thought of two kings:
the one who was trading her away
and the one he was sending her to marry.

On the eighth day, the mountains.
The road climbed. The horses slowed.
Her brother ordered her from the chariot.
Crossing the clear bright ceiling
of the world, her father's words,
her past, her future all folded small.

*

King Xau met them in the foothills.
Younger than she, barely seventeen,
already he had the same assurance as her father.
He swept Shazia and her brother
inside the circle of his soldiers.

"They told us," Xau said,
looking at her directly,
"that you speak our language."

A gray-bearded man beside him
translated his words as he spoke.

Shazia raised her chin.
"Yes. I speak five languages fluently."

"But your brother doesn't?"

"He speaks only Ritan and Sumbrese."

"Good. We are to be married tomorrow.
If you wish, it can be a paper marriage.
You may live near our sister
in a separate part of the palace."

Instead of translating what Xau said,
the gray-bearded man substituted
a pleasantry about the weather
to which Shazia's brother nodded.

For the space of two drawn breaths,
Shazia thought of agreeing.
She pictured herself alone in a room,
reading in late afternoon light:
a quiet and inconsequential life,
nothing save her marriage of any import.

"No," she said. "Without sex—"
she used the word deliberately
"—there can be no children. Without children,
I would have half a life, a paper life.
And the peace between our countries
would be a paper peace, easily torn."

*

Three months later,
the night before Xau rode to war,
he gave Shazia a black kitten,
a purring softness.

"We found her in the stables," said Xau,
"half-starved, but fierce, determined.
She reminds us of you. If you don't want her,
our sister has offered to take her."

"No! She's mine. I won't let her go."
She didn't weep, didn't beg Xau to stay.
She raised her chin and said,
"Come back safe to me."

WEDDING GIFTS

Bows, breastplates, broadswords,
spears, scabbards, shields,
helmets, horses, harnesses.

Salt, saffron, cinnamon,
incense, silver, silk,
ivory, jade, a dragon's egg.

Bowls, bottles, bells,
masks, mirrors, music.
One treaty, long-sought.

TRAINING: SPARRING

Queen Shazia should not have come—
useless to pretend she came
for her husband's sake—

   Each day King Xau's guards
   took turns attacking him.

With fist, foot, knee, elbow;
with dagger, sword, spear.

Swift, serious, silent:
slashing, stabbing, strangling.

(Did all skill possess grace?
The guards like dancers.)

She should not have come—
a single time, perhaps,
not over and over—

Moves too fast for her to follow,
but even in such swiftness

skill steered strength,
softened the final strike:

Xau bruised, not bloodied
by bare hands, wooden weapons.

The guards' skill mortal
but contained, constrained.

Each attack reenacted
until Xau could counter it.

She should not have come—
but useless to dissemble:
this the apex of her day—

That first time Xau lunged
swifter than his guard:

the guard on his back,
grinning like a fool,

like Shazia, unable to
stop herself from clapping.

WOLF MOON

The first full moon of summer,
beneath the ancient stone arch:
Donal the Red King, red-haired,
red-handed in war, and his queen.

His bare back against cold stone;
Queen Fian's breath, her moist mouth,
her pale hair unbound, gleaming,
moonlit, under the dark arch.

Her hands warm, Donal hard as iron:
Fian screamed in the old language,
the words unknown to him,
surging through him like blood.

Fian knelt, licked him clean,
said, in plain Innish,
"Kill him. Kill Xau the Usurper.
Take back my country for me."

Then from the hills a yowling,
older than language,
as a hundred wolves
raised their heads in answer—

He woke an hour past dawn,
naked, no memory of the night
save Fian's pale hair gleaming.
He must have drunk too much.

Donal pissed against the arch.
He had a mind to go to war,
to kill the fucking Horse Boy
before the year was out.

CROSSING

Who saw them raft over the river,
three hours before daybreak?
Who saw their half-darked lanterns
glimmer on helmet and shield?

> The heron in the reeds,
> the crane startled to air.

Who heard the drip of oars,
water dropping on water?
Who heard the horses nicker,
the jangle of bridles?

> The otter curled in her holt,
> the rat warm in his burrow.

PIGEON SIX

Pigeon Six: no rank,
no name beyond her number,
but she the soldier sent
with news of the invasion.

Pigeon Six: no honors,
her message all that mattered
to any but the pigeon-girl
who cleaned her empty perch.

SETTING OUT

Ten men, ten horses, hooves ringing
on the straight street from the capital,
day brightening about them—

Half his army at the Innish border,
but King Xau himself eight days away
even if he rode from dawn to dusk,
changing horses at every way-fort—

Half his army might be lost in eight days:
Xau tried to turn that thought aside.
Failed. He should have been there.
Should have set out weeks ago—

Ten men, ten horses, no baggage
but swords, bows, arrows, knives;
day warming about them—

Ten men: Xau should have set out weeks ago,
would not waste more time shepherding
the valets, aides, scribes, cook (a cook!)
that his steward thought his rank demanded—

Ten men: Xau, his personal guards,
and Khyert, lately a stableboy,
now promoted to factotum:
valet, aide, groom all in one—

Ten men, ten horses, no armor,
no tents, no grain, no time:
the day hastening by—

Xau looked at Khyert riding beside him.
The boy beamed back, eyes bright.
If any harm came to Khyert
that, too, would be Xau's fault—

Time wasted negotiating with envoys
who'd been sent to waste his time.
Half his army now at risk
and nothing Xau could do but ride.

THIRTY-EIGHTH WAR BETWEEN INNIS AND MEQING

FIRST BATTLE

Before:
    Waiting. Listening to the veterans brag,
    the captain's bad jokes.
    Lunch (stew), but Brennan couldn't eat,
    him being, it turned out, a coward.
    Waiting.
    Packing up for the night.
    Equipping in the morning.
    Bowl, cup, spoon, shield, sling, stones, knife.
    Waiting.
    Moving camp. (No one told Brennan why.)
    Waiting.
    Rain. Sent to the tents to sit
    in steaming sweaty smelly damp.
    Day after day after day waiting.

Battle:
    King Donal shouted,
    "Kill the fucking Horse Boy!"
    Drums, trumpets, horns
    as the captain led the slingers
    toward the enemy's left flank.
    Arrows, crossbolts whirred overhead,
    thunked into flesh
    as Brennan ran from side to side
    to confuse anyone
    who might be shooting at him,
    certain he was about to be hit.
    He chose a target, an archer—

black hair, wide nose, dark eyes—
scared-looking—
scared as Brennan, who balked,
couldn't aim at that scared face.
He sent the stone wide,
saw the archer's gloved hand release,
saw the man's dark eyes—
Brennan swallowed bile,
zigzagged, slung stone after stone,
not aiming, throwing wildly.
Worthless.
Useless.
Off to his right, Diarmid screamed,
clutched at a crossbolt in his thigh,
collapsed.
Horses charged toward them.
"Retreat!" yelled the captain.
Men ran past Brennan
as he helped Diarmid stand.
Diarmid took one step, swayed.
Brennan looked at the oncoming horses,
dropped his shield,
hoisted Diarmid over his shoulder,
staggered away,
expecting a crossbolt in his back
with each slowed step he took.

ROSE

Rose heard the horn call,
one drawn-out note
carried on the wind:
King Donal had lost the battle.

Two months she'd been the king's woman,
had heard all the stories about Donal,
the Red King—red-haired, red-handed in war,
who gutted enemies and left them to die.
He had never hit Rose,
but she hadn't seen him
lose a battle before.

She should run—
she grabbed her coat, two jeweled rings,
lifted the tent flap, let it drop. No.

She would not go back to being nobody,
a whore's unwanted daughter.

She paced the tent,
rebraided her hair,
checked she had linen for bandages,
boiling water, wine, cold meats,
the honey cakes Donal favored.

When Donal came at last,
he shouted at his guards to keep out,
grabbed the cup of wine, drank half,
tipped the rest on the ground:
"Get rid of the fucking wine."

Hastily, Rose put the flagon outside the tent.

"A boy. A fucking boy."
Donal sat down on the bed.
"A fucking boy and his fucking horses.
I've never seen cavalry like that."

Mutely, Rose offered the honey cakes,
the plate trembling in her hands.

"My boots," said Donal.

Rose knelt down,
but her hands shook so much
she couldn't unlace his boots.

"Stop shaking. I won't hurt you."
He kissed her, gently, on her forehead.
He was not usually a gentle man,
and she didn't know how to respond.
Tentatively, she kissed him back,
opening her mouth.

"Later, Rose. I want you to listen."

"Yes, Your Majesty."

"I won't hurt you.
I've hurt men, hurt my enemies,
but I've never hurt a woman.
And when I'm done with you,
if I'm ever done with you"—
he loosed her hair from its braid,

and tangled his fingers in it—
"I'll buy you a small house,
and you can grow old telling tall tales
about King Donal. All right?"

Rose nodded. She couldn't speak.
In all the tales about Donal,
no one had ever warned her
that he could be kind.

KHYERT

Outside: six soldiers, trained,
deadly, guarded King Xau's tent.
Inside: Khyert.

Khyert, lately a stableboy,
stood as generals, advisors, lords
met with the king.

Stood, quiet, after they left,
while the king cleaned his sword,
over and over and over.

"Horses," said the king,
wiping his sword, "lay in the mud,
legs broken.

"But we fought. We left them lying.
We did not stop. After the battle,
we killed them."

The king hung up his sword.
"Men were dying too.
We cannot think about them."

He sat on the edge of the bed
and started unlacing his jacket.
Khyert came over.

He helped the king undress,
turned down the wick in the lantern,
blew out the flame.

He stood in the dark,
hesitated before saying,
"It's not your fault. You had to fight."

He sat down cross-legged in his spot
by the king's bed, listening to the
small sounds of wakefulness.

After a while, when the king still
fidgeted, Khyert sang, too softly
for those outside to hear.

Eventually, the king slept.

MOON SWAN

Beyond the army encampment,
a tented market of wine sellers,
fortune tellers, a hundred harlots
hawking a hundred pleasures.

Among them, Moon Swan:
artist, musician, courtesan,
a woman long past her youth,
but at the height of her fame.

She whose fountained gardens
were tended by a dozen servants
left her walled estate
to follow the army.

She whose mastery of the zither
was unmatched in all Meqing
sang comic ballads to men afraid
they'd never make it home.

She who'd sold her time to kings
offered it now to boys
who'd never been to war before,
who brought nothing but their need.

Her need as great as theirs.
Only in wartime, only beneath
the grunts of the soldiers
did she hear his voice again.

And at night's end, he'd bow
to her across the tent,
her son, her soldier boy,
dawn shining through his shoulders.

THIRTY-EIGHTH WAR BETWEEN INNIS AND MEQING

SECOND BATTLE

Before:
    The captain's quiet praise
    for carrying Diarmid to safety.
    Undeserved praise.
    Brennan had failed the captain,
    had thrown wildly the whole battle,
    not aiming,
    though he'd been slinging
    since he was five,
    could take down a rabbit
    at three hundred yards.

Battle:
    Brennan useless as last time.
    Each time he chose a target—
    saw their face, their eyes—
    bile rose in his gorge.
    So he slung wild.
    Horses charged toward them.
    Men broke, ran past Brennan,
    who waited for the captain
    to order the retreat—
    saw him: askew on the dirt,
    arrow through his neck.
    A stone fitted to Brennan's sling,
    hurled at an oncoming horse
    before he thought.
    He aimed for the horses
    until he was out of stones,
    turned and ran.

Dusk:
    Went back with Finn and a shovel.
    Found the captain's body,
    blood-sodden, eyes staring upward.
    Brennan pulled the captain's eyes shut,
    but they wouldn't stay closed.
    Took turns digging with Finn.
    Neither of them about

to let the captain
be buried in a heap
with the other dead.

LEONG

Battle:
    Leong, who served double duty
    as both king's guard and surgeon,
    rode into battle at King Xau's left,
    the boy he'd been guarding
    for the past eight months
    and had grown to like.
    A fact Leong set aside.
    Fought.
    Targeted those with the range
    to reach the king: archers, slingers—
    drew, aimed, released;
    drew, aimed, released.
    Permitted himself neither triumph nor remorse.
    Downed perhaps twenty men.

After:
    Leong joined the surgeons
    in their tents.
    Applied scalpel, saw, forceps
    to soldiers skewered by spears,
    pierced by arrows,
    hacked by sword and axe.
    Permitted himself neither triumph nor anguish.
    Dispassionate. Skilled.

    Hours into it, he saw King Xau—
    a momentary lapse of Leong's control
    when he saw the king in the tents,
    when he thought the boy might be hurt,
    but the boy was well,
    had returned to talk to the injured
    for the second time that long day,
    now night.

    The boy, seeing him, came over, said,
    "Thank you for your work here,
    a service beyond your duties,
    but much needed."

Leong bowed. "I'm glad to help.
There are too few surgeons."

Xau looked searchingly at Leong.
"Until the war is over,
we release you from guard duty.
You are needed here more."

"No!" The word out before he thought.
He went to one knee.
"Forgive me, Your Majesty.
I would ride into battle beside you."

"We know.
You have done so twice.
This is only a temporary assignment."
The boy's voice soft,
his hand briefly on Leong's shoulder.
"But so long as this war lasts,
we would have you serve here."

As if a shadow lifted.
A moment before he understood why,
before he understood
what the king had given him.
If Leong ever had children, he'd tell them
what he'd done in these tents,
not what he'd done in battle.

Leong stood and bowed to the king.
"Thank you, Your Majesty."

Xau bowed back as deeply
as if Leong were a king,
headed back to the injured.

Leong took one slow breath,
reached for dispassion. Found it.
Returned to work.

MIDNIGHT

Tsung should not have come—
useless to pretend he came
to celebrate—
he stood in darkness

by Moon Swan's tent.

Two battles. Two victories.
In the distance,
a soldier's drunken laughter.

Nearer, from Moon Swan's tent,
rustlings, the murmur of her voice,
the sound of a man
celebrating.

Tsung, captain of the king's guards,
waited outside.

Soon enough, the man left
and Moon Swan stepped out
to hang the purple-shaded lantern
that advertised her availability,
her long hair pinned in a bun,
a faint fragrance of jasmine
as she moved.

"Captain Tsung." She bowed.
"An unanticipated pleasure.
*Seeing you after so long,
my heart lifts like the wings
of the swallows the day we met.*"

Lantern still in her hand,
she led him inside.

She who'd sold her time to kings,
gestured to the bamboo mat
on the dirt floor of the tent.
(The mat, a bed roll, the lantern,
water boiling on a brazier,
a chest, a teapot, two tea bowls.
Nothing else.)

Tsung set his weapons down,
sat cross-legged on the mat.

Moon Swan poured Tsung a bowl of tea,
sat down opposite him.
"What is wrong?"

"Nothing. I am well."

He took a sip of tea,
noticing neither the taste
nor its heat,
only Moon Swan's face,
his own confusion.

She reached over,
laid her fingers lightly
on the pulse of his wrist.
"The young king,
is that what troubles you?"

Tsung shook his head,
though Moon Swan was correct.
Tsung's duty to protect King Xau,
the king but a boy of seventeen,
a boy who might be killed
a hundred ways—

Tsung made himself smile.
"King Xau is well."

"Is he like his father?"
Moon Swan unpinned her hair,
as Tsung had seen her do
the first night Xau's father visited her,
years ago,
when Tsung was the youngest
of King Hao's guards,
left to stand in a corner
not knowing whether to watch
(in case the king was attacked)
or look away—

"No, he is not like his father."

"A weaker king?"

"A better king."
Tsung did not elaborate.
He took another sip of tea,
set the bowl down.
He should not have come,
should have stayed near the boy—
he got to his feet,
bowed. "I must leave."

Moon Swan stood,
placed her hand on Tsung's jacket
over his pounding heart.
"Stay, Captain. Rest.
You will do the king poor service
if you are worn out."

A truth there,
but he hadn't come
seeking rest—
Moon Swan standing so close,
her hand over his heart,
her long hair unbound,
the smell of her
mingled with jasmine—
heat in Tsung's face,
heat hard below.

He put one hand to her long hair.

     *

Later
    (after he was done,
    after he'd told Moon Swan
    such things as men said
    when they thought
    themselves in love,
    after she'd told him
    that she loved him
    and he'd smiled
    thinking that she said that
    to all her customers
    yet liking it anyway,
    after he'd fallen asleep
    beside her)
Moon Swan lay awake,
breathing him in,
watching over the man
who watched over the king.

THIRTY-EIGHTH WAR BETWEEN INNIS AND MEQING

THIRD BATTLE

Before:
    The retreat back to Innis
    harried by enemy cavalry.
    Pitching camp. Waiting.

Further back:
    Brennan's first two battles.
    Fitting stones to his sling.
    Unmanned each time he chose a target—
    saw their face, their eyes—
    so he'd slung wild, not aiming.
    His captain killed.

Further back:
    Herding sheep,
    slinging stones at rabbits,
    fancying himself a warrior.

Battle:
    Chance. Fate. Luck.
    Enemy cavalry neared Brennan's position.
    Men ran. Brennan stayed put:
    he couldn't aim at men,
    but he could aim at horses.
    No thought to it,
    stone, sling, arm, body: one motion.
    Hard to judge moving targets,
    yet he struck horse after horse.
    Ducked a javelin.
    Saw, then, the enemy king,
    the Horse Boy in his fine armor,
    the one who'd led the charge
    that killed Brennan's captain.
    No thought to it,
    stone, sling, arm, body: one motion.
    The slingstone struck the Horse Boy
    hard on his greave
    as the boy leaned over,
    drove the boy's foot clear out of the stirrup.

The Horse Boy toppled from his horse—
Brennan whooped in victory—
the boy—
a boy—
younger than Brennan's little brother—
Brennan bent over double. Vomited.
An arrow meant for his head
passed through emptied air.
Brennan ran.

TSUNG'S BATTLE

—stopped

—each arrow halted in its flight

—the pounding of Tsung's pulse suspended

—the boy, the king, Tsung's charge,
    toppling from his horse,
    struck by a rock

—between the rock's impact on the king
    and the king's impact on the ground
    that stuttered dread

(Before, an instant earlier,
Tsung's pulse pounded loud
as the wind's wet rush,
as the clash of metal on metal,
as the screams, the battle drums,
whilst Tsung rode beside the king,
the horses maneuvering
as if they were a thousand shadows
of a single faultless form—
a thing out of legend,
out of the old times
when dragons aided King Nariz—)

—stopped

—each drum halted between beats

—Tsung's breath paused

—the boy falling

—Tsung, captain of the king's guards, forsworn,
   the king he took an oath to guard
   unguarded

—between the rock's impact on the king
   and the king's impact on the ground
   no excuse
   no absolution

DOWN

In the tumult of battle,
the boy, the king, Tsung's charge
toppled from his horse,
lay askew in the dirt.

The cavalry faltered.
Drums beat. The wind blew hard.

Tsung, captain of King Xau's guards,
jumped from his horse,
yelled at General Qiang
to circle the horses about the boy.

Xau struggled to sit—
the boy armored so that Tsung
could not tell if he was bleeding,
how badly he was hurt—

The king looked at Tsung: "Help us up."
Tsung helped the king stand.
Five other guards round them now,
the cavalry ringed beyond that.

Drums, trumpets, shouts,
a volley of incoming arrows.
Tsung grabbed the king's shield,
offered it to him.

King Xau shook his head.
"We cannot hold it. Help us mount."

Tsung hoisted him up,
heard the small swallowed sound
the boy made at the jolt.

Xau refused bow, arrows, spear,

his left arm hanging loose.
Took his sword in his right hand,
dipped his head to Tsung:
"Thank you, Captain."

Tsung remounted beside him
as the king lifted his head
and shouted to his cavalry,
"Ride with us!"

Wind turned to rain
as the king rode forward.

DONAL

"Dismount! Kill your horses!"
King Donal yelled at his cavalry—
his cavalry? Hardly—

He sliced the neck of his warhorse
and it floundered in its own blood.

"Form a shield wall!"
Donal grabbed a fallen pike from the mud,
the shaft slick with rain,
and took a spot in the front line.
Xau's cavalry charged toward them.
Donal braced himself, pike ready,
but the wave of enemy horsemen split,
poured round to their flanks.

Several horses slipped in the mud.
Through the rain, pouring now,
Donal saw the horses halt,
then maneuver again, more slowly, and withdraw.

Rain. He laughed,
water running under his helmet.
Xau was pulling his cavalry back
to save his horses,
his precious, unbeatable horses—

Donal squelched through the mud,
the mud that had saved him,
and ordered his own soldiers to fall back.

He'd lost the first two battles

holding his few cavalry in reserve.
Today he'd tried to use his cavalry
and the fucking horses
stopped. Mid-charge.
And just stood,
immobile.

After today, Donal was ready to swear
that Xau was King of the Horses,
that the stories were all true—
that ten thousand wild horses
had galloped up to Xau
and begged to help him—
but Donal was buggered if his own horses
were going to follow suit.

He passed one of his cavalrymen
still standing, uncertain, beside his horse:
his horse that still refused to move.
Donal swung round and killed the horse himself.
Horse blood dripped from his sword,
his gauntlet, his greaves.

Enough. Time to talk peace, to play at truces,
then go back home and recalculate.
There would be other years to fight Xau,
to kill the fucking Horse Boy
and end his fucking legend.

SURGEON

Hurried across the tent, distracted,
wiping blood from his hands, his arms,
bowed as he walked past King Xau—

the king had visited the wounded
after each battle, chatting now
to the man with fractured tibia, lacerations—

walked past, but Tsung,
captain of the king's guards,
stepped in his path: "The king is hurt."

The king, seated by the injured man,
glanced up at the surgeon:
"We will wait our turn."

"Your turn is now," said the surgeon.
That much clear to everyone in the tent
except the king himself.

He appraised the king before touching him:
color good, breath uneven,
a boy of seventeen, not yet full grown.

He took the king's pulses,
both wrists, the twelve positions,
bared his left shoulder (dislocated, bruised).

Five tries to correct the shoulder joint,
the boy's color poor by the end,
hardly surprising.

But it did surprise the surgeon
that the king refused a sleeping draft,
refused to retire to his own tent,

that he stayed all night, talking to the men;
the war won, but half the injured
never to return home.

THE MATTER OF THE HORSES

General Qiang stood in King Xau's tent
with the king's other generals
and the king's advisors
and the king's guards
and the king's serving boy
and the king himself,
the tent crowded with men,
rank with sweat.

The young king sat on a stool,
his left arm in a sling,
a grimness about him
that matched Qiang's own mood
though the war was over,
the victory theirs,
the king's advisors jubilant.

Qiang hadn't slept last night.
Had tried to sleep. Failed.
Yesterday's battle still with him.
The horses. Mud, rain, blood.

In the tent, the talk moved
to the matter of the horses,
to how it could be exploited
for conquest.

"No," said the king.
One word enough to quiet the tent.
"We do not crave conquest."

"Even so," said an advisor,
"we should test the limits
of your control over the horses,
the better to employ it for defense."

The advisor turned to Qiang.
"General, how would you proceed?"

Qiang looked at the advisor,
a man who'd never fought a single battle,
who'd sheltered in a tent yesterday,
warm and dry,
while rain cascaded from Qiang's saddle, his armor,
turning earth and horse-shit to stinking mud,
Qiang riding on the king's right
(the king, injured, unable to hold a shield,
but still riding),
Qiang's horse maneuvering beneath him
before he even gave the commands,
all the horses in perfect unison
as if they were a thousand shadows
of a single faultless form—
a thing out of legend,
out of the old times
when dragons flew to King Nariz
and demons walked the earth—
the stench,
the pounding of hooves, of Qiang's pulse,
as he rode beside the king,
as the enemy charged full at them—

And stopped.

Every horse in the Red King's army
rooted to the spot
though their riders kicked them.
Whereupon the Red King,
red-haired and red-handed in war,

screamed in his barbarous language.
And then the enemy had slaughtered
their own horses,
slitting their necks,
the horses floundering in blood—

Qiang looked at the advisor and said,
"If it were my decision,
I wouldn't test the horses.
I would let them be."

"Even if inaction now leads to defeat later?"

"Even then."

Into the stretching silence,
the king spoke:
"What happened with the horses
is not a trick to practice and parade,
but a gift. A gift the horses gave.
A gift for which many of them died."

The king's gaze rested on Qiang, anchoring him.

Qiang touched his hand to his heart,
offered it palm-up to the king,
a gesture Qiang had never made before,
the sign of allegiance of warriors
in the old tales.

The tent crowded with men,
but for that moment
only the two of them.

TRAINING: RUNNING

On their ninth day back
within their own borders,
Tsung, captain of King Xau's guards,
watched that king run round and round
the fort's largest room,
a set look on the boy's face,
a look that held nothing
of triumph.

(Three battles. Three victories.
The invaders routed.)

At length, Tsung called out, "Enough!"

Xau dipped his head to Tsung, but said,
"We would run further."

"You have run enough. Rest.
Let Leong examine your shoulder."

The barest pause—
a fraction of a fraction of a breath—
Tsung holding the boy's gaze,
aware that Xau wished to defy him—
but before the other guards took notice,
Xau bowed low to Tsung.

The boy ran from something,
that much Tsung perceived.
Not Tsung's place to ask
what that might be.

His duty only to serve his king
as long as the boy allowed him.
His duty and his pride.

WHAT XAU RAN FROM

The sound of battle—
drum rolls, the blare of trumpets;
battle cries, screams, groans, pleas;
metal clashing metal.

The soldiers who died for him.
Quick or slow. The horses.
Bones, teeth, shit, blood.
The stench.

The man, after, in the surgeon's tent,
half-choking on his own blood,
but beaming wide, because Xau
clasped his hand. His red grin.

How Xau's soldiers cheered
when he rode back, victorious—
No. Not their cheers,
but how he'd liked it.

THE QUEEN'S WAR

A short war.
Thirty-one days
from when King Xau
rode away from her
to the day she learned
of his victory.

Thirty-one days
that Shazia ran the palace
as if unafraid,
juggling ministers,
ambassadors, servants
with deft assurance,
ensuring palace and city alike
were fully provisioned
in case of siege.

A long war.
Thirty-one nights
that she went to sleep
not knowing whether Xau would return;
whether, if he did not return,
the enemy would advance
to the capital,
to the palace—

With only her guards as witness,
she sat up in her bed
half the night, reading;
reading each page
twice, three times
before she fathomed
what it said,
the kitten Xau had given her
curled on the pillow beside her.

(The enemy would kill her if they came,
or rape her and then kill her,
but the cat—
maybe they would let the cat live.)

A month of nights,
but she wept only once,

when she thought
of the kitten,
how some man,
some war-drunk man,
might kill it—
a small death,
paltry beside
the battle-dead,
but she could not hold it.

Three weeks after
the news of his victory,
Xau returned,
intact, unscarred,
yet not as he was:
the lightness in him gone,
or buried so deep
he could not find it.

But he was home.
Let that be enough.

NIGHT

That night,
King Xau's first night home from war,
with their guards
in the hall outside,
Shazia undressed Xau.

Between them,
between her hand and his skin,
unasked questions:
Did he kill anyone?
How many people?
How many did his army kill?

Shazia undressed Xau,
but he did not reach for her.
(Did he watch men die?
How many men?
How many did he lead to their deaths?)

She told him how the kitten
had chased a moth,
the kitten's tail puffed up

as if the moth were a wolf.
He nodded, but did not smile.

All that night,
he spoke only once,
when they were first alone,
when he told her he loved her,
staring at her oddly
as if she were a fragile thing,
as if she might break
were he to touch her.

They lay six inches apart
in the dimness
of a half-darked lantern.

An hour or more
before Xau reached
for her hand.

Two more nights
before he held her against his body.

A month before he told her
a part of what he'd seen.

MEMORIALS

On the third day after his return,
after King Xau had seen every other minister,
after he had spoken (at length)
to each visiting ambassador,
after five separate requests,
King Xau granted the Finance Minister
a private audience.

The minister, a man three times Xau's age,
resplendent in gold-embroidered silk,
bowed three times.
"Your Majesty, the magnificence
and swiftness of your victory
enriched the treasury
beyond expectation."

Xau, lacking splendor,
his leather jerkin well-worn,
his trousers unpatterned and undyed,

neither stood, nor bowed, nor nodded,
but fished a sheet from the paperwork
littering his desk.
"Explain this."

The minister beamed.
"It is my authorization
for your triumphal arch,
awaiting your countersignature—"

"No." Xau tore the sheet in half.

"Your Majesty?"
The minister looked about
as if searching for support,
but there was no one present
save the king and two guards.
"Would Your Majesty prefer a grander edifice,
one befitting the greatness
of your accomplishment?"

"We do not want an arch at all."

"If Your Majesty is concerned about the cost,
rest assured that the reparations rendered
by the Innish more than suffice—"

"No. No arch. No monument. Leave us."

The minister bowed three more times on his way out.

Tsung, captain of Xau's guards,
who had watched in silence,
said quietly,
though it was not his place to say it,
"The minister thought to please you."

"We know."
Xau took a blank sheet of paper,
glanced over at Tsung.
"Thank you."

The king started to write,
stopped, looked at Tsung again.
"We should learn patience,
but the minister measures war
in ounces of gold."

Tsung said nothing further,
neither that the Finance Minister
would be baffled by Xau's disapproval,
nor that the capital was littered
with triumphal monuments,
nor that Xau needed rest.

In silence, Tsung stood
while the king wrote
in his own hand
(breaking tradition)
to the parents of a common foot soldier,
a handful of sentences
about their son Guo
and how he had died.

STABLES

In the stables,
King Xau found himself again,
or found the man
he might have been
if he had never been crowned,
never gone to war,
never led other men
to their deaths.

Half an hour at a time
squeezed between meetings
and training exercises,
the stables secured by his guards.
Only Khyert, once his stableboy,
inside to watch him groom Micha
or Pica or Narson or Romer,
to sit beside him on the feed sacks
breathing leather, manure, dust,
the scent of the horses.

Xau's words already spent
on rice farmers, ministers,
ambassadors, advisors;
on irrigation, taxation,
alliances, strategy,
so that sometimes
he had no more

than a handful of words
for the boy—
Khyert, younger even than Xau,
turned fifteen that autumn.

But sometimes they spoke
at length about the horses,
both Xau's own mounts
and the others in the stable,
about the condition of the pastures,
the chafing of a girth,
a horse off its feed,
while Khyert rubbed oil
into the saddles,
asking nothing of Xau,
then or later.

Xau listened
more than he spoke,
received more than he gave,
though he asked nothing of boy or horses
beyond their company,
but boy and horses alike offering him,
unasked and without restriction,
their hearts.

TRAINING: DARK

No reason to be afraid:
the courtyard so dark
King Xau couldn't see the walls,
couldn't see his own hands.

No reason to be afraid:
all eight of his guards
circled about him,
armed with sword, bow,
dagger, knife, staff, ji—

Xau barefoot in his pajamas,
weaponless,
cold and getting colder,
afraid,
though he should not have been—

"Begin."

Tsung's voice,
captain of Xau's guards,
Tsung who had decided
it was time Xau learned
to fight in the dark
(though it would doubtless be months
before Tsung judged Xau ready
to actually fight).

Xau ran into freezing darkness,
trying to remember the size
of the courtyard,
trying to make out the walls,
(failing),
forcing his breathing to steady
though with each step
he grew more uneasy,
afraid he'd crash into stone
or slip on ice.

"Turn."
Tsung's voice level.

Xau stretched his arm out
as he turned:
his fingertips brushed stone.
An effort to steady
his breathing again,
but Xau would rather hit a wall
than slow down.
One thing to be afraid,
another to show it.

Eight times round the courtyard,
Tsung's voice catching him twice more
when Xau would otherwise
have run into stone.

"Now stretch."
Tsung's voice easy.

Xau stretched,
moving from one stance to another,
trying not to shiver,
the sky perhaps a lesser darkness
than the courtyard round him,

but his guards, his own body
still lost to him
in the moonless, cloudy, freezing dark,
one week past winter solstice.

The flagstones cold, hard
beneath his cold bare feet,
the air moving chill about him,
the faint sound of another man's breath,
of what might have been footfalls—
Xau abruptly certain
that his guards had moved closer,
that they were almost touching him—

Eight men armed with sword, bow,
dagger, knife, staff, ji:
deadly, trained—

Each of them capable
of killing Xau barehanded,
with ease—

A fraction of a fraction of a breath
while Xau considered that,
and, having done so,
relaxed for the first time
since he stepped into the courtyard.
His guards deadly,
but their loyalty
as sure as the flagstones
beneath him.

So that Xau neither screamed
nor struggled
when someone seized him
and hoisted him high in the air,
holding him up there
while Tsung lit a lantern.

Xau, blinking back brightness,
saw that it was Li lifting him,
Xau's newest guard,
one month in his service,
a man who fought as if weapons
were an extension of his body,
as if he were dancing.

Li set him down gently.

"A good beginning."
Tsung bowed to Xau.
"What did you learn?"

"Trust. Why Li and not you at the end?"
Xau had to press his teeth together
to stop them chattering.

"Li has better night vision.
I might have hurt you
if you had struggled."

Xau bowed then to each of his guards in turn,
feeling a little foolish
and very cold
in his pajamas.

Li took off his jacket
and handed it to Xau
as if it were a simple matter,
as if Li had forgotten
that Xau was the king
or had set that fact aside,
as if Li cared only
that Xau was cold.

A year since Xau came to the throne
and very little since then simple.

He nodded his thanks to Li
as he went indoors
with his guards.

DRAGONSLAYER

It's true enough,
I killed a dragon—
an old dragon with a maimed wing, mind you,
crippled by some foreign prince.

The dragon came down the mountainside
after it was injured,
right into our village.
I remember women screaming. And men.

The smell of roast meat.
Then the dragon came up to my smithy
and fired the roof,
and I filled up with fire myself
and ran at it with an axe in one hand,
a spear in the other.

Three days afterward
the king's soldiers arrived.
Too late to bury the dead,
but the captain offered me
a place in the army,
and, being a young fool,
I said yes.

Oh, I've done well enough,
but most of that's luck—
I've seen better men than me
killed quick by arrows
or slow by gangrene.

So. I've had my moments.
Lots of harlots, no wife—
I will say this for dragon-killing:
the harlots like it.
I never fought for honor
or any such nonsense,
just for my men, my pay,
food, drink, and, yes, the harlots.

But the new king,
now that's different.
They say he bested a dragon himself,
and what if he did?
I can still get fired up,
rage into battle.
Like when I fought that dragon,
rushing at it like a young fool.
Not for honor,
nor glory,
not thinking much at all.

But that's the smaller part
of what makes a king.

You should have seen him this summer.
Not much more than a boy,

but he rode at the front of the charge
in his first battle
like a king should,
and afterward he got down off his warhorse
and walked in the mud,
looking for survivors,
and went into the surgeons' tent
and spoke to those waiting
for the knife.

He came out of that tent
and vomited.
I know. I was there,
checking on one of my soldiers.
The king looked right at me and said,
"Next time I won't throw up. I promise."

Now that's a king.

COMPANIONSHIP

Fall. Winter. Spring.
The birth of their first child.
Quiet days that quickly slip behind them.
His hand reaching for hers
after supper is cleared.
Her arm reaching for him
in her sleep.

A strategic marriage,
a political marriage.
Unasked-for, unnegotiated,
this friendship.

Shazia softly singing to their soft-cheeked son
in her own language, the words unknown to Xau,
but the string of sounds stored in his memory,
so that one night,
far from her,
on the eve of his second war,
he will remember each rolling syllable,
the way she smelled,
his son's hand fisted
round his finger.

TRAINING: CARRY

An escape,
that was how it felt to Leong,
as he rode with the king's other guards
and King Xau himself
away from the palace
and the three-day-long celebration
of the king's eighteenth birthday.

(Leong refused to contemplate
the panoply that would attend
the king's coming-of-age
in two years' time.)

Early morning,
the air green-gold beneath the leafing trees,
clear, crisp, fragrant with honeysuckle—
a few squirrels, a solitary deer, rabbits,
a cacophony of birds—
Leong, King Xau, the other guards,
even the horses in high spirits.

Only Tsung, captain of the guards, severe,
eyeing each bush as if it might attack.

(Leong was glad not to be captain,
suspicion not something
that came to him naturally.)

They rode for half an hour,
stopped in a clearing bounded by oak trees,
dismounted,
watered and tethered their horses.

Tsung bowed to Xau.
"In honor of your birthday,
we will do the work for you today.
We will take turns carrying you
as if you were injured or ill—"

"We are!" Xau coughed theatrically.
"We have a cold. Our throat hurts."

Tsung glanced at Leong,
who served double duty
as both guard and field surgeon.

"The king," said Leong,
"has a mild cold,
hardly worth even calling it a cold,
but if he feels weak
we could return to the palace."

"Remarkable," said Xau,
"how much improved we feel
after Leong's sympathy."

"Then Leong may carry you first."

Leong lifted the king
over his shoulders,
clasped the king's right hand
firmly in his own right hand,
and headed round the clearing at a jog.

"Be still!" said Leong
when the king squirmed.

Xau stilled, but he said,
"Your bow keeps bumping us."

"That's a fine bow," said Leong.
"Make sure not to damage it."

"We are not damaging it.
It is too busy battering us—"

Leong clambered onto a boulder
and jumped down.

Xau grunted as they landed.
"Your shoulders are nothing but bone."

"They are fine shoulders.
Make sure not to damage them."
Leong scrambled awkwardly over a log,
and set off round the clearing
for a second time, panting:
Leong the least fit
of the king's guards,
a deficiency Tsung tolerated
because Leong was both their best archer
and their only surgeon.

"We would prefer if you refrained

from banging us against the branches,"
said Xau reproachfully.

"Hardly a bang. More of a scrape."
Leong looked over at Tsung.
"Is that far enough, Captain?
The king has evidently put on weight."

Tsung nodded. "Dao, your turn."

One after another
the guards carried the king
round and round the clearing,
the king voluble
(and increasingly imaginative)
in his complaints,
except at the end,
the king entirely silent
while Tsung carried him,
an inward look to his face
even when the captain jolted him.

Leong frowned,
wondering whether the king
had somehow been injured—
though Xau grumbled endlessly
about minor ailments,
the king had made almost no complaint
the one time he was seriously hurt.

Tsung set the king down.
"Now we will eat."

"No," said Xau.
Darkness then in the king's eyes.
"First we will practice carrying you."

"That is not required," said Tsung.

"It is required," said Xau.
He looked at each of his guards in turn,
a look that passed into Leong
and would never leave him.

Six years Leong had served Xau's father,
had been willing to die for him,
had known himself valued,

but never equal.

Yet Xau looked at Leong
as if he had misplaced
the boundary between them,
or set it aside.

"It is required," said Xau.
"We will not leave you behind
if you are hurt."

A weight in Xau's voice,
in Tsung's face,
in Leong,
who had ridden into battle
with both of them.

A bird sang out,
loud and sweet
in the spring air.

"If it comes to that," said Tsung,
"you must leave us.
That is the way of things."

"No," said Xau.

Tsung bowed very low then,
and Leong followed Tsung,
and about them the other guards bowed also.

Gan, a giant of a man,
six and a half feet tall
and heavily muscled,
stepped forward.
"Carry me, Your Majesty.
If you can manage that,
you can carry anyone."

Xau half-staggered, half-walked
once round the clearing
with Gan over his shoulders,
before lowering Gan with a groan.

"Now we will eat," said Xau.
"Except for Gan, who needs to diet.
Leong, help us—we have hurt our back.

We may never walk upright again."

Leong knew the king was joking,
but he placed his fingers
on the king's wrists anyhow
whilst the other guards set out
meat and pastries.

He took the king's twelve pulses:
some agitation,
but the king well enough,
all well enough,
the air green-gold
beneath the leafing trees.

ROPE SKIPPING CHANT

Higher, higher,
demon fire.

Darkest night,
flaming bright.
Jump too low,
in you go.

Higher, higher,
demon fire.

Pick a town,
burn it down.
Ash and stone,
brick and bone.

Higher, higher,
demon fire.

NAMING

Had it been up to King Xau,
he would have been outdoors
with Shazia and their hundred-day-old son,
their son wrapped in a blanket,
safe in Shazia's arms;
no sound but a river running over stone
as Xau told his son
(who would not have understood)

that he, Xau, was sorry,
sorry for every difficulty, every grief
that would ever come to his son,
and then Xau would have lifted
the end of the blanket
and tickled his son's feet.

Instead King Xau stood in a hall
filled with dignitaries and their wives,
a sea of red silks and gold embroidery,
perfumed, painted, posed.

Beside him, Shazia,
their son safe in her arms,
wrapped in a red blanket.

When the time came,
Xau announced the baby's name:
Tan Soon Keng.

(Xau looked at his sister as he spoke.
Keng had been their brother's name,
Keng who had let Xau ride his horse,
who'd taught him to wield a sword,
who'd called him Little Crane.)

The ceremony over at last,
Xau put his arm around Shazia
and led her into the garden.

A cloudy autumn day,
the oak trees yellowing,
the palace staff waiting outside
to see the baby prince,
red ribbons round the men's arms,
red ribbons in the women's hair.

In the sky behind them, nearing,
a flock of cranes,
white with black wingtips,
long necks outstretched.

Men and women pointed, called out,
cranes a sign of good luck, long life.

Xau could not speak,
could not move—

where the cranes flew
he saw his brother,
saw him in the quick upward flick
of the birds' wings,
in the gaps of air between,
in the patterning of cloud.
His brother's voice under the wind,
heard only by Xau,
offering benediction—

Xau's throat raw, his sight blurred
as the cranes passed him
so low, so near
that twice a feathered softness
flicked his hair.

Then the sky stood empty. Silent.
His brother gone.

Xau caught his breath,
looked down at his round-faced son,
who stared back,
alert, intent,
sucking his index finger.

Xau lifted the blanket,
tickled his son's feet,
bent down and whispered
into Keng's tiny, perfect ear.

Then the king wiped his face
with the sleeve of his robe,
put his arm around Shazia,
went back indoors to the reception.

DECORATION

In the royal palace of Meqing:
five hundred paintings, a thousand ornaments;
a daily fragrant shifting from peony,
to magnolia, to jasmine, to plum blossom
arrayed in vases of porcelain, silver, jade.

Holly branch with berries:
    In the second week of King Xau's reign,
    the morning after his guards removed

the old woman dusting his rooms
so Xau might have peace,
and Xau said to let her be:
a holly branch by his slippers.

Pine bough:
In the second month,
the day after the king asked
the cleaning woman her name:
a freshly cut bough of pine
placed on his desk.
A smell of forests.

Mint leaves with rounded stone:
Fourth month,
after Xau introduced Tian
to his foreign-born queen
and the pair of them bowed to her:
mint leaves on the wash basin.

Maple, chestnuts, herbs:
Ninth month, tenth month,
after she saw how the king looked
when he returned from war:
maple leaves, roasted chestnuts,
bay leaves, sage, mint,
fresh-crushed lemon balm.

Paper flower:
Eleventh month,
after Xau came—
unannounced, no commotion,
only two guards as escort—
to the funeral of Tian's husband:
an intricately folded paper flower.

Shell:
Second year,
each of the five mornings
that Xau stayed in bed,
cantankerous, coughing,
littering handkerchiefs
on floor, table, bedcovers,
more trouble than his infant son:
assorted sea shells,
the pickled cucumbers

the king favored,
the sound of Tian humming
as she cleaned.

A HANDFUL OF NIGHTS

Zither under one arm,
Moon Swan walked toward
King Xau and his guards,
the men sitting beneath the maples
in a spill of lantern-light,
this celebration in honor of Tsung,
captain of the king's guards—

Tsung whom Moon Swan had first seen
back when he'd been the youngest
of King Hao's guards,
left to stand in a corner
while she pleasured the king—

A long time ago, that king dead,
his son now crowned.
The foolishness of her youth
to have wanted the king's guard,
not the king;
the foolishness of age
to want him still.

Tsung, sitting on King Xau's right,
started when he recognized Moon Swan,
glancing from her to the young king
in evident confusion.

"Thank you for coming."
King Xau dipped his head,
a clean-shaven youth, slightly built,
dressed like his guards
in black pants, black tunic.
Not his father's equal.

Moon Swan sat down on the grass,
adjusted her zither,
opened with an old love song,
looking neither at the king nor Tsung,
but the other guards,
holding each man's gaze in turn,

slowly, tenderly,
a thing she'd done a thousand times
for men of lesser worth but greater wealth,
the guards' lives bent like a bow
to the king's service.

She let the zither's plucked notes
float into silence,
sang the next piece unaccompanied.
When the girl in the song proclaimed her love,
Moon Swan sang the words to Tsung.

Tsung flushed, his eyes fixed on her.

Moon Swan's pulse leapt,
foolish and giddy and eager.
Later, when they were alone,
she would ask Tsung to stay with her,
not for one night or a handful of nights,
but every night—

The guard on sentry duty called out—

All the guards jumped to their feet
and the young king likewise—

Moon Swan sat frozen,
not knowing what was happening—

Guards drew their swords,
and the young king likewise—

An archer fitted an arrow,
targeted the far bushes—

Tsung placed himself
between the king and those bushes—

Leaves rustled. An arrow sounded—

On the dark grass,
difficult to distinguish,
a small, still, darker shadow.

A guard ran and picked it up. "A rabbit!
Leong, you saved the king from a rabbit!"

Moon Swan stared up at Tsung.
Not her whom he had leapt to defend,

but the king.

If she changed that,
if, later, when they were alone,
she asked Tsung to choose her over the king,
not for one night or a handful of nights,
but every night, and if Tsung agreed,
she would like him less for doing so,
would like herself less
for asking.

So she would not ask,
not yet,
would wait as long as Tsung needed,
would wait until he retired
from the king's service
in his own time.

In the spill of lantern-light,
Xau bowed very low to Tsung.
"For twenty years, you have shielded
first our father, then ourself.
Thank you." Xau bowed again.
"Thank you for teaching us
to be a better king.
We learned by watching you."

At least the king was worthy of Tsung—

Clear as lantern-light,
yet Moon Swan hadn't seen the difference
between Xau and his father,
the difference between a king
who honored his soldiers,
and one who had ordered her
to suck him
while his young guard
waited in the corner—

Xau grinned. "Now go away, Captain.
You're off duty for a week."

Tsung beside her then,
his breath warm on her skin.
"Will you come with me?"

She nodded, stood,

set her arms about his neck,
kissed him full on the lips
in the view of his king.

For now,
they had only this handful of nights.
She would not waste one single moment.

ARTOCH

"We have acquiesced to all
your other recommendations."
King Xau spoke mildly,
which was not,
in Artoch's experience,
an auspicious sign.

Artoch did not bow,
nor offer any apology.
The king came to him
for advice, not admiration.

Even so, Artoch hesitated.
Sixty-one years old,
over two decades counseling kings,
and still there were many days
when he doubted his aptitude.
It was one matter to assess
the correct course of action,
and quite another to convince
those you counseled.

He took a sip of tea before he offered:
"A man will punish his gardener
for the single wilted flower
in an otherwise perfect display."

"Meaning that the Sumbrese will be
so offended by our choice of translator
that they will ignore all else."

"Very possibly."
Artoch took another sip of tea.
"They will be insulted
that you chose a mere woman—"

"Hardly a mere woman! Our wife.
The daughter of their own king.
The person who headed our court
while we were away at war."

Artoch studied his tea bowl,
the delicacy of the heron
painted on its side, flawless.
An awkward matter, this.

"The Sumbrese prince," said Artoch,
"is likely to see only the insult."

"The Sumbrese prince," said Xau,
"should see that we hold his sister
in the highest esteem."

"But the breaking of tradition—"

"Tradition!" Xau stood up
and paced rapidly
around Artoch's office,
another inauspicious sign.
"We have spent three years
attempting to break certain traditions,
including the ancient tradition
of enmity with Sumbral."

"A shame then," said Artoch,
"to undo those efforts
with one misplaced gesture."

Xau stopped by the tall window,
looked out into the sunlit courtyard.
After a short, strained silence
the set of his shoulders eased
and he turned to Artoch:
"Would the Sumbrese prince
take offense if his sister
is present at the negotiations,
provided she does not speak?"

"If she is silent,
if she stays in the background,
that should be acceptable."

Xau walked over to the doorway,

paused. "Keep on annoying us."

Artoch raised his eyebrows. "Your Majesty?"

"We have found that your most valuable advice
is usually the most annoying. Keep on."

Artoch bowed then as the king left,
partly in respect and gratitude,
partly to hide the emotion
flushing his face.

An old man should not care about praise,
should have learned that a task
well executed is its own reward.

Artoch still had much to learn.

AFTERWARD

After the opening pleasantries,
after the exchange of gifts,
after the trade negotiations,
after the concluding pleasantries,
only then did Tahj, crown prince of Sumbral,
acknowledge the presence of his sister,
a mere woman.

Even then, he did not address Shazia,
but rather her husband, King Xau:
"I trust my sister pleases you."

"Beyond words."

"Good." Tahj bowed.

"If you wish, Shazia could walk with you
in the Sunken Garden and introduce you
to our son."

"Perhaps another time." Tahj bowed again.
"When my nephew is a few years older,
I would be glad to meet him."

Xau bowed back,
a fraction less deeply than usual,
but only his wife, a mere woman, noticed.

*

After Prince Tahj had left,
after Xau played hide and seek with his son,
after Xau trained with spear and ji,
after Xau met with the head carpenter,
after Xau consulted his steward,
after Xau ate a late supper with his guards,
only then, the midsummer sky long since dark,
did Xau speak to Shazia alone.

"Why does Tahj dislike you?"

"He doesn't. Tahj doesn't bother himself
with either liking or disliking me."

"We are sorry." Xau sat on the end of the bed
and rubbed Shazia's feet gently.
Little by little, the tautness left her face.

"They're not all like that," said Shazia.
"My brothers. Two were kind to me,
and one is far worse than Tahj."

"If we meet the one worse than Tahj,
we won't promise to behave ourself."

"Good," said Shazia,
and then she undid Xau's tunic
and let her hands speak for her.

After that, too, was done,
Xau fell asleep beside her.
Shazia lay for a while
just looking at him,
his face unguarded in sleep, vulnerable,
before she blew out the lamps.

WHAT XAU REMEMBERED

Not the Ritan court,
nor the twenty-foot-tall mural
round the banquet chamber;
not the Ritan princesses dancing,
nor his own queen's laughter;
but a glint of light,

a hand yanking his shoulder,
the bench toppling,
floor knocking the air from him,
so that he lay sideways,
dazed, unable to breathe,
staring at pastry crumbs on polished planks
before he understood
why two of his guards
were covering him with their bodies,
why a third guard—
Shang, his youngest guard—
sat on the floor,
an arrow wedged in his chest.

Not the Ritan soldiers
taking down the assassin,
nor the guests being
cleared from the room;
not the Ritan king
promising vengeance,
nor his own queen
checking him for injury;
but Tsung, the captain of his guards,
saying to Shang, "You're dying. You did well,"
and then, nightmare sharp,
how he and Tsung knelt either side of Shang,
trying to ease him when he coughed,
but no help possible,
blood puddling on the floor,
and how the young guard's fingers
clutched at Xau's like a child's
as his lips went blue.

ONE WEEK

In the long truce,
in the fifth year of his reign,
at the end of summer:
one week with his son.

One week stolen
from army, court, negotiations;
one week stolen
from queen and baby daughter.

Riding Micha,
his son in front of him—
three years old,
balance already perfect.

Damming a stream,
his son muddy and soaked,
running for more stones,
splashing him.

His son pointing
at the guards, asking
why the men were there.
—"To keep you safe."

The boy falling asleep
by the campfire;
keeping him on his lap,
the smell of smoke.

In the long truce,
in the fifth year of his reign,
at the start of autumn:
one week with his son.

BEDTIME

Lie still and listen well.

"Yes, Mama, I know," said Prince Keng.

Before the dragons flew to King Nariz,
before the time of demons,
Batar was the greatest horse lord
who ever rode the eastern plains,
yet he thirsted for more power.
So Batar fell upon the towns.
The lines of his horse archers
stretched a mile wide, six men deep,
and the towns bowed down to Batar
and gave him grain and gold and women,
but that did not content Batar,
so he rode north to Jian-Jian.

"That's where Papa's gone.
Because it had an earthquake."

Shazia nodded. Unbidden,
she thought of Xau waking Keng
before dawn to say goodbye.

Jian-Jian, city of a thousand bells,
and each of the thousand bells rang
as Batar rode up, as the city rulers
prepared to surrender their treasure.
But a sewing-girl, ten years old,
ran up onto the ramparts
and shouted, "Leave us alone!"
Batar laughed and his men laughed.
He fitted an arrow to his bowstring
to silence the sewing-girl,
but his horse turned under him
and galloped away from Jian-Jian.
And all the horses in Batar's army
turned likewise and galloped away.

(Xau hadn't woken their baby daughter,
but he had lifted the blanket
and kissed her toes.)

Next morning Batar returned
with the full might of his army.
Before the city rulers could surrender,
the sewing-girl ran onto the ramparts
and shouted at Batar, "Leave us alone!"
And Batar's horse lay down under him
so suddenly that Batar fell off,
and all the horses of his army
lay down likewise.

"Like Papa in the battle
when the enemy horses stopped."

Shazia nodded.

Batar was the greatest horse lord
who ever rode the eastern plains,
great enough to recognize an equal.
He stood up, bowed to the girl,
led his army away,
and never again troubled Jian-Jian.

Keng yawned. "When will Papa be back?"

"I don't know. Close your eyes."
Shazia didn't finish the story,
didn't tell Keng how the rulers
of Jian-Jian waited a month
in case Batar should return,
then drove the girl from the city.

She kissed Keng on the forehead,
tucked the blanket about him,
and tried not to think of Xau.

HELP

Cold in the tent where Lieutenant Honghui
made tiny notes on scraps of paper,
trying to calculate how long he had
before hunger tipped to starvation.

The twelfth morning since the earthquake:
six thousand three hundred and twelve still alive,
of whom perhaps five thousand could walk,
if he had anywhere to send them,
or supplies to send them with,
or soldiers to escort them.
The roads at best rubble,
at worst sheered into crevasses;
the bridges out;
Honghui's commanding officers killed
when the barracks collapsed.

The least of his worries that his aide
burst into the tent without announcing himself.
"Lieutenant! The king!"

Honghui raised his eyebrows and said mildly,
"King Xau? Has he sent a message?"

"No! He's here! Outside the tent."

Honghui jumped up,
tugged his uniform
into a semblance of order,
went outside.

Seven men in black pants, black jackets,
all armed, all travel-stained,
none of them dressed more finely than the rest,

but Honghui remembered King Xau
from the war against Innis.
No man in that third battle
would ever forget the young king.

He bowed to the lanky youth.
"Your Majesty—
I didn't expect you—
I only hoped you might send help—"

King Xau bowed back. "Lieutenant Honghui,
one of your pigeons reached us.
We have brought what we could."

Honghui looked beyond the king and his guards,
saw perhaps forty soldiers
with as many laden packhorses.
Laden with what?
Honghui had barely been able to steady his hand
when he wrote reporting disaster,
less than an hour after the earthquake,
before he realized they wouldn't find
any other carrier pigeons alive,
before he knew what they most needed.
Forty packhorses couldn't carry food for six thousand,
but if they had bandages, or rope, or axes—

Honghui looked back at the king.
"Your Majesty, thank you—
would you like refreshment?"

"We're fine. Tell us how to help."

Xau's voice gentle,
and that gentleness almost undid Honghui,
who had not known what to do,
but had done the best he could
for the past eleven days;
it took him a while
before he could compose himself
and tell the king what they needed.

WHAT THEY BROUGHT

Salt, sugar, spice, oil, oats,
dried meat, pots, pans, paper,

maps, thread, string, rope,
candles, canvas, coins;

nails, needles, nets, knives,
tents, tongs, wrenches, anvil,
axes, augers, gimlets, chisels,
hooks, hammers, pickaxes, shovels;

blankets, bandages, ointment,
pestles, mortars, forceps, clamps,
curettes, scissors, specula,
scalpels, saws, surgeons.

ROUTE

A brief break snatched
between a dozen pressing tasks,
the map spread out on rubble
where the city walls of Jian-Jian
had stood, the walls largely leveled
along with the city.

Lieutenant Honghui followed
as King Xau pointed out his route:
the main road north from the capital,
wagons, fresh horses every fifteen miles;
then by boat along the river,
the king and his soldiers
still making good speed,
changing oarsmen whenever possible;
then east, slow-going,
a hundred miles along worsening roads,
running into bandits, looters, refugees;
then across the Blue Snake river—

"How?" asked Honghui. "The bridges are out.
I sent scouts, hoping for a supply route."

Xau shrugged. "We had three sampan boats.
It took twenty-eight crossings
and we had to abandon the wagons."

The captain of Xau's guards,
who had shadowed the king all day,
said, "It is not a safe crossing point.
We nearly lost two of the sampans."

"You crossed here?"
Honghui tapped the map,
the river fast-flowing at that point,
not as bad as the rapids, but dangerous,
and, in February, near-freezing.

Xau nodded.

"In sampans? With forty packhorses?"

"The horses swam."

"Swam the Blue Snake river, in winter?"

Xau looked up at Honghui,
his eyes alight, smiling
for the first time that day.
"They are good horses."

"But—How—?"

The captain of Xau's guards said,
"The king swam. They followed him."

Honghui stared at the king.
"*You* swam across the river?"

Xau nodded, turned back to the map.
"We left six men to guard supplies
that we couldn't load onto the horses.
Tomorrow, when the horses are rested,
you can send back for those."

Quickly, the king discussed the worst spots
on the road (what was left of the road)
between the river and Jian-Jian
(what was left of Jian-Jian).

Honghui forced himself to pay attention,
but half his mind back at the river,
imagining the king swimming across,
the horses following him,
a sight Honghui would have given much to see.

CAMP

A brutal day,
and Gan exhausted,

mud, dirt, brick-dust clinging
to his hair, his pants, his jacket,
in his nose, his boots, under his nails,
so that when they got back to the army campsite
and found Leong already there,
their tent up,
he would have hugged him,
save that Leong was decorated not merely with dirt,
but also with a spattering of blood
from his patients.

King Xau went into the tent,
and Gan, a giant of a man,
bent almost double to follow him.

Dao outside, condemned to sentry duty,
five guards and the king inside:
a cramped confusion
of blankets, water bottles, weapons,
men taking off their boots,
the sharp smell of sweat, of feet,
the wavering light of the lantern.

Gan, out of the cold wind, boots off,
chewing a stick of unidentifiable smoked meat,
looked to Leong: "The girl?"

Leong shrugged. "Dead."

No more than Gan had expected
when he'd lifted her out of the rubble,
a scrawny thing, all skin and broken bone.
Twelve days since the earthquake,
they weren't searching for more survivors.

No more than Gan had expected,
but his appetite gone.
He abandoned the stick of meat,
looked for King Xau's boots to clean,
but the king already scraping them himself.

King Xau,
dirty and smelly as the rest of them,
nodded to Gan,
"You did the work of three men today."

"Not enough," said Gan,

before his wits caught up with his tongue,
before he added, "Thank you, Your Majesty."

"You're right," said the king. "It's not enough.
Our whole army would not be enough
to do what needs to be done."

A truth that Gan had been avoiding
since they arrived that morning.
The city of Jian-Jian leveled;
thousands without shelter, food, clean water;
winter not yet over.

(And the girl he'd found in the rubble,
the girl who'd demanded, "What took you so long?"
then clung to him so tightly
he had to pry her fingers loose
when he got her to Leong,
that girl now dead.)

"Our whole army," the king said quietly,
"would not be enough,
but that does not diminish what you did.
We have never seen anybody exert
such sustained strength."

Tired as Gan was,
a flicker of pride
at the king's words.

He took the stack of blankets,
handed one to the king,
one each to the other guards,
took one himself, lay down, shut his eyes.

AFTERSHOCK

A dry clear chill day
in the ruined city of Jian-Jian,
its thousand bells buried with its buildings
beneath brick and mud and wood and stone,
even the great city walls largely reduced to rubble
by the earthquake two weeks earlier;
the stench worse than a battlefield,
putrefying corpses buried with the bells.

King Xau walked, cautiously, across the rubble,
accompanied by three of his guards and three soldiers.
In front of them, incautious, running back and forth,
a boy who'd said he could lead them
to one of the city's granaries:
thousands of survivors,
little food,
winter not yet over.

"Hurry up! Over here!"
The boy jumped, and tripped,
the ground tilting—

—Odd, how that instant stretched,
the boy screaming, high-pitched, as he tumbled.

—Odd, how the ground shifted,
rolled like a wave beneath King Xau
as he dropped, lay face down.

—Odd, the loose, grinding, creaking,
splintering of the debris under him.
Xau blinked back dust, looked right:
two of his guards, Dao, Li, prostrate,
Li staring at him,
Dao's eyes squeezed tight.
Xau looked to his left:
the three soldiers and Tsung,
captain of his guards.

—Odd, the wave tilted left,
Xau slid downslope
where no slope had been,
coughing, dust choking him, in his eyes.
Stopped.
To his right, uphill now: Dao, Li.
Left—a chasm.

—Xau stared down,
ten, twelve feet down into a pit.
Where the three soldiers had been.
Where Tsung had been.

—The ground steadied. Settled.
Xau pushed himself to hands and knees.
He saw Li walking toward him, testing each step,
saw the boy running away

along the ridge of the new slope.

Li stopped just above Xau,
gripped onto a plank with one hand,
grabbed Xau's arm with the other hand.

"Tsung's down there," said Xau.

Li nodded. "First we get you to safety,
then we fetch help."

From below, from out of the pit,
an animal groan, horrifying, inhuman.

"Tsung!" Xau shouted. "Tsung!"

No answer.
No movement in the pit.
Li's hand anchored to Xau's arm.

Xau looked at Li. "Let go of us.
Fetch ropes, men, digging equipment."

Li let go,
called to Dao, "Fetch help."

Xau swung his body down,
dangled over the edge, dropped.
Li beside him.

Xau and Li scrabbled
through brick and mud and wood,
time running out like air under rubble,
like a man's blood,
stuff shifting loosely beneath Xau
as he dug with his hands—
no shovels,
shovels with the soldiers—
Xau shouted and dug and lifted
and dug and shouted and scraped—
his fingers left bloody imprints
on the planks he twisted free,
the bricks he lifted away.
Blue cloth—blue, a soldier, not Tsung—
Xau and Li dug the man out with their hands,
the man groaning like a wild animal
as Li checked him for bleeding,

as Xau groped in the rubble,
found the shovel, tried to remember
how the men had been positioned
before the ground fell. Moved left.
What chance of air under this stuff?
This stuff that shifted,
filled in holes as he dug them?
He shouted, "Tsung! Tsung!"
Over and over.
He dug. A boot.
Xau dropped the shovel,
scraped with his hands, feeling for flesh,
Li beside him again:
a man's head, crushed in, not Tsung—
Xau grabbed the shovel, moved on, dug,
shouted and dug and lifted and bent.
Black cloth—Tsung—
Xau dropped the shovel,
scrabbled with his hands, Li with him,
touched a knob, an elbow,
dug with his hands, exposed one side of Tsung,
wedged horizontally in a gap,
unconscious, breathing,
blood dripping from his legs, his torso,
Li trying to stop the blood
as Xau strained against the planks
that pinned Tsung in place.
Wood splintered, Tsung loose in Li's arms;
Li laid the captain flat,
used his jacket to bandage Tsung.
Xau doubled over, hacking up dust,
back throbbing, arms throbbing, hands throbbing.
He took the shovel, went forward,
digging for the third soldier.
The smell of putrefying corpses
intruded on Xau for the first time in—
how long?—
no, not the stench of corpses, but shit.
It stank of shit.
He dug toward the smell, Li helping.
A slant of wood, the top of a platform.
They dug down: tall ceramic jars,
one broken, rice everywhere,
a soldier curled round the broken jar,
fist in his mouth, pants soiled, breathing.

*

A dry clear freezing night
in the ruined city of Jian-Jian,
another fifty people dead,
the bells silent.

Beyond the city,
in one of the surgeons' tents,
King Xau nodded to sleep where he sat,
cross-legged, hands bandaged,
beside Tsung's mat.
His guard, Li, picked up a blanket,
fumbling, his fingers also bandaged,
set the blanket over the king's shoulders.

SCALPEL

Before Leong examined King Xau,
he knew the infection had spread,
knew by Xau's febrile flush,
his very lack of complaint.

The king grumbled about minor ailments,
but had been likewise quiet
last time he was seriously hurt
(four years ago, the king only a boy,
shoulder dislocated, severe bruising).

The king sat cross-legged,
making no fuss,
in the overcrowded shelter,
nineteen other patients nearby.

Leong unwrapped the king's right hand first,
inspected the lacerations: no swelling,
no discharge. "This hand's healing well."

Xau nodded. "How is Tsung?
We went to see, but he was sleeping."

"Recovering rapidly.
In a day or two, he'll be up
and causing trouble."

"That's good. Very good."

Leong applied ointment,
rebandaged Xau's right hand.
Then, gently as he could,
he unwrapped the king's left hand,
the odor foul,
the king unable to hold still.
The wound bright red, purulent, hot.

So. Leong took a breath,
tried for the same detachment
that came to him so easily
when he treated strangers.

It did not come.

An effort to meet the king's eyes,
to say, quietly,
affording the king what privacy he could,
"The infection has spread.
If it does not improve,
I will need to amputate your left hand."

The king started,
dread on his face in the briefness
before he shuttered it away.
"Thank you for telling us."

To be thanked when he had failed,
that almost the worst part.
Leong took a breath, said,
"I can clear this area, give you privacy."

Xau shook his head,
both of them aware
that there was too little shelter
and too much need.

"Very well. I need to debride the wound.
It will hurt. You are permitted to scream."
Leong tried for lightness,
but his voice failed him.

He had the king lie down,
called Gan to hold him still,
prepared his instruments.
A moment before his fingers
steadied enough to wield the scalpel.

Then the worst part,
working with scalpel, forceps, scissors,
the king's solitary stifled scream,
the look that Gan gave him.

SCARED

Bad enough standing guard
while King Xau tossed
in fitful, fevered sleep.

Worse when the king woke
and nodded in thanks to Dao,
who deserved no thanks.

"Dao, what's wrong?"

The king's concern unbearable.
"Your Majesty, once you are well,
find a better guard than me."

"We do not want other guards.
We could not ask for better
than those we have."

"No! When the ground quaked,
I was so scared I couldn't think—
I left you—"

No reproach in the king's eyes.
"You fetched help, came back.
All men are scared."

"Not you."

"We are scared to sleep,
scared we will wake
to the surgeon's saw."

Nothing Dao could say.
He helped the king to drink.
He stood guard.

GIRL

Hour by slow hour
the burning candle marked
the progress of the night
as Gan, acting captain of King Xau's guards,
paced back and forth past
the twenty mats with their twenty patients,
stopping each seventh time
to wet the cloths
that failed to quench King Xau's fever;
Gan a giant of a man,
but his strength useless,
his skill useless.

Back and forth,
back and forth,
watching the candle creep
toward the sixth hour mark
when Leong would change
the king's reeking bandages.
If the infection had advanced
the king's hand would be amputated,
and nothing Gan would be able to do
but hold Xau down.

Back and forth,
back and forth,
stopping each seventh time
to check on the king,
to wet the cloths,
so that it came as a relief
when Peng entered with her pails
and towels and blankets
and matter-of-fact efficiency,
when she set to work emptying piss bowls,
turning patients to wipe them clean.

Peng wiping a patient
when she straightened up suddenly,
looked past Gan. "Back again?"

Gan spun round
but no one there.
"What—?"

"Your girl's here."

Gan baffled, blunt:
"I don't have a girl. I prefer men."

"The dead girl. The girl you rescued."

Not what Peng said,
but her brisk impatience
that made Gan believe her.
The girl he'd rescued
from earthquake rubble,
all skin and broken bone.
The girl who died a few hours later.

"I'll tell him."
Peng nodded.
"She says to thank you.
For coming to help, for being gentle."

"She's welcome—"
Gan stopped, looked where Peng looked,
addressed empty air.
"You're welcome. I'm sorry
I couldn't do more."

A sweetness like the scent
of the blue-flowered weeds
in the town where Gan grew up.

Hope stung him.
He fell to his knees.
"If you can heal King Xau—
if there's something you want—please—"

The sweetness faded.

"She's gone," said Peng.
"She said what she wanted."

Gan hurried to the king,
laid his hand on Xau's forehead: still hot.
He sank down on the ground.

"She couldn't help," said Peng.
"The dead can't heal."

Peng cleaned her hands, came over,

touched Gan briefly on his shoulder.
"The king's young.
He may get well on his own."

Gan said nothing.

After a time, when Peng
was picking up her things to leave,
Gan asked, "Peng, what was her name?"

"She didn't say."

Peng left.

Gan wet the cloths,
laid them over the king,
paced back and forth,
watching the candle creep downward,
hour by slow hour.

CURE

Not healing herb, nor dragon's wing,
nor surgeon's skill, nor serpent's sting,
nor spell, nor ghost that healed the king.

But that the surgeon, tired, distraught,
still heard the mumbling woman out;
abandoned pride; considered; thought.

A hundred hook-mouthed maggots mined
the king's fouled flesh, devoured, dined:
a feast that left no taint behind.

THE WAY OF THINGS

Tsung, captain of King Xau's guards,
paced outside the king's tent,
ice-sheeted snow crunching
beneath his boots,
working over the words
he wished to say—

Xau had risked himself to save Tsung,
an ill-judged, unacceptable act,
an act that had jeopardized the kingdom,

that had nearly cost Xau
his left hand—

Tsung braced himself as if for battle,
nodded to Dao, standing duty
at the tent's entrance,
went in.

Xau sat cross-legged, haggard,
a blanket over his shoulders,
his left hand swaddled in bandages.

Li, king's guard,
the finest warrior Tsung knew,
crouched beside the king,
shaving away the last scraps
of Xau's straggly stubble.

"You were starting," said Li,
"to resemble a goat."

"A very fine goat, no doubt."
Xau looked from Li to Tsung.
"Captain?"

"I need to talk to you
once Li is done."

Li finished up quickly, left.

"Your Majesty," Tsung began.
Stopped. Went to one knee.
Stared down at the snow melting
from the tip of his boot, said,
"Thank you for saving me,
but you should not have done so.
In risking yourself,
you put Meqing at risk."

"In guarding us," said Xau,
"you put yourself at risk.
Every day."

"That is my duty,
yours is to safeguard Meqing.
That is the way of things—
I've told you that before,"
Tsung said, more harshly

than he'd meant.
"You could have died—
your hand—"

Tsung stared down at his snowy boot,
made himself repeat what Leong
had said that morning,
"You have lost the use
of two fingers."

"We know. We know we are lucky
not to have lost the hand.
We know what we were meant to do.
We couldn't do it, couldn't leave you."
Xau's voice collapsed.

Tsung looked up at the king,
Xau dry-eyed but trembling—

Tsung should have delayed,
should not have spoken so soon,
the king worn out, weak—

"It's all right,"
Tsung said softly, helplessly.
"It's all right, Xau.
It's all right."

A while before the young king
collected himself.

IN HONOR OF THE KING

No amphitheater, no gilded concert hall,
no stage, no roof, no carpet.
Instead a stretch of downtrodden grass
on a chilly February afternoon.

Still, it would sound well, would it not?
That Enlai, the master minstrel,
had rushed to Jian-Jian in its hour of need.
Enlai sniffed as he appraised his audience.

Grubby men and women with grubby children
on their laps, those who'd survived earthquake,
fire, the nights with no shelter, no food,
nothing but the paltry belongings they'd salvaged.

(Judging by the smell, few had salvaged perfume.)

Among them, sitting cross-legged on the grass,
distinguished only by the men guarding him,
King Xau, his clothes plain, face haggard,
left hand heavily bandaged.

The young king burnished with legends
yet in person so ordinary that Enlai suspected
the tales were a clever concoction
of distortion, exaggeration and fabrication.

(The king, frankly, a disappointment.)

Enlai positioned his harp comfortably,
adjusted his velvet sleeves.
From the first plucked notes,
he knew he had them:

their eyes following his every motion,
faces flushed, fingers tapping time
to the old heroic ballads,
laughing till they wept at comic ditties.

He sang for an hour, looking often
at one marginally less grubby woman
who might demonstrate her appreciation later
in the warmth of Enlai's tent.

He finished with a flourish,
bowed to the deplorably disheveled king
as the crowd clapped and clamored,
"Another song, Master Enlai, please!"

"One more," said Enlai, "in honor of the king."

He played the opening of a ballad
about hundreds of wild horses
coming to this young king—
who lifted his head and looked at Enlai.

Something then in the king's eyes,
a flash of what? Rage? Rebuke?
No. Rather as if the king raised a weight
that he had set aside.

Perhaps Enlai had misstepped, but too late now.
So Enlai sang of the coming of the horses,

and, singing, saw the moment when the king
thought of commanding him to stop:

and the following moment
when Xau looked at the people round him
and stayed his tongue,
bowed his head.

So, at last, by the ruins of Jian-Jian
Enlai apprehended the truth:
the wild horses *had* come to Xau
following no command but their own hearts.

And maybe the other tales were true as well,
maybe the king had bested a dragon,
maybe enemy cavalry halted mid-charge
if the king raised his hand.

The final note floated into silence.
Then a scuffling of shoes
as men, women, children got to their feet,
turned and bowed, very low, to the king.

The king said,
still sitting cross-legged
on the downtrodden grass,
"Too many died here. We cannot undo that.

"Those who stay will have a hard winter.
We cannot change that.
But we will stay here ourself until spring,
until the rebuilding of Jian-Jian begins."

The king got to his feet awkwardly,
cradling his bandaged hand;
headed back toward the campsite,
his guards close about him.

Enlai covered his harp.
Upstaged by the king.
Not what he'd hoped,
but other ways to turn this to advantage.

Perhaps he'd stay long enough
to write a song of Xau and the earthquake,
something in the heroic vein, he fancied.
The right song could make a man's reputation.

TRAINING: INJURY

The first day of March,
sun rising over rubble and ruin,
the remains of Jian-Jian,
city of a thousand bells,
those bells buried by earthquake
five weeks earlier.

On a frosty stretch of grass,
King Xau's first training session
since he was injured,
his left hand swathed in bandages,
his guards hovering round him
like ruffled mother hens.

Xau wobbled from *Leaning Horse* to *Crane*
and two guards grabbed to steady him.

"Enough for today," said Tsung,
captain of the king's guards.

King Xau raised his eyebrows.
"We have barely begun."

"Enough."

 *

The first day of April,
the ruins of Jian-Jian overcast
as Xau ran round them with his guards,
looking down from the remnants
of the great city walls
on men clearing debris,
building roads, laying pipes.

Halfway round the city
a single drop of rain.

"Enough running," said Tsung. "Walk."

 *

The first day of May,
lilacs in bloom in the palace gardens:
purple, pale pink, a perfumed profusion,
King Xau back home,

sparring outdoors with Leong
while the other guards watched,
both Xau and Leong fighting one-armed,
the scars on Xau's left hand
raised, red, rough.

Xau pivoted, kicked at Leong's shin,
overbalanced onto the grass.

"Again!" said Leong.
"One leg only this time!"

One-legged, one-armed
Leong and Xau hopped about,
disabled by laughter.

The lilacs in bloom,
the kingdom safe,
the king safe.

MICHA

Beneath the silver river of stars,
under the spreading maple trees,
the mare pacing, grazing, pacing.
Two men watching. No words.

On the horse-cropped grass,
Micha lies down, whinnying.
Khyert, once a stableboy,
watches beside his king.

Under the wind-stirred leaves,
Micha strains, rests, strains.
King Xau looks a question at Khyert,
who nods back his reassurance.

Under the crescent moon,
emerging, wrapped in membrane,
one small foot, then another.
Two men watching.

Dawn floods the river of stars;
the foal born, the mare resting.
Khyert beside his king, his heart full.
A night worth a month of days.

THRESHOLD

As King Xau raised his hand
to knock on his guard's door, doubt:

knocking would be an intrusion
upon Li's scant privacy,
upon the portion of his life
not bent to his duty.

A dozen possible reasons
Li might have skipped
the daily training session.
None of them Xau's business.

It was Li's day off,
his one day off in the month.
It was Li's day off,
yet Li never skipped training.

Three of Xau's other guards
watched as he hesitated.
Xau weighed his worry
that Li was in trouble.

Knocked.

"Your Majesty. Come in."
Li bowed, opened his door wide.
A chair. A table. A narrow bed.
Weapons, books, a stack of clothes.

Xau bowed, but did not enter.
Li's uniform rumpled
as if he'd slept in it.
"Are you all right?"

"Yes. No. My mother is ill.
I'm fine. I heard last night.
I was writing to her,
trying to write to her."

Li gestured at the table,
inkstone, brushes, water,
a single sheet of paper,
the paper bare, blank.

Xau considered how to proceed.
He had seen Li exhausted before,
but never shaken, discomposed.
"Li, go and see her."

Li shook his head.
"It's ten days away.
Thank you. No. I'm fine.
I'll write to her."

Xau touched Li's hand,
repeated, "Go and see her."

Li glanced past Xau to Tsung,
captain of the guards.
"I can't. The timing is poor.
The midsummer ceremonies."

"Your family lives near Qingzi?"

Li nodded.

"A happy coincidence," said Xau.
"It is too long since we visited
the coast. We ourself will travel
to Qingzi for midsummer."

Behind Xau, noisily, pointedly,
Captain Tsung cleared his throat.
"Your Majesty! It is far too late
to change your plans—"

"Either," said Xau, looking at Li,
"you will accompany us to Qingzi
as part of your duty to us,
or you will go to your mother."

"I'll go. She asked to see me."
Li's face crumpled like a child's.

"Stay as long as you need."
Xau bowed very deeply,
pulled the door closed,
left Li what privacy he could.

RIDDLE: TWINS

A summer morning,
the tall paper windows opened wide,
the king, as was his custom,
taking breakfast with Queen Shazia,
their two children, his sister,
and all eight of his guards:
Prince Keng too excited to eat,
too excited to sit still
on the grand occasion
of his fourth birthday.

"Your Highness," said Dao,
king's guard, seated that morning
between King Xau and Prince Keng,
"now that you are four years old,
I have a question for you."

"A question?" said Keng.

"Yes," said Dao, bowing.
"Twin brothers, strong and thin,
both the same height,
always working side by side,
always eating the same food,
but skipping the soup.
Who are they?"

Keng frowned. "I don't know."

"It's a riddle," said Queen Shazia.
"A puzzle question. Think hard.
What eats food, but not soup?"

"A rabbit?"

Dao tapped the edge of Keng's plate
with his chopsticks.
"Twin brothers, strong and thin,
both the same height—"

"Chopsticks!" shouted Keng.

Demon

ABSENCE

Five years in,
the truce with Innis frayed.
The Innish ambassador demanded
concessions of land, grain, silk.
King Xau declined.

When Xau left for the border,
war threatening,
Queen Shazia refused to miss him.
Xau often away;
no cause to admit
that this was any different.

She concentrated on her duties:
dined with dignitaries,
entertained envoys,
met Xau's ministers.

Reserved her afternoons
for their two young children—
hard not to think of Xau
when she saw him in Keng.

Woke, a week after Xau left,
to a queasiness familiar
from her earlier pregnancies,
yet unanticipated. New.

A child Xau might never see.

With only her guards as witness,
she fought to compose herself
before her official wake-up.
Bowed, dry-eyed, to her attendants.
Carried out her duties.

LETTER TO HIS YOUNG SON

Dearest Keng,
Thank you for your painting of Micha.
She looks very happy.

King Xau's brush blotted the sheet.

He paused, gazed at Keng's picture:
a horse with four stick legs
and an oversized, smiling mouth.

Thank you for visiting Micha.
It snowed all day yesterday.

The first heavy snow in the two months
Xau had been at the border.
Snow that would hinder Xau's cavalry,
a fact which might tip Donal
from hostility to open war.
Not a thought to share with Keng.

A knock at the door.
Tsung, captain of Xau's guards,
announced General Qiang.
Xau stood, bowed to the general,
tucked the thought of Keng away.

THIRTY-NINTH WAR BETWEEN INNIS AND MEQING

COMMENCEMENT

Not a battle, but a raid,
not on impulse, but under orders—

Prince Connol would have risked
his brother's anger
and questioned those orders
had he judged it would do any good,
but King Donal was set on war,
so war it would be.
And Connol would start it.

Connol and twenty of his soldiers
trudged through snow and wind,
crossed the border
somewhere inside a forest
that had been renamed six times
in the past hundred years
as war shifted it from one king to another,
or, as now, carved it in two.

Rested until dark,
then off again, light snow falling
as they went from farmstead to farmstead.
Burning, killing.
Setting the Innish banner by each burnt farm.

They didn't kill or rape the women,
just bound them and left them in the snow.
One woman nearly naked,
Connol worried she'd freeze.
He wrestled a coat from a corpse,
put it on the woman as she spat at him.

Not many women, no young children,
for which Connol was grateful.

Wherever the women and children
had fled, the men hadn't followed.
Peasants with pitchforks and shovels
that Connol and his men
killed with brutal ease.
Some of them not armed at all.
Some trying to surrender.

Armed or unarmed,
resisting or cowering:
all killed.

Three hours before dawn, the sky cleared.
Snow gleamed under the half moon
as they happened upon a larger farmstead.
Stone house and outbuildings.
Connol gave the signal to halt.

None of his soldiers injured,
but all of them tired.
He weighed it up, said quietly,
"We're heading home."

Fergus gave him a look.
"King Donal won't like it."

That the only protest,
Connol started back.
Before he'd gone a hundred yards,
a scream.
Connol spun round,

saw Tamhas collapse, arrow through his neck.
Saw the pair of archers.
Helmets. Cuirasses.
Not peasants, but Horse Boy's soldiers.
A large group of farmers assembled behind them.

Well then. A fight after all:
"Kill the fucking bastards!"

Connol ran, shield up,
straight for the pair of archers,
Fergus alongside him, the others following.
A cut-off yelp behind him.
Connol didn't turn. Ran on.
Drew his sword as he reached the archers,
slashed one in the shin.
The man staggered, fell.
Connol cut the man's throat,
looked round: Fergus and Iain
fighting the second archer,
most of his men attacking farmers.
He stepped toward Fergus,
lost his sword to a blow from a shovel.
Grabbed his axe,
took down the farmer with the shovel.
Looked round again: the second archer
face down in the trampled snow,
Iain sprawled beside him.
No farmers standing.

Connol tallied his soldiers. Iain dead.
Tamhas, Dunne, Liam downed by arrows. Dead.
Muiredach with an arrow in his shoulder.

Connol took his axe.
Went to the archer he'd killed,
chopped the archer's hands off.
Opened the archer's jaws,
set a severed hand in their bite.
Did the same to the second archer.

Less than Donal would have done,
and he took no satisfaction from it,
but a message for Horse Boy.

Headed back to Innis
with his remaining men.

FAULT

Seventy-eight men—

    King Xau lay still,
    eyes closed.

Seventy-eight men.
Seventy-six of them farmers
or farmhands. Two soldiers.

    Xau lay still,
    trying not to disturb Khyert,
    once his stableboy,
    now valet, aide, groom,
    sleeping on a mat by the door.

Seventy-eight men.
Burnt. Stabbed. Mutilated.
To provoke Xau to war.
Seventy-eight deaths to start a war
that might kill tens of thousands.

    Xau's throat dry.
    He lay still.
    Forced himself to relax his muscles.

No good options.
To go to war in the bitter heart of winter,
try to maintain a supply line
despite snow and ice.
Or to stay put
as if nothing had happened,
perhaps persuade the other farmers to evacuate,
to follow their children to the towns.
Or to retaliate in kind:
to raid Donal's farms,
order his soldiers to burn Donal's farmers—

    Xau sat up.
    Reached for the water. Drank.

    Khyert stood, came over.
    "Can I get you anything?"

    "No. Thank you.
    Get some rest if you can."

No good options,
but he'd chosen anyhow.
Tomorrow he would lead his army
to the Muir river to take out the bridges—

"It's not your fault."
Khyert's voice quiet, diffident,
worried about him,
but all this was, in the end,
Xau's fault.

Believing he could stop a war
that had continued,
overtly or surreptitiously,
for the past three hundred years—

Khyert still standing there,
watching him.

"Try to rest," said Xau, again.

But Khyert sat,
cross-legged, by Xau's bed.
Looked down at the floor.
Sang, very soft,
too quiet for the guards
stationed outside the door to hear,
a shepherd's song about the greening trees,
the lambing ewes.

Xau closed his eyes.

POLTON

No survivors. Not even a dog.
A handful of stone buildings
jutted out of desolation,
snow falling over ash and bone.

King Donal had thought the reports
exaggerated until he stood there,
stood in the burnt remains
of what had once been a town.

Rourk, chief of his guards,
kicked the snowy ash with his boot.
"I'll say this for Horse Boy.

He's thorough."

"Too thorough," said Donal.
"I don't see how he did it.
Unless his fucking horses
breathe fire now."

That the lesser puzzle,
how Xau had razed Polton.
The greater puzzle,
that Xau had wanted to.

He'd misread Xau, thought him
constrained by moral qualms.
Donal ruthless enough himself,
but this more than he could stomach.

That one skeleton clutching another
so small it must have been newborn.

JUSTICE

Pilfering food.
Improper care of weapons.
Drunk during picket duty.

Flanked by two of his guards,
King Xau sat on a stool
in the camp's practice area
on a freezing February morning,
heard the charges,
dispensed judgment.

(Hardly the Hall of Justice
where every case was considered
by five judges enthroned in gilded glory.
Xau had been there twice.
Hadn't cared for the pomp,
but the verdicts dispassionate, well-reasoned,
so he had let the judges be.)

The fourth and final offender
was hauled in front of Xau:
a foot soldier solid as a tree trunk,
hands tied, head up, uncowed,
breath clouding in the chill air.

A lieutenant bowed twice to Xau.
"Soldier Tang punched a washerwoman,
breaking her nose. Six witnesses."

A slight shifting of the assembled soldiers,
some two thousand men, then stillness,
so that Xau's voice carried clearly,
"Soldier Tang, do you admit the charge?"

"Yes." Tang stood at ease.
Any misgivings the man had hidden.

"Do you wish to add anything?"

"She said my jacket wasn't ready."

Bravado or defiance?
Either way, Xau doubted Tang
would be reformed by corporal punishment.

Xau's voice iron,
"You will apologize to the washerwoman
and give her two months' pay."

"I'd sooner be flogged. Your Majesty."
Tang bowed to the required degree.
"She's only a washerwoman by day.
At night she's a cheap whore."

"Enough." Xau did not turn his head,
did not look to Gan, the guard on his left,
Gan whose mother had been a harlot,
Gan who put himself in danger every day
to safeguard Xau.

A moment to master his distaste for Tang,
to say merely what was necessary.
"You are dismissed from the army.
You may not take any weapons."

"But—Your Majesty—"
Tang looked around as if expecting support,
the assembled soldiers motionless,
though some (how many?) must sympathize.

Tang started again.
"Your Majesty—we're in enemy territory—"

"As is the washerwoman.
As is every man and woman
who follows our army,
who washes clothes,
or cooks, or mends,
or helps the surgeons."

Perhaps one chance in two that Tang
would make it back to Meqing.

Xau walked past Tang,
headed for his tent,
Gan at his left, Li at his right.

WINTER REAPING

The winter war barely begun
but Eirdre's husband home.
Brought back like baggage.
Declan's bloodied body frozen,
his beard ice-beaded.
Her warrior bard made mute.

A mark of Eirdre's rank—
sister to Queen Fian herself—
that they'd carted Declan
across half the kingdom.
Most men buried or abandoned
in the fields where they died.

Fian came to comfort Eirdre,
bringing the old, bright tales,
the tales their mother had told,
of the time before kings,
before Horse Boy's people
claimed the wolf country.

Fian came to strengthen Eirdre,
vowing vengeance,
bearing sweet bright lies:
that Declan died in glory,
died to free hill and river,
forest and wolf.

The winter too bitter
to grant Eirdre such solace;

the truth preserved by frost.
She washed Declan's corpse.
The arrow had entered
his back, not his breast.

A coward's wound.
Declan died for nothing,
or, worse, died for her,
trying to come home.
The winter nights long.
The bed too large.

MESSENGERS

No herald, no envoy, no messenger of state.
A girl of thirteen, her boots too small,
running and walking, walking and running
to the enemy's gate, shouting Open. Help.

A fisherman, the first back that night,
returning to where his town used to be,
then rowing for the border, for the enemy port,
shouting Help. Demon. Fire. Mercy. Help.

BROTHERS

Connol met his brother, King Donal,
outside the pig barn in the fort's bailey.
The swineherd, well used to them,
walked out, and Connol followed Donal
into the grunting, stinking dimness,
away from any eavesdroppers.

"Another town lost."
Donal spat in the trough.
"Burnt to the ground."

"Horse Boy's work?" asked Connol.

"No. Last month, when Polton burnt,
I guessed it must be Horse Boy,
though I couldn't fathom how.
I was wrong."

"If not Horse Boy, then what?"

"Demons."

"Demons?" said Connol.
The barn seemed darker,
his brother smaller.
"Demons are stories for children."

"The stories have woken.
They left their sign—
the demon sign."

Donal's voice faltered, stopped,
Donal who was never spooked,
never nervous.

Not since they were boys.

Behind Connol, a guttural growl.
He jumped, drew his sword—
The pig grunted again.
Only a pig.

Connol shoved his sword
back in the scabbard.
"Maybe it's Horse Boy after all,
hoping to scare us."

"No. That war's done.
I'm going to bend my knee
to fucking Horse Boy
and beg him for help."

Donal laughed then,
an empty, barren laugh,
near to despair.

Connol had seen his brother in a fury,
seen him castrate men who'd betrayed him.
That empty laughter worse
than Donal's rage.

Connol tried to think, to steady himself.
"Wait—you can't go to Horse Boy.
If he learns we're weak,
he'll attack."

"I doubt it.
He's the kind of noble prick

who'll fall over himself to help."

"If you're wrong—"

"If I'm wrong, it doesn't matter,
because there's nothing else
I can think of to save us."

DEMON FIRE

Outside: the harbor,
the town wall, both extant.

Inside: No trace of wood.
No leather. No cloth.
No birds, no insects.
The wells dried out.
The mud burnt brick hard.
A few stone buildings.
Ash. Charred bones.
Two kings (alive),
their guards
at a short distance.

"Too few bones," said Donal,
the Red King: red-haired,
red-handed in war.
"We think most people
were taken prisoner,
or killed elsewhere."

"Several escaped," said Xau,
"and fled to us eight days ago."

"At moon dark," said Donal.
"And last month, the same thing—
a town obliterated at moon dark."

He led Xau to the town center.
The stone fountain bowl
had cracked in two.
On the flagstones in front:
a black circle,
wide as a man's height,
wavy lines radiating from it.

"Demon sign," said Xau.

"Yes." Donal spat on the sign.
"Help us. Name your terms."

"We'll help. No terms," said Xau.
"But how? What can we do?"

"I don't know," said Donal.
"I knew how to fight you.
I have no idea how to fight this."

They stood, silent,
by the dry fountain
at the center of what
had once been a town.

NECROMANCER

Ven spoke and dead men heard him.
Ven spoke and rich men paid.

Silver to pass the dead a message;
gold to know what they replied.

Ven feasted, drank, fucked girls
before an audience of ghosts.

A year, two years, and then it palled;
he tired of gold, of limber flesh.

He cut girls, cut boys, killed.
Nothing answered, nothing thrilled.

He corrupted scholars, raised bones,
demanded: "What pleasured you?"

In the tombs of a fallen empire,
the dust whispered: *Demon fire.*

*

The darkness striding through the town
was once a man, but now is not.

Afire, each man, each woman, each child,
each scorched scream fresh, fabulous.

Their thoughts, terrors, torments
unfolding in his mind: tangible, tasty.

A flaring feast that briefly fills
the darkness striding through the town.

RANK AND FILE

To not show his despair,
his fear, his helplessness.
To be what they need him
to be.

At night, on sentry duty,
every shifting shadow
speaks of demons
until the king makes his rounds.
Stops by each sentry,
hears their reports,
remembers their names,
the fragments of their lives
they shared on other nights.
The darkness lifted.

Rice gruel for breakfast
every day for a month
but the soldiers don't complain,
King Xau eating the same.
Only colder.
He and his guards the last
to serve themselves.

To worry about them all—
their boots, blankets, food,
how long it's been since
they last heard from home.

LINNY

"It's only for one night!"
Linny glared at Tirron,
who sat on their bed,
scratching his feet.

"Go if you're scared. I'm staying."

"Of course I'm scared—it's moon dark.
What are you planning to do?
Fight demons?"

"Nope. I'll cook porridge and go to bed."

Linny so furious she wanted to shake him.
Instead she squashed a blanket into her pack,
fastened the straps, said, her voice level,
"Everyone's to leave. King Donal's orders.
The mayor set up a guarded area north of town."

"Not everyone'll go, and some that stay
will be looting. I'll protect our things."

"So you're not planning to fight demons,
just ruffians. That's smart, really smart."

A bell tolled in the distance,
followed by a chorus of other bells,
the chimes overlaying each other
in the dwindling afternoon light,
the last warning to leave.

Linny hoisted her pack.
At the door, her back to him,
she said, "I love you."

Afterward, she clung to that fact,
that she'd told him she loved him.

NIGHT ATTACK

The king away at war—

The palace sentries oblivious
to the enemy infiltration
of his bedchamber—

A feline operative
thwarted the incursion:
the intruder captured, released,
captured, released, recaptured.
Remains deposited on the queen's slippers—

Next assignment: The Pigeon Problem.

ANGSHAN

Safe, they thought they were safe,
safe across the border,
safe from demons,
safe from fire.

The towns of Innis,
their enemy, burning,
but their town, Angshan, safe.
Many flouted the evacuation order.

At moon dark, demon fire.
Indigo flame leapt like lightning
toward a moonless sky.

Burnt, the town of Angshan
burnt down to stone, ash.
Bridges, boats, buildings
all burnt.

Burnt—
the silk market,
the wooden warehouses,
a wealth of cloth, embroidered, dyed.

Bodies burnt to bone.
King Xau stood, silent,
staring down at skeletons.
His fault, his failure.

Later, the king listened to all
who wished to meet with him.
No answers to offer them.
His hands empty.

MOON DARK

Moon dark,
the border town of Ningxi
evacuated in fear of demons.
The moonless night so dark that Tsung,
captain of King Xau's guards,
could barely make out the six men
forming a perimeter round Xau

while he and Li flanked
the young king.

No lamps lit.
Fire of any kind
shunned at moon dark
in the wake of Polton, Harmouth,
Lare, Aldford, Angshan.
All five towns demon-burnt
on moonless nights
like this one.

Little left but stone, ash, bones.

Tsung shivered despite the night's warmth.
Four squads of soldiers patrolling
in case the demons attacked Ningxi,
Xau and his guards operating
as a fifth squad.

"Ware!" yelled Dao,
ahead and left of Tsung—

Tsung and Li shifted
between Dao and the king—

A shadow sped over Tsung.
He swung round. Relaxed.

"Easy," said Tsung. "Just a bat."

"So," said Leong.
"Do we have a defense plan
against rogue bats?"

"Try not to look like
a juicy mosquito," said Gan.

They walked on,
down dark street after dark street.
The town meant to be empty
save for the soldiers,
but Tsung wary of every doorway,
every alley, every window.
Twice they met squads of soldiers,
the king pausing to talk
to the men.

Unclear what soldiers could do
against demon fire.
Unclear what anything could do.

The dark pressed against Tsung
as they moved into the marketplace,
threading their way past stalls
smelling of ginger, cloves, cardamom.

A faint creaking ahead
like a bow being drawn—

"Ware!" Li hurled himself onto Xau
a fraction before Tsung reacted—

Xau and Li thudded down,
Li on top of Xau—

The whoosh of an arrow—
a rap as it struck brick—

Tsung glanced to make sure
Li was shielding Xau—

Ran into darkness
with the other guards—

Ran toward an unseen archer
as a second arrow flew—

"Got him!" shouted Gan,
a man pinioned in his grip.
Probably an Innish patriot
who opposed the temporary truce,
who reviled King Xau.

"Gan and Shuen, tie him up," said Tsung.
"Chong, Dao, Tai Seng, search
for accomplices. Leong, with me."

Tsung raced back—
Li still covering Xau with his body.
"Li. Report."

"He landed hard. Bruised, maybe worse."

"Li was hit." Xau's voice muffled.
"He's bleeding. Leong!"

Leong, who doubled as field surgeon
as well as guard, bent down by them.
Tsung forced his gaze away,
scanning the area, listening.

Dao ran over. "No one else nearby."

"Stand guard."
Tsung crouched by Leong,
Xau and Li now sitting side by side
while Leong evaluated them.
"How are they?"

"Middling. The king's badly bruised.
An arrow grazed Li's arm,
bloody but shallow."

"All right, let's get them back
to the campsite."

"No," said Xau,
pushing himself upright.
"We will not leave our soldiers
to face a threat
we will not face ourselves."

In the king's voice
the weight of the burnt towns.
Tsung responsible for the king,
the king responsible
for a country.

Tsung set his hand gently
on Xau's shoulder, said,
"At least rest a while."

Xau nodded,
sat back down without protest,
proof that the king was shaken.
Tsung not that calm himself.
Hours until dawn.

Demons out there somewhere.

MIDSUMMER'S DAY

Plump bees clung to the clover
in the stretch of meadowland
between Donal's encampment and Xau's,
both armies allied against the demons,
but ready to fight each other
if the demons ever fell.

Midsummer's Day,
but the soldiers inside their tents.
No feasting, no celebration,
the demon fire, the burnt towns
had marked them all.

> *

A messenger came to Donal's tent.
"Your Majesty, a package from King Xau."

Donal undid the long, heavy bundle:
bamboo, colored silks, paper, string.
"What is this?"

"String," said the messenger, "paper—"

"I can fucking see that. What's it for?"

The messenger, prudently, said nothing.

"Get out," said Donal.
He tossed the bundle to Rose, his woman,
went to the entrance flap.
Over at Xau's encampment,
a scrap of purple lifted into the air—
a kite, a fucking kite—

The purple diamond climbed higher.
Donal's sentries shouted,
more animated than they'd been in weeks.
Other soldiers peered from their tents,
saw the kite, came outside.

"Fuck." Donal turned to Rose.
"Have you ever made a fucking kite?"

> *

As the long day wore on
more kites dipped and rose
on the skittish breeze.

At dusk, they held a contest.
Two boys, one from Meqing, one from Innis,
unable to speak each other's language,
between them crafted a paper wolf head
that darted and soared,
hunting the wind,
outflying all the other kites.

Two hundred years later,
when Xau and Donal and their soldiers
were long buried,
their deeds reduced to song,
the children of Innis and of Meqing
flew kites each Midsummer's Day.

BURNT

First went Polton, home to tanners,
skinners, saddlers, cobblers.
Not one hide, one shoe left
of all their wares.

Next Harmouth, the deep harbor
and the dry-stone walls unscathed.
Within the town little left
but stone, ash, bones.

Then Lare, Aldford, Angshan:
linen, sheep, the silk market;
Balimar of the horse races;
Jozhou of the flowered courtesans.

All burnt, and with them a convoy
of Sumbrese merchant galleys,
four triremes from the Ritan fleet,
unnumbered fishing boats.

TRAINING: ENDURANCE

In humid heat,
up and down a low hill

along a goat track,
carrying shield and sword,
sweating, ran King Xau,
his guard Li at his side.

Another town burnt.
Nothing Xau could do.

Stationed along the way,
his other seven guards
and twenty of his cavalrymen
(horseless, standing guard).

Another town burnt—
How many heeded the warnings and left?
How many stayed and burned?

Up and down the hill;
Tsung, captain of his guards,
watched from the summit,
gave Xau and Li water
each time they crested the hill.

Demon signs left on stonework.
Demon fire sighted from afar,
indigo flame leaping like lightning.

People gathered on the hillside,
wide hats shading their heads,
casting circles like demon signs
onto the short grass.
They bowed as Xau passed,
a swaying wave of men and women.

Men and women who looked to him
to save them,
who trusted him,
who thought him more than he was.

An hour and a half in,
sweaty, sweltering, smelly,
his arm chafed raw by the shield straps,
his calves protesting each stride,
Tsung said to him, "Stop if you wish."
Xau shook his head,
ran on, Li at his side,
past the growing crowd.

Would have run until he fell
if it would help,
but he couldn't fight demons,
couldn't even find the demons,
couldn't find anyone who had seen a demon
and survived.

Men and women stretched in continuous lines
either side of the goat track,
bowing as he passed,
their shadows slowly lengthening.

The demons woken out of story,
out of nightmare.
A hundred dark legends, but no mention
of how to defeat demons,
of what Xau could do.
Or try to do.

Up and down the hill,
Li at his side, sweating,
but Li's gait, Li's breath as easy
as when they began.
(Xau gasping.)

Another town burnt.
Xau's soldiers, Xau's people, Donal's people
all looking to Xau
as if he were King Nariz himself
come with a hundred dragons to save them—
A dragon—
Maybe.

He glanced at Li,
saw Li's steady gaze on him.
"Better?" asked Li,
the first word he had said all that afternoon.
"Maybe," said Xau.
Li touched him lightly on the shoulder
as they reached the top of the hill,
as Xau stopped, bowed to Tsung.
Stretched. Drank. Considered.

DRAGON

Unarmed and unarmored, alone,
he walked up the mountain
as he had six years ago.

Then as now, it snowed.
Then as now, she landed beside him,
snow steaming from her wings.

"I gave you a kingdom,"
she said, her breath ash.
"What more do you want?"

"A way to save that kingdom."
He knelt to her, his knees in the snow,
snow creeping into the tops of his boots.
"The demons have returned—"

"Not *demons*. Demon, singular.
One demon, many servants.
And he did not *return*;
he was born a man, a man like you:
eating and pissing and farting.
Now he does none of those things."

Still kneeling, he stared into
the inscrutable gold of her eyes.
"Will you help us defeat him?"

She flamed. Heat stung his face.
"I came. I am speaking to you.
What do you think I am doing?
I despise the demon,
as I despised the one before him."

"The one before?"

"Yes. Eleven hundred years ago.
How quickly your people forget."

He leaned forward until his head brushed the snow.
"Please. Help us. He is burning the towns.
We cannot stop him. We do not know how."

"Get up. Don't beg. It doesn't suit you."

He stood.

"The demon is a foul and spreading stain
in my thoughts. If he comes here, I will kill him."
She turned her head to the side and flamed hugely,
her breath lighting the slope below them.

"*If* he comes here—will you not seek him out?"

"No. My power is in these mountains.
The last demon came here
when she ran out of towns to burn.
Perhaps this one will too."

"That's your advice: to wait until every town
has burnt to the ground, and *then* kill him?"

She laughed, a sound like an anvil dropped on granite.
"Good. I like it better when you spit.
I advise you to kill him yourself."

"How? We are outmatched."

"Are you? Do not men follow you?
Did not the horses come to you?"

"If we knew which town he would attack,
if we had any way to defend it—"

"As to which town, I cannot help.
But remember two things:
an army will not help against a demon,
and demons are strongest in darkness."

"Thank you. We are in your debt—"

"Spare me the speech. Go. Hurry.
Save what's left of your kingdom."

ALDFORD

Thirty feet down,
months after Aldford burned,
old Nial shoveled dirt,
digging out a new well.

His back hurt. His arms hurt.

He took a break, straightened up,
stared at the small circle
of gray sky.

Linny, his son's wife,
grunted beside him,
a woman doing man's work.
Both of them fools.

Should have stayed gone,
left for another town,
like most of the others
who fled before the fire.

Nial bent back over,
pried loose a rock
with swollen painful fingers.
Shoveled more dirt.

He wasn't going anywhere,
at least not while his son
lay up top, his bones
lost among other bones.

BEFORE

Khyert, once King Xau's stableboy,
now valet, aide, groom,
handed the king pants, tunic, belt—
Khyert's hands shaking—
said in a sudden burst,
"Do not send me from your side!"

Xau adjusted his belt, looked to Khyert.
"If we ourself are killed,
we would have you live."

     *

Artoch, senior advisor to King Xau,
lifted his tea bowl,
set it down again without drinking.
"Your Majesty, I recommend—I ask—
that you take your guards.
Please."

Xau shook his head.

Artoch knelt then,
he who never knelt to Xau,
he who offered the young king
advice not adulation.

"Thank you," said Artoch,
"for your service to Meqing."
His voice deserted him.
The king a blur who came over
and gently raised him up.

                    *

Tsung, captain of King Xau's guards,
checked Xau's sword for the third time,
stared long at Xau before he said,
"Your father undervalued you.
It has been the honor
of my life to serve you."

Xau took his sword,
laid his hand briefly
on Tsung's shoulder.

                    *

Xau's guard Li hummed a fishing chanty
until Xau raised his eyebrows,
said, mildly, "What, no parting words?"

"There is much I would say."
Li looked at him steadily.
"Tomorrow. When you return."

DEMON

At noon, the armies withdrew.
King Xau stood on the town wall,
watching the train of men
and wagons and horses head north.

"Behold our great plan,"
said Donal, the Red King,
from his place at Xau's left.
"I can't say I like our chances."

Xau said nothing.
Either the demon would come,

or he would not.
Either they would defeat him,
or they would not.

"I've never liked waiting,"
said Donal. "Let's walk."

Together they walked
the circuit of the town wall.
Inside the town, a few cats,
pigeons, gulls; no people,
no one left for the demon to burn
except the kings themselves.

Xau stopped at a crenel
overlooking the sea.
The air smelt of salt.
Fishing boats rocked on the water.
He squinted at the horizon
until his eyes smarted,
looking for movement, a sail,
a demon ship. Nothing.

When they had walked
twice round the wall,
they sat and shared a meal
of fruit and dried meat.
Neither ate much.

"Let's light the torches,"
said Donal, and they walked
the circuit once more,
lighting the tall, smoky torches.
Then down into the empty town,
where they lit more torches
as the day wore on.

Without discussion,
they ended by the fountain
at the center of the town.
Deserted shops and market stalls
lined the wide street up to the fountain.

They stretched. They pissed.

They played a children's game
of tossing sticks and stones.

They sharpened their sharp swords.

Above, the sky darkened. No moon.

The torches kept the town
bright as a rainy day,
yet the night pressed against Xau
as if the dark behind the stars
reached down for him.

In Donal's face, the same uneasiness.

"If the demon is coming," said Xau,
"let us greet him." Tentatively,
he sang the first words
of a song of Donal's people,
"*My brother, he taught me*
to fight with a sword—"

Donal joined in, "*My brother,*
he taught me to follow our lord."
Afterward, he looked at Xau.
"I'm ready. Let him come."

Xau nodded.
If the demon did not come,
if he did not lust to kill
two undefended kings
in their fragile arrogance,
then he would burn a different town.
Better here.

Xau dipped his hands into
the fountain's water,
splashed his cheeks and drank.

The water rippled in a rising wind.
The torches gusted.

In the empty street of empty shops,
a door opened. A man ran out,
his face lit by the gusting torches
so that Xau saw him clear: Khyert,
who was once Xau's stableboy,
who had left with the army,
who could not be here.

Donal drew his sword.

"Stay!" said Xau. "We know him."

Khyert ran to him and knelt.
Down the street, a torch blew out.

Xau hauled Khyert upright. "Run!"

"No. I won't leave you—"

"We command you."
The wind flattened Xau's hair.
"Go!"

But already a darkness strode toward them,
shaped like a man, but void of color;
a hole, a gap, a horror.

"Kneel to me," said the demon,
"and I will protect you."

His voice was the voice
of Xau's favorite brother. Hearing him,
Xau was a yearning child again,
who had only to kneel,
a small thing,
a gesture.

He put one hand
on the rim of the fountain basin
to hold himself upright.

"Kneel to me," said that voice,
familiar, loved. "Let me help you."

Beyond Xau, Donal knelt.
Closer, right beside Xau, Khyert knelt too.

Xau put his other hand
on the fountain basin and held on.
His brother was dead.
The demon lied.

"Kneel and I will raise
you up as my captains.
Together we will rule a kingdom
greater than any you have dreamed."

Xau let go of the fountain basin.

Slowly, he drew his sword.
He had not wanted a kingdom,
but one had come to him,
one that he would die for.

As the demon neared,
Xau thought,
incongruously,
of the first horse
he had ever had,
the moistness as she lipped up
a piece of apple from his hand.

"Kneel or burn," said the demon.
A ribbon of indigo flame curled
in the void of the demon's left hand.

The demon cast the fire
and in that instant
Khyert pushed himself upright
in front of Xau,
straight onto the flame:
a man-torch, a skeleton of fire,
ash and bone crumbling.

Xau lunged at the demon,
his sword catching
on a thickness like honey,
hot as fire,
searing his sword,
the hilt scorching his hand.
He sliced again and again into a darkness
that broke apart on his blade.
He thrust though he could barely
force himself to hold the fiery sword,
thrust though the darkness cried out
in his brother's voice,
thrust when there was nothing
left to thrust at,
when the flames
and the darkness
had gone.

A hand took his sword from him.
Donal said, "It's over. You won.
You fucking won."

Xau took his sword back.
He noted distantly how the sword shook
in his grip,
how it hurt to clasp it,
his hand red, blistered.

Donal went to one knee. "I, Donal,
King of Innis, pledge peace,
never to attack your lands—
draw up a treaty.
I'll sign it."

Xau nodded.
He supposed he should feel glad, triumphant.
Maybe later he would.

"Who was that man?" asked Donal.

"Khyert. His name was Khyert."

Xau walked away from Donal,
away from where the demon had been,
away from the bones
of what had once
been a friend.

THE DEMON'S CREW

Kneel to me,
and I will protect you.

Black-robed, in thrall,
the demon's crew
knelt as one
on the unlit ship
on the moonless sea.

The demon ashore,
a mile away,
but his words
reverberated
in the twenty men:
soft as a swan's wing,
beloved as the women
whose voices he borrowed.

Kneel or burn.

Twenty throats screamed,
transfixed, transcendent,
afire with the flame
in the demon's hand.
Twenty hands cast
that flame with him:
unbearable ecstasy,
burning, purified—

Severed.

Cords cut.

The demon gone. Gone.
Dead? They knew not.

Twenty men unmoored,
rocking on the moonless sea.

Night? Day? No meaning now.
Each man alone, separate,
sailing uncharted seas;
hourglass stopped, broken,
overboard.

A dawn came,
but they did not heed it.

A ship came,
but they did not hail it.

Voices called,
but not his voice.

Came, last, aboard their ship,
a king:
    In the dark lost compass
    of their souls,
    a man's hand
    laid to their chest,
    bare skin to bare skin;
    a man's voice—
    rough, tired, hoarse,
    a coarse thing,
    but certain as daybreak,
    sure as an anchor,
    calling them home.

DEBT

On the deck of the demon's ship,
twenty sailors, sprawled as if dead.

Left to himself,
King Donal would have finished the job,
killed them for aiding the demon.

But King Xau was determined
to try to save them,
and Donal in Xau's debt.
So Donal shouted at a sailor,
upended a bucket of water over him.
The man stayed still as a stuffed sack,
breathing but senseless.

Xau, his burnt hand heavily bandaged,
knelt down on the planks,
touched the sailor,
spoke to him,
too soft for Donal to catch the words,
and the man stirred. Woke.

Might have been happenstance,
except that neither Donal,
nor his guards,
nor Xau's guards,
could duplicate Xau's feat.

In the end,
Xau the one who woke
all twenty men,
and by the end
Xau huddled on the deck,
hunched over like an old man,
haggard, harrowed, shaking.

Donal crouched beside him—
Xau a fucking noble prick
who'd been fucking easy to hate
when they were enemies,
but last night that fucking noble prick
had killed a demon,
a debt Donal couldn't repay.
"Xau? Can I help?"

Xau shook his head.

Across the deck, commotion:
"The king! King Xau!"
the sailors, roped like prisoners,
shouted, demanding Xau.

Xau set his good hand
on one of his guards,
hauled himself upright. Went over.

The oldest sailor bowed to Xau,
"Your Majesty, what about the others?"

"Others?"

"The demon's other servants, sir.
At his fortress. Who'll wake them?"

"You believe there are men lying there,
insensible as you were?"

"Yes, sir. Men, women, children."

Xau took a breath.
"If you will take us there,
we will try to help—"

"Hold up," said Donal. "How many people?"

The man shrugged. "Two, three thousand."

"No," said Donal flatly.
He turned to Xau.
"You can't save thousands.
You barely managed twenty."

"We must try."

Donal spat on the deck.
"I'll go in your place, do what I can.
You saved both our fucking kingdoms.
That's enough."

"No," said Xau. "Too many have died,
in battle or demon-burnt.
We will do this."

Xau didn't look like much,

wounded, worn out, scrawny,
yet Donal the one who'd knelt to the demon,
Xau the one who'd defied it.

Xau didn't look like much,
but the set of his face uncompromising
as he held Donal's gaze.
Donal the one who looked away,
who dipped his head, defeated.

Xau a stubborn prick.
He'd make a good ally,
if he didn't get himself killed.

DAYBREAK

Northeast by east
along the curve of the world
sailed the demon's ship
back to his fortress.

Behind the ship,
dawn spread over
the burnt towns—
Angshan, Jozhou, Aldford,
Lare, Harmouth, Polton—
the third dawn
since the demon's death.

Northeast by east
sailed the demon's crew,
bringing the king
who slew the demon,
the king who saved them
from the demon's spell,
King Xau, who stared down
at the heaving ocean
into which he heaved,
miserably, his breakfast.

Swiftly they closed on
the demon's fortress,
day already bright
on its battlements.
Within, the demon's servants
—unbound, undone by his undoing—

lay, parched, on the stones,
the men, women, children
who had knelt to the demon
as he burnt their towns
(Polton, Harmouth, Lare,
Aldford, Jozhou, Angshan).

To save them, the sailors
brought the king,
the king who would
call them home.

NUMBERS

Later, a historian, striving for the appearance of candor, said he couldn't de-termine precisely how many people the demon burnt in their towns, but that, by using the most meticulous methods, he estimated between 16,020 and 16,150 perished thus.

Seeking the authority of precision, the historian next stated that 18,272 men, 16,164 women, and 4,769 children followed the demon to his island fortress and there served him in dubious ways.

When the demon died,
fewer than two thousand
of his servants remained alive
within his fortress.

He had not hoarded his human treasure,
but spent it, singly or by the dozen,
setting servants aflame
in the dining hall.

Fewer than two thousand left
when King Xau came,
yet still the number
seemed overwhelming—

people lay collapsed in chambers,
passages, stairwells;
inert, parched, many injured,
all dying of thirst.

The same historian, a soured and stunted specimen, dismissed King Xau's part in a peevish paragraph. He said that doubtless the king visited the fortress, but that the king himself saved no one, merely ordered his soldiers to wake the dazed sufferers.

The king's guards tried
to rouse the survivors;
the sailors who had brought
the king to the island tried:

they could not rouse
one man, woman, child.
Instead they wet the sufferers' lips
(most swallowed, some did not),

and took them to the king—
who did not look kingly
(a fact the historian would have reported
gleefully had he guessed it).

Xau slouched, slovenly, sweat-soaked
over body after body;
his hands on chest, face, neck;
speaking, whispering, croaking.

Five died before the king
had time to help them.
Thirteen more (injured, weak)
woke, but died within days.

A few of the survivors
achieved distinction:
the glassblower from Angshan
rose to the head of his guild;

the china bowls made by one
female potter were hailed
(over a century later)
as the greatest of their age;

thirty-two men enlisted in the army,
of whom one became a captain of note.
Most returned, their names unrecorded
by history, to ordinary lives.

Curiously, when they remembered
the king kneeling over them,
each recalled a heroic figure:
young, handsome, clean, richly dressed.

Many described him as crowned,
the crowns as various as the speakers—

plain or jeweled, arched or unarched,
gold or silver or iron.

Only the guard who carried the king
back to the ship accurately remembered
the man in his arms: smelly, shaking,
stammering, crownless but a king.

DARKNESS

Xau woke in the rocking wooden cabin of the ship, his guards about him,
his sheets twisted, soaked in sweat. He shook, and could not stop from shaking, could not speak, could not answer his guards. Tsung stood over him, an
oil lantern swinging in his hand. Xau stared up at its small and insufficient
light. The ship a scrap tossed atop vast darkness. Above the dark ocean, above
the swinging lantern, unbounded night. Gan and Shuen lit more lanterns,
brought them near, but it was Li who lifted Xau in his arms, who carried
him out onto the rocking deck. Before them, the waxing moon and all the
patterned stars hung over the sea. The darkness broken. The demon dead.

MENDING

King Xau's strength spent,
the demon's voice—
his brother's borrowed voice—
a battering wave Xau drowned beneath.

Held under by the foundering weight
of men, women, children
in hopeless, helpless hundreds,
Xau lost as those he'd tried to save.

Asleep, awake. Memory, nightmare.
Against that joint assault,
his guards at first a whisper,
seeking to let him rest.

Their hushed deference shifted
to insistence, persistence.
They changed his clothes,
his bandages, his sheets.

Li sat by him, stitching a tunic,
humming as he worked.
Li's hands, his voice snagged

Xau's drifted thoughts.

Xau watched each stitch:
needle, thread, cloth.
The rhythm of Li's hands,
Li's voice held Xau afloat.

Xau watched, unquestioning,
as Li undid the work he'd done,
sewed the same seam, over and over,
to keep Xau safe.

TRAINING: SHIELD

"No more delays. No more fucking games."
King Donal strode past Artoch,
the old man who served
as senior advisor to King Xau.

Donal did not like Artoch,
did not like men who spoke
but never fought.
No sword on Artoch's belt,
no fire in the man's belly.

Artoch's voice behind him, apologetic.

Before the translator
could parrot whatever platitudes
the old man mouthed,
Donal said, "Don't bother translating.
King Xau got back two days ago.
I'm seeing him now."

The guards outside the room
where Xau was closeted
took Donal's sword, his dagger,
the knife from his boot.

Within, a cool dimness.
Stone walls. High windows.
King Xau in the slanted light
from one of the windows,
swordless, shield up,
opposite a guard
with a wooden practice sword,

four more guards at a little distance.

A bleakness in the younger king's face
that harrowed Donal,
exhaustion in Xau's stance,
under his eyes—"Are you hurt?"

Xau stared at Donal,
but did not answer.

Tsung, captain of Xau's guards,
said, "The king's burns are healing."

"Can't he—" Donal looked to Xau.
"Can you speak?"

Artoch, the old man,
spoke up from the doorway,
echoed by the translator,
"The king labored six days
calling men, women, children
back from the demon.
His words are spent for now."

Xau stood in slanted light,
but shadow and darkness
between them, behind them.

Donal dipped his head to Xau.
"Thirteen nights ago,
I watched you kill that demon.
I'll sign any treaty you give me,
but I won't negotiate with minions."

Xau said, haltingly,
as if he had to dig each word
from frozen ground,
"Then. Wait."

From the doorway,
Artoch bowed to Xau, said,
"Your Majesty, I recommend
that you show King Donal
the training routine."

Xau stared at Artoch,
made a gesture with his hand

of resignation or consent,
before bowing to the guard
with the wooden sword.

The guard lunged forward.
Xau blocked with his shield.
The guard lunged again,
his arm a fraction higher.
Then again. And again.

Move and countermove.
The clash of wood on iron.
Xau awkward, hesitant.
The guard like a dancer.
Time and again, the wooden sword
tapped Xau on wrist, knee, shin.

Tsung, the guard captain,
spoke as the two men fought,
"This is a warm-up drill.
Move and response are fixed.
King Xau has done this a thousand times.
Never as poorly."

"Fuck."

Move and countermove.
Xau too slow,
only the guard's care
saving him from injury
when the wooden sword struck him.

When the two men stopped,
Donal looked at Artoch.
"Why did you have me watch that?"

"Because a treaty is worthless
without your trust.
I'm not here to play games
or to delay you without cause."
Flame in the old man's voice.

"I stand corrected."
Donal bowed to the old man,
turned back to Xau.
Shadow and darkness behind them,
and a debt Donal couldn't repay,

his kingdom saved.

He touched his hand to his heart,
offered it palm-up to Xau
in the old sign of allegiance.
"I'll wait. As long as you need."

Xau nodded. Wordless. Bleak.

TIRRON

In the ashy ruins of Aldford,
Tirron found and held his Linny.

Her face pressed into his shoulder;
her gulping sobs shook him.

"I thought you burnt," she gulped.
"I thought you dead."

He shuddered hearing her voice—
the voice the demon had borrowed,

the voice he'd served,
the voice he'd knelt to.

(Better men than he had burnt
instead of kneeling:

collapsing skeletons of fire,
scorched screams.)

He shuddered, but didn't let go,
only clutched Linny tighter.

He'd rehearsed what to say,
but couldn't get the words out,

couldn't make promises,
or tell her what he'd done.

"It's all right, Tirron,"
she said, "It'll be all right."

Wordless, he held onto Linny
and tried to believe her.

RETURNING

Through darkness,
King Xau rode with his guards,
changing horses at every way-fort—
hurrying the startled staff,
following them into the warm stables,
that smell of horse, of hay, of leather
as he helped tack up the horses—
his heart pounding as if time
were running out,
but the demon dead,
the kingdom safe.

Through freshening wind,
Xau rode with the eight men
who had shielded him
when he could not speak,
who'd woken him when nightmare wracked him,
when the demon called in his brother's voice,
night after night—
his guards beside him,
then as now.

Under moonlight,
Xau rode, not quite himself yet,
wind drying his face.
Khyert dead.
Khyert, who should have been
riding beside him.
Xau rode,
home within reach;
his children, his wife,
the thought of them,
the need for them
driving him on.

HAN CHEN

When the king returned a full day early,
Han Chen, his steward,
did not quite run through the palace
in order to speak to him—

that would have been unseemly—
but he walked so briskly
that the boy attending him
had to run to keep up—
King Xau must have ridden
through the night—
Why such haste?
The demon dead, the war over—

Ahead, Tsung, captain of Xau's guards,
travel-soiled, rank with sweat,
blocked the door to the king's rooms.

Han Chen raised his eyebrows:
"Captain, is there a problem?"

"No." Tsung paused, added,
"Unless your business is urgent,
give the king time."

Not Tsung's place
to come between steward and king,
not unless the matter bore
on the king's safety,
which Tsung would have told him.

Nor, by custom, should the king
have delayed before seeing Han Chen—
the king's father had never done so—
the running of a kingdom to discuss—
"I will see the king. Now."

Within, two more of the king's guards,
and the king sitting cross-legged
on the floor, disheveled, dirty,
Prince Keng on his lap.

As Han Chen entered, Prince Keng demanded,
"Papa, why are you so smelly?"

"We were in a hurry to see you."
The king's voice hoarse
as he hugged his son,
looked up at Han Chen.

Who bowed to him,
turned round, left the room.

He had sons of his own,
but had never gone to war,
never had to leave them
for months at a time.

The king's father had erred.
The kingdom could wait.

RIDDLE: MAIDEN

The king hadn't slept.

Dao, who'd had the night shift,
had watched the king's wakefulness
from across the room,
the king still harrowed by the demon,
and by the days he'd labored
calling men, women, children
back from their dark service
to that demon.

So that morning,
taking breakfast with King Xau
and Xau's family and Xau's other guards,
Dao unobtrusively filled in the spaces
in the conversation,
distracted Prince Keng and little Ying:

"This tiny maiden dines on leaves,
spins and weaves so you may wear
beautiful clothes, yet wears
no clothes herself.
Who is she?"

"Mama!" shouted Ying.

"That's wrong," said Keng.
"Mama wears clothes."

Dao cleared his throat.
"This tiny maiden spins so you may wear
beautiful, soft, *silky* clothes—"

"A silkworm!" said Keng. "Another. Please."

After breakfast,
as Dao was leaving for his quarters,

the king's hand on his arm:

"This warrior worked all night," said Xau,
"then, unasked, served extra duty."

King Xau bowed low to him.

AFTER

Triumph. Demon dead.
Yet the young king woke each night
fighting him again.

> Back to the burnt towns
> straggled men, women, children
> with their lice, fleas, horses.

High on her mountain
the dragon yawned, vastly pleased
with her chosen king.

> Bracelets, rings, flowers
> placed in the ashy ruins;
> a child's stuffed rabbit.

VICTORY

When King Donal returned, triumphant,
the whole town came out to cheer.
Trumpets sounded, pipes blew,
children whistled, dogs barked.

Donal rode up to the castle,
throwing honeyed almonds to the children,
but he did not smile, nor speak, nor wave.

In the castle gatehouse,
Connol, his brother, gave him a bear-hug.
"It's been dull here.
You can have your throne back."

Donal nodded, but said nothing.

"I hear you had more excitement. You were right.
Horse Boy brought us victory."

"Don't call him that," said Donal.

"What? Xau?"

"King Xau."

"But you call him Horse Boy—"

"Not anymore." Donal walked past Connol,
past the people waiting to meet him,
and up the spiral stairs.

Connol sprinted after him:
"Did I say something wrong?"

"King Xau slew the demon."
Donal came out onto the wall-walk.
"I won't call him names.
Nor will any man in my army."

"How did he kill the demon?" asked Connol.

Donal walked on without answering.
He had no mind to tell anyone,
even Connol, about the demon,
its voice like their uncle's voice.
How Donal knelt to it.
How he would have taken
what the demon offered.

Connol caught Donal's arm. "Are you all right?"

"I'm fine. We won. King Xau won."
Donal shook himself free of Connol's grip.
He stared out of an embrasure,
seeing neither the hillside
nor the town below,
but the demon's men,
found the morning after the demon died.

Men who didn't speak,
didn't look at anyone,
didn't react. Lost.

As he might have been.

"Xau saved the demon's men," said Donal.

"I don't believe it," said Connol.
"You like Xau now. You fucking like him."

"I fucking do," said Donal—
and the saying of it,
and Connol beside him,
and the town below them safe once more—
set something right inside him.

"So," said Donal, "did you fetch women?
Rewards for the valiant?"

"Your wife is visiting her sister."
Connol grinned. "So yes, I fetched women."

"Don't delay then," said Donal. "Lead on."

QUEEN FIAN

Fian said, rubbing oil onto Donal's back:
Such a great victory,
such a victory as they will sing of,
the victory of our age.

Fian, giving Donal spiced wine:
You saved your country,
and now, at last,
you will save mine.

Fian, massaging his legs:
Xau the Usurper trusts you,
thinks you his grateful pawn,
ambition lost, fire quenched—
hush, my king, be easy.
Forget my words,
they are nothing but air.
Going, gone.

Fian, turning him over and oiling his chest:
My people are crushed.
So long, it has been so long
they do not remember freedom.
My mother, and my mother's mother,
and their mothers before them,
waiting, always waiting.

Fian, atop him:
Now. Waiting. Ends.

Fian, licking him clean:
The great victory is already yours.
Done. Won.

Fian, giving him more spiced wine:
I ask only a token:
two kings out hunting,
an accident, a tragic fall,
poor young king Xau—
hush, be easy! Hush.

Fian, rubbing his arms, his shoulders:
Hush, there are other ways.
Forget my words,
they are nothing but air. Going, gone.
Let it be as your heart wishes.
Go to Xau, become his friend.

Fian, kissing Donal's closed eyes:
Only invite him here.
Only that.

Fian, whispering, hand on his forehead:
My words are air.
Only bring Xau to me.

DEMON STAIN

Dusk on a moonless evening,
Queen Fian herself
went down on her knees
to scrub flagstones,

squeezed black water
into a silver bucket,
lifted her head
to smile at the crowd.

Men and women cheered:
their Queen herself
had come to rinse away
the stain of the demon.

*

Midnight at moon dark,
unattended, unwatched,
the Queen placed a hair
in a vial of black liquid,

one strand of her hair—
the demon liquid hissed
in a foam of bubbles.
The hair dissolved.

She stoppered the vial,
thinking of her mother,
and her mother's mother,
of vengeance coming.

DARK HARVEST

High on her mountain,
the dragon woke—

A fell foulness flared
at the far periphery
of her awareness,
north and east of her,
across the Innish border.

As if the demon walked again.

No, not quite.
The corruption tainted, altered,
as if someone had harvested
the demon's strength,
claimed it for their own.

The dragon's eyes black,
the gold in them gone.
The night dark, moonless,
the stars obscured.

BRIGHID

Six years old,
youngest of the demon's servants,
didn't cry when the king
roused her after the demon's death;
nor when, an hour later, she remembered

her father's scorched scream,
his flesh aflame;
nor when, toward evening,
a fishmonger recognized her
and offered to see her back to her aunt;
nor when, weeks later, the fishmonger
delivered her to her aunt, who hugged her—
and hugged the fishmonger—
and wept.

That night the farm tomcat,
a gray and surly mouser
not inclined to affection,
lay down on Brighid's blanket
and matter-of-factly licked her arm,
her bare shoulder, her face,
his rough tongue rasping her skin,
and she cried,
thinking not of her father,
or their burnt home, their burnt town,
but of her mother's voice,
a voice she'd forgotten
until the demon borrowed it,
that she'd known to be a lie
but followed anyhow.

MATTERS OF STATE

"This is the *shortened* guest list?"
King Xau waved three closely-inked sheets
at Artoch, his senior advisor.

"Yes, if you wish to treat King Donal
as your equal, then he must be
introduced to everyone of importance
on his first official visit."

Xau skimmed the list.
"Ministers, yes. Guild heads, yes.
Generals, yes. But every judge?
Every scholar?"

"A mere twelve scholars."

"Twelve scholars."
Xau imagined Ang Su raising a point

of abstruse logic and Donal's likely reaction
(a word no translator could render
both politely and accurately).
All Xau could do not to laugh,
but Artoch had worked tirelessly,
so Xau mastered himself.
"Very good."

"Your Majesty. One more detail."
Artoch looked down at his sleeves
as if suddenly fascinated by them.
"King Donal said he would bring
just five men with him—
Queen Fian is not accompanying him."

"We know. And so?"

Artoch, a man who'd intimidated generals,
hesitated, cleared his throat.
"Five men, no women.
King Donal is said to be a man
of considerable appetites."

Xau had spent too many nights
sharing a tent with his guards
to be shy about such matters:
"If you want to offer him harlots,
we will approve it.
Speak to Captain Tsung."

"Thank you, Your Majesty."
Artoch's eyes fixed on his sleeves
as he retreated from the room.

TWO KINGS

Side by side rode the two kings:
Donal, the Red King,
red-haired and red-handed in war,
and Xau, the Horse King.

Donal come now in peace, welcomed,
to the land he twice attacked,
come at Xau's request,
sooner than he himself
would have chosen.

Barely a week at home
before it was time to leave.
But he would have turned round
and ridden back to Xau
the same hour he'd reached home
had the younger king asked it.

Shadow and darkness behind them
and a debt Donal couldn't repay.

"You're looking better."
Donal searched Xau's face,
found no sign of the harrowing
that had marked him five weeks ago.
"Are you better?"

"Largely."

"And this is what you want?
That I come to the memorial?"

"Yes." Finality in Xau's voice.

Donal noted the soldiers
riding in advance,
the scouts on their flanks,
his own men and Xau's guards
following behind them.

At length, Xau looked over at Donal.
"Though we cannot forget
and will not ignore
what happened, we seek an end to it.
Peace in place of war.
Friendship in place of fear.
Let it start with the two of us."

"You think we can be friends?"
Donal shook his head inadvertently.
He owed Xau his kingdom.
A demon slain,
hundreds of Donal's people
freed from the demon's service
at a cost that had nearly broken
the younger king.
Yet they had little in common—
by all his informants had ever heard,

Xau neither drank, nor gambled,
nor even whored.

Unexpectedly, Xau grinned.
"Why not? What are you thinking?
That we are nothing like each other?"

"That, and wondering why you speak Innish."

"By our father's command."

"King Hao? He called us barbarians."
Had, in fact, addressed Donal
as *King of the Barbarians*
the one time they met.
A meeting that had not ended well.
"Why would he want his son
to speak like a barbarian?"

"His fourth and least important son.
He planned to marry off
ourself or our sister
to an Innish ruler
and so pacify the barbarians."

"Your sister speaks Innish too?"

Xau nodded. "And learned it faster.
For three years we studied together.
Both of us unwilling.
Then two years by ourself alone,
after Mei was judged fluent
and we were not.
We were a slow student."

A mile of silence,
but an easy silence.
Half Donal's attention on the land,
noting defensible ridges,
the scant cover—
a few isolated stands of trees.
Half his attention on Xau,
the younger king's posture relaxed,
yet Xau eyeing the selfsame stands of trees.
Not everyone in Meqing
glad of Donal's visit.

Side by side rode the two kings.

RESPECT

Cheong stood apart from the other mourners
on the cropped grass inside the ring of graves.
A waste of his time,
waiting for the two kings,
and Cheong too old to have much time
left to waste.

Seventy-seven sandstone slabs,
each garlanded with paper flowers,
each with a chiseled name.
The seventy-eighth slab
void of flowers,
his son's name standing alone.

Cheong had incised the name himself,
back in the spring,
the fields ready for planting,
but Cheong practicing
on fragments of sandstone,
working with hammer and chisel
until he was certain
his hand would not slip,
that each character would be properly formed.
April when he'd chipped out the name.

Fall now,
the war over,
a demon slain,
though it hadn't been a demon
that killed his son,
but men,
the Red King's men, raiding,
the raid that started the war.

A waste of Cheong's time, waiting.
No king, no gold, no paper flowers
of any use to his son.

Cheong was contemplating leaving
when the two kings arrived,
bare-headed, white-robed,
walking ahead of a company of soldiers.

King Xau, Cheong's king,

stopped at the far edge
of the ring of graves,
bowed three times to the mourners,
said, "We are sorry we failed you."

Not much of a speech,
but the young king's voice
hefted with loss.

The other king, the Red King,
the one whose soldiers
slaughtered Cheong's son,
said nothing at all.

King Xau went to the nearest grave,
read aloud the chiseled name,
bowed three times, very deeply,
said the name once more,
looked to the Red King,
who echoed the name.

King Xau moved to the next grave,
read aloud the chiseled name.

Men said that Xau slew the demon,
that when the Red King saw him do so,
then the Red King knelt to Xau
and pledged peace.
Cheong old enough to remember eight wars.
Words as worthless as paper flowers.

Xau came to Cheong's son's grave,
said the name aloud,
put his hand to the bare stone,
touched each chiseled character.

The king a white-robed blur.
Cheong's son dead.

DIVERSION

One moment, King Donal rode beside King Xau,
wondering when the mock ambush would be,

the autumn air clear and cool,
glossy-leaved bushes bright with berries.

Next moment, the hill ahead heaved,
men jumping from a camouflaged ditch.

Donal's horse reared. He slipped
—saw clouds, bushes, an arrow—

landed on his butt, clambered upright
to be hauled bodily onto Xau's horse,

lay like a sack of winded flour,
Xau shooting blunt arrows over him.

Xau's guards galloped toward them
—to help?—grinning like boys,

all except their captain,
a stern, lean figure in the lead.

A blunt arrow struck Xau's chest,
dropped past Donal.

The captain shouted, came alongside,
pulled Xau onto his horse

(a second sack of flour)—bumping Donal,
who slid, feet first, landed,

drew a wooden sword, hacked an ambusher,
who fell with dramatic flair.

A grinning guard galloped across,
hoisted Donal up—a sack again.

His horse joined Xau's:
two sacks of flour stared at each other.

"This." Donal spat out horse hair.
"Wasn't what I meant by fun."

"Oh?" said Xau. "A horse ride.
Fresh air. Nothing better."

"I had whores in mind, not horses.
Gambling. Wine...."

Odd. For a moment, Donal thought
he heard a woman whispering,

but there was no woman in sight.

He shook his head to clear it.

"Come visit in the spring.
I'll show you what I mean."

"We would like to come." Xau squirmed
as if to sit, but the captain pinned him.

"Our captain is making a point."
Xau glanced at the grim figure.

"He said we should not have
wasted time rescuing you,

"that had the attack been real,
we would have an arrow in our chest."

"He's right," said Donal.
"What were you thinking?"

"We were thinking," panted Xau,
"that we were having fun."

Donal grunted. He'd never guessed
how uncomfortable a sack could get.

The horses halted in a clearing:
blankets spread out on the ground.

Ambushers and guards alike bowed
to Xau and Donal as they dismounted.

Donal unsaddled his horse, rubbed it dry,
led it to a water bucket, tethered it.

He was sitting, watching the guards
set out food, when the horses panicked—

snorting, tugging their ropes, rearing:
Xau sprinted for the horses.

The captain yelled, Xau yelled back,
right up to the horses now.

Donal scrambled to his feet,
brandished his toy wooden sword.

The horses, quiet now, quivering,
clustered round Xau,

eyed the bushes to their left,
bright with berries.

The captain, a sword in each hand,
raced for Xau—thirty yards away

when the bushes heaved apart,
branches breaking, a brown hugeness—

eight, ten feet tall—a bear—
rearing up, roaring.

The captain screamed, ten yards from Xau.
Xau swung round, seized a sword from him.

Other guards ran for the two of them.
An archer angled for a shot.

Roaring, the bear plunged down,
down onto a horse, Xau's silhouette.

Two men stood, the bear on its side.
Still. The horse downed, throat torn.

Still. All the horses perfectly still.
Red running the length of Xau's sword.

The captain grabbed Xau,
yanked off his jacket, his tunic,

checked his chest, his back,
his legs, his arms. Stepped away.

Xau said something;
the captain stepped forward again,

stood while Xau checked him,
methodically, for injuries.

Xau pulled his tunic back on,
led two of the horses to Donal.

"We're riding back immediately.
There might be more bears."

"A horse ride," said Donal.
"Fresh air. Nothing better."

They rode back to the palace,
the guards circled around them.

ENLAI

Enlai was in the palace stables
when King Xau's guards burst in.
He surrendered sword, boot-knife
at their discourteous demands.

An indignity amply rewarded
when not only King Xau
but also his barbarian guest
led their horses past.

(The barbarian king rather splendid
in green riding leathers,
King Xau as scruffy as ever,
his jacket horribly besmirched.)

Enlai peered. Surely that was blood?
He stepped from Shira's stall,
gave his most elaborate bow:
"Your Majesty, I trust you are well?"

"Quite well, Master Enlai."
King Xau took the stall opposite.
The barbarian handed his horse to a groom,
joined Xau in the stall.

Enlai looked pointedly at the king's jacket.
"An invigorating ride?"

"We killed a bear."
Clear the king had no wish to elaborate.

Enlai bowed again,
withdrew to check Shira's hooves.
He could have left her care to a groom,
but he loved her. A weakness of his.

"Who was that?"

(The barbarian, speaking Innish,
which Enlai, apt with languages
and widely traveled, understood.
A fact he chose not to point out.)

"A minstrel." King Xau, also in Innish.
"He will sing for you tonight."

"But you don't like him?"

"He wrote a song about us last year
that we did not care for."

(Enlai sniffed: that song—
a singularly fine song—
had made his reputation,
had been sung in every inn in Meqing.)

Xau: "Now Artoch wants us to commission him
to write a ballad about the demon."

Shira neighed—
Enlai startled to clumsiness—
a royal commission—
the first of Xau's reign—

King Xau's sigh quite audible
and quite uncalled-for.
"Enlai would do as he did before,
turn us into a hero."

The barbarian king: "Fuck it, Xau.
You are a fucking hero.
You killed a fucking demon
and saved both our fucking kingdoms."

"After Khyert—after Khyert saved us."

Too much. Enlai had heard too much.
He must either speak up,
or spend the rest of his life
pretending not to know Innish.

He left Shira's stall,
cleared his throat to attract attention.
"Your Majesties, I speak Innish.
Perhaps I should have told you."

Surprise shifted fast to fury
on the barbarian's face,
then the barbarian lunged forward:
"You fucking should have."

Enlai backed up against Shira's stall,
his heart thumping, his legs shaky,
recalling the barbarian's reputation:

ruthless, red-handed in war.

The barbarian grinned at him,
which was, if anything, more terrifying.
"Stop quaking. I won't kill you without
your king's permission. Xau?"

Xau unsaddled his horse
before looking at Enlai,
a long, appraising look that held
neither rage nor hostility.

"Master Enlai," said Xau,
"we will not punish you,
but there will be no commission.
Not for you, not for anyone else."

Enlai bowed, a plain bow this time.
He returned to Shira's stall,
tried to calm himself—
that look on the barbarian's face—

He gave Shira a piece of carrot,
told himself he wasn't disappointed.
Heard Xau say, "We should have guessed.
He's a minstrel. He travels."

He was a minstrel.
He would travel to the burnt towns,
talk to the soldiers,
talk to those who'd served the demon.

And then he would return
and write such a ballad
as men would still sing
a hundred years hence.

And since the king wasn't paying,
Enlai could embellish Xau's every deed
to heroic proportions—he looked forward
to the young king's reaction.

BOYS

"Tell me about him," said Donal. Xau said nothing. He did not wish to speak
of Khyert. What use in words? He finished rubbing Narson down, checked
his hooves, left the stall. Donal nudged his shoulder, steering him not toward

the stable exit, but toward the tack room, said again, "Tell me about him." So. Donal set on this, and Xau set on friendship between the two of them, between their kingdoms. For that reason only, Xau said, "We knew him when we were both boys. He worked here in the stables." Xau paused. "Twice we noticed he was badly bruised, both face and arms, and Khyert already better with horses than men who'd worked here many years. We did not think a horse had kicked him. The second time, we asked. He'd been beaten by his brother. He had two broken ribs, but he was mucking out the stalls." Xau could not firm up his voice. "We helped him in the stables until our father ordered us to stop. Later, when we were made king, Khyert was kind to us when we most needed it." The tale not finished, but Donal had been there at its ending. Xau turned away. Donal said, matter-of-factly, "In Innis too, warriors weep when brave men die. Then most often we get drunk." And Donal waited for Xau to be done.

MEI

"What is it, Princess? What's wrong?"

No one had asked Mei that in years,
she who was King Xau's only sister:
prospering, privileged, protected.

"Nothing. Nothing is wrong."
Mei answered the barbarian prince
in his own language, and gave him
a carefully correct smile.

Prince Connol pushed his plate away,
leaned toward her across the table,
ignoring the other banquet guests.
He laid his hand over her wrist.
"I see bones. When I look at you,
I see bones on a mountain."

Mei jerked her wrist free.
"My three oldest brothers died
on a mountain. Years ago.
It is well known."

"Not to me."

"Indeed?" Mei raised her eyebrows
without offering outright insult.

The barbarian grabbed a wine jar
from a passing server.

"Princess, I know how it is
to be the king's sister,
or the king's brother,
to always take second place."

"I am fine. I am fortunate."
Mei kept her voice level,
grateful that no one else in earshot
spoke Innish, a barbarous language
for a barbarous people.

"You're fortunate, I'm fortunate."
Connol gulped straight from the wine jar.
"My sister died when she was eight.
Years ago, so of course
it doesn't matter anymore.
Just like your brothers' bones.
You're fine. I'm fine.
We're both fucking fine."

"You're drunk."

"Drunk is fine.
Good night, Princess."
He thumped the wine jar down,
stared brazenly at her bust,
stood up and walked away.

Mei, furious, seized the wine jar,
ran headlong after him,
heedless of who watched.
"You forgot this."

Connol took the wine jar.
"Thanks, Princess."

"You also forgot your manners,
forgot the debt your people
owe to my brother, King Xau,
forgot that you know nothing,
nothing about who I am."

He looked at her oddly,
as if she were a fragile thing,
a sparrow with broken wings.
"I know who you are,
not important enough to matter,

but too important to be allowed
to make choices for yourself.
I'm sorry your brothers died."

He raised the wine jar in salute. Left.

Slowly, carefully,
as if she walked along a cliff edge,
Mei returned to her seat.
She would not let that man,
that barbarian, upset her.

She nodded to the guest on her left,
painted a smile on her face.

SECOND SIGHT

He's having visions, or he's drunk,
or he's drunk and having visions.

He sees her hands, the thin wrist he held,
her hair, unbound, falling to her waist.

Sees her, grown old, devouring a peach;
her face, its bones, a bird in a cage.

Her shadow leans against a moonlit wall;
he crosses the courtyard to reach her.

Moonlight on swords. Guards.
Thrown to the ground, bruised, bound.

The cell is filled. The cell is empty.
He cannot see her. He cannot see her.

INCIDENT

King Xau sprinted headlong down the halls,
guards hastening at his heels,
sword belted over his pajamas,
to his sister.

Held Mei
as she buried her face
in the silk-sleeved encircling
of his arms.

Held her
as her guards stated the foreign prince
had not touched her below the waist
nor undone his pants
before they downed him.

Held her
as Leong, gentle, took her twelve pulses,
as his own heart rate slowed,
as he ordered Mei's day-guards woken,
as his advisors descended upon them.

    *

Later,
after he'd left her,
the ramifications and diplomatic repercussions;
the prince's incarceration, interrogation;
subsequent complications, decisions, consequences.

BLAME

King Donal furious,
heart pounding, head pounding,
woken in the middle of the night
because his brother fucked up—

"He's badly bruised," said Xau.
"He never drew his sword
so the guards didn't kill him,
but they weren't gentle."

Fucking stupid Connol—
Whores aplenty, but Connol
determined to stick his prick
into a fucking princess—

Xau set his hand on Donal's arm.
"Do not blame your brother yet.
We were angry just as you are,
but he is... not himself."

Donal shrugged off Xau's grip.
He didn't need a lecture.
This whole fucking mess
Connol's own fucking fault.

—Stairs spiraled underground,
rough-set stone, torch-lit,
soldiers either side
of a barred iron door—

Within, curled on a mattress,
chained by both ankles, Connol:
one eye swollen shut,
red fist marks on his stomach.

Fuck. His little brother.
Donal hadn't seen him like that
in twenty years, not since
their father—fuck. Fuck. Fuck.

The soldiers unbolted the door.
Two steps to cross the cell.
"You fucking idiot—
What were you fucking thinking?"

Connol fixed his good eye on him.
"I saw her, a bird in a cage,
a little girl with pigtails.
I saw her, bones and all."

A moment's doubt, then Donal
shook his head to clear it.
"Connol, King Xau is here.
Beg him for your life."

Xau stirred, said, softly,
"That is not required.
We will not execute a man
who is... unbalanced."

Connol looked past Donal, smiled.
"I see you, I see you, Princess.
I see you young, I see you old.
I see you dancing, hair flying."

Donal followed Connol's gaze.
No one on that side of him.
Not Xau. Not the guards.
Only air. Only madness.

Donal's rage doused to dread.
Bile in his throat,

the same sick feeling
he'd had years ago.

"Hush, hush now."
He crouched down,
clasped Connol's hands.
"I'm sorry, little brother."

"We will wait outside." Xau's voice.
Footsteps. The door.
Then Donal alone with what
remained of his brother.

THE HOUSE OF MEMORY

Princess Mei folded the barbarian's drawing.
But it was no use. She had seen it.
Rough strokes on rice paper.

> A willow tree on an island,
> a fisherman and his little girl
> in a sampan boat;
> in the girl's hand,
> dangling by one ear,
> a toy rabbit.

Poorly rendered. Sentimental.
Composition crowded.
Also, impossible. And intolerable.

Impossible because that scene
had been Mei's childhood daydream.
Years back. Private. Never told.

> (She who hadn't wanted
> a king for her father,
> because kings were too busy.)

Intolerable that any man,
least of all *that* man,
had invaded her very thoughts.

She placed the drawing carefully,
precisely atop the one
of bones on a mountain.

Both kings—

his brother, her brother—
had decreed the barbarian mad.

Yet these drawings proved
Mei's own mind breached.
The house of her memory ransacked.

Defiled as he had tried
to defile her body—
his hands on her hair, his heated breath—

Her guards had stopped him then,
but no soldiers could ward
the doors to her mind.

Her brother must be told—at once—
and the barbarian executed
for his transgression.

PETITION

Fish darted beneath the bridge
where King Xau stood: gold, silver, orange,
bright as jewels, trapped.

"Kill him. Please." Mei, his sister,
dropped to her knees on the rocks
by the edge of the pond.

"He does not deserve death."

   "He broke into my mind."

"Not by his choice."

   "You will let him violate me!"

"We will let him live."
Xau crossed the bridge,
and Mei reached for him.

Gently, saying nothing,
he held her in his arms.
He had no answers to offer.

One could not demand happiness,
neither for oneself,
nor for those one loved.

HER THOUSAND FACES

This is not true love.
This is not a fairy tale.

The prince met his princess,
swore, got drunk, walked out.

No use. The thought of her
unhinged him. No, her thoughts

unhinged him. Her thoughts
inside his thoughts: visions,

phantasms, figments, fragments
of future, present, past.

Fractured by her thousand faces,
obsessed, possessed. Jailed.

At last, the thousand aspects
collapsed into a single image,

which stood, silk-robed,
within his cell, lantern in hand.

Her fingers, gentle, sketched
the contours of his bruises.

But in her eyes, he read ruin:
scorn melted not to love, but pity.

How pitiless the pity
of her black and midnight eyes.

He will not inherit the throne.
He will not live happily ever after.

DUTY

Mei found Queen Shazia in the nursery,
the baby, Mei's nephew,
swaddled in a sling, suckling.

"You saw Prince Connol?" asked Shazia.

"Yes. Just now."

Mei picked up a tiny pair of red socks,
folded them, put them down.

The barbarian prince still jailed, chained,
but more lucid this time.
Enough himself to know himself half-mad.
Which he deserved for what he'd done to her.
Which he did not deserve,
because he had not known
what he was doing.

Mei had thought this through,
had not slept for thinking on it.
She unfolded the same tiny pair of socks,
said, "Maybe Xau should release Connol
as a gesture of good will."

"But you wanted him punished!
You wanted him condemned."
Shazia stared at her.

"I still do."
She wanted more,
wanted Connol gone,
wanted him never to have been.
She was twenty-one years old;
it was time she looked
beyond what she wanted.

"But what I want," said Mei,
"is not what must happen.
He is King Donal's brother."

As Mei was King Xau's sister,
the peace between their kingdoms
recent, tentative, jeopardized
by the prince's imprisonment.

"Oh, Mei, poor Mei."
Shazia came over,
made awkward by the baby
stirring in the sling,
took Mei's hand in hers.
"It will be all right.
Connol will return to Innis.
You'll never have to see him."

Shazia's sympathy unbearable.

Mei looked away,
looked down at her baby nephew,
his perfect happiness.
If she went thus far and no further,
she might find happiness. In time.

"At least Artoch will be relieved."
Shazia spoke lightly,
but concern clear on her face.
"He suggested freeing Connol
and Xau yelled at him:
I heard your brother from two rooms away.
He said you'd endured enough."

Her brother who bent his life to duty,
yet never asked the same of Mei.

Therefore she must ask it of herself.

Mei straightened her back,
painted a smile on her face.
"I will ask my brother
if it would benefit Meqing
were I to marry Prince Connol."

WHAT KING DONAL SAID TO HIS BROTHER,

PRINCE CONNOL, CONCERNING A POSSIBLE WEDDING BETWEEN PRINCE CONNOL AND THE PRINCESS MEI

You're fucking marrying her.

SOLSTICE

Their wedding,
hastily arranged,
hastily performed,
took place in the courtyard
where the bride,
one week earlier,
had begged
that the groom
be executed.

Four guests,
three officials,
eighteen guards.
No musicians,
no attendants,
no dancing, no feast, no kiss.

Then a twelve-day ride
to the burnt ruins of Harmouth,
the marriage unconsummated,
and Mei (the bride) appalled
by the groom's (Connol's)
lackluster horsemanship.

At Harmouth,
winter drawing in,
Connol spent his days
out in the frost,
planning the reconstruction of the town;
came back each night
to his cold bride,
the fire of her past
an open book through which he leafed
(the hundred passions, tantrums, generosities
of her privileged, protected youth)—
all quenched now,
frozen.

Mei married him
out of duty.
She ran the house for him
out of duty.
She offered her body to him
out of duty.

He used her body
out of duty,
to beget sons,
he who had lusted for each inch
of her flesh:
the soft inside of her elbows,
her earlobes, fingers, buttocks, breasts,
nipples, neck, knees, navel,
but his lust lost
in the cold wasteland
of her disdain.

On the shortest day,
the longest night,
Connol handed her sheepskin boots,
a sheepskin coat
(she who had come to him in silk
embroidered in gold and scarlet),
led her down to the deep harbor,
the fishing boats rocking
on the dark water,
the fishermen standing
on the stone quay.

Connol and the fishermen
and the handful of other townspeople
and every farmer within a day's walk
and the two dozen soldiers under Connol's command
sang the sun back,
as it had been sung back in Harmouth
each winter solstice
since the first stone
was laid in the harbor wall.

No musical instruments,
only the voices raised,
over and over,
in chorus and chant,
canon, counterpoint, call-and-response,
and, twice, Connol sang
the long solos
in his rusty baritone.

Mei, listening,
forgot the smell
of fish and sweat and smoke and salt,

forgot how cold her nose was.
There, in the dark,
as she sang, softly, unobtrusively,
the words as she learned them.

SCHEDULE

"Draw up next week's guard schedule."
Tsung, captain of King Xau's guards,
offered no further explanation,
merely handed Li a copy
of the king's projected schedule.

If the younger guard was nervous,
he showed no sign of it.
Li studied the king's appointments,
helped himself to paper and brush,
gridded the paper into shifts,
added Leong's name in six places.

"Why Leong first?" asked Tsung.
"And why those times?"

"Because he doubles as surgeon.
When the king leaves the palace,
Leong should accompany him."

Li waited a moment,
a questioning look on his face,
but the captain said no more
and Li bent back to his task.

Tsung reviewed Li's effort, asked,
"You assigned me nine shifts. Why?"

"I judged that those occasions
offered more threat to the king.
Should I have done differently?"

"No," said Tsung. "That is exactly
what I would have done. Until today."

Tsung took the brush,
crossed out his name
from one of the shifts,
wrote Li's in its place—

the brush trembled in Tsung's hand,
threatened to blot the paper.
He set the brush down,
thought of Moon Swan
with her hair unbound,
the scent of jasmine,
of how he might see her
while Li stood his shift,
of how the closing of one gate
might open another—

That questioning look on Li's face again.
Tsung did not explain himself, said only,
"A good job, Li. You may go."

After Li had left, Tsung sat alone.
The man was the finest warrior
Tsung had ever known,
a man who fought as if weapons
were an extension of his body,
as if he were dancing.

Tsung not quite ready to tell Li
he was seeking more, seeking someone
to replace him as captain.

Tsung not quite ready
to admit that to himself.

RIDDLE: AUSPICIOUS

Prince Keng, age five,
ran into the breakfast room,
bowed hastily to his parents,
then took the seat by Dao,
one of the king's eight guards.

"Master Dao," said Keng,
"I made a riddle for you,
because it's your birthday."

"I am honored," said Dao,
bowing his head to Keng.

"These men are soldiers,
but aren't in the army,

and their number is auspicious.
Who are they?"

"Hmmm. Soldiers but not in the army?"

Keng nodded. "Eight soldiers:
eight is an auspicious number.
Would you like a clue?"

"Yes, please."

"They protect my father."

King Xau said nothing,
but his eyes alight
as he watched Keng and Dao.

"Hmmm. Do you mean us,
the king's guards?"

"Yes! Yes!" Keng bounced in his seat.

"Thank you, Prince Keng," said Dao.
"No one has ever given me
a riddle for my birthday before."

Allies

SUMMONS

Identical message carried by three separate pigeons:

From the High Honorable Lady Nya,
mother of the Ninety-Fifth King of Meqing,
may his memory be exalted:

To Xau, Ninety-Sixth King of Meqing:

Grandson, I require you to visit me.
Depart at once.

JUMBLE

Twilight.
Two men on the snow.
Tsung's thoughts jumbled,
snow below him, above him,
branches thickened by white.
King Xau bent over him,
blood trickling from the king's shoulder.
Red blood, white snow
as Tsung drifted in and out,
the king's hands on his stomach—
pressure, no pain—
the king trying to hold together
what could not hold.

Little sign left of the boy
that king had been,
the boy Tsung had been given charge of,
seven years ago—
un-muscled, unassuming,
easy to underestimate.
As Tsung had done.

"Leong!" Xau's hands on him,
the king shouting. "Leong! Help!"

But Leong not there,
none of the other guards there—
Tsung's fault—

Sun sinking, setting,
now the colors gone

except the red trickling
from the king's shoulder.
Hard to breathe,
to shape a word.
"Xau?"

"Don't try to speak," said Xau.
"Leong will come—"

"Xau. Leave me."

"No." Flat.

"I'm dying. Leong can't help."
Each word a battle.
"Xau, bind up your shoulder. Go."

"No."

Both of them silent, then the king:
"We will not leave you to die alone."

A puny boy, Xau,
not a natural warrior.
Unlike his father, his eldest brother.
But Xau had acquitted himself well today.
Had fought as Tsung had taught him.
Efficient, effective.
Two of them against seven.

The boy. A boy no longer. The king.
Twilight.
Tsung tried to sort out time:
he'd told the other guards
to set up camp,
had walked into the forest
with the king—
stupid, no backup, Tsung's fault.
A mile? Two miles?
before he'd told the king
he'd be stepping down as captain.
How far? How far did they walk?

Cold now.
The press of the king's hands.
Seven men who fought like soldiers,
pale-skinned Innish men.

Maybe brigands who'd crossed the border.
Clear that the seven hadn't guessed who Xau was.
Mere bad luck to run into them.
No, not bad luck, Tsung's fault,
because he'd ordered the other guards
to stay behind,
had wanted (stupidly) to speak
to the king alone.

Darker,
twilight fading,
and, at the last, pain after all.
As if the sword
were in his belly still. Twisting.
Tsung turned his head,
out of breath,
sucked in air.
A dark puddle under him.

"Leong!" Xau's hands pushing, hurting
—why was the king hurting him?—
the king shouting, "Leong! Here! Help!"

Tsung shaped a word.
No breath in him to sound it.
The pain hard to bear,
hard to keep his eyes open.
He looked at Xau, his king,
his king whom he loved.
No breath to tell him so.

"Tsung." Xau's voice very gentle.
"You were a better father to us—"
The king stopped, restarted.
"A better father to me
than my father ever was.
Tsung? I love you."

Tsung closed his eyes for a moment.

FALLEN

A fire made, the tent up,
last light dimming in the west,
when Leong and the other guards
followed Li under the snow-heavy trees—

Captain Tsung had ordered them
to remain at camp,
but if Tsung had meant
to stay out past dark,
he would have taken backup—

The captain's prints,
the king's prints plain on the snow,
the pace close to a run,
Leong's pack digging into his back.

Lantern-light bobbed ahead,
more lantern-light behind
as Shuen brought up the rear,
leading a horse, ropes:
Leong refused to think on that.

Ahead, what might have been a shout.
Then, carried clearly,
King Xau's voice, "Help! Leong!"

Leong ran to that voice
faster than he'd ever run,
despite his pack, the snow,
ran past Gan, past Dao.

Li's lantern stopped,
Li shouted, "Leong! Hurry!"

—King Xau crouched in the snow,
bent over Captain Tsung,
blood pooled all about them,
the king's hands red with it,
pushing down on Tsung's stomach.

(Li set the lantern down by Leong.)

Too much blood,
yet still Leong took the time
to assess the captain:
skin clammy, lips blue-tinged;
breath shallow, fast;
four of the twelve pulses imperceptible,
the other eight erratic, faint, racing;
Tsung unresponsive to touch, to pressure,
to Leong calling his name.

Time wasted. Tsung beyond help.
Leong looked to the king,
saw the gash in his jacket,
his left shoulder,
the steady trickle of blood.

"Xau. Let go of him."
Leong softened his voice,
laid his hands over the king's.

The king would not let go of Tsung.
"Leong, he'll bleed to death."

"I know. I can't save him."
Leong prised the king's hands loose,
pulled the king's jacket off.
Xau's shoulder lacerated deep into muscle,
bleeding freely,
the king's breath quickened,
his skin clammy—
Leong looked up—
Gan bent over one of several bodies
(killed by Tsung and the king?),
Shuen tying up the horse,
Li and Dao on guard, bows readied—
"I need some help!"

Li the first there.

Leong grabbed a bandage from his pack,
pressed it to the king's shoulder,
set Li's hand over the bandage.
"Apply pressure. Don't release."

"How are they?"

"Tsung's dying."

"Xau?"

"Hold his shoulder."
Which was no answer.
Leong would not lie outright,
but spoke as best he could to calm the king,
"Xau, the cut to your shoulder looks clean.
Which is good, very good.
Stay still for me.
You'll feel my hands."

Leong kept his voice soft, continuous,
as he probed the king scalp to foot.
No other injury Leong could find,
but the king's pulses racing, weak, disordered,
the king shivering—
How much of the blood on the snow his?

"Xau, let's warm you up a bit."
Leong took his jacket off,
put it over the king,
and the king's jacket over that,
and the blanket from the pack.
All futile if the king had lost
as much blood as Leong thought.

The king's eyes on him.
Leong could not meet that gaze.

Dispassion. Detachment.
The mark of a good surgeon,
a good physician.
Leong fallen short.

"Li, hold on tight.
Xau, I'm going to lie you down."
His voice calm, his voice a lie.
"You'll feel my hands again.
Take deep breaths. That's it."

He took the king's twelve pulses,
once, then again. Firmer.
A hopeful sign.

"Leong." Li insistent. "How is Xau?"

"How do you think?!
He lost a lot of blood—"
Leong stopped. Looked down.
Observed his hands shaking.
Looked up.
Saw, fleetingly,
so brief he almost missed it,
fear on the king's face.

"Xau—I'm sorry. You'll be fine."
He met the king's eyes properly.
"You lost a lot of blood,
but I think you'll be fine."

"Tsung?" Xau strained to lift his head.
Leong took a breath. Let it out.
Helped the king look.
Tsung still, his chest still.

Xau closed his eyes, said,
"The men who attacked. Were Innish.
Swore in Innish. Tsung fought.
As we have never seen."

So. Leong silent.
Hard to summon words.

"Li, you may let go now.
I'll hold his shoulder."
He gripped the king's shoulder.
"Xau, I'm going to sit with you.
Shuen made a fire for us,
back at the camp."

Beyond, tied to a tree,
the horse waited for Tsung's body.

CAPTAIN

The king badly injured,
the captain dead,
a two-mile hike
at night
in a snowy forest.
Li, king's guard, led the way,
startled to false alert
by every falling clump of snow,
King Xau behind him on an improvised litter.
The captain's corpse tied to a packhorse.

Back at camp,
Li helped Shuen unload Captain Tsung's body,
set it on the snow,
laid the captain's sword atop him.
Told Shuen to tend to the horses.
Gan and Dao already on sentry duty.

Li went in the tent.
Various ointments spread out,
King Xau flat on his back,

conscious but very pale,
Leong stitching his shoulder.

"Leong, do you need help?"

Leong shook his head.

(The larger question,
the question in Li's heart,
he left unasked this time.
Either the king would live.
Or he would not.)

Li unrolled the map,
tilted it toward the lantern.
The nearest fort a full day's ride away,
no closer than their original destination.

"Li. When you have a moment."
King Xau's voice uneven.

Li went to him at once.

Darkness then in the king's eyes.
"Li, if you are willing,
we would appoint you
captain of our guards."

"I am willing."

"Be certain. It is—"
Xau paused, pressed his lips together
while Leong finished up.
"It is hard enough to be our guard.
Harder to be the captain."

Li bowed. "I am certain."
No duty he would rather choose.
No man he would rather serve.

"Thank you."
The king lifted his head, dipped it to Li,
closed his eyes.
"We need a second witness...
paper... ink...."

The king's voice trailed off. He lay still.

Li looked sharply at Leong,
who made the hand signal for *asleep*,
started clearing away his ointments.

Li stood quietly, watching the king,
before he went back to the map.

OUTSPOKEN

Scene: Library of Nya's estate.
Enter King Xau and his guards.

XAU
Good evening, Grandmother.

NYA
Is that all the manners they taught you?
To sit before your grandmother does?
Poor behavior even in a barbarian.
Unacceptable in the ruler of Meqing.

SHUEN
The king must sit—
he rode since dawn despite injury.
The last two hours, he'd have fallen
off the horse if I hadn't held onto him.

XAU
Shuen, it's all right.
Her words do us no hurt.

NYA
An unmannerly guard for an unmannerly king.

XAU
You sent three separate pigeons
requesting our presence.
Are you in difficulty?
How can we help?

NYA
You can't. I am dying of a malignancy.

XAU
Our guard Leong is a physician.
Let him examine you.

NYA
No. I want no more hands upon me.

XAU
Then why send for us?

NYA
Is it not enough that I wish
to meet my grandson before I die?

XAU
We invited you to our palace. Repeatedly.

NYA
I never liked travel. You're here now.
Tell me about your father,
who was my son before he fathered you.

XAU
He was a strong king,
an excellent tactician.
We have studied his campaigns.

NYA
He was your father.
Did you not love him?

XAU
Once.

NYA
A cold answer.
Your father had more passion.
Your father looked like a king. You?
It's hard to believe you won two wars.
Did your generals fight
your battles for you?

XAU
They fought beside us.

NYA
And did they fight the demon too?

XAU
The demon—
the demon we slew alone,
after a friend died to save us.

NYA
Tell me what happened.

XAU
No.

NYA
I am your father's mother.
I am dying.
Yet you refuse me.

LEONG
He is the king.
He is injured and in pain.
Yet he has been patient.

NYA
Another of your men speaks out of turn.
Have they no shred of discipline?

XAU
That is the second time
you have insulted our guards.
Do not do so again.
They are each of them better men
than our father, your son, ever was.

NYA
Hah! At last some spirit.
And in your men's defense.
That speaks well of you, Xau.

XAU
We care little what you think of us,
but our guards have suffered greatly.
Their captain died three days ago
in our defense.

NYA
I did not know. I am sorry.

XAU
He... showed us how to be a king.

NYA
You grieve for him. That is fitting.
Where is his body?

XAU
Outside your stables,
watched over by our guard Gan.

NYA
I note you didn't ask permission.

XAU
His body stays where it is. Undisturbed.
Or we will leave and take it with us.

NYA
Oh, relax. I'm old. My sons are dead.
I'm entitled to be cantankerous.
Eat. Rest. We will talk tomorrow.

Xau stands up unsteadily. His guards assist him.

SICKBED

Scene: Nya's bedroom.
Enter King Xau and his guards.

XAU
Good morning, Grandmother.

NYA
Only two guards today?
Am I less fearsome lying abed?

XAU
Gan and Shuen are sleeping.
They stood guard overnight.

NYA
Oh, go ahead. Sit.
Did your father ever talk of me?

XAU
No. Our mother said you—

NYA
Your mother! An upstart
from an uncivilized backwater.

XAU
Our mother spoke six languages,

kept every empty point of etiquette,
yet had the trick of making
those about her happy.

NYA
A veritable paragon!
No, keep your seat. I'll curb my tongue.
Listen. I maintain a large correspondence,
and have learned, besides much else,
that Shazia's father, King Vihaz,
is beset by envy of your fame.

XAU
No rumor of this has reached us.

NYA
Vihaz minds his words in public,
then airs his grievances
to his junior wives.
A moment. Hand me that bowl.

XAU
Let us wipe your face.
You are in pain. We can return later.

NYA
Stay. Listen.
For now, Vihaz's envy is outweighed
by desire to see your son, his grandson,
sit the throne of Meqing.
If that changes, beware.

XAU
We will tell Artoch.

NYA
Good. Now tell me how you bend
the horses to your command.

XAU
I do not know.

NYA
Oh come, you can do better.
I am your grandmother,
and, moreover, I am dying.

XAU
You are exploiting your situation.

NYA
Of course. So answer.

XAU
We would rather not.

NYA
Answer anyhow.

XAU
When the wild horses came to us,
we asked nothing, yet they came.

NYA
And, later, controlling
your cavalry in battle?

XAU
We thought of what we wanted,
the maneuvers. It was... hard.
When we wished one group of horses
to veer left, another to veer right,
we had to hold those thoughts apart,
which proved exhausting.

NYA
Hmmm. A cost to it then.
Was it harder to control
the enemy's horses?

XAU
We didn't.
We didn't ask for what they gave,
but their deaths lie on our conscience.

NYA
As well they might.

XAU
Our soldiers also are on our conscience.
Those who died.
Though there we did no more
than any general in any war.

NYA
Did you not?
You are tiresomely, relentlessly principled,
a trait that incites loyalty.
Enough. I tire.
Sit with me, but do not speak.

Xau holds her hand.

LETTERS

Scene: Kitchen, Nya's estate.
Enter Nya.

XAU
Grandmother—

NYA
Why are you eating with the servants?

XAU
It's not yet dawn. We didn't want
to cause them extra work.

NYA
That *is* what they are paid for.
Here, I kept your father's letters.
You should know more about him
than his military campaigns.
The paragon's letters are there too.

XAU
Mama's letters?
We never thought—thank you.

NYA
(To Li) You are the captain
of Xau's guards? Shield him well.

LI
That *is* what I am paid for.

NYA
Hmmph. It takes more than gold
to induce a man to die for you.

LI
The king has paid more.

NYA
He still looks pale.
Is he well enough to ride?

XAU
We can ride. We had not guessed
you would worry about us.

NYA
A passing weakness. Safe travel, Xau.

Xau bows to her, then hugs her.

BESPEAKING: RIDDLES

Dialogue, debate, diatribe, anecdote,
sarcasm, insults, politics, gossip,
a sporadic conversation carried out
across a divide of hundreds of miles.
Both participants ancient, inhuman—
one a creature of fire and flight;
the other a six-eyed, six-mouthed,
tentacled monstrosity.

High on her mountain,
the dragon bespoke the Hidden Queen,
"What bears no weapons,
has neither talons nor teeth,
yet can bring down kingdoms
or foster alliances?"

Hundreds of miles away,
deep in her underground chamber,
the Hidden Queen snorted.
"Feeble. The answer is *words*.
What grows when you feed it,
dies when you give it water?"

"*Fire.* Pathetic. Utterly pathetic.
That one was old before I hatched."

"True, you are horribly old. Try this.
What's the smallest square number

that is the sum of two
non-zero square numbers?"

"What?!" bespoke the dragon.
"That doesn't sound like a riddle."

"You know all the riddles."

"I am indeed wise."
Then a lengthy pause.
"How can numbers be square?"

In her underground chamber
the Hidden Queen laughed,
a discordant sixfold creaking.
"A square number is one obtained
by multiplying a number by itself.
One, four, nine, sixteen....
Do you give up?"

"It's not a riddle!"

"So you're giving up?"

"No!"
A lengthier pause.
A tree stump flamed to ash
before the dragon answered,
"Twenty-five."

Complaints, commiserations, confessions,
conjectures, strategy, philosophy,
riddles, rumor, friendship
traded across hundreds of miles
over the course of centuries.

FIRST DAY

"My stomach hurts,"
announced Prince Keng
when King Xau collected him.

King Xau crouched down,
felt Keng's forehead.
No fever, no sign of pain
when Xau pressed Keng's belly.
"Are you worried about lessons?"

"Noooo."

"Are you worried about something else?"

"The others," said Keng.

"The other children?"

Keng nodded.

"It's all right to be worried."
Xau stood, took Keng's hand in his,
started down the corridor.
"But maybe you'll become friends."

That was why Xau had arranged this.
All Keng's life, people would defer to him,
yet these three—one girl, two boys—
might see him as their classmate,
not their prince.

Xau would have preferred a larger group,
but few families lived at the palace,
and of those few, fewer still
that would not try to please Xau
by having their children
please his son.

The fathers of these three
all men who'd spoken up
when they disagreed with Xau,
all men he trusted
with his life.

He'd been lucky to find
as many as three.

"Why can't Mama keep teaching me?"

"Mama will still teach you Sumbrese.
The tutor will teach mathematics,
history, reading, writing—"

"I can write already."
Pride in Keng's voice,
though his fingers
clutched tight to Xau's.
"I can write my name

and the numbers and the colors
and lots of animals."

"That's a good beginning."

Then they were at the classroom,
and Keng, spotting Chee, a girl
with whom he had played twice,
the daughter of Xau's guard Shuen,
let go Xau's hand and ran to her.

Xau stood in the doorway,
his hand empty.

FOREBODING

A stolen day, the air golden,
sweet with honeysuckle,
his children playing under the greening trees,
the sound of his wife laughing.

A shadow on the day, on King Xau's heart
as he sat cross-legged on the grass,
helping Ying, his two-year-old,
pick the small yellow flowers
all about them.

Xau looked up at Li, captain of his guards,
standing, watchful, within arm's reach.
"Li, which guards will stay behind
when we go to Innis?"

"Dao and Shuen.
Dao's off-wrist is not yet at full strength.
Would you like to bring Shuen?"

"No."

A centuries-old history of war with Innis;
the peace recent;
that Xau would have enemies there
beyond doubt.

And Shuen the only one
of Xau's guards with children—
a son Ying's age, a girl Keng's age—
despite which Xau had risked Shuen

in war, earthquake, the demon's onslaught.

But now, today,
Xau glad Shuen would stay behind.

"You expect trouble," said Li.
"As do I. We could take twenty
of the palace guard. Or more."

"No. We go not to prove our strength,
but our friendship."

Xau watched Ying,
the way her mouth opened
as she took a flower from his hand.

He watched
and could not stop the thought
that if he died,
her death would follow.
Hers, and Keng's, and Chye's.
His children too young
to hold a throne.

A thought he'd had before.
A thought he could not afford.

Li gave him a penetrating look.
"If you seek to clear your mind
and cannot do so, spar with me.
Your children have never seen you fight."

"We don't have practice blades."

"Sticks will serve."

*

A stolen hour, the air golden,
Ying and Keng watching, mouths agape,
as Xau fought each of his guards in turn,
defeating two out of eight.

At the end,
a pile of broken sticks,
their baby son asleep in Shazia's lap,
Xau sweaty, his heart full.

EVER AFTER

"Mei, do you want me to stay?"
asked Prince Connol,
already sitting his horse (poorly),
his men mounted beside him.

"Sit straight," said Mei.
"Your shoulders are too far forward."

"Do you want me to stay?" repeated Connol.

"No. We've discussed this."
Mei's tone sharp.
She'd hoped to accompany him to court
for her brother's visit,
but this pregnancy, her first,
not proving easy.

"If you need help—"

"Orla can clean up after me."

"Mei, I love you."

She did not love him,
would not say those words.

And he,
he who had wandered
through her mind, unasked,
throwing wide the doors
to her memories:
did he not know
how she felt?

He did not look as if he knew.

"I will miss you," said Mei,
because that much was true.
"I will miss having tea with you
after your work is done,
and losing to you at dice,
and how you brush my hair
last thing at night."

Connol's eyes awash.

"Sit straight," said Mei,
and turned away
before he wept.

WELCOME

"Welcome." Queen Fian stood beside King Donal,
a tall woman, tall as her husband Donal.

She wore a green gown, green as her eyes.
Her pale hair gleamed in the spring sun.

She smiled then at King Xau, a smile
such as no woman had ever given him—

as if he had slain a dragon single-handed
so she might string its teeth around her neck.

"I have looked forward to this day all winter,"
said Fian. "It gave me joy on the darkest day."

"As it gave us joy," Xau said, bowing low,
"to know that we would be coming to Innis."

He judged she had spoken the truth. Why then
did her silvered words unsettle him so?

LI

Li, captain of King Xau's guards,
appraises his predicament.
The windows are too large,
the hallway vulnerable.
Five guards plus Li himself. Too few.
For one night, they could stay awake,
but they will be here for twelve.

> Fighting,
> one must first master the elements:
> to pierce, to pivot, to punch.
> Later, the dance:
> from the choice of opening pose
> through the sequence
> of following moves.

So. Two men outdoors.
One man in the hallway.

One man sleeping inside, blocking the door.
One man sleeping below each window.

It is both art and skill, fighting:
the body a shaped tool,
waiting for the first note
of the dance.

Li positions his men,
pulls two blankets from the bed,
spreads them in an inner corner.
King Xau, watching him,
raises his eyebrows,
but says nothing.
They have traveled
this road before.

Li spent twenty years
forming himself into a weapon,
his body lethal with sword,
staff, arrow, knife, naked.
But this new art,
the art of protecting another,
he has yet to master.
Sometimes the music begins
before the dancer is ready.

The king bows to each guard
and last to Li,
then lies down in the corner.
Li takes his place
on the floor by the door,
relaxes his muscles, breathes.
It is necessary that he sleep.
He cannot sleep.

A long road.
Son of a fisherman,
but the town soldiers chose him—
he alone of all the boys his age—
to be their cook, apprentice,
then, later, comrade, captain,
promoted to the city,
the capital, the palace.

He opens his eyes,

sees the king
staring back at him.
A year ago, this country
was at war with King Xau.
Many here still hate the king.
Breathe. He must sleep.

    A long road,
    and he has been back only once.
    The king told him to return
    when his mother was ill.
    Li refused.
    The king announced
    he was traveling to Qingzi himself.
    It is not easy to fight
    both your king and your heart.
    He saw his mother
    before she died.

Li watches the king
until the younger man
settles into sleep.
Li closes his eyes,
breathes,
and, at length,
sleeps.

BEFORE KINGS

Queen Fian knelt on the cliff top,
head pressed to the stone toes
of an ancient rock figure, twice her height,
that peered down at a plunging waterfall.

"Ean-the-Watcher, I offer you power."
She unstoppered the vial
she carried next to her skin,
let one black drop fall.

She spoke in the old language,
a language almost forgotten,
passed down to Fian by her mother
and her mother's mother.

The wind rose,
flapping the shirts of Fian's guards

who waited, motionless, expressionless,
fifty feet back.

"Two kings will come soon:
one who is my enemy,
one who is my husband.
I offer you their lives."

Beneath Fian's fingers,
a flare of sudden heat.
Wind whipped her pale hair
as she stood up.

She leaned far out over the cliff,
held up by rushing air, the gods.
"I swear that if I come to power,
your worship will be revived."

She stared down at the tumbling water,
the wooden overlook
where the two kings would be,
the river far below.

Her mother's mother
had told her of the time before kings,
before men claimed ownership
over hill and river, forest and wolf.

No man should own a hill,
or a river, or the wind.
Fian laughed then,
and went to her guards.

"You were never here," said Fian.
The guards nodded, blank-faced.
"You took me to the bluebell woods.
I picked flowers, then threw them away."

She touched each man's forehead.
"Forget my words,
they are nothing but air.
Going, gone."

Fian left with her guards.

She didn't wait for the kings.

VIEWPOINT

In every bowl of tea,
a chance of poison.

Li saw:
King Xau and King Donal
standing, spattered by spray,
on the opposite side
of the wooden overlook;
Rourk, Donal's guard,
armed with sword and crossbow;
snow-melt plunging
in twisted braids
to the river below.
No backup.
No guard save him
to protect King Xau.

Beyond each doorway
may stand an assassin.

Li saw:
an ancient stone wolf
carved in the rock-face
(sacred to Donal's people:
the reason no other guards
were permitted);
above, on the cliff top,
a giant stone figure
(also deemed sacred);
the narrow, exposed path
back to the horses.

Risk can be reduced,
but not eliminated.

A shadow shifted—Li looked up—
the giant stone figure tilted.
Li leapt toward Xau, yelling,
as the stone figure crashed down—
the platform splintering,
shearing, tipping.

If a rock tumbles,
look for he who pushed it.

Underwater. Icy. Bubbles.
Li tried to kick up.
The water shoved him down.
He dropped his bow, his sword,
running out of air.
Yanked up by his jacket,
he surfaced, coughing water.
Xau, gripping him,
slammed into a boulder
at the river's edge.
Li heaved them out.

    Lightning kills,
    but men are killers.

Li saw:
Xau beside him,
left arm bent back, broken;
floating debris (planks, splinters);
a rock, upstream,
with the smashed body
of Donal's guard;
Donal sprawled on the far bank,
red on his shirt.

"Swim to Donal. Help him."
Xau had to say it twice
before Li understood him,
the king panting shallowly,
his teeth chattering.

"No. You're hurt and in danger."
Li opened Xau's jacket,
the king jerking at the touch,
breath gasping, rapid.
No blood on his tunic.
"Your arm's broken,
maybe some ribs."

"That can wait," said Xau.
"Li, go. Help Donal.
We fought to gain this peace.
Worth risk to keep it."

Li stared at Xau,
then dipped his head
in acknowledgement.

A man must learn
which risks to take.

So. Li would have to trust
that no assailant descended
from the cliff top.
He took off his boots and jacket,
plunged into the water,
swam, diagonally, swept downstream,
for the far side.

To die for Xau, one matter.
To die for Donal, another.

Ripples, swirls, rocks.
Li fetched up on the bank,
sprinted to King Donal—
the king groaning,
a long gash across his chest—
used the king's soaking shirt
to bandage him,
helped him into the river.
Swam, supporting King Donal.
Slower, too slow, freezing,
not even halfway across.
Li's head went under.
He kicked, holding Donal,
surfaced, gasped. Air.

He had not realized how much
he still valued his life.

The river stronger than him,
Donal clutching him, heavy.
Water closed over him.
He kicked, couldn't surface,
couldn't breathe, cold.
Looming darkness rushed at him—
rock—no—
he hurtled into the flank
of a horse, Xau on its back,
the king struggling, one-armed,
to haul Li up;
the horse swimming for the edge;
the three men clutching
the horse, each other,
the riverbank. Alive.

THE RIDE BACK

Each breath stabbed Xau,
each footfall of the horse.
Li, seated behind him, steadying him,
nudged Narson faster.

Xau looked round,
saw Donal, the extra horses.
No other movement.

"Do you think. We're being chased?"
Xau asked, taking a breath
between each few words.

"No. I think our attackers
want to avoid a direct assault,
but it's not a risk we should take
if you can keep riding."

"We can ride."

Rourk dead, Donal's guard.
His broken body outstretched
on a rock, mid-river—

Donal had turned to look back
at Rourk as they rode away,
the fury on his face
shifting to grief—

Likely the guard was one of the men
that had been closest to Donal,
as Li was close to Xau.

Xau struggled to stop
his thoughts drifting.
He had to apologize to Li.
That was important.
"Li. Sorry. For ordering you
to swim to Donal."

"It was the right decision."

"We should have asked. Not ordered."
Xau shut his eyes, fighting pain,
weighing whether to say more,

surely Li already knew.
Yet, riding away from one guard's death,
Xau wanted to tell Li
how much he valued him.

Two men close to Xau
killed this past year.
Khyert, once his stableboy.
And Captain Tsung.
And before them, seven years ago,
his brother Keng.

He was drifting again.
"Li, how much further?"

"About an hour."
A pause, then Li said,
"I advise downplaying your injuries.
If you can ride unsupported,
I'll change to my own horse
before we reach the fort."

"Agreed."

Then neither of them spoke
for a long time,
and what Xau might have said
was left unvoiced.

POSTPONED

Queen Fian stood on the fort's outer dike,
her pale unbound hair windblown,
watching three riders approach
across the muddy flats.

Long before they neared her,
she had masked both disappointment and triumph:
disappointment that both kings had survived
(their guards didn't matter),
triumph that the gods
had heard her.

When the riders reached the gap in the dike,
she called down, "Husband, where is Rourk?"

"Dead." King Donal reined in his horse.

"Dead?" She caught her breath, feigning dismay,
and ran down to him. "And you are hurt!"

"It's minor. Comfort me later."

"What happened?"

"The stone figure above the waterfall fell."

Donal rode on past her,
unaware that he rode past his death,
for though he had postponed death that day,
the gods had answered Fian.

And if she but served those gods better,
surely they would help her kill both kings—
then she would have vengeance,
and more than vengeance,
since her son—
her young, malleable son—
would inherit a throne.

And Fian would rule
from behind that throne.

DISTRACTION

Leong turned to the door's scrape:
saw Li and King Xau,
the king's left arm in a sling.

Then Leong in motion, grabbing his bag,
cutting Xau's clothes free,
probing, palpating,
the king unable to mask his pain.
Distraction indicated.

Leong bowed.
"Congratulations, Your Majesty.
Your first broken bones, I believe.
Your left humerus—"

Leong indicated Xau's arm.
"Plus at least two ribs. Here and here.
How did you manage all this?"

"We hit a rock."

"Next time avoid rocks."

"The king hit a rock," clarified Li,
"saving me from drowning."

"Next time don't let Li swim."
Leong splinted Xau's arm
quickly but carefully.

"Besides, it's cold for swimming.
Better to wait until summer."
He handed Xau a cup. "Drink."

"Leong, what is this?"

"A sleeping draft."

"No," said Xau flatly.
"Rourk died. Donal's guard.
We will attend his wake tonight."

"Your strength is spent. You need rest."

"We will rest tomorrow."
The darkness in the king's eyes
unanswerable. Final.

WAKE

Gaer was caught between grief and fury:
Rourk dead, a good man,
a strong warrior.

Rourk dead,
and the Horse King, Xau,
who fought against them a year ago,
come to his wake.
King Donal had made peace with Xau;
Gaer not so quick to forgive.

Six guards hovered round Xau like nursemaids.
Xau thin, only lightly muscled,
his left arm in a sling.
Donal, a warrior king;
Xau, a weakling.

Gaer ground his teeth together.
Nursemaids or not, he'd have challenged Xau,
except that this was a wake.
Instead, he pushed past Xau to Rourk's bier,
centered in the fort's dining hall.

Grief won then.
Gaer stared long at Rourk's smashed face,
his body hidden beneath wolf skins,
offerings heaped over the skins.
Gold rings, a bronze torc, knives, daggers.

Gaer had campaigned with Rourk, years ago,
but it wasn't Rourk's strength Gaer thought of,
rather how Rourk would sing on the march.
Every word heartfelt
though his voice was rough.
A warrior singing of warriors.

Gaer laid his dagger on Rourk.

Prince Connol, Donal's brother,
put a rubied ring beside Gaer's dagger.

"You and Fergus got the body?" asked Gaer.

Connol nodded.

"Who killed him?"

"Cowards who fled."
Connol spat on the floor.

At midnight, the beating of drums.
King Donal raised a bronze urn.
"To Rourk," said Donal,
tears running down his cheeks.
"Who fought at my side.
Who twice saved my life."

Donal lifted the urn to his lips. Drank.
Passed the urn to Prince Connol.

"To Rourk," said Connol.
"Who protected my brother like a brother."

One by one, the soldiers toasted Rourk.
Queen Fian, the only woman present,
said, "To Rourk. A brave warrior,"

drank as deep as any man,
then left for her bed.

The Horse King
(who couldn't even hold the urn
with his left arm in a sling),
said, "To Rourk. Defender of Innis.
Who put his king before himself."

One of his nursemaids held the urn
while Xau drank.

Gaer stepped forward,
took the urn from Xau's guard.
"To Rourk. Who never needed
a fucking nursemaid."

A flicker of reaction from Xau,
so brief Gaer couldn't name it,
then Xau nodded to him
as if unaware he'd been insulted.

When all had toasted Rourk,
Donal led the way to the feasting table.
Food. Talk. Drink. (Gaer drank a lot.)

At dawn, they went outside,
walked the path to the inner dike.
Cold. The ground wet with dew.
Four men to carry the bier,
Donal and Connol at the head.

No widow to weep.
No one to send the body home to,
Rourk childless, wifeless.
So they put him in mud and stone
near other soldiers
who'd died without family.

Gaer helped to fill in the grave.
King Donal shoveled,
all the soldiers took turns,
even Xau's nursemaids,
but fucking Xau did fucking nothing.

Then it was finished;
Rourk buried, the sky paling above them.

A good man dead,
and Xau, who had barely known Rourk,
who had fought against him,
standing by his grave,
just six feet away from Gaer,
fucking nursemaids beside him—

Fuck Xau. Funeral done. Time to fight.
Gaer lunged at Xau
to knock his teeth out.

Xau backed sideways a step,
deflected Gaer's fist with his injured arm
while his other hand grabbed onto Gaer—
grabbed Gaer's right arm—
pulling Gaer forward, then left, off-balance,
Gaer's wrist bending.

Fuck. Gaer crashed down onto the dirt,
not sure what happened,
how it happened.

Xau looked down at him.
"Are you hurt?"

"I'm fine."
Gaer got up, slowly,
sobering up just enough to realize
he was in trouble.

"Gaer." Fire in Donal's voice,
his sword drawn.
"Anything you want to say?"

"No, Your Majesty."
Gaer stood straight as a spear,
trying to sort out what had gone wrong.
Xau not the man he'd taken him for.

"You're demoted," said Donal,
"and sentenced to fifty lashes."

                    *

Later, much later,
Gaer worked out that the nursemaids—
standing right by Xau when Gaer attacked—
would have killed him

save that Xau had signaled them not to.

He was never certain
why Xau had done that.

EIRDRE

Four foreigners in the stables
when Eirdre, sister to Queen Fian,
arrived with her escort.

She handed her horse off,
looked hard at King Xau's men:
all four plainly dressed
in black pants, black jackets,
three of the four armed with sword,
bow, dagger, studying her
as she studied them.

The fourth, his left arm in a sling,
sword at his belt,
but no bow on his back,
had evidently been relegated
to the menial work,
brushing the horse—King Xau's horse?—
the horse inclining its head toward him.

She liked his unhurried gentleness,
the quiet way he spoke to the horse
as he worked.
Not the man's fault
what his king had done.

      *

That evening in the castle's great hall
a crowd of people waited to meet King Xau.

King Donal led Eirdre past the crowd
to the fourth man from the stables,
the man's clothes plain as before,
but a silver crown on his head.
Xau, their former enemy.
Xau, who had widowed her,
Eirdre's husband killed by Xau's army.

"This is Lady Eirdre," said Donal,

"Queen Fian's sister."

Xau bowed to her,
and Eirdre,
who had meant to hate him,
found herself unequal to the task.
She saw the man from the stables
and held out her hand.

BENCH

Bustle, noise, light,
the castle's great hall crowded
with guests vying to meet
Xau the Horse King,
Xau the Demon Slayer,
lately their enemy, now named a friend.

King Donal himself at Xau's side,
resplendent in green velvet,
emeralds inset in his golden crown.

King Xau in black,
his crown silver, undecorated,
his left arm in a sling,
tired and in pain,
though he showed neither—
smiled, bowed, offered his hand
to soldiers, merchants, guild heads,
to women dressed in every color,
answered the same questions
over and over
as if they were new.

When all the guests
had had their chance at him,
Xau retreated to a bench
at the side of the hall,
flanked by his guards.
A soldier followed him over,
one of the many who'd met Xau earlier.
Xau remembered his face,
the raised scar half-hidden
by his beard, though not his name.

"I'm Captain Tadhg.

I was born in Aldford."
Tadhg's voice cracked.
Aldford the fourth town
that the demon had burnt.
Tadhg went to his knees,
bowed his head.

"Thank you," said Tadhg.
"Without you, without what you did,
the demon would still be burning Innis."

Xau said quietly, "We were not alone.
King Donal was there,
and a man called Khyert, who died."

Eight months ago, yet still at times
Xau could not sleep, remembering.
He touched Tadhg's arm. "Sit with us.
Had you family in Aldford?"

"Three sisters, a nephew. They left in time."
Tadhg sat, fished something out of his pocket,
said in a rush, "My father made this.
Gave it to me when I joined the army.
I want you to have it."

He handed Xau a wooden wolf
the length of a finger,
minutely detailed,
a listening look on its face.

A moment before Xau could speak.
"Thank you, Captain."

Xau's guards turned
at the roughness in his voice.
He set the little wolf
beside him on the bench,
made the hand sign for all-well,
picked the wolf back up.

Tadhg the first of two dozen
who came over to Xau
and thanked him as privately
as the assembly permitted:
men and women, old and young,
ranking from a cousin of King Donal's
down to a serving-girl.

They knelt to him,
or touched his face,
or kissed his hand;
offered gifts they'd made themselves
and small treasures passed down
through their families;
not gold, nor jewels, nor furs,
but cloth they'd dyed,
an old brass bell,
a bracelet for Xau's daughter
strung with shells.

Xau took their gifts,
placed them on the bench beside him;
took their thanks far into his heart.

And after, when the guests had left,
when the servants were clearing up,
King Donal came over,
looked at Xau closely.
"Your arm is hurting you."

Xau silent. Nothing to be said.

Donal shifted the gifts to make a space,
sat on the bench by Xau.
"I saw them coming to you, and kneeling.
I would have stopped them bothering you,
but that they were right.
Every fucking man and woman
in the fucking room
should have knelt to you.
Myself included."

"No—" Xau spoke too sharply.
He took a breath, tried again.
"We do not want you to kneel to us.
Better to have a friend."

Donal leaned back against the wall.
"If you were any other friend of mine,
we'd get drunk together.
Or go to a brothel.
Or both."

"Not a brothel," said Xau.
"But we could drink with you."

Donal raised his eyebrows.
"I didn't think you ever got drunk."

"We don't. We will try it once.
For educational purposes."

With the guards' help,
they carried the gifts
plus liquor to Xau's room,
and then set about the business
of educating him.

TIARNAN

The horses and dogs ready
when Connol arrived. Late.
His brother—King Donal—
plus a dozen other men,
and Queen Fian and her sister
all waiting for him.

"Sorry. Where's Xau?"

"King Xau chose not to hunt with us."
A hint of scorn in Fian's voice.

"Anything wrong?" asked Connol.

Donal shrugged. "He drank a lot last night."

"He got drunk? Xau doesn't drink."

"He drank. He sang. I sang with him."

Connol so preoccupied imagining this
that they were a mile out
before he noticed that Tiarnan,
Donal's fourteen-year-old son,
wasn't there either.

*

Tiarnan searched half the castle
before finding King Xau outdoors,
drilling with his guards.

Xau, his off arm in a sling,
paused midway through a footwork drill.

"Tiarnan, do you want to join in?"

"I'd like that."

Tiarnan warmed up,
borrowed a practice sword.
Once he had the patterns down,
they went faster and faster
until Tiarnan ran with sweat.
Xau's guards tirelessly, infuriatingly faultless;
Xau's form almost the match of his guards
but the king's face set with effort.

When they finally stopped,
Xau gave Tiarnan an easy, friendly smile.
"You're a far better swordsman
than we were at fourteen."

"Thanks." Tiarnan tried not to show
how pleased he was—
he wanted Xau to like him—
didn't want Xau to *know*
that he wanted him to like him.

"We were lazy," said Xau.
"We didn't practice."

"But I thought you were—
I thought you always did
exactly what you were meant to.
My father said, years ago,
that you were 'hideously honorable.'"

Xau silent a moment.
"We... tried to do what was right."

"And you did it!"
Tiarnan couldn't understand
Xau's hesitation. "You won the war,
saved the demon's servants,
you did everything."

Xau looked at him,
not the look a man gives a child,
even a child he is proud of,
but the look of one man to an equal.
"We tried, but men still died.

Men. Women. Children.
Innish and Meqingese alike.
In battle or demon-burnt."

Lead in Tiarnan's stomach,
a weight he'd never shared.
"What happens, when I'm king,
if I don't know what to do?
Or if I'm bad at doing it?"

Xau laid his hand briefly on Tiarnan's arm.
"For what it's worth, we think—I think—
you will be a good king, Tiarnan."

Tiarnan ducked his head,
said nothing,
but he remembered Xau's words.
Tried to live up to them later.

DREAM

He looses Rose's long brown hair from its braid, runs his hands through it,
but she pulls away saying, "Rourk," and Donal, frantic, must rebraid her hair
to rescue Rourk. His hands entangle: Rourk's body broken, buried. "Hush,
be easy," says Rose in a voice that is not her own. Donal turns on his side,
reaching in sleep for that voice, for Fian his wife. Fian speaks with Rose's face,
says, "Go to the tombs. My words are air. Going, gone." And Donal lets go of
Rose, slides far from fret or thought.

SWORDS

Under the castle,
delved in earth and rock,
a burial ground.

Donal, King of Innis,
walked down to the tombs
of the kings who came before him
with Xau, King of Meqing,
lately an enemy,
now a friend.
With them came Connol, Donal's brother,
and Xau's guard, shadowing his king.

At Donal's side hung his longsword, Raid,

the sword with which his father
slew foes, wolves, whores, wretches:
a brutal man, a brutal king,
and Donal, the Red King,
red-haired, red-handed in war,
had fought all his years
to hold that selfsame rage in check.

Donal stopped in the passage
by a bare earthen mound:
he'd ordered his father buried
without even a namestone.

Donal spat on the mound,
his fingers curling round Raid's hilt,
the hilt his father once smashed
against Connol's head,
knocking his young son to his knees,
and bringing Donal at a run
to hurl himself upon his father.

He would have died that day,
but that his uncle deflected
Raid's heavy blade.
His uncle lost three fingers
and Donal lost the last of his affection
for his sire.

                    *

Connol walked past Donal and Xau,
wasting neither spit nor glance
upon their father's mound.

Torches burned on the walls,
the damp air smelling of oil and smoke,
and Connol wondered what servant
lit torches underground
for dead men.

The passage widened into a cavern.
Water dripped from rock above
onto a circle of seven stone tombs.
A stain darkened the dank dirt at Connol's feet.
He followed the stain behind a tomb:
a woman's spread-eagled corpse,
dagger in her chest.

He yelled, drew his sword
in the moment before he recognized her—
Eirdre, Queen Fian's sister—
a moment in which he saw
neither Eirdre's body,
nor the sword in his hand,
but a vision of his wife, Mei,
a baby suckling at her breast,
a vision he'd had a dozen times before,
though no child had yet been born.

Connol came back to himself
as the others caught up to him.
Beneath his boots, a trembling,
then a rending din
as the tombs split wide.

Bones rose from out the gaping tombs.
Dirt rushed in streams toward the bones,
settled over the skeletons like skin
as they rose to their feet:
seven dead kings with earth for flesh,
their jaws grinning open.

Eirdre's corpse rose too,
the dagger still in her chest.

Connol frozen in horror,
his scalp crawling
as Eirdre took a smoky torch
from the cavern wall.

"Fian did this," said Eirdre.
"I will not be her servant,
her abomination."

She set the torch to her bloody robes.
As flames leapt, as her hair caught fire,
she screamed.

Beside Connol, Xau shifted,
undoing his jacket—
to put the flames out?—
but Xau's left arm in a sling,
his movements awkward.

Blue light flashed, dazzling,

outlining the seven dead kings.
When the light faded,
the seven figures stood side by side.
In each dead king's grasp, a blue sword.
On each eyeless head, a blue crown.

One still moment,
then the dead kings attacked.

*

"Back to back!" shouted Donal
as the seven kings encircled them.

Donal swept Raid
clear through one king's torso.
The two halves fell apart,
then, having fallen,
slithered back together,
bone rejoining bone.
The dead king stood up,
raised its blue sword.

Donal already beset by two others.
He parried one,
would have been skewered by the second
save that Xau lunged,
chopped off its sword hand.

Hand and sword
clattered jointly onto rock.
Xau yelled, "Take the sword."

Xau's guard scooped up the blue sword
in his off hand,
sliced one king's head from its shoulders.
The blue crown rolled past Donal,
but the headless king fought on.

Around the living men,
the dead kings fell and rose again.
And again.
And again.

Donal cut the sword from one,
grabbed it. He laughed then,
laughed though he might die here,

because he finally knew the distance
between his father's brutality
and his own violence—
a violence Donal had tempered,
battled, constrained.
That had not swallowed him whole.

     *

Connol heard his brother's laugh,
but could not look round,
his boots slipping on the damp ground,
the king he faced outmatching him.

Xau sidestepped,
hacked off the dead king's arm,
shouted, "Get the sword!"

Connol bent down,
yanked the blue sword loose
as the severed arm slithered
toward its body.

Three swords taken.
Four left between seven dead kings.

Turning to slash at the nearest king,
Connol saw his brother on one knee,
blood running from his thigh,
saw a dead king pivot
to lunge at Donal.
No time.

Connol stepped into the path
of the blue sword,
saw his own innards spill forth
in the instant before the dead king
lopped off his head;
saw then,
in the breathless end of his life,
his wife Mei,
pouring a bowl of tea,
her black hair shining.

     *

Seeing Connol decapitated,
Donal rose, roaring, to his feet.

He cleaved his brother's killer
neck to groin,
cleaved another
as Xau kicked both swords
away from the grasping weaponless kings.

Xau's guard sent a blue sword flying
from a dead king's grip.

Together, Donal and Xau
took down the last armed king.

As the king fell,
blue light dazzled from its crown, its sword,
from the blue sword in Donal's off hand.

Donal blinked,
his off hand empty.
The crowns, the blue swords gone.
The seven kings reduced
to piles of bones.
Motionless.

Donal's breath loud, hard,
his thigh throbbing,
coated in blood.

Neither he, nor Xau, nor the guard spoke.
The guard bound up Donal's thigh.

Donal hoisted Connol's body
over his shoulder,
picked his brother's head up
by the hair,
and limped his way
out of the cavern.

WOLF THRONE

No attendants, no witnesses
as Queen Fian sat in the wolf throne,
clasping the heads of the wolves
that formed the throne's sides.

Soon it would be her throne
in all but name:

King Donal dead,
their young son crowned,
Fian the force behind the throne.
And behind Fian, the old gods.

So close—
both Donal and Xau must be dying even now
in the caverns under the castle,
their deaths her doing
though hers not the hand
upon the sword.

Fian bowed her head,
rehearsed receiving word of Donal's death,
how disbelief would turn to grief—
her only true grief
her sister's death,
a sacrifice demanded by the gods.

The doors swung open.
Fian jumped from the throne
as King Donal limped in,
his brother's head dangling from his hand,
blood dripping on the marble floor.

Fian screamed—
how could Donal be alive?!—
screamed again as King Xau
walked in with a dozen soldiers.

"Seize her," said Donal.

Only when a soldier
set his clammy fingers round her wrist
did she think to dissemble.
She trembled, let tears brim.
"Husband, please, I love you."

Donal set his brother's dripping head
on the wolf throne.

"You killed my brother," said Donal.
"You killed your sister—"

"Eirdre is dead?!"

"You fucking know it. She fucking named you."

"But if she's dead—"

"She woke up."

Fian gaped at him
before she understood.
The gods had done as she asked,
had raised the cavern's dead,
and Eirdre, dead too, had risen too.

"Put her in the dungeon," said Donal.

"Wait! Let me see Eirdre—"

"Shut up," said Donal,
"or I'll cut out your tongue."

That voice, that look,
his ruthlessness
well known to her,
but this the first time
she had been the target.

Fear dried her throat
as the soldiers blindfolded her
and dragged her away.

HARP

Bustle, noise, light,
the castle crowded with guests.
In the center of the great hall,
covered in wolf skins, laid out on a bier,
the corpse of Connol, Prince of Innis,
killed in defense of his brother, Donal.

Donal, King of Innis,
who sat on a bench,
his thigh heavily bandaged,
listening to an old man
play the harp.

An old man whose fingers, whose breath
had once conjured storm and battle,
dragon and demon,
every night in this great hall.

Faolan, his back bent with age,
played and thought of the boy
who used to sit on the floor
listening to him practice,
almost the only time that boy held still;
the boy now grown into a king.

Thought of the boy's younger brother,
fastened to him like a shadow;
a shadow who had squirmed
when Faolan practiced fingerwork.

That shadow now covered in wolf skins,
heaped with gold rings, swords, daggers,
a silver torc, a linden shield.

At midnight, the beating of drums.
Donal got up with help from King Xau.
He raised a silver urn.
"To Connol. Who died for me. Who—"

Donal stopped, shook his head.
Tears ran down his face.
He drank from the urn,
handed it to Fergus.

"To Connol," said Fergus.
"My commander and my friend.
Who died with sword in hand,
his brother's shield."

One by one, they drank to Connol.

When Faolan's turn came,
he stood as straight
as his back would allow.
"To Connol, Prince of Innis,
who loved a marching tune."

Faolan drank deep,
laid his harp on top of Connol.

WIDOW

Carrying Prince Connol's shrouded body
down to the moonlit harbor,
the fishermen and the soldiers sang.

Mei, waiting in the largest fishing boat,
neither wailed nor wept for her husband.

Softly the men sang Connol's dirge
as they positioned his body
in a wicker coracle within the large boat.

Mei, pregnant, queasy, gagged on the smell
of myrrh, mackerel, decay.

Six men rowed her to sea,
singing the dirge in time to the stroke,
the fleet of fishing boats following.

Mei blinked away sea spray,
not tears. She hadn't loved Connol.

The men rowed, their voices rising
the further out they went,
the song echoed from the other boats.

Mei had scorned Connol as a barbarian:
insolent, insulting, insufferable.

The men stopped. Stopped singing.
Stopped rowing.
One man handed Mei a flaming torch.

Slowly Connol's patience, his kindness,
had crept in upon Mei.

Wind, water against the hull. No voices.
The men lowered the coracle
into the waves and rowed clear.

Mei tossed the torch down on Connol.
The flame caught on his shroud.

All the men on all the boats
turned then to Mei,
and she sang, clear-voiced,

not the funeral dirge, but a lullaby,
not in Connol's language, but her own,
while the fire burnt out.

HARMOUTH

King Xau came to the ruins of Harmouth
with the corpse of Prince Connol,
his sister's husband;
came to comfort his sister
and bring her home,
but Mei declined,
declined though she could not articulate
her reasons, reasons as incomplete
as the child in her belly;
stayed on in the burnt border-town
though it meant living among barbarians;
birthed her son in the five-room stone house
of her short, strained marriage;
noticed only then,
in the colorless days of illness
following that birth,
the barbarians waiting, openhanded, patient,
offering friendship.

Turned her shame and their friendship
to a purpose, founded a school:
taught Meqingese to fishermen
and fishermen's wives, and sailors,
soldiers, traders, craftsmen.

Never did return to Meqing but that once
when Xau could not come to her,
when men and women journeyed
from half the world away
to honor him.

OPUS

Magnificent in deep blue velvet,
his harp gleaming in a slant of sunlight,
entirely pleased with himself,
Enlai sang to an audience
of ministers, dignitaries, advisors,
their families, and King Xau himself.

By darkest night, no moon in sight,
armored with flame, the demon came.

Two kings alone opposed his might,
two kings against the fire.

"Kneel thou to me!" the demon cried,
his hands ablaze with searing light.
Two kings his victory denied,
two kings against the fire.

Eighty-nine verses thus far performed,
Enlai's audience enraptured;
King Xau's son eyeing his father in awe,
but King Xau himself appalled,
delightfully, conspicuously appalled,
his cheeks stained red.

"Kneel thou to me!" again he roared,
and one king knelt, the other fought.
Two kingdoms balanced on one sword,
one king against the fire.

That sapling king alone he fought,
alone opposed the demon lord,
bereft of hope, but stern of thought,
one king against the fire.

King Xau, that sapling king,
buried his face in his hands.
Hah! That served him right
for refusing Enlai a royal commission:
the king chronically reluctant
to be cast as a hero.

"Kneel thou to me and call me Lord!"
The demon's spite in searing waves
engulfed the king; pain his reward,
that king who fought the fire.

Each breath, each step an agony,
yet still fought on that sapling king,
so young, yet none as brave as he,
that king who battled fire.

All Enlai's labors amply rewarded:
eight months of tedious exertion,
gathering accounts of the demon.
Admittedly, he'd taken a few liberties,
an opus of such stature demanded

a hero of equal proportion.

> *All night he fought that Lord of Flame*
> *till he could scarcely raise his sword,*
> *yet would not yield: acclaim his name,*
> *King Xau who fought the fire.*

> *With his last strength as morning came,*
> *his sword-hilt scorching in his grip,*
> *he thrust clear through the Lord of Flame*
> *and proved the demon's bane.*

> *His limbs undone, his vision dim,*
> *his foe now slain, the young king fell,*
> *but Donal knelt and tended him,*
> *the king who'd conquered fire.*

A rustle of silk, a creaking of chairs
as the audience rose and applauded,
bowing first to Enlai, then to Xau,
who sat, head hidden in his hands.
Doubtless the others thought him
overcome by his memories.

All in all, quite satisfactory.

RIDDLE: INSTRUMENT

"I hear," said Leong,
over breakfast with King Xau,
Xau's family, Xau's other guards,
"that I missed a fine ballad."

"Better than fine," said Gan.
"Gripping. Inspiring. Magnificent."

Leong caught the reproachful look
that the king gave him—
Xau's cheeks turning red,
the king perennially discomfited
by his heroic reputation.

"It was all about Papa," said Prince Keng.

With studied innocence, Leong asked,
"What was the best bit?"

Gan sang in his clear sweet bass:
*"Two kingdoms balanced on one sword,
one king against the fire!"*

"Dao!" said the king,
as soon as Gan paused for breath.
"This would be an excellent time
for a riddle. Please."

"Let's see," said Dao.
"Man or woman, old or young,
we can all play this instrument,
but we cannot touch it,
cannot see it.
What is it?"

Princess Ying, three years old,
said, "A panda!"

Leong hid his smile behind his napkin.
All week long, Ying had guessed *panda*.

"Not a panda," said Dao.

Gan sang, *"One king against the fire—"*

"Singing!" said Keng.

HANDS

In the dusk,
her daughter ran to her,
abandoning the other children
with their yo-yos, jump ropes, spinning tops,
straight through a bed of peonies.

"He doesn't! He doesn't!" wailed Ying.
"Papa doesn't have horrible hands!"

Shazia lifted her daughter up,
kissed her small grubby fingers,
searching for a truth
measured to Ying's need.
"Papa's left hand was hurt
saving Captain Tsung and two soldiers."

Ying's face burrowed into her

and Shazia held onto her
as if that holding could shield Ying.
"His right hand was burnt fighting a demon.
His hands are ugly,
but they are the bravest hands I know."

"I wish he had nice hands," said Ying.   .

Then Ying wriggled free
and ran—straight through the peonies—
back toward the other children.

Shazia stood, arms empty,
watching her daughter run.

SHADE

His years of duty ended,
still the captain stood watch
over his king,
night after night.

Hung in honor on the wall,
the iron-forged blade
the captain once wielded
in the king's defense.

In the captain's hands
that blade's twinned shadow,
both sword and man reduced
to air and captured moonlight.

LIPOH

Seven years since Atun
lay prostrate on the dirt
beside his mother and sisters,
face sideways so he could peek at the horses,
hundreds upon hundreds of wild horses,
and the boy-king they followed.
The greatest day of Atun's life,
though he had done nothing
but watch.

Now, seven years later,

Atun sat astride his favorite horse,
his silver armbands bright-polished,
his hair braided with crimson ribbons,
his three spare mounts alongside him
on the East Bridge into Lipoh,
the Ringed City, capital of Meqing.

Lipoh's massive walls loomed before him,
taller than any building he'd ever seen,
taller than any building he'd ever imagined,
five times the height of Atun astride his horse,
but their hugeness left him undaunted.
He was Atun, son of Anikha,
a warrior of the horse tribes,
and he had come to serve King Xau.

    Had known seven years ago
    that he wanted to follow King Xau
    even as the wild horses had done,
    even though it would mean
    leaving the horse country,
    leaving his kin.

Atun gazed down at the deep moat,
gazed round at the other travelers,
gazed at the marble dragons
lining the bridge,
well-pleased by all he saw.
Seven years and seven hundred miles
behind him,
the city and the king just ahead.

Eight soldiers armed
with sword and bow and ji
guarded the far end of the bridge,
their helmets bright as Atun's armbands.

The old woman in front of him
stammered as the soldiers
asked her business.
Bowing low to the soldiers,
she stumbled and dropped her basket,
bundles of herbs scattering.

The soldiers shouted at her
as she scrabbled for her herbs,

and Atun jumped down from his horse,
helped her pick them up.

Not the soldiers' shouts
that shook Atun,
but rather the indifference
with which they then waved him through,
as if he, a warrior of the horse tribes,
scarcely mattered.

For seven years he had worked toward this day.
Now he wondered if King Xau
would deem his service
of little consequence.

MISTAKEN

The soldier on the left
of the palace entrance
eyed Atun dubiously.
"Name and business?"

"Atun, son of Anikha.
I've come to serve King Xau."

"Is the king expecting you?"

"No." Atun's cheeks flushed,
but he didn't look down.

"How do you plan to serve the king?"

"To be his guard, his oathsworn."

"You mean, join the army?"

"No. To protect the king himself."

"The king," said the soldier slowly,
"has eight personal guards. Handpicked.
From the best men in the army.
I don't think he's looking for more."

Atun's cheeks now afire.
Among the horse lords,
it was a mark of honor
to have as many oathsworn as possible.

Not an army, not soldiers paid
to fight at your command,
but men who freely chose
to protect you.
He had thought—
he had assumed—
he had been mistaken.

A second soldier, an older man,
spoke for the first time.
"You're from the horse tribes?"

Atun nodded stiffly.

"Then you might try the royal stables.
Might be they could use another groom."

"Thank you." Atun bowed deeply,
aware that the man meant to help.
But it didn't help.

Seven years and seven hundred miles
for nothing.

HUANG

Not much startled Huang anymore,
but he was taken aback
when he first saw Atun—

his silver armbands catching the sun,
his long hair braided,
nervous as a yearling colt—

No weapons, the guards had taken those,
yet the young man unquestionably
a warrior from the horse tribes.

"I'm Huang, the stablemaster.
They told me you're looking for work."

"Yes, sir."

"Hmmm." Pointless wasting time
quizzing him about horses.
He'd know as much as Huang.

But why had he left the horse lords?
Huang had never heard of such a thing.
Unless the man treated horses cruelly—

"Did you bring your horses to Lipoh?"

Atun nodded. "They're stabled at an inn."

"May I see them?"

"Yes, but it's two miles away."

Which would be a hot and sticky walk,
even this early, but Huang said only,
"That's fine. We'll go there now."

Huang saw the worry on Atun's face,
would have liked to reassure him,
but he couldn't make promises.

Not until he'd seen the horses.
"Is this your first time in Lipoh?"

"Yes, sir."

"There's a bridle path by the river.
You could take your horses there later."

Huang talked of this and that,
not pressing the young man
with any further questions.

At the inn, Atun's horses
were in as fine condition
as Huang had hoped.

Better yet, they were clearly
glad to see Atun, nickering,
bringing their heads toward him.

"Your horses do you great credit.
I'll take you to Captain Li next."

"Captain Li?"

"The head of King Xau's personal guards.
I'd like to hire you, and Li checks
everyone who works in the royal stables."

"Thank you, sir." Atun's eyes alight.

Well then, a good morning's work.
Huang fussed with his tunic a little
while the young man composed himself.

DECISION

Four hours before Li,
captain of King Xau's guards,
had time to question Atun.

Late afternoon by then,
the sun a hole of fire overhead,
Atun in the shade of the sentry station,
sweat dripping from his silver armbands,
standing still as a statue
precisely where Li had left him,
as if he had not moved all afternoon.
Perhaps he hadn't.

Li handed him a water bottle,
led him across to a stand of junipers.
"Huang said you want to work
in the stables."

"Yes, sir."

"You were a horse warrior,
but now you want to be a stablehand?"
Li didn't try to hide his skepticism.
Anyone with access to the stables
was a potential threat to the king.

"Yes, sir."

"Why?"

"To serve King Xau."

"Why?"

Atun silent,
a look of desperation on his face.

"Why did you leave?
Because you're a poor warrior?"

"No!" Fury in that single syllable
before the man mastered himself.
"I'm the third best archer
in the horse tribes."

"Then why leave?"

Atun lowered his gaze,
said all in a rush,
"When I was twelve,
I saw the king with the horses,
the wild horses,
hundreds and hundreds of horses,
so many that their hooves
on the grass were a thunder.
He was only a boy,
but they came from the hills
to follow him. To serve him.
As I would do."

A rawness to that spill of words.

Li's tunic stuck damply to his back.
He dipped his head to Atun, said gently,
"And so, having seen this, you wished
to look after the king's horses?"

Atun looked at Li. "No, sir.
I wanted to be his guard—
I didn't know there are only eight of you—
I'll serve him any way I can."

Li silent then a long while.
Huang eager to hire Atun as a groom.
To approve that an easy decision,
a safe decision.

That did not make it the right one.

*

Dusk deepening to night
in the Peach Courtyard
as King Xau ran up to the tree
his daughter was hiding behind.
He made a show of searching
high up in the branches,
the ripening peaches swaying.

Ying giggled and he darted round,
picked her up: "There you are!"

"How did you find me?! I stayed still!"

"You giggled."
He kissed the top of her head.
"Time to sleep."

"I'm not tired!" said Ying,
but her head drooped on his shoulder
as he carried her over to Shazia,
who was reading by lantern-light.

Ying a sweetness in his arms
that he did not want to set down,
that he set down anyhow;
he had hours of work left.
He touched his hand to Shazia's,
watched her lead Ying away.

Footsteps behind him—
Li, who should have been off-duty by now—

"Your Majesty." Li knelt to him,
a thing he had not done in years.

Xau set his hand under Li's arm,
raised him up, studied him in the dusk,
Li's breath too fast. "What's wrong?"

"Eight is an auspicious number," said Li.

Xau raised his eyebrows. "And so?"

"Meqing has eight ministries.
The palace has eight wings.
You have eight guards,
as did your father,
and all the kings before him."

Xau waited.

"Your Majesty, there's a man
I'd like to test for a place
as a ninth guard. His name is Atun."

ATUN

He was the wind,
the bow in his hand,
the galloping horse beneath him.
At the top of the horse's rising run,
in that suspended instant
when all four hooves
left the ground,
he had no fear, no need;
he was the air-drawn line
between eye and target,
the string releasing,
the arrow in flight.

    Earlier,
    one hour into his first day
    working as a stablehand,
    Atun was a pending storm:
    he hadn't striven seven years
    so he could muck out stalls—
    had dreamt of shielding the king
    with sword and bow and blood and muscle.
    One hour then Captain Li appeared—
    Atun's first thought
    that Li had decided to dismiss him—
    but no,
    the captain wished to test him
    for a position as king's guard.
    One last chance for Atun
    to earn what he most wanted.

He was the rush of air,
the cool jade hardness
of his thumb ring;
no thought to it
as he fitted another arrow to the string;
no past, no future,
nothing beyond the bow, the horse,
the stirrups under his feet
as he turned his body,
loosed the arrow.

Over. Done.
Atun wheeled his horse round,

rode to the captain,
fear and need rushing back,
the bow trembling,
his limbs trembling.

"Good enough," said Li.
"Your sword skills need work,
but I've never seen a finer archer."

Atun unable to do more than nod.

WHAT ATUN LEARNED

In his first month as King Xau's guard,
Atun learned:

That the other guards outmatched Atun
with every weapon save the bow;
that Li, their captain, outmatched him
as easily as a horse outruns a beetle.

That in every ten-hour duty shift
the guards spent two hours training;
that Atun would train for twice as long
until he met the captain's standards.

That, in matters concerning
the king's safety, the king's guards
(including Atun, new though he was)
outranked every officer in the army.

That King Xau was not the hero
Atun had imagined: in all that month,
no demon defeated, no magic wrought,
no monster slain, no battle fought.

That Xau bruised as easily
as other men, and, in private,
nursed a mosquito bite
as if it were a war wound.

That, in public, Xau never complained,
never showed when he was tired;
listened more than he spoke,
noticed more than he said.

That the guards ate breakfast

with the king and his family;
that Princess Ying, age three,
loathed rice gruel, craved sesame balls.

That the king took Prince Keng riding
twice a week, no matter how busy he was.
That the king trained with his guards
every day, no matter how busy he was.

That the king was busy every day;
that the king would sooner talk
to Tian, his elderly cleaning woman,
than to the dignitaries vying for his time.

That the dignitaries
were unlikely to guess this—
Xau attentive to all who approached,
high or low, man or woman.

That, in private, the guards bantered
with each other; that Li and Leong and Gan
bantered even with the king;
that, in public, the guards held silence.

That at the close of every shift
the king bowed more deeply
to his guards than he did
to visiting princes.

Even to Atun,
the least and most junior
of his guards,
Xau bowed as if to a king.

JUN XI

No raised voices, no open dissent,
yet something amiss—
Atun, newest and most junior
of King Xau's guards,
scanned the eight ministers,
their assistants, the king's advisors,
King Xau himself—

King Xau whose gaze rested
on Finance Minister Jun Xi,
even though Jun Xi had not spoken—

Jun Xi's posture perhaps too rigid,
Jun Xi who had argued against the king
at two previous meetings.
Resentment there?
Enough to endanger the king?
Atun gave a finger signal to Dao,
who stood guard across the room.

Another minister gave his report,
the king looking often at Jun Xi,
Jun Xi agitated,
Atun uneasy—

Jun Xi appeared to be unarmed,
no sword at his belt,
the red sash of his office
perfectly aligned atop his silk robes;
an aging, argumentative man
who had eyed Atun dismissively
when he became a king's guard,
as if Atun's braided hair, his armbands
marked him as a savage—

"Your Majesty," said Jun Xi,
beginning the treasury report,
"trade with Innis continues to increase
with a concomitant rise in revenue."

—A slew of numbers followed, then—

"A most regrettable incident occurred
in the district department of Weizhou.
Five men, including an inspector,
have been accused of fraud in the exams
to enter the finance ministry.
It appears likely they will be convicted."

Jun Xi stood up,
lifted the red sash of office
over his head, clutched it.
"I therefore offer my resignation."

Which explained the minister's agitation.
Atun relaxed fractionally.

"Had you met any of these men?"
King Xau's voice quiet, even,

his expression hard to read.

"No."

"Do you know of anything
connecting you to this incident
beyond the fact that it took place
within your ministry?"

"No."

"When did you first learn about it?"

"Two days ago."

"You should have informed us at once.
That is a serious error of judgment."

Jun Xi bowed deeply, his hands trembling.
Atun had no cause to like the man,
yet the minister's misery so evident
that he felt sorry for him.

"However," said the king,
"we find no other fault in your actions.
You are dedicated and highly capable,
and we refuse your resignation.
Be seated."

Jun Xi sat down,
fumbled the sash back on.
The rest of the meeting subdued.

Jun Xi waited at the end
until the other officials had filed out.
The minister bowed again to Xau.
"Your Majesty, I let you down.
I'm sorry. I—"

"It's all right,"
the king said gently.
"We need you. We need someone
who will point out our mistakes."

"That should keep me busy."
Jun Xi's words disrespectful,
the look on his face quite otherwise.

The king reached for Jun Xi's arm,
clasped it briefly,
a history between them
that Atun could only guess at.

TRAVELING

Traveling,
day after day after day,
something unfolds
inside Shazia, quiet.
Call it gladness.

No attendants to dress her;
no one to style her hair;
no flower arrangements
at the breakfast table.
No table at all.

The guards setting up camp,
the smell of wood smoke,
eating supper with her fingers,
the horses nickering
to each other.

In the tent, Shazia touches
the scars on Xau's hands, his shoulder,
permits herself to imagine
that he will never
be hurt again.

If it were up to her,
they would circle round and round,
never reach an end,
grow old traveling together,
day after day after day.

DISCRETION

Li, captain of King Xau's guards,
stood thirty feet from Xau:
too far for Li's liking,
too many people in the room,
too many entrances.

This the second day
of a state visit to Ritany,
a visit intended to further
the alliance first forged
by King Xau's father.

Xau's duty to represent Meqing,
to hunt, dance, dine, negotiate;
to remember names, faces,
every point of protocol.
Li's duty to keep him alive.

Too many people at the reception:
King Memnor, the Ritan king,
gray-haired and great-hearted;
King Xau; the two queens;
much of Memnor's court.

Only Li and Gan to guard Xau.
All nine of King Xau's guards
had accompanied him on the journey,
but here, within the palace,
diplomacy dictated discretion.

Discretion conferred risk.
Li alert for anything awry,
motions sudden or surreptitious;
he ranked guests by proximity to Xau,
places weapons might be concealed.

He assessed the attendants
offering refreshments;
tracked the tone and timbre
of overlapping conversations
though he spoke no Ritan.

—Boots sounded in the hall.
—Running, approaching.
Li discarded discretion,
sprinted to Xau's side
as the east door opened.

A messenger—unarmed—
uniformed in Ritan livery—
raced over to King Memnor.
Spoke. Urgent. Gulping.
Hands punctuating his words.

Li looked at Xau—
too straight, too still—
Xau who understood Ritan.

"There's been a disaster,"
said Xau. "A huge flood."

FORD

Rain, wind, water, mud—
men and horses slowed
so that the two-day journey
took three days,
though they set out before dawn
and rode past sunset.

Wind, water, mud, rain—
the last light lingering in the west
when they climbed the ridge
overlooking the ford,
the wide river swollen,
the plain across the river flooded.
Diminished shapes of survivors
struggled toward the ford
where thousands of people
already stood, stranded, sodden,
on the far side of the river.

Water, mud, rain, wind—
Memnor, King of Ritany,
gray-haired and great-hearted,
ruler of that underwater plain,
rode down the ridge to the ford
followed by sixty of his cavalry
and his guest, King Xau,
who had offered his help,
though it seemed unlikely
that Xau and his guards
could make much difference,
the scale of the disaster inhuman.

Mud, rain, wind, water—
Memnor's horse refused to put one hoof
into the churning brown water,
so Memnor dismounted and strode in,
the cold water pummeling him.

He made it thirty yards,
thigh-deep, fighting for balance,
before he turned round.

Rain, wind, water, mud—
Memnor waded back to his soldiers
beneath the darkening October sky.
Wind whipped his wet hair.
His guest, King Xau,
only twenty-four years old
yet already burnished with legends,
dismounted and joined him.

Memnor turned to Havnar,
his army commander (and more than that),
a muscled man with a shaven scalp.
"What can you do?"

"Nothing until the main army reaches us."
Havnar shrugged, his habitual response.

Memnor gazed across the water
at his stranded people.
A man on the far side
waded into the river toward them.
Partway across, hip-deep,
the man was knocked off his feet.

The man's head bobbed up once, twice,
before Memnor lost all sight of him.
"Ropes?" asked Memnor.

"Ropes are with the supply train."
Havnar wore the same look he'd worn,
years ago, when his soldiers
were dying of a fever.

King Xau said, "Perhaps the horses."

Memnor looked at him sharply.
He didn't point out that his own horse
had refused to set foot in the river.
He'd heard the tales about Xau—
demon-killer, dragonslayer,
he who tamed wild horses.
Tales were usually exaggerated,
but Xau had always struck him
as levelheaded.

Xau said, "If the horses stand,
each bracing each, a rope of horses,
people to walk beside them."

Xau gestured as he spoke,
compensating for his awkward grammar
(just as well since the translator
was back with the supply train).
A rope, or chain, of horses
lined up across the river,
the horses anchoring each other,
people wading, holding onto them.
Perhaps.

Havnar shrugged. "I doubt it's possible."

"It's all we have," said Memnor.

Xau nodded. "We are not sure your horses
to do this for us. May we try with him?"
Xau laid his hand on Havnar's horse,
a sturdy brown gelding.

Havnar shrugged again. "Go ahead."

Xau unsaddled the horse,
handed the saddle to one of his guards,
walked the horse into the river.
Through the rain and dark
it was hard to make him out
when he paused, over halfway across,
turned the horse, came back.

Memnor stepped forward
and hugged the younger man,
surprising both of them.

Mud, water, wind, rain—
a chain of horses across the ford,
people struggling through the water,
clinging to the horses.
Soldiers in the water with them,
carrying children.

Rain, mud, water, wind—
Memnor helped people—his people—
up the ridge, many of them crying,

all of them exhausted, cold, hungry,
yet those who could helping
the children, the elderly,
so that Memnor's heart swelled
with pride and love for all of them,
for the whole soggy expanse of Ritany.

Wind, rain, mud, water—
two hours in, Memnor shook with cold
as he ordered the soldiers
to rotate and take breaks.
Havnar strode over
and handed him a mug of soup.

Memnor drank the soup,
standing by Havnar,
shoulders touching,
no need of words
after all these years.

Water, wind, rain, mud—
four hours in, Memnor estimated
half the people had crossed the ford.
Progress, but not fast enough.
The surgeon thought many
would die by morning without shelter.
"Half done," he said to Havnar.

Havnar surprised him by frowning
instead of giving his habitual shrug.
"King Xau's half done too.
He won't leave the horses,
but he can scarcely stand."

"Would the horses stay without him?"

Havnar did shrug this time.
"I doubt it. The horses look at him
like he's their foal—no, their leader."

Memnor peered into rainswept dark,
shook his head. "Get across the river.
Send the small children first,
then the babies and nursing mothers,
then the elderly. If there's time."

Havnar shrugged and went.

Mud, water, wind, rain—
most of the children over.
Two horses lost down the river,
the other horses struggling.
Memnor waded into the water himself,
stopped in the middle by Xau,
who looked three quarters dead,
the current pushing both of them
against the wet black flank
of one of the horses.

Memnor gripped Xau's arm.
"We're done until morning."

Xau mumbled something
that Memnor couldn't decipher,
and pointed at the people
waiting to cross.

The horse edged its head round,
rubbing its cheek against Xau.

Xau looked at the horse,
its nostrils flared,
sides heaving, and nodded.
"The horses are tired."

Water, wind, rain, mud—
all the horses out of the river,
Xau clinging to a horse for support.
Memnor exchanged a look
with one of Xau's guards,
and then the two men
hoisted Xau up between them
and carried him to the surgeon's tent.

Wind, rain, mud, water—
Memnor, too old for nights like this,
checked on his soldiers,
checked on Xau (fast asleep under two blankets
and the watchful gaze of his guards),
walked down to the river,
pissed into the rushing water,
then walked back up to the tent
where Havnar waited for him.

A CHAIN OF HORSES

Too little sleep,
too much beyond his control.
Havnar, commander of King Memnor's army,
stared across the ford's foaming fury.
Thousands of refugees still stranded
on the far side of the river,
more straggling to join them.
No shelter, rain pouring down.

As Havnar watched, another corpse—
painfully small, a child—
was laid in the churning river
by a taller figure. Father? Uncle?

Havnar turned away from the sight,
bowed to their guest, King Xau.
"Eighty more of my cavalry have arrived."

"Good. The horses to take turns.
Sixty horses for one hour. Then sixty more,"
Xau said in fractured Ritan.

"You'll take breaks too," said Havnar.
"Come out of the river and warm up
while my men ready fresh horses."

Xau gestured and one of his guards—
the savage with armbands and braided hair—
stepped forward.

"Our guard Atun," said Xau,
"to be in charge of the horses."

Havnar reined back a retort
that the man was uncivilized.
"He doesn't know my men.
Does he even speak Ritan?"

"No. He understands horses.
Atun to be in charge."

Havnar shrugged.
One more thing beyond his control.
He was helpless without Xau.

Havnar's own men unable
to persuade so much as one horse
into the churning brown water.

And yet the horses had followed Xau,
had lined up across the ford,
bracing each other for support,
a chain of horses along which refugees
had inched their way to safety.

Havnar called his cavalry captain over,
introduced him to Atun. Whilst he did so,
Xau took off his jacket, his tunic,
passed them to another of his guards,
stood there in the drenching rain.

Havnar frowned.
Xau was brave, no question of that.
Bravery not the same as judgment.
Xau had spent half the night in the river,
had pushed himself close to collapse.

Havnar had commanded too many young men
who'd hurled themselves at danger
without weighing the risk.
He put his hand on Xau's bare arm.
"If you feel ill, stop.
Get straight out of the water."

Xau looked away,
looked across the river,
said, "They are dying over there."

Sharp as pain that moment,
knowing Xau understood the risk
that he was taking.

He stood by the young king
and stared at the small figures
waiting on the far side.

NOT LIKE THIS

Not like this,
it wasn't meant to be like this:
　　rain, wind, water, night,
　　King Xau staggering

out of the churning river
beside a staggering, stricken horse,
the horse's foreleg spurting blood,
skin hanging in ribbons;
Atun examining the mare
by wavering torchlight,
shaking his head;
the look the king gave him then.

Like this,
it was meant to be like this:
 Atun, one of King Xau's guards,
 accompanying king, queen, princeling
 on a state visit to Ritany,
 his bow ready but unneeded,
 the arrow of his life
 flown straight.

Not like this:
 their visit to Ritany
 coinciding with its worst flood
 in three hundred years;
 refugees struggling mile on mile to the ford,
 but the river fickle, furious, fast,
 too powerful to cross
 even at the ford,
 the Ritan army overmatched,
 King Xau and his guards
 trying to help.

How the world should be:
 as it was, seven years ago,
 when eighteen hundred wild horses
 followed the king from the hills
 of the horse country,
 and Atun, twelve years old,
 prostrated himself on the ground;
 the leader of the horse lords
 bowing so low to Xau
 his braid brushed the dirt;
 the greatest day of Atun's life,
 though he did nothing
 but watch.

Not as it was at dawn:
 the Ritan commander eyeing
 Atun's braid, Atun's silver armbands

as though Atun were a savage.
The Ritan cavalry, Xau's guards
trying to persuade horses
into the ford's foaming fury.
Failing.

Nor as it was at noon:
supports shearing, splitting, splintering,
the army's attempt to build
a wooden bridge over the river.
Failed.

Perhaps this, an hour after dawn:
sixty horses followed the king
into the churning water;
stood, stoic, one in front of another
—a chain across the ford—
people wading along that chain to safety.

And then, repeated all day into night:
Xau leading spent horses from the river
into Atun's care (the horses exhausted, cold)
while others tended the king (exhausted, cold)
before Xau led fresh horses into the river,
staying with them, speaking to them.
Over and over, six times over,
and each time the king put his hand
on Atun's shoulder and thanked him,
and Atun (weary, shivering, rain running
down his braid, down his back)
filled then with pride.

But not like this,
it wasn't meant to be like this:
rain, wind, water, night
when the king staggered out
beside the torn horse.
Only the stricken horse
and the two of them then,
all else shadows, torchlight, wind.
Shadows that shouted
that there were other horses,
that the king must rest,
that did not understand;
what the horses had given must be honored.
Atun inspected the horse's leg,
shook his head,

offered his sword to the king.
The shadows shouted,
the king swayed on his feet,
but Atun steadied him
so Xau could raise the sword.
The horse's neck divided on the blade.
Shadows. Water. Wind. Blood.

SURFACING

A sound.
A sound that disturbed.
A sound that disturbed him.

(Tired, too tired to stir.)

"Xau! King Xau!"

Xau. His name.
The sound a voice,
a voice he knew.
He climbed up from a great depth,
forced his eyes open. "L-Leong?"

His teeth rattled.
A weight on top of him.
A blanket covered with stones.
Hot. Hot stones over him.
Yet he shook, freezing.

(Too tired to sort it out.)

"Drink," said Leong, raising Xau's head.

A honeyed warmth.
A bearded man beside Leong,
a man he'd seen before,
a man who laid his fingers
against Xau's wrist, nodded.

"Drink all of it," said Leong.

He drank.
The hot stones shook in time
with his shivering.

Tired. The man,

the bearded man,
was King Memnor's surgeon—
King Memnor—the flood—
the chain of horses—
he had to get up—had to help—

"Lie still!" said Leong.

Hands on his shoulders,
holding him in place.

The honeyed warmth,
the weight of stones,
the heat
conspired against him,
pushed him back down into sleep.

BUSY

"The king is busy," said Atun,
the least and most junior
of King Xau's guards,
his silver armbands bright
in the first sun in two weeks.

"Busy? Busy?!" said Havnar,
a muscled man with a shaven scalp,
commander of King Memnor's army.
Havnar's disbelief plain
even through his translator.

Atun neither bowed,
nor dipped his head,
nor offered explanation.
He stood, straight-backed,
outside King Xau's tent.

Havnar eyed Atun's armbands,
his braided hair,
said, dismissively,
as if the task took little skill,
"You looked after the horses well, boy."

Atun made no acknowledgement.
That Xau had entrusted Atun
with the horses, had praised him,

a great matter.
Havnar's opinion, small.

A bearded man,
King Memnor's surgeon,
stepped out of Xau's tent.
Havnar's expression shifted to concern:
"Is King Xau not yet recovered?"

"The king is... busy."
The surgeon glanced at Atun,
who bowed low to him.
They didn't speak the same language,
but they understood each other.

Havnar frowned. "When it suits the king,
Memnor and I wish to thank him."
Havnar slapped his hand twice
against the sheath of his sword,
and left with the translator.

                    *

Inside the tent, silent,
sitting cross-legged on the dirt,
his guards around him,
King Xau wept.

WHY THE KING WEPT

For the horse that died
by his hand, and the horses
swept down the river;
for the infants dead
before they reached the ford,
and the childless mothers,
and the wifeless men;
because he had spent
all his strength,
yet many died anyhow;
because they knelt to him
and called him valiant,
but he knew himself fallible;
because he wished his brother
had been king instead of him;
because he had not forgiven

his father, but had come
to understand him;
because he had run out
of strength to stop
from weeping.

DREAD

Memnor, King of Ritany,
gray-haired and great-hearted,
surveyed the meal,
such as it was.
Dried meat and beet soup.
"My apologies."

"This is fine, this is good."
His guest, King Xau,
sitting on a rug on the floor of the tent—
not even a cushion to offer him—
took a strip of dried leathery meat.

"It's wretched," said Havnar,
commander of Memnor's army.
"There'll be a feast in your honor
once we're back at the palace."

"That is not to be needed.
This is all we want."
Xau's Ritan awkward.

"*This* is what you want?"
Havnar brandished the leathery meat.

"This. The food is fine.
The food is not to be important.
This. The three of us, eating together."

Havnar dipped his head to Xau,
then looked at Memnor. "You were right,
he's not like his father."

Xau stilled,
a slight hardening
to the lines of his face
that Memnor might have missed

except that the captain of Xau's guards—
a lean, black-uniformed figure
on the far side of the tent—
alerted, the captain's attention
centering on Xau.

Memnor handed Xau a cup of water.
"I knew your father quite well.
Havnar did too."

Xau nodded. "You fought,
and then to become allies,
and then fought together."

"Fought together,
and hunted together,
and drank together,
and, at times, made fools
of ourselves together.
Hao was a charismatic man,
a strong king, a superb warrior,
yet he would not have done what you did,
would not have risked himself
on behalf of people he'd never met,
people with no influence,
not even from his own country."

Memnor stopped.
Still that hardness
to the young king's face.

Havnar shrugged, filled the silence.
"Your father would have loved
a feast given in his honor.
He liked attention,
liked his own importance,
spoke so men might hear him.
You say less, but it means more."

"And Havnar should know," said Memnor.
"That's probably the longest speech
I've ever heard from him."

Havnar shrugged.
"You speak enough for both of us."

Xau grinned.
Relaxed, he looked like any young man,

ready to get drunk or get laid.
A moment only,
then Xau was himself again,
his kingdom on his shoulders.

Memnor knew.
Memnor had been twenty-four,
Xau's age now,
when he came to the throne,
a burden eased both by his wife,
who had never once asked
for more than he could give,
and by Havnar,
who'd given more
than Memnor had asked.

"One more speech tonight,"
said Memnor. "Not the one my advisors
will draft in your praise.
Rather a speech they would
counsel against,
but it has weighed on me,
and I will say it."

Would say it not in gratitude,
though that cause enough—
Xau having pushed himself
almost to his death
saving Memnor's people—
but because a dread oppressed Memnor,
a dread that darkness stirred anew,
that Xau, who had defeated a demon,
would yet face a malevolence
greater even that that.

So Memnor stood,
took the three steps over to Xau,
knelt.

"I, Memnor, King of Ritany,
son of Mithron, son of Marnas,
do swear to you, Xau,
without impediment or restriction,
my aid whenever and however
you request it:
my sword, my strength,
my army at your command."

Memnor touched his hand to his heart,
offered it palm-up to Xau,
a gesture of allegiance older
than either of their kingdoms.

A weight in Xau's eyes
as the young king set his hand
on Memnor's forehead.
"We, Xau, to accept your oath,
knowing there may come the day
when we have need of it."

The rest of the night uneventful.
They chewed on the leathery meat,
chatted of this and that.

Later, when the time came,
Memnor kept his oath.

HERO

To wait.

To answer
when their children ask
when Papa will be back.

To nod when people, well-meaning people
tell her she must be so proud
of her husband—
that he's a hero—
that word—

To wake.
That space beside her in the bed.

To meet with those
he isn't there to meet.

To eat.
The food delicious.
The guilt of that.

To hear his deeds
cast into story, song
and he the hero—
a word she's come to hate—

To sleep
curled around his old jacket,
the smell of him.

To decipher the tiny cramped characters
of a note sent on a pigeon's leg.

To write
and to not beg him
to return.

To speak with soldiers
shaken by what they've seen,
exhausted by their horses' haste,
their news partial, dated;
though they do not voice the word,
it's written on their faces
when they speak of him.
That light.

To find an answer
the first time Keng, their eldest,
asks not when, but whether
Papa will be back.

To lie awake,
wondering how it would be
to hold the sword herself.

HOMING PIGEONS

By all natural rights,
they are hers,
hers to stalk, startle
strip from their feathers.

Likewise, the palace is hers,
though she condescends
to share her territory
with the king.

The sentries her servants,
tall uniformed door-openers
with paltry swords
in place of claws.

Recalcitrant servants
who deny her one door.
Behind it, irresistible,
the flapping of pigeons.

Feathered frumps!

VENGEANCE

They stole the daylight, stole her throne,
cast Fian down upon cold stone.

They think her nothing, think her beaten,
think the dungeon holds her in.

But hers the will which woke the dead,
hers the wrath, the wolves' wild tread.

They think that's her: defeated, lamed,
thrown to the floor, tethered, tamed;

think her trapped, her limbs bound tight,
think the blindfold stops her sight.

But hers the will that does not yield,
hunting allies, eyes tight-sealed,

finding in far-off desert sands
a beast to bend to her commands.

Her life the cost to spur that beast
to wreak, in time, her vengeance feast.

Hers the guile her bonds to loose,
hers the hand to knot the noose.

Hers the airless swinging death.
Hers the rain, the wind's wet breath.

DARK ARROW

Airless dark, jaws agape.
Vengeance vaunted, flaunted,
arrowing to a target—

High on her mountain,
the dragon choked. Woke.

Bespoke the Hidden Queen:
"What happened?!"

Hundreds of miles away,
deep in her underground chamber,
the Hidden Queen dropped a fish—
fresh, still flailing—
into one of her six mouths.
"What happened? Nothing happened."

"No." The dragon gathered herself,
reviewed that fleeting impression—
more than nightmare—
fell, foul—
"Something, someone,
worked a terrible magic."

"Who? Where? What manner of magic?"

"I don't know."
The dragon's tail lashed
against granite.
"Someone with a strength,
a malice to match the demon's."

DIPLOMATIC COMMUNIQUÉ

Xau—

I think I'm in fucking trouble—
Fian killed herself,
and she wouldn't have done so
without a fucking good reason.

I need a couple of weeks here.
Tiarnan's a mess, blames himself.
As if he could have stopped
his mother. The fucking bitch.

At the end of December,
I'm heading to the Hidden Queen,
see if she can work out
what the fuck Fian was up to.

Come if you can.

Donal

MEETING

Even in midwinter,
the Crescent Dining Hall
of the city-kingdom of Trillium
was crowded with traders, travelers, lovers,
soldiers, scholars, spies
gathered for gossip, passion, profit.
Many of the encounters louder, lustier,
far more delightfully scandalous
than when the two kings met.

"Fuck, Xau, you made good time—"

"We had eighteen horses
between the six of us."

"Eighteen horses—
How far did you ride today?"

"From the fort at Guanshan."

"Fuck."

Donal took Xau's sodden cloak,
Xau looked him up and down,
their hands clasped.

"Sit. Eat. Your guards too."

"How is Tiarnan?"

"Doing better."

"That's good. Very good. And you?"

A shrug.

"When did you arrive?"

"Two days ago.
I went to Harmouth first.
Told Mei. Saw the baby,
one of the fattest babies I've seen.
She named him Connol."

"We know. We're glad."

A pause then,
both of them remembering
the other Connol,
Donal's brother.

More in that silence
than in the little they'd said.

THE VOICE

Through the spy-hole,
the Voice studied the two kings:

The seats slanted subtly sideways,
and Donal, the older king,
fidgeted, as did most petitioners;
Xau, the younger king,
sat as if entirely at his ease.

The Voice lowered her veil,
entered the room.
Both men stood.

"You may sit," said the Voice.
"I speak for the Hidden Queen."

A thousand times
the Voice had done this,
yet still that strangeness
when, from a chamber far below,
the Hidden Queen extended
the tendrils of her thoughts
into the Voice's mind,
borrowed her lips, her tongue,
spoke through her:

"You requested a meeting. Why?"

Donal shifted in his seat.
"Fian, my wife, used witchcraft.
She raised the dead—"

"By killing her sister. So I heard."

"A month ago, Fian hung herself.
Could she have worked a spell
as she died?"

"Yes, and it's your own fault."

"My fault? How?"

"You allowed her to kill herself—"

"Allowed?!"
Donal spat on the floor.
"She was bound, blindfolded,
yet she hung herself
from a lamp hook."

"Careless of you to leave
a hook within reach,
careless and unfortunate.
Dark magic took place
the night Fian died,
almost certainly her handiwork."

"Fuck. *Fuck*."

Xau spoke for the first time,
his voice quiet, level.
"What did she do?"

"I don't know,
only that it was an act
of purposeful malevolence."

The Voice stepped right up to Xau,
gazed at him from behind her veil.
"I was asked to tell you this, King Xau."

"Asked?"

"By one well known to you.
She wished you to have warning."

Recognition, comprehension,
then a momentary gentling
to the set of Xau's face.
"Thank her for us."

The Voice nodded.
"I am in your debt
for slaying the demon."

Her hand lifted—

not by her own will, but the queen's—
almost, she almost touched him,
then her hand dropped.
She stepped back, said,
"Tell me whose voice you each heard
when the demon spoke to you."

"My uncle's," said Donal.

Xau said nothing.

"Come now, King Xau,
my vices are simple,
gluttony and curiosity.
Tell me whom you heard."

Still Xau said nothing.

"What do you desire
in return for your answer?
Treasure? Knowledge?"

"Peace and prosperity for our kingdom."

Laughter. Discordant, creaking.
"Is it contagious,
this worthiness of yours?
What do you, Xau, wish for?"

"We are curious to see you."

A maelstrom within the Voice,
not her own, but the queen's—

None but her servants had viewed her
in three hundred years,
yet Xau a fascination—

"If you will answer my question,
I will let you see me."

Xau nodded. "Agreed."

"Very well. I await you."
The queen withdrew.

Released, herself again,
the Voice gave the ritual phrase,

"So spoke the Queen."

Xau stood, bowed low.
"Thank you for speaking for her.
We appreciate it."

Behind her veil, disconcerted,
she who had once been Farahnaz hesitated—
men never noticed her,
never considered her as more
than a mere mouthpiece—
"That is my purpose," she said at length.
"I am the Voice of the Hidden Queen.
Follow me. I will take you to her."

THE HIDDEN QUEEN

King Xau smelled the queen
before he saw her—
a noxious mix of fish,
rotten eggs and perfume
permeated the passage
to her underground chamber.

The Voice opened the door.
A vast gelatinous bulk sagged
on a grate in the floor:
six-eyed, six-mouthed
with suckered tentacles
that glistened with slime.

Xau bowed deeply,
schooling his expression
to polite neutrality,
though his stomach roiled.
"Thank you for letting us
come to meet you."

The queen flicked a tentacle
and her servants left.
"Tell me," said the queen
in a six-mouthed echoing,
"whose voice the demon used
when he spoke to you."

"Keng's," said Xau.

"Our second oldest brother,
after whom we named our son."

"Aaaah," she sighed,
moistly, malodorously.
"Tell me about this brother."

"We loved him," said Xau.
"We loved him before
we could write our name.
He was the first to teach us
how to wield a sword.
He let us ride his horse."

Four scant sentences,
all he could manage
in a level tone.

"Aaaah," she sighed again.
"How then did you find
the will to slay the demon?"

"We were desperate.
We knew no other way
to save our kingdom."
Memory, sharp, cut him.
"Khyert, our friend, threw himself
upon flames meant for us."

"Khyert," sighed the queen.
"He is not in the ballad."

"No. Nor did the battle
last till dawn, and nor
was the fight glorious.
The ballad is wrong.
We are not the equal
of our reputation."

"Are you not? I am."
A yellow fist-sized glob
wriggled from the base
of the queen's corpulence
and slithered across
the floor toward Xau.

With unexpected speed,

the queen seized the glob
with a suckered tentacle,
dropped it in a mouth
and swallowed noisily.
"As ever, I am delicious."

Xau raised his eyebrows.

"Well, not exactly myself.
I believe that what I ate
was one of my offspring."

Xau struggled to compose himself.
"You just ate your child?"

"If that is what it was.
I've never been certain.
I don't remember my beginnings,
nor others of my kind,
nothing until I was goat-sized
and slithered from a desert cave."

"You've never let any of your
… children… survive?"

"No. I am not yet so vile as that."

"Explain," said Xau.

"People think me a freak,
a weird gluttonous creature
controlling hundreds of servants,
seeing through their eyes,
hearing what they hear,
ruling my city-kingdom—

"Skills akin to the demon's,
but vile though I am,
I do not force my servants.
They choose to obey me.
My offspring might not
exercise such restraint."

Xau bowed. "You are greater
than your reputation."

"More hideous yet wiser?"
She laughed, a sixfold creaking.

Xau waited until she was done,
then said quietly,
"You have great power.
You could have wielded it
to shatter men's lives.
But you did not."

"Thank you, King Xau."
Six eyes considered him.
"Is there anything else
you would ask of me?"

"May we know your name?"

Six different notes
sounded from six mouths,
and then again, and again,
a strange and lonely sound.
"That is what I name myself.
Leave me for now."

Xau bowed again and left.

FRAUGHT

Donal waited for Xau
in thick-falling snow,
white settling over the paths,
the steps of the west entrance
to the Hidden Queen's palace.

His ears grew numb, his breath plumed
as he stamped back and forth—
he'd fucked up—
the Hidden Queen had made
that much abundantly clear—

"Warmer indoors," said Fergus,
chief of his guards,
pacing Donal on his left.

Donal gave him a look
and Fergus shut up.

Xau took just long enough
for Donal's short temper
to shorten further.

"Well?" said Donal.
"Did you learn any more?"

"Not about Queen Fian."

"Shit," said Donal.
"I should have fucking killed her
when I had the fucking chance."

"Yes," said Xau.
Straightforward. Blunt.

Donal grunted,
set off on the path
that circled the palace,
headed nowhere, needing to move—
he'd let Fian lead him
by his balls not his brains—
had known for years
that she was ambitious, even vicious,
yet never doubted her loyalty—
Connol hadn't liked her—
Connol. Shit. *Shit.*

Halfway round the palace,
he stopped, turned to Xau.
"We don't even know
what the fuck Fian did.
How can we mount a defense?"

Xau shrugged.
"Strengthen our kingdoms.
Rule as best we can."

Donal spat in the trodden snow.
"That's not much use.
What do we do right now?"

"Pack. Get our horses.
Go to Black Mink Falls."

"Why the fuck would—
That's two days' ride.
If the snow lets up."

Xau said quietly, "You look ragged,
as if you haven't slept in a week.

We, I, am worried about you.
I think the excursion might help."

"Traveling through
a fucking snowstorm
is going to help?"

"Maybe," said Xau. "A horse ride.
Fresh air. Nothing better."

*

The ride proved rough,
the camping rougher,
the waterfall overrated
(an apathetic trickle).

The hills snow-swept, desolate,
slate escarpments slick with ice.
The few trees gleamed,
branches bright-burnished.

The company good.

MONSTER

Six-eyed, six-mouthed, unnamed, unknown,
beneath the sand, he dwelt alone.

By night he hunted desert prey,
then in his cave slept light away.

His touch a trap that linked his mind
to any creature he would bind;

his will the force that held them still,
while, quick or slow, he made his kill.

His hunger vast, a brutish need,
no goal beyond six mouths to feed.

Into that dark and formless greed,
Queen Fian cast her evil seed:

her death the cost to spur in him
a taste for torture, vile and grim.

No creature safe, his touch a chain
that bound his pleasure to their pain.

TRAINING: HOSTAGE

Artoch, senior advisor to King Xau,
screamed as Gan wrenched his arm
up behind his back.

This practice session Artoch's idea.
Perhaps, in hindsight,
not his best.

From halfway across the throne room
King Xau said sharply,
"Gan. Ease up. You're hurting him."

Gan's hold relaxed fractionally,
Gan the burliest of the king's guards,
and, right now, terrifying.

"You want him back in one piece,
come and get him," snarled Gan,
rather too convincingly.

The hostage protocol clear.
Xau meant to head for safety.
He did not. He stood immobile.

Li, captain of Xau's guards,
touched the king's arm.
"You have to walk away. Now."

Still Xau stayed put, his reluctance
part of why Artoch liked him,
but a failing in a ruler.

"Your capture," said Artoch,
"would threaten the kingdom.
Other hostages are expendable."

Artoch hardened himself, went on,
"Think of your children.
If you are killed—"

—The king's children too young
to take the throne. If Xau died,
their deaths would follow—

"We know what would happen."

Xau's voice hollow, colorless.
"As we knew it when we rode to war."

At last the king moved.
He walked away from Artoch,
stopped by the tall paired doors.

"Enough that we may one day
need to do this," said Xau.
"We will not rehearse."

He yanked a door open. Left.

ANOTHER WEEK

At the end of summer,
when Prince Keng was seven,
one week with his father.

One week of riding,
hunting, walking, climbing,
standing atop a limestone arch,
the grazing horses far below,
tiny as toys,
his father's hand
on his shoulder.

One week without school,
without people fussing
over his clothes,
without Ying or Chye
or his baby sister,
with his father
to himself—
except for his father's guards,
seven guards with them that week,
that almost the best part:
watching Atun shooting
from a galloping horse,
fencing with Captain Li,
helping them set up camp,
their conversations, their jokes
sometimes baffling
but never condescending.

One week of campfire suppers,

his father helping him
skin his first rabbit,
roasted pears, the smell of smoke,
Dao and Gan singing duets,
three warm nights sleeping on grass,
the patterned stars.

And the day they did nothing
but laze in a two-man fishing boat on a lake,
chatting and dozing in the heat,
jumping into the water to cool off,
the dip of the oars
rippling the still surface,
the lake's depths undisturbed,
his father wearing a conical bamboo hat
like a rice farmer;
a memory he dipped into, later,
time and time again,
unable to recall what they'd talked about,
only the easy back-and-forth of it,
and beneath, undisturbed,
his father's love.

BASICS

Donal, the Red King,
red-haired and red-handed in war,
battles behind him, restless in peace,
decided to learn Meqingese
in proof of friendship.

Cut his temper against erudite tutors:
raged, roared, railed,
without retaining the rudiments
of pitch and tone.
Regrouped. Reconsidered.
Rented a mixed-race whore.

Practiced basics in the bedroom:
between, beneath, belt, button,
strap, skirt, shirt, silk, satin,
open, closed, finger, thumb;
the rising, falling, dipping tones
of woman, man, mouth, lips, hips, ribs,
breast, buttock, belly, balls,
hot, heat, hand, hold, hard;

repetition and variation:
standing, lying, table, chair,
front, back, over, under,
in, in, in.

Then wine, honey cakes,
a master class of pillow talk.

Months later,
speaking Meqingese to Xau
for the first time,
Donal, flustered,
complimented Xau's clothes,
his hair, the fineness of his eyes,
while Xau, perplexed,
inquired how heavily
Donal had been drinking.

FOR HER BIRTHDAY

To Queen Shazia from King Xau:
books, a jade bracelet;
a painting of the southern vista
from the palace she grew up in;
eight mornings together
in the royal greenhouses.

   (An extravagance of glass
   cast by Ulixian craftsmen
   two hundred and thirty years ago:
   eight arched greenhouses,
   eight being an auspicious number,
   ringed round a bronze dragon.)

Eight winter mornings,
the willows sagging with snow,
the palace stonework clad in white,
the tiled greenhouse floors
heated, warm against
Shazia's bare feet.

Eight mornings
with no meetings, no duties,
with only baby Suyin
and four of Xau's guards—
the tallest, Gan, a giant of a man,

trying to blend into foliage. Failing.

Eight mornings that Shazia
walked through spring:
peonies, chrysanthemums, camellias;
mandarin trees tricked into blossom;
the scent of sage, saffron, sesame leaves,
cinnamon, mint, cardamom, coriander, cloves.

Strolling, talking, playing cards;
the baby suckling as they sat
by the small perfection
of the lotus pond;
Xau as relaxed as she'd ever seen him,
his arm around her back.

Eight unhurried mornings,
and then, each night,
Xau's guards briefly banished
to hallway and courtyard.
The messy, urgent merging press
of hands, mouths, skin.

INHERITANCE

High above, the dragon watched
the king and his young son
approach through deepening snow.
Flew down when they drew close.

Her laughter boomed from the rocks
like an anvil dropped on granite.
"Back again, Xau? And bringing
your princeling with you?"

King Xau knelt, weaponless, crownless.
He bowed so far forward
that his hair brushed snow.
"Thank you for coming."

"Oh, get up off your knees.
I take it this is sufficient?
That you just wanted to show
your son my magnificence?"

Xau stood. He placed his hand

on his son's shoulder. "Sufficient,
but it would be preferable if you
explained matters to him."

"You want me to frighten him?"
The dragon turned her head sideways
and flamed hugely,
sending steam from the snow.

"Not to frighten him. To warn him."

The dragon made an explosive sound
that might have been a snort.
"In eleven hundred years,
I have never done so."

Xau stared at her levelly.
"We would tell Keng ourself,
but you laid an oath on us
that we cannot break."

The dragon flamed again.
Heat stung the two humans.
Keng jumped,
moved right beside his father.

"Very well," said the dragon.
"Since you once rid me of a demon
that fouled my thoughts,
I will tell him."

She turned her golden eyes to Keng.
"Princeling, your father wishes you to know
that I chew up princes and spit out kings.
Come closer."

Keng took six steps forward,
so close he could have touched her.
He trembled, but held his head up
and looked straight at her.

"Well enough," she said. "To clarify:
when your father dies, his steward
will send you here. If I deem you adequate,
you will become the new king.

"If not, I will eat you,
and the steward will send me

another prince to sample.
Any questions?"

"What happens," said Keng,
"if you run out of princes?"

The anvil boomed from the rocks again.
"When the king's sons are gone,
they send brothers, cousins, uncles.
Occasionally princesses. More questions?"

"No," said Keng.
After a moment, he added, "Thank you."

The dragon burped, her breath ash,
and looked back to Xau.
"Are you troubled by your past?
Are you planning to die soon?"

"Not planning on it," said Xau.
"But death may come anyhow."

"I asked two questions."
Darker gold surfaced
in the dragon's eyes.
"You answered only one."

Xau said nothing.

"We will talk more," said the dragon.
"First I will take your son's oath,
then he can walk back by himself—
oh, don't bleat at me! He'll be fine."

Then the dragon took Keng's oath
and the boy went down the mountain alone.

As for what the dragon said to the king
and what he said to her
in the day and night that followed,
that is no one else's business.

KENG

Prince Keng came down the mountain alone,
and they descended upon him:
his father's advisors,

his father's guards,
his own guards—

—"Where is your father?"
—"Where is the king?"
—"What happened?"
—"What happened?!"

And Keng, a boy of eight,
his head full of fire,
of the dragon he'd seen,
the dragon who'd told him
she chewed up princes and spat out kings—
Keng said, "I cannot say."

Because he could not,
because the dragon
had stopped his tongue
from speaking of her,
but they didn't know that
and they repeated their questions
until Keng, exhausted, worried,
said, "I cannot say. I'm sorry.
I'd say if I could. I can't."

A pause.

Then Captain Li nodded,
said to the others, "Let him be."

Keng stood,
his stomach hollow,
his father still up the mountain.
With *her*, the dragon.
And it was all Keng's fault,
because Papa wouldn't have gone
up there in the first place
except for Keng's sake—

"Prince Keng, are you hungry?"
asked Dao, one of his father's guards,
Dao who knew more riddles than anyone,
Dao who had used one of his free days
to take Keng carp-fishing.

Keng nodded.

Dao led him back
to the mountain fastness,
sat him down in the kitchen,
fetched a bowl of dumpling soup,
said, firmly, "Your father will be fine."

Which Dao could not have known:
Dao who hadn't seen the dragon,
how her flame turned snow to steam,
hadn't smelled the ash of her breath—
the dragon who might as easily
chew up a king
as a prince—

Still, it helped, a little.
And next morning, Keng's father
came down the mountain.
Unburnt. Unhurt.
Safe.

RIDDLE: HOUSE

A spring morning,
warm and windswept,
the tall paper windows
of the royal breakfast room closed,
but the room filled with their light,
crowded with King Xau, Queen Shazia,
their four children,
all nine of the king's guards,
the two serving women.

Shazia, heavily pregnant,
feeling as large as an elephant,
listened as Dao, king's guard,
asked the children a riddle.

"In his coat of scales,"
said Dao, "he lives in a house
with no doors, no windows.
To leave his home,
he must break the walls.
What is he?"

Suyin, the youngest, sucked her thumb.

Chye, almost five now,
frowned thoughtfully.

"A fish?" said Ying.

"A fish has scales," said Dao,
"but the answer is not a fish. Keng?"

"A dragon in an egg," said Keng promptly.

Dao bowed. "Correct."

A kicking inside Shazia's belly.
She reached for Xau's hand,
laid it on her stomach,
their child nearly ready
to... hatch.

Xau's face lit up by his smile.

STAY

In the twelfth year
of King Xau's reign,
on a windswept spring morning,
the palace gardens littered
with peach blossom,
Queen Shazia went into labor
with their fifth child.

A day, a night, a day.
On the second night,
waiting in the hallway,
Xau heard Shazia scream. Repeatedly.
An hour after midnight,
the royal physician came out to Xau:
"Your Majesty, the baby
is facing forward, not backward.
The labor is not progressing well."

Two drawn breaths before the man's words
made any sense—
Xau saw the red-and-gold dragon
embroidered upon the shoulder
of the physician's robes,
saw how the lamplight

glinted from the polished scabbards
of Xau's watching guards—
these things, these details
unaltered, unaffected—
and then Xau's heart thumped
like a galloping horse—
"Can you help her?"

The physician shook his head.
"I can cut the baby
from Queen Shazia's belly,
but it would kill her."

"No."

"Sire, neither I nor the midwife
think your wife can be saved.
The baby might live."

"No. Try. Try to save her.
Try everything you can."
Clearly, concisely,
so that there might be no
misunderstanding, Xau said,
"Shazia is more important
than our child."

The physician bowed and left.

The slow passing of the night. Dawn.
More of Xau's guards came on duty,
gathered about him. None left.

In the early morning, the midwife came out.
"Your Majesty, your son was stillborn."

"Shazia?"

"We can't stop the bleeding."
The midwife led Xau into the room.

The window open,
the scent of peach blossom,
sunlight touching the edge of the bed
where Shazia lay:
pale, her hair damp, sweaty,
cradling their son on her chest,

the physician pushing something
between her legs—
the sheets down there red—

"Shazia—"
Xau knelt beside her,
kissed her damp forehead—
"Shazia, we, I, I love you."

"Xau." Her eyes brimmed.

He kissed her again,
touched their son's cheek. Cold.
Their son's lips purple,
his nose so small, so perfect.

"I'm sorry," said Shazia.

He bent over her,
held both her and their son.
"Don't be. Don't be sorry. I'm sorry."
He wanted to lie,
wanted to soothe her,
wanted to say it would be all right.
He wanted to ask her,
wanted to beg her
to stay.
He did not.
He said, inadequately,
"Our son is beautiful."

She closed her eyes,
panting for breath. "Xau?"

"I'm here. I love you," said Xau.
He held her, held their son
until she stopped panting,
stopped breathing,
her skin emptying of color.

The physician stood up
and moved away from the bed.

Xau let go of Shazia,
anchored the baby
beneath her arms.
He had to get up,

had to tell the children.

First—
He looked for the physician,
the midwife.
"Thank you for attending our wife. Let—"
His voice crumbled.
He wrestled the words out.
"Let the baby stay with her."

EVERYWOMAN

When Shazia cradles
her stillborn child,
she is no longer a queen:
she is a weaver,
measuring her son
for a shroud.

When they stuff bandages
up her bleeding body,
she is not a queen:
she is a washerwoman
tallying bloodied sheets,
a cook oozing clotted soup.

When they bury her,
when every bell sounds,
when the white-robed king
lights a white candle
for their white-wound child,
then she will be a queen.

Before,
when she gave suck
to her firstborn,
when she sang to him,
when she pressed her face
in the fold of his neck
and smelled her milk,
then she was richer
than kings.

TRAINING: GUARDS

In the innermost courtyard of the palace,
Li, captain of King Xau's guards,
observed the training session
dissolve into a shambles.

The warm-up routine
completed without disgrace,
but the six-on-three combat wretched.

That the king was off-form:
anticipated and unavoidable.
Grief not a matter to be rushed.

That the guards were off-form:
a threat to the king's safety.

Gan and Dao,
assigned to fight alongside Xau
whilst the other six attacked,
were both overly protective,
hardly letting the king
parry a single thrust,
an extravagance they could ill afford
when thus outnumbered.

Of the six attackers:
four guards too tentative,
not only failing to attack the king,
but scarcely even engaging
with Gan and Dao.

The remaining two, Atun and Leong,
on-form, formidable—
those two, like Li himself,
able to disregard all distraction
when they fought.

Dao would have bruised ribs
despite his padded jacket.
Had the blades not been blunted,
had Atun and Leong used full force,
the pair of them would have killed
Gan, Dao, and the king.

"Halt!" Li bowed to the king.
"Xau, take turns sparring one-on-one
with Leong and Atun."

Li gestured the remaining six guards to him,
looked at each man in turn.
"You cannot defend the king
if you are dead,
cannot fight effectively
unless you can concentrate.
If there is anything that
you cannot set aside when you fight,
you must deal with it now. Today."

Silence.

Gan broke it. "How?
We can't talk to the king.
He doesn't want to speak about her."

Three days since the queen died,
yet Xau had not spoken about Shazia
except to his children;
had not slept except for the night
Leong gave him a sleeping draft;
had not wept, yet his grief naked.

Li stared at Gan.
"If you can find no other way,
then you must speak to Xau."

Gan's face almost as anguished
as the king's, but he nodded,
walked over to Xau,
waited for the king
to finish sparring with Leong.

Li couldn't hear what Gan said,
but he saw the king set his hand,
briefly,
on Gan's shoulder.

A stillness in the five men with Li,
then first Tai Seng, and then Dao,
and Chong, and Wen Xun, and Shuen
went to the king.

After,
when they were done,
Li set two of the guards on watch,
dismissed the others,
and sparred with the king himself,
neither of them speaking,
Li using a dagger against the king's sword
so that they were more evenly matched,
Xau struggling nonetheless,
but stepping to keep Li
out of dagger-reach,
perhaps forgetting,
for a moment or two,
anything beyond the placement
of hand and foot,
the changing positions
of sword and dagger.

Little else Li could do for Xau
but to stay near him,
which he did,
fourteen hours a day
for the next six weeks;
speaking rarely,
and then mostly of small matters,
the shape of a tree,
a hawk in the sky;
Li at the king's side
the one time he wept.

UNDONE

"How would you punish him?"
demanded King Xau, staring down
from the massive dragon throne
upon the gray-haired woman
kneeling before him.
"A beating? A caning?"

The woman raised her head.
If she was intimidated by the king,
by the marbled magnificence of the room,
by the armed menace of the guards,
she did not show it.
"Your Majesty is grieving."

"Irrelevant," snapped Xau.

She looked straight at him
without dropping her gaze.
"Your Majesty has many other concerns.
Your Majesty may have overlooked
your son's age.
Prince Chye is only four—"

"Almost five," said Xau,
hardening his features.
"Old enough to be disciplined."

"Old enough to be reprimanded,
not beaten," she said quietly,
no defiance on her face,
merely dissent,
a dissent Xau had despaired
of ever finding.

Hard to argue against a king.
Of the twenty-two previous applicants
for the position as senior amah
to Xau's children,
not one had dared oppose him.

Xau leaned forward.
"And what age would be old enough?
Six years? Eight?"

"Your Majesty, some would say six,
some would say eight,
but I would not beat the prince
even if he were fourteen."

That moment,
the moment Xau knew
he had found someone
who would look after his children,
who would care about them,
who would stand up for them
no matter how powerful the forces
arrayed against her—
that moment almost undid him.

"That's good, very good."
He worked to steady his voice.

"Ignore what we said earlier.
We do not wish you
to ever hurt our children."

But not that moment that undid him,
nor at breakfast, two days later,
when Chye climbed onto his lap
and asked if Mama was still dead;
nor the letter from Shazia's mother
(King Vihaz's senior wife)
thanking Xau for sending her
a painting of her daughter.

Instead a stupid thing,
his own fault,
opening a bottle of the perfume
Shazia used to use:
that scent,
as if she were right behind him;
how he couldn't stop himself
from looking round—

AMBER

Xau held Micha to a trot
though she had caught his mood
and wanted to gallop over the grasslands.
Keng, his oldest son, followed close,
all eagerness and pride at accompanying him.
Behind Keng, six of their guards.

Autumn and all well in the kingdom,
the harvest gathered,
the land at peace;
five months, two weeks, one day
since Shazia died—

Half a life,
Shazia had said when they met,
that she didn't want half a life,
a safe life.
So he had swept her along with him,
a son, a daughter, a son, a daughter,
and then the stillborn child
she died birthing,
so that she had half a life after all—

Xau bid Micha gallop.
Wind, air, grass, the smell of leather.
For a moment, a drawn breath,
he was nearly happy.

He slowed Micha to a walk,
led her to a stream,
dismounted, watered her.

His son, joining him,
chattered about the ride.
Xau showed him a frog
half-submerged in the mud,
watched Keng try to catch it.

Xau walked upstream,
away from Keng and the horses,
four of his guards following
at a distance.

Movement.
Under a bush,
across the stream,
a gray shape, big. Wolf.
The wolf looked at him,
amber eyes steady,
and waded into the stream
straight for Xau.

In the wolf's eyes: recognition.

Xau let his hand
drop from his sword.
He knew, knew beyond doubt,
that the wolf would not harm him.

He made the arm signal
to his guards to stay back,
saw Atun ready his bow,
watching him,
watching the wolf.

Xau crouched down,
and the wolf came, dripping wet,
to the reach of his hand.
She sniffed him,
licked the inside of his wrists

as Shazia used to do,
and lay down beside him.

Xau's heart pounded,
those amber eyes fixed on him.
He caught his breath,
said goodbye to Shazia,
his words barely louder
than the small noise of the water.

When he was done
the wolf stood up, shook herself,
before crossing the stream
away from him.

PORTRAITS

Only two official portraits
ever made of King Xau:
the one in the throne room
depicts him after he won his first war—
seventeen years old,
robed in red, crowned in gold,
no hint of triumph
on the boy's stern face.

They caught Tian off guard.
She'd finished cleaning
the king's rooms,
had an armful of dirty cloths
as she stepped out into the hall—

The king and his guards
were lined up along the wall.
They all bowed to her—
to *her*—
and led her into the breakfast room,
the table laid with plates,
tea bowls, a single mooncake.
King Xau pulled out a chair for her,
the king beaming, Tian speechless.

The king cut the mooncake
into little pieces, scattering crumbs.
He handed the first piece to her.
"Happy Birthday, Tian."

Tian sniffed noisily
as the king gave bits of mooncake
to his guards, poured tea.
If she tried thanking the king,
she'd end up in tears.
So instead she gestured at the crumbs,
the plates, the bowls, said sharply,
"Who'll clear all this up?"

"Captain Li will," said Xau.
"He's getting lazy."

"The king will," said Captain Li.
"I will incorporate the clean up
into today's training session."

"You see?" said Xau. "He's lazy."

The second portrait,
painted by the master Pei Tsu,
given, in a gesture of outlandish generosity,
to an elderly cleaning woman:
black ink wash on silk,
the king in profile,
smiling as if at a friend.

MONSTER: PUPPETEER

The splintered scrape of broken bone,
forced to and fro across sharp stone.

No one to see, no one to care
how slowly died the desert hare.

No accident, no slip, no trip,
its mind caught in a monster's grip.

Six-eyed, six-mouthed, the monster foul
controlled each scraping move, each howl.

Hare and lizard, dove and sparrow,
lowly beasts he chose to harrow.

The monster's link a ghastly chain
that bound his pleasure to their pain.

Year after year small prey he hunted,
till such thrills at length grew blunted.

In search of richer meat to snare,
he slithered, cautious, from his lair.

And trapped a child to his delight;
fed on her hurts, fed on her fright.

His will the whip that steered her hand
to all the evils he had planned—

The burning branch, the severed thumb,
the screams to make her mother come—

Then what rapture, what doubled joys!
Mother and child now both his toys.

Forced the girl to scar her mother,
each one aching for the other.

Watched the mother grope her daughter,
stronger fodder than mere slaughter.

Nothing ignored, nothing wasted,
such games sweetened all he tasted.

ELIGIBLE

Every day more invitations:
inked in gold or silver,
scented with peony and jasmine,
carved into rosewood, ivory, jade.

Notes from the king's cousins,
from ministers, from magistrates.
Deputations from foreign powers,
direct or veiled in discretion.

Would King Xau attend a concert?
A festival? A tournament?
Would he name a ship?
Hunt tigers with the Ulixian court?

No, no, no, no. And no.
(Xau wished to see a tiger,
but not as a pretext for meeting
the five Ulixian princesses.)

Not yet thirty, widowed so young,

a strong king, a fair king,
burnished with legends.
The most eligible man in the world.

Alas for the world,
alas for Xau's advisors,
for all who advocated the advantages
of matrimony (political, psychological).

Xau, contrary, conversed with men
deficient in daughters; danced
with women in possession of husbands;
told tales about tigers to his children.

THE NINE

Not what Dao had expected.

King Xau had promised
his guards a surprise,
and Dao had guessed at, maybe,
new uniforms or new weapons.

Instead, seated on a stool,
a semicircle of chairs around him,
resplendent in lavender silk:
Master Enlai the minstrel.

King Xau dipped his head to Enlai,
then turned, beaming, to his guards.
"In thanks for your service,
a special performance."

Eagerly, Dao took a seat.
He'd heard Enlai twice before—
the man massively conceited,
yet his music magnificent.

The harp's first notes flowed
like a mountain river,
the rhythm slowly building
until Enlai began singing.

> *When to peril Xau rides, who rides*
> *at his side though danger abides?*

> *Nine men who shield him with their blood*

from clashing swords, from foaming flood.

Steadfast and loyal, brave they be,
the king's guards led by Captain Li.

Dao's vision blurred.
He blinked, looked down.
Stupid, stupid to be overcome,
only a song.

King Xau's right hand, valiant as he,
deadly in battle, Captain Li.

Muscled and tall, the strongest man,
speedy to help, good-hearted Gan.

Sworn to his king, true to his vow,
skillful riddler, the dauntless Dao.

The king's gaze rested on Dao,
warm, approving, glad;
the man Dao most honored,
honoring him, honoring them.

Barefoot sprinter, fleetest of men,
father of two, daring Shuen.

Duty doubled, surgeon and guard,
Leong holds fast when times turn hard.

Peerless bowman, equaled by none,
braided his hair, handsome Atun.

After naming each guard in turn,
Enlai let the last notes die out,
sang unaccompanied,
his voice his instrument.

And with these nine, two more I'd sing,
the two who died to save their king.

Swift with a blade and swift of thought,
quiet Shang died before he ought.

The young king's mentor, Tsung the wise,
in honor now his body lies.

Enlai silent, the harp silent,

tears running down Dao's face,
Gan sobbing audibly,
the king's head bowed.

Enlai strummed his harp,
launched into a glorified retelling
of the guards' deeds,
closed with the opening couplets.

> *When to peril Xau rides, who rides*
> *at his side though danger abides?*

> *Nine men who shield him with their blood*
> *from clashing swords, from foaming flood.*

> *Steadfast and loyal, brave they be,*
> *the king's guards led by Captain Li.*

Enlai finished with a flourish.
A moment before Dao collected himself,
before he joined in the applause,
clapping till his hands hurt.

                    *

Dao on duty that night.
The king up late,
writing to his sister,
reviewing reports.

"So," said Xau, sighing,
pushing the reports away,
"what did you think
of Enlai's latest?"

"I liked it very much."
Dao hesitated, continued,
"Even though I'm not,
not dauntless like he said."

"No?" said Xau. "You stood with us
in the flood's fury in Ritany.
You walked the streets of Ningxi
when the demon threatened."

And Xau stood, bowed to Dao,
as deeply as though to a king.

TOMB SWEEPING DAY

Rain spatters on chopsticks,
a barley grass dumpling,
a bowl of tea,
a bamboo dragonfly.

Grief will not help her.
The king cannot set it down
beside their children's gifts.

Fire Bones

ARROW

Late April,
   hills overrun
      with flowering azaleas—
         pink, white, red, magenta—
      the air bright with their scent,
   King Xau's mood dark
as December.

He galloped
   past his guards.
     Li, his captain, shouted,
       but Xau kept riding. He would spend this day,
     this one day as far away as possible
   from the relentless matchmakers
and their wares:

flirts, flatterers, coquettes,
   twelve-year-old girls with painted faces.
     An onslaught of replacement wives
   who couldn't replace
Shazia.

Air bright
   with the fragrance of flowers,
     his horse crested a hill, and there, below him,
       galloping on a gray horse, an archer:
    black hair beaded, braided,
   riding away from Xau,
bow in hand.

Xau halted
   as the rider arced round,
     black braids swinging as she—
       demonstrably, conspicuously female,
    full breasts rounding her chest guard—
   loosed an arrow. A hawk fell.
Dead.

One arrow, double duty.
Xau as stricken as the hawk.

NOTHING

It was nothing to Hana
when the man rode over,

less than nothing that
four hired guards followed.

(The horse lords didn't bribe
their oathsworn to protect them.)

The man sat his horse well,
Hana did notice that,

as she noticed him eyeing
her face, her chest,

her bare legs against
her mare's gray flanks.

Gerel, Hana's mare, edged closer,
nickered as if she knew the man.

He gave his name, King Xau,
which complicated matters.

Her brothers would disown her
if she displeased Xau.

(The horse lords honored Xau
beyond reason, beyond endurance.)

Thinking to get rid of him
Hana said she was hunting—

extracting the dead hawk
from her pouch as proof—

but he asked to come too
and she perforce agreed.

Trapped, nettled, she asked him,
"Will your guards come to assist you?"

He laughed, a clear, bright sound,
free of the rancor Hana harbored.

"Yes. They can retrieve our body
once you fell us with your scorn."

"I do not scorn you."
Lightly, easily, she lied,

but the words shifted
as she looked at him:

thin, beardless, plainly dressed.
No gold armbands, no jewels.

Not his fault that men had
inflated his deeds to legends.

Xau ordered his guards
to keep at a distance,

and then they rode
across the rolling hills.

His company was nothing to Hana;
she preferred to hunt alone.

They passed two deer, a rabbit,
pheasants, an antlered stag.

She saw Xau spot the stag,
but he didn't reach for his bow.

She brought her mare alongside him.
"I thought you wanted to hunt."

"We wanted to watch you hunt.
We saw you shoot that hawk as it flew.

"We would like to be with you
every day, every hour of our life."

She snorted, couldn't hold it in.
"For one hour maybe. On top of me."

He flushed, his cheeks reddening
though he was no pale Innish man.

His embarrassment nothing to her.
"Are there no women in your palace?"

"None like you." Xau hesitated,
reddened still further, went on,

"None who can outshoot us.
None who dare scorn us.

"None who ride as if they
and their horse were one."

Xau's gaze fixed on her,
his approval all too clear.

A complication she did not need.
She urged her mare forward, away.

Heard Xau's horse follow,
not too close, not pressing her.

The hills thick with azaleas,
the air bright with their scent.

Hana paused by a stream
to let her mare drink.

Xau rode up. "Are you hungry?
Our guards have red bean cakes."

Hana's belly betrayed her,
rumbled loudly and pointedly.

Xau signaled his men over,
introduced them to her.

They ate sitting on the grass,
the bean cakes sweet, delicious.

Xau made sure that each guard
had a chance to rest, to eat.

Something disconcerting there:
how the guards looked at Xau,

how the king looked at them.
As if they were brothers.

Afterward, when they rode on,
an easing between Hana and Xau.

She told him about herding sheep,
the spring shearing, making felt;

about the winter the snow melted,
then refroze, the ice iron-hard;

told him about her sister, mother,
brothers, her three horses.

Xau listened more than he spoke.
Quiet, alert, intent on her.

Dusk settling onto the hills
when Xau halted his horse.

He dipped his head to her, said,
"Will you marry us? Please."

As if she could not breathe.
As if a wall closed in on her,

relentless, remorseless,
to seal her within Xau's palace,

far from these open hills,
the rushing air of a gallop.

"No!" She shook her head fiercely
as if that could silence him.

"Marry my sister instead.
She would fall at your feet—"

"—We don't want a woman
who falls at our feet,

"who mistakes us for more
than we are. We want you."

The trap closed. Walled in.
She was walled in by his words,

by the intolerable possibility
that he meant what he said.

"No. I'm sorry. I do not want you."
She turned her horse. She rode away.

RIPPLES

"A woman from the horse tribes?"
Artoch spoke quietly,
so that the king's guards
on the far side of the pond

wouldn't overhear.
"You asked her to marry you?"

"Yes," said King Xau. "She refused,
but we hope to change her mind."

A silence awkward as any
in Artoch's twelve years
advising the young king.

At length, Artoch offered,
"That may be... unwise.
Such a marriage would further no alliances.
The horse lords already support you fully.
The Sumbrese would interpret it
as an insult—"

"The Sumbrese interpret everything
as an insult. What more does King Vihaz
expect of us? We married his daughter—"

Xau stopped.

The king stared into the fish pond,
but Artoch doubted he even noticed
the fish darting below him—
gold, silver, orange, bright as jewels.
For the first time in months,
Artoch saw grief plain
in the king's face,
and, seeing it,
understood that it had been
there all along.

The king had never talked to him
about the death of Shazia,
Vihaz's daughter.
Oh, Xau had done what was needed:
approved funeral arrangements and so forth.
But beyond that, nothing,
not one sentence.
Only that the king,
always tender to his children,
became even gentler.

Sunlight glinted on the water.
Tiny blue flowers, whose name Artoch
did not know, edged the pond.

Instead of continuing to discuss
the matter of Xau's future second wife,
Artoch found himself saying,
inadequately,
"Shazia loved you."

Xau stared at the water
for the space of two drawn breaths.
The grief had left his face
but was still in his voice
when he looked up at Artoch.
"We know. Thank you."

Artoch bowed.

The king left.

Artoch stared into the pond
without seeing the fish.
Ripples beyond ripples
if Xau married this woman
from the horse tribes,
and very little of it
favorable for the kingdom.

HONOR

*If it is true,
I will have Xau killed.*

Cyrus, fourth prince of Sumbral,
stood alone on his balcony
in the hour before dawn,
his father's words repeating,
unshakable, inescapable,
as they had repeated all night.

*If it is true,
I will order my assassins
to kill Xau for scorning me.*

Trumpets sounded the dawn.
Below him, Cyrus saw the servants
enter the courtyard to make obeisance.
They crossed their hands

over their chests three times:
once to honor Sumbral,
once to honor King Vihaz,
once to honor their fathers.

Alone on the balcony,
Cyrus turned and went inside.
He had offered the triple obeisance
at dawn and sunset every day since infancy.
But not today.

> *Either quickly, by blade or arrow,*
> *or slowly, writhing,*
> *poison burning his veins.*

Cyrus's father and king
one and the same man.
Unworthy. Shameful.

Cyrus sat down at his desk,
dipped his quill in ink.
How could his father
stoop to assassination?
Acts perpetrated by night,
by stealth, by trickery.

Ink blotched the paper
as Cyrus scrawled:
Renounce the horse woman
before Vihaz exacts revenge.

A single treasonous sentence.
No signature. No elaboration.

Thus Cyrus, like his father,
stooped to stealth,
rather than offering open challenge
before the eyes of men,
beneath the eye of the sun.

A man's first duty
to honor his country;
all else second to that,
and Sumbral's honor at stake.

He folded the note,
scrawled Xau's name on the outside,

dripped wax on it,
set the royal seal of Sumbral into the wax.

DELAYED

Renounce the horse woman
before Vihaz exacts revenge.

A single sentence scrawled in haste,
then by a Sumbrese agent raced
to the mountains from the palace
to thwart Vihaz's bitter malice.

At the border, haste laid to waste:
the portentous message misplaced
by a distracted customs clerk
worn out by perpetual overwork.

Chance, mischance, or the hand of fate.
The note unread until too late.

FERRY

Well past midnight,
the ferry-raft rocked gently
as Dao, king's guard,
sat on the bench by King Xau,
glad that the day's heat
was finally dissipating.

Reflexively,
Dao scanned the far riverbank,
but no one waiting to cross;
no sound but the splash
of the three ferrymen
working the long wooden poles.

Light from the oil lamp
caught on the wet poles,
on the medallion round the neck
of Nahr, the senior ferryman,
a Sumbrese man who'd been working
this crossing for years.

Neither King Xau

nor the other three guards spoke.
Probably they were as relieved as Dao
to be out of the minister's house,
the party too noisy,
too crowded.

—a ferry pole, all three poles
    split lengthways
—the ferrymen yanked out
    thin sticks
—blades

Dao shouted. Captain Li shouted.
Dao scrambled to stand.
The three ferrymen on them.
Chong, seated in front of the king,
downed before his sword was out.

"Xau!" shouted Li. "Run! Swim!"

—the rightmost man
    held off by Captain Li
—the leftmost man blocked by Gan
—the center man, Nahr, advancing
—Nahr's stance
—the shift of his feet

Dao lunged,
parried Nahr's thrust—
Dao off-balance—

—Nahr pivoted
—Gan exposed

"Gan!" yelled Dao.
Too late, too slow,
but the king deflected the blade
as Dao got his balance back,
stepped clear of a bench—

"Xau!" shouted Li. "Go! We will slow them—"

—Gan disarmed by the leftmost man
—Nahr fast, faster than Dao
—the king blocked a cut aimed at Li
—Nahr sidestepped, feinted, lunged
—the blade speeding at the king

Dao in the wrong position.
Nothing he could do, except:

Dao fell.
Fell deliberately.
Fell onto the blade's sharp sweep.
Fell down onto the planks.
The blade yanked back, up,
clear through Dao's side. Pain.

Dao turned his head,
saw Xau on his feet.
A single drop of blood
beaded the king's neck
where the blade had nicked him,
but the king was well.

Dao closed his eyes.

THE RIDE

Xau offered Hana his kingdom;
she declined.

The horse lord who ruled her tribe
ordered her to marry Xau.
Hana lay face down in the dirt
at the horse lord's feet. And declined.

A second king,
father to Xau's dead queen,
took such offense at the possibility
of Xau replacing his daughter
with a barbarian horse woman
that he unleashed
his assassins.

Not on Hana herself,
honorably, in open challenge—
barbarian that she was,
she would have met them
with bow and knife,
without fear, gladly—
but against King Xau by night,
by stealth, by trickery.

The captain of Xau's guards
yelled at him to flee.
Instead Xau fought
beside his men.

No mannered fencing match, no rules.
Three assassins, two guards slain.
Xau himself barely scratched,
but the assassins' blades
sticky with a poison
that crept along Xau's veins
and burned him from within.
He tossed, tormented,
in the moonless country
between death and breath.

So Hana rode,
rode to marry Xau
if she could reach him in time,
if he could still mouth her name.

Rode,
willing Xau to fight as hard
for his own life
as he'd fought for his guards.

No man would tell her
whom she would or would not marry.
Not her brothers.
Not the horse lords.
Not the craven King Vihaz
whose name she cursed
as she rode—

Vihaz who hid behind walls
whilst others fought his battles,
Vihaz who thought Hana less
than his daughters,
Vihaz whom she defied
by choosing Xau—

Hana rode,
rode with her brothers
and two horse lords
and thirty spare horses.
No tents, no pack animals,

drinking their mares' milk,
four hundred and ninety miles
in four days;
by dawn, day, dusk, dark,
across the grasslands
into the interior of Meqing
with its paved roads
and bricks and peasants
(the peasants abandoning
their wheelbarrows to gawp
at Hana and the others).

Rode,
the horses failing one by one,
until only Hana, her eldest brother,
and six horses remained.

Rode,
not knowing if she would ever
ride again:
if Xau, should he live,
would then, having won her,
wall her up like treasure
inside his palace,
until her heart died
remembering the plains,
the smell and sound and touch
of the horses she rode to reach him.

Rode faster
than the news of her coming,
so that, at the last,
Xau's soldiers delayed her,
blocking her approach to the palace,
to Xau—who yet lived—
until she explained,
four times over,
who she was.

Surrendered her bow, her arrows,
her knife, her past,
her future
to come to the king.

VIGIL

Hard as battle this duty.
Li, captain of King Xau's guards,
stood—useless—
as the king tossed, fevered,
pain-wracked, poisoned.

Day and night,
day after night after day after night,
sleeping only when the king slept,
starting awake each time
the king stirred.

Over the doctors' objections,
Xau insisted on dictating letters
to the families of the two guards
killed protecting him.
If Xau had fled when Li shouted
more guards would likely have died,
but the king would have been unhurt.
A large matter,
but one understood
between them years ago.
That Xau would let his guards fight
for him, beside him,
but refused to run
while his guards fought.

Night after day after night
with nothing that needed to be said,
but Li could not watch, silent,
while Xau labored not to scream.

So Li spoke.
He spoke of his childhood,
of his father, a fisherman,
of hooks and baits and nets,
of gutting fish, cooking fish,
the price of fish, the smell of fish,
of oiling his father's boots,
and the tunes his father played
on a wooden flute,
and his father's pride
when Li became a soldier.

Day after night after day.
Holding Xau so the king
could piss into a pot.
Holding him so he could vomit
into a different pot.

Night after day after night,
until Li had no stories left,
neither his own,
nor the folk tales
his mother once told him.

Li shouted at Leong for saying,
ten days in,
that the king had no strength left,
that perhaps the time had come
to offer an easier death.

Li quit the king's room
and fetched Xau's firstborn son,
Keng, a boy just ten years old.

Li positioned the boy
on a stool by his father,
and watched Xau battle
to give his hand
and a dozen words
to his son.

And Keng,
valiant as any soldier,
smiled as if all were well,
as if the weight of the kingdom
were not crashing upon him,
and told his father
about his lessons,
his sisters and brother,
his horse and the new cook.

Li kept Keng there five hours,
until the boy was hoarse
and the king unable
to mask his pain.
So low had Li fallen
that he was considering fetching
the king's younger children,

but Xau, spent, slid into sleep,
the first untroubled rest he'd had.

Twelve hours later, fever broken,
the king woke, saw Li, frowned:
"Li, go get some rest.
You look terrible."

"As do you, Your Majesty."
Li laid his hand
on the king's arm briefly,
bowed and left.

PARTNERS

Hana hears him before she sees him,
the gentleness in his voice a puzzle
until she sees the child on his lap.

    Xau inhales her before he sees her:
    the sweat of her mixed with grass
    and the smells of horses.

He is too thin, too pale.
Sitting, propped up,
in his sickbed.

    She is dusty, dirty,
    her long braids coming undone,
    bow and arrows gone.

She kneels on the floor beside him
(the little girl buries her head
against her father's chest).

    He is afraid to breathe,
    afraid she is a figment
    of his longing.

Ignoring the guards, advisors, steward
who have followed her in,
she says, "I would be your queen."

    "Are you certain?" He gestures
    at the guards, advisors, steward.
    "This is how it will be.
    Staff, soldiers, ambassadors.

And war likely coming."

"I am certain."

> He looks at his steward.
> "Fetch a magistrate.
> We will be married this hour."

> One arm about his daughter,
> he clasps Hana's fingers
> in his free hand.

He is less than his legend:
mortal, frangible, worn. Good.
She could not love a legend.

UNSAID

Morning. Hana pulls the covers off,
looks at Xau's gaunt body slatted by light
from the window shutters.

> Xau inhales her before he sees her,
> the smell of her faintly mixed
> with leather, grass, horses.

She fingers the stark jut of his ribs,
but doesn't voice that he looks
too weak to ride to war.

> When he touches her,
> he is not the king,
> he is as nervous as a boy.

When he touches her,
she feels the pull of him,
the reason men follow him.

> He kisses her, tastes her,
> tries to be slow, to be gentle,
> but he is neither.

Hana pushes him onto his back,
rides him on that brief wild gallop;
she is not gentle either.

> Afterward, he doesn't promise

to come back safely,
only tells her he loves her.

Easy then to lie,
to say she loves him.
But she does not say it.

If he comes back,
if they are given time,
he is a man she might love.

If he does not return,
maybe she will wish
that she had lied.

REMEMBRANCE

In his doubled role
as both king's guard
and king's field surgeon,
Leong watched King Xau as they rode—
watched Artoch and the generals
ride up to confer with him:
a debate that lasted all morning,
through the midday break,
well into the afternoon;
watched Xau, who usually said little,
say less and less;
watched Xau finally dismiss
the others to ride alone.
Too thin. Too pale.
Still afflicted by the remnants
of the assassins' poison.

Leong brought his mare alongside Xau.
"Are you in pain? Nauseated?"

"The same as yesterday."
A pause. "Thank you, Leong."

The clatter of hooves
on the stone road.
A horse neighing ahead of them.
Xau said, "We were thinking
of Dao and Chong."

The guards killed
by the same assassins
who had poisoned Xau.
Chong cut down before
he'd even drawn his sword.

Leong said quietly,
"Dao was born near here."

Xau nodded. "In Weizhou."

Three sparrows foraged
in the dry grass
off to their left.

Xau and Leong silent.

PROPHECY

"You lied," spat King Vihaz,
entering with his soldiers.
"The assassins failed me.
You failed me. Xau lives."

Mehev, soothsayer, knelt, shaking,
pressed his forehead to the floor.
Fading daylight slanted across
the tiles an inch below his nose.

Mehev's mouth had dried up
so he could scarcely swallow,
but his tongue babbled away,
seeking to placate the king—

"Not, not for long, Your Majesty.
As the sun sets outside,
so King Xau's day is surely ending.
I, I received a message."

"A message? What powers spoke to you?"
A catch of eagerness in the king's voice.
Perhaps the fragrant agarwood incense
had stilled Vihaz's anger.

Mehev lifted his head a fraction.
He stared at the king's sandals,
heavily embroidered with gold.

"Who can name the powers? I cannot."

...that was because the message
hadn't come from the powers beyond,
but in the morning mail, unsigned,
a sage leaf embedded in the paper.

He had received such notes before,
four times, the startling accuracy
of their predictions instrumental
in establishing his reputation.

"What did the powers say? Tell me."

Mehev raised his head enough
to gaze on the king's oiled knees,
raised his head further still
and dared to look on Vihaz's face.

"That if you lead your army
into the Shahness Mountains,
the hundred dragons of Sumbral
will fly to meet you."

The king flung back his head
and laughed in open delight.
"As they did for King Nariz!
What else did the powers say?"

A bead of sweat rolled down
Mehev's nose, dripped to the floor.
The message had said nothing else,
but the king expected more.

"Your son," said Mehev, frantic,
pulling words out of nowhere,
out of the agarwood fumes,
out of the dying day.

"A son of your line will spill
royal blood, king's blood,
if you lead your army
into the Shahness Mountains."

"Xau will die." Vihaz beamed.
"I will go to war. And triumph.
If your words prove true,

I'll shower you with gold."

Mehev pressed his forehead to the tiles.
"Your Majesty is the greatest,
wisest, most generous ruler
beneath the eye of the sun."

He lifted his head just enough
to see the king's embroidered sandals
pivot, walk away, then pause.
Mehev dropped his head hastily.

"If your words prove lies,"
King Vihaz's voice was soft,
"I'll cut your balls off
and make you swallow them."

Mehev tried to speak,
but a gulping croak emerged
before he managed to say,
"Your Majesty is great."

And then the king was gone.

MEDDLING

Deep in her underground chamber,
the Hidden Queen, her six eyes shut,
tentacles still, opened her servants' minds:

She was a weaver buying yarn,
a harlot oiling a soldier's back....

... A merchant told the weaver
that King Xau fought off
five attackers (inaccurate).
The soldier told the harlot
that Xau and a bare-breasted barbarian
had sex on horseback (improbable).

Footsteps sounded.
The queen opened her eyes
as the Voice, head of her servants,
carried in a sweet-smelling pail.

The queen sighed sixfold. "Skip my bath."

"What's wrong? Are you ill?"

"Not ill. I tried to help King Xau,
called in favors,
fabricated a prophecy."
The queen sighed again,
swished a tentacle in the pail.
"Centuries of limiting my meddling
to minor matters. Abandoned."

Abandoned after the first moment
she saw war looming between Vihaz and Xau,
saw war looming and relished it—
relished the prospect
of Xau at battle,
his wits and nerve made manifest—

A darkness in her to wish for war,
a darkness she had quashed,
and interfered instead.

"Well," said the Voice,
"it could have been worse.
At least you didn't help Vihaz."

The Hidden Queen laughed,
a discordant sixfold creaking.
"Thank you. Leave me for now."

She closed her eyes,
reached for her servants,
for news of Xau.

QUESTIONS

King Xau's soldiers took Donal's weapons
before they let him enter the mountain fort.

Inside, Xau's guards searched him again,
taking the dagger from his boot
and the jacket from his back.

Given what had happened,
Donal offered no protest.

Finally they led him to a square room
at the top of a turret.
Xau sat at a desk,

staring down at a map:
too thin, too pale,
the bones in his face standing out,
tunic hanging loose.
Twenty-nine years old,
but he looked like
a man of forty.

Guards, soldiers, advisors all about.
From the doorway, Donal said,
"Don't they feed you?"

Xau's face lit up,
bringing back a part of his youth.
He stood, went to Donal, hugged him.

Xau nodded to an attendant.
"Bring King Donal his weapons,
a hot meal, wine, water...
Do you want anything else?"

"Vihaz's head," said Donal.

Xau sat down again, looked at his men.
"Leave us."

Two guards stayed by the door,
but the other men left.

Donal sat down on the bench opposite Xau.
"For the first week, I thought
I was riding to your funeral."

"Near enough," said Xau.

Donal held Xau's gaze long enough
to let Xau read in his face those things
that Rose (Donal's woman)
would have had him say aloud.

Then Donal pulled the map over,
looked down at the mountain ranges
between Sumbral and Meqing,
the year-round passes marked in red,
the summer-only passes marked in blue.

The fort they were in had been circled,
and stood atop one of the passes.

"My troops are two weeks behind me,"
said Donal. "Will there be war?"

Xau shrugged.
"Vihaz is marshaling his army.
We are marshaling ours."

"You think they'll come over the mountains,
not round through Ritany?"

"We think so.
King Memnor has closed his border
to Vihaz, even to trade."
Xau tapped the map,
traced the blue line
leading to the circled fort.
"We think they'll take the Shahness Pass
right up to where we're waiting."

"Why?"

"The Hidden Queen wrote to us," said Xau.
"She seemed certain of it."

Xau stopped talking as attendants entered.
One handed Donal his weapons.
Others set out two empty bowls,
stew, broth, bread, rice, drink.

Donal heaped stew into a bowl.

Xau broke off a piece of bread,
scowled down at it
as if it were a conundrum
he couldn't solve.

"What's wrong?" asked Donal, mouth full of stew.

With his foot,
Xau pushed a pot out
from beneath the desk. "We eat.
And then half the time, we vomit."

"I thought you were better."

"We are getting better. Slowly."
Xau dipped his bread in the broth,
took a small bite,

chewed determinedly
as if eating rancid meat.

Donal stared at Xau,
thought of questions
better left unvoiced,
and one he had to ask:
"Can you fight?"

"We can sit a horse in battle," said Xau.

Years since they'd fought
on opposite sides,
but it wasn't a thing
Donal would ever forget,
Xau leading his cavalry,
men and horses alike
following him
as if he were a godling,
and Donal's own horses
refusing to lift a hoof against him.

A huge, unnatural advantage.

The captain of Xau's guards,
Li, a man whom Donal had fought beside,
stirred in his position by the door.
In poorly accented Innish, the captain said,
"The king can ride, but cannot wield
shield or spear or sword."

"Then you will ride on his right,"
said Donal, "and I will ride on his left."

Li bowed to Donal.

"Thank you."
Xau reached across the desk,
but stopped,
the gesture incomplete,
an inch short of Donal's hand.

Donal gripped Xau's hand firmly,
then helped himself to more stew.

"So," said Donal,
"I heard you found a woman.
What's she like?"

YING

"I'm not hungry, so I'm not eating."
Princess Ying, eight years old,
glared up at the new queen.
Nothing was right anymore. Nothing.

The queen didn't say anything.
She took the knife from her belt,
cut Ying's honey cake in two,
and popped half in her mouth.

"You took my cake!"

"You aren't hungry." The queen
spoke with her mouth full,
which was very bad manners,
and turned to leave.

The steward, waiting in the doorway,
cleared his throat noisily.
"Queen Hana, I had hoped
you might talk to the princess."

"I didn't have much to say.
The child is selfish.
How can I change that?"
The queen strode from the room.

Ying ran after her: "I'm not selfish!"

"Yes, you are. I'm selfish too."

"You are?"

"Yes." The queen led her entourage
out into the gardens, past the fish pond,
past lavender bushes thick with bees.
There were bees everywhere.

The queen sat down on the grass
(which she should not have done)
beside a row of thrumming beehives.
"He will worry about you."

Ying frowned. "Who?"

"Your father," said the queen.
"They will write to tell him
you refuse to eat, and then,
in a few days, to say you're ill."

"They shouldn't write!"

The queen shrugged. "If they do not,
how will your father trust them
the next time he goes away?"

Ying scowled. She didn't want
her father ever to go away again.
But he would. If he came back,
he would leave again. And again.

The queen said nothing more.
Bees bobbed on the blue flowers
in the grass at Ying's feet.
"You're trying to get me to eat."

"Yes."

"Why?"

The queen shrugged.
"For your father, mostly."

A bee landed on Ying's thumb.
She held as still as she could.
If there was war, her father
might never come back.

Thinking about it did no good,
but she hadn't been able to stop
since he left. "I'll try to eat."

"Good." The queen stood up.
She did not take Ying's hand,
or hug her, or claim
to be her friend.

THE HUNDRED DRAGONS OF SUMBRAL

*And King Nariz entered the Shahness Pass with the full might of his army.
Whereupon winged shapes, like unto birds, approached, but as they flew near,
men saw that the greatest of the beasts was more than eight times the length of a
horse. Thus came the hundred dragons of Sumbral to honor King Nariz and to
fight alongside him. And such a gathering and such an honor had not been known
in all the days of men.*

Tahj, crown prince of Sumbral,
rode, silent, filled with doubt,
beside his father, King Vihaz,
as they entered the Shahness Pass.

Vihaz wore a golden winged crown
set with diamonds and rubies,
his horse arrayed in silver,
his armor burnished bright.

Behind them came the lesser princes,
captains, heralds, horse, foot soldiers,
workmen, attendants, pack animals,
and camp followers of Vihaz's army.

Tahj scowled up at the mountains.
The way was steep, but Vihaz
had severed the tongue of a captain
who suggested another route.

A man of honor must honor his father,
but Tahj had been humiliated
when Vihaz grasped openly
at the soothsayer's prophecy:

*If you lead your army
into the Shahness Mountains,
the hundred dragons of Sumbral
will fly to meet you.*

Unbalanced by hatred of Xau,
Tahj's father now mistook himself
for a second King Nariz.
Should Tahj therefore challenge him?

As Tahj, doubting thus, looked up
at the mountains, he beheld dark specks
shifting against the blue-white peaks.
The army stopped. Tahj stopped.

The dark specks flew toward them,
their wings moving like hinges,
the largest of them greater by far
than any creature Tahj had known.

Ten, twenty, thirty winged beasts,
their color resolving from darkness
to deep wine-red, their scales agleam,
steam issuing from their nares.

One of the king's heralds
called out Vihaz's name,
once, twice, three times,
and the army shouted after him.

Tahj, silent, sat his horse
(the horse's flanks heaving
but the horse rooted in place),
as the soldiers shouted behind him.

Then neared the greatest beast.
Its shadow darkened the ground
below Tahj as its clawed foot
reached and seized Vihaz's crown.

The great dragon wheeled about,
the crown dangling in its claws,
as a second dragon, near as large
as the first, descended.

The second beast grabbed up
Vihaz's purple-and-gold banner
and, ripping it to shreds,
dropped the pieces to the ground.

So, at last, seeing the dragons
thus repudiate Vihaz,
doubt left Tahj and he cried out,
"I call challenge upon you, Father!"

At which the winged beasts
climbed the air and circled far above,

watching as Tahj dismounted
and as Vihaz dismounted also.

Then Tahj bowed to his father,
his sword still sheathed,
but Vihaz, who did not bow,
rushed upon his son.

And Tahj, hearing him come,
flung himself to the ground,
rolled, drew his sword,
and smote his father.

Thus fell Vihaz, King of Sumbral,
and the herald called out,
"Vihaz is dead. All glory
to Tahj, King of Sumbral!"

And there before the eyes of men,
beneath the eye of the sun,
the greatest beast descended
clasping the golden winged crown.

Tahj stood, his sword dripping,
his hair flattened to his scalp
by the beat of the beast's wings,
his eyes fixed upon the crown.

But as he watched, the beast
crushed and crumpled the crown,
dropped the twisted mangled metal
on Vihaz's corpse, and flew away.

THE PATH TO PEACE

A son of your line will spill
royal blood, king's blood,
if you lead your army
into the Shahness Mountains.

Standing, sword dripping,
over his father's corpse,
Tahj laughed bitterly.
His father had thought
the prophecy promised victory.

But truth had proved as twisted
as the mangled crown
that lay atop his father,
atop the slit still spilling
its proof of Tahj's betrayal.

Tahj laughed on, unable to stop.
He was King of Sumbral now.
He could lead his army against Xau
despite the dragons
who had repudiated his father.

Or he could end his father's war,
dispatch his envoys
to grovel at Xau's feet:
buy a bloodstained, bitter peace.
Tahj's laughter died.

He bent down to claim
the crushed and crimsoned crown.
Let a smith reshape the mangled metal
as Tahj would reshape Sumbral,
as he would offer peace to King Xau.

Peace, but never friendship.

DRAGON BREATH

"Thought you that this was over?"
Anuk uncoiled himself from the fire pit
at the back of Selaz's lair.

"Let be. Twice-told is old and cold."
Selaz hinged her wine-red wings
to fit through the entrance hole.

Anuk rumbled, shaking the stones:
"The Hidden Queen should not
have asked such a thing of us."

"Let be, Anuk! It's done."
She entwined her neck round his,
wrapped her tail about his tail.

She breathed full on Anuk then,
wreathing his head in fire
so that he shut his eyes.

When the tantalizing heat faded,
he pushed her into the fire pit,
her belly flat to the coals.

Holding her in place,
he breathed on her wine-red scales
until they glowed like rubies.

Groaning, she rolled on her side
and he flamed her belly,
the bump of her unlaid eggs.

No words, only their breath
wreathing round each other,
his fire inside hers.

A GIFT

King Xau couldn't sleep,
couldn't feign sleep,
couldn't lie still.

He rose, dressed,
bowed to the two of his guards
on night duty,
told the others to rest,
but none would,
so that his wakefulness
led to all nine guards
following him into the corridors
of the mountain border fort.

He walked the circuit of corridors,
past rooms of sleeping soldiers,
round and round again,
his pace deliberate, measured,
but his pulse galloping.

Up the stairs,
out onto the observation platform.
Chill air,
no lanterns,
but the crescent moon low in the west,
the constellations strung like decorations,
the mountains falling away
beneath him.

Down to the wall walk,
where he spoke to each of the sentries,
walked round twice,
stopped, finally, at an arrow loop
with a view down the Shahness Pass,
down toward his enemy
who had retreated,
beyond expectation,
beyond his hope.

A gift,
if he could trust the envoy.
The war over,
over before it began,
but he couldn't set it aside,
his heart agallop,
braced for battle,
for death,
his death that walked away
down the pass, below the snow line.

He had not wanted any part of this.
A crown, war, duty,
that his death should mean more
than another man's.

Back to the observation platform,
the flamboyant beauty of the stars.
He looked down the other side of the pass
toward his kingdom,
toward Hana, his children,
whom he had not allowed himself
to think about.

Then down to the lanterned warmth of his room,
where he offered tea to his guards
and asked after their families.

FIRE BONES

Heng stood, a shadow
beside King Xau, King Donal,
and their generals, advisors, guards.

King Xau handed him the letter, and Heng,
though he wished himself invisible,

though he had never aspired
to more than the background,
the turning of pages,
the calm of a library,
nonetheless Heng had to translate,
for Siak had pneumonia
and Kwang was two hundred miles away.

"It opens 'Beneath the eye of the sun,
in the glorious presence of King Tahj,
these words are transcribed.'"
Heng's voice was a susurration,
a breeze stirring a leaf.

King Xau, too thin, too pale,
seated in the room's one chair,
leaned toward Heng to catch his words.

Heng raised his voice a fraction.
"'But the words are not King Tahj's,
rather those of three elders'
—literally *old men*, however, the term
connotes respect—'Three elders
who are undone by the deaths
of their sons, the warriors who died
a week before the summer solstice
in combat against King Xau.'"

"Vihaz's fucking assassins,"
interrupted King Donal.

Heng nodded. "The term means *warriors*,
but, yes, it refers to the assassins."

"Warriors?!" said King Donal.
"They were fucking cowards
with fucking poisoned swords."

"Continue," said King Xau, his tone level,
his steady gaze steadying Heng.

"'The elders beg the king,
who is a four-times father himself,
to give back, in clemency, the fire bones'
—that is the cremated ashes—
'of their fallen sons.'"

Darkness then in the king's eyes.

The letter trembled in Heng's grip.
"Then the scribe's signature
and the royal seal of Sumbral."

"Anything further we should know?" asked Xau.

"It is... notable... that King Tahj
expresses no regret for his father's actions,
and, in addition, it is a clear insult
that the letter was written in Sumbrese."

Xau looked at his senior advisor. "Artoch?"

"Tahj seeks to discredit you.
If you refuse, he will use that
to justify renewed hostilities.
If you agree, he may dispose of the ashes,
and likewise claim that you refused."

Heng, withdrawn to a corner,
a shadow gladly overshadowed,
bowed his head, dismayed.
Vihaz had proven contemptible;
perhaps his son Tahj
would prove no better.
Yet Heng loved Sumbral,
had met only kindness
all the years he studied there.

"We will return the ashes,"
said Xau, "not to thwart Tahj,
but because it is right.
We will ride into Sumbral ourself,
ourself plus three guards,
to bring the fire bones
home to their fathers."

Heng raised his head
and looked at the king,
an anchor of calm
in a sea of uproar—
advisors and generals alike protesting
that Xau should take, at minimum,
three hundred soldiers
for his protection.

Oddly, the loud-mouthed King Donal
stayed quiet, his hand resting
on the younger king's shoulder.

Into the uproar, Xau spoke,
the room stilling about him.
"Our children are half-Sumbrese.
We would not have them judge
their mother's country
by Vihaz and his assassins,
nor judge us by what
we knew to be right
yet feared to do."

Something stirred in Heng
that he could not name
in any language.

"To bring hundreds of soldiers,"
said Xau, "would be a show of force.
To come with three guards
is a gesture of trust,
a gesture that may bring us
nearer to lasting peace.
Artoch?"

"A powerful gesture,
but a powerful risk also.
Vihaz had many supporters—"

"A risk we will take."
Xau looked over at Heng.
"Thank you. You may leave."

Heng bowed, turned to go,
turned back, knelt down, hastily,
his heart thumping as if it, too,
wished to escape the eyes
of all those people.

Heng said, "Your Majesty,
you may need a translator.
Let me come."

"Thank you," said Xau.
"We accept your offer."

Xau's gaze on him then,
steadying Heng as he rose to his feet,
as he stepped out of the shadow.

TRAINING: STAFF

King Donal's staff struck Li's.
Donal grunted, stepped back
into the drill's next move,
shifted his grip: "Keep—"
Donal swung his staff, "him—"
wood hammered wood, "safe."

"I will try," answered Li,
captain of Xau's guards,
in his poorly accented Innish.
Xau had been teaching
all his guards Innish: Li fluent
despite his terrible accent.

"Do more than try."
Donal shoved hard on the staff,
straining to drive Li back,
but Li matched his force
as if it were child's play.
Move. Countermove. Response.

Li stopped, no warning, mid-drill.
Donal overbalanced, recovered,
followed Li's gaze
to Leong and King Xau—
Leong holding both men's staffs,
Xau's arms trembling.

Xau looked from Leong
to Li and then to Donal,
and raised his eyebrows.
"We are fine," said Xau.
"Li, you're like a mother hen.
Cluck, cluck, cluck."

"Leong?" asked Li.

"His strength is improving,
but he is still weak.
He should rest now."

Xau held up his hands in defeat.
"Continue. We will watch."

Donal bowed to Li, resumed the drill.
Move. Countermove. Response.
Vihaz. And his fucking assassins.
Donal shifted. Wood hammered wood.
Tomorrow, Xau would be in Sumbral—
Tomorrow, Xau could be dead—

Donal's staff cracked in two.
He fell onto Li's staff,
staggered back upright,
stared at his broken staff,
tossed the pieces to the side,
bowed to Li. "I'm done."

Donal took off the padded jacket,
walked over to Xau.
"If you don't come back,
if this fire-bone business
is a trick of Tahj's,
if he hurts you—"

Donal stopped.

Xau waited.

"If Tahj harms you, I will crush him
beneath the boots of both our armies."

"We are counting on it."
The lightness left Xau's voice.
"Tahj knows your reputation,
knows you will have command
of our combined armies.
It may give him pause."

"It had better," said Donal.

They helped the guards clear up;
went to the barracks dining room;
ate with a squad of skirmishers
who could hardly get the food
from their plates to their mouths
for gaping at the two kings.

ESCORT

Underwhelmed and unimpressed,
Prince Cyrus, commander of Tahj's cavalry,
escorted King Xau down the Shahness Pass.

Hard to credit
that the gaunt man
riding ahead of him
was the legendary king.
Hard even to tell Xau apart
from his three guards,
all four men dressed alike
in plain black pants and tunics;
the fifth man,
Xau's translator,
wearing flowing silk robes
finished with gold embroidery,
so that Cyrus had at first mistaken
the translator for the king.

It is a point of honor,
Cyrus's brother, King Tahj, had said,
that your cavalry are seen to protect Xau.
I neither require nor desire
any more than that.
Do not be overzealous.

And so Cyrus had sixty of his cavalry
ride well in advance of Xau,
with sixty more, Cyrus among them,
forming a rearguard.
No flanking scouts,
no zealous overexertions.

Had an archer sought to target Xau,
they'd have had ample opportunity.

But nothing happened;
no one attacked;
the lone point of interest
was the matter of Xau's extra horses.

Five spare mounts and three packhorses,
not one of them on a lead rope.
Yet the horses followed Xau

in perfect order,
as if invisible riders
sat astride them.

An oddity that struck Cyrus
more and more as they descended
from the chill of the high mountain
into the heat of the foothills.

An oddity that conjured
the myriad tall tales
of Xau the Horse King,
until Cyrus half-expected
his own horse to ride up to Xau,
whether he wished it or not,
and offer itself to the king.

THE DEAD

Before the eyes of men,
beneath the eye of the sun,
rode King Xau and his four men.

Ahead, resplendent, in the Lotus Crescent,
at the entrance to King Tahj's palace,
a thousand of Tahj's Royal Guard.

But Tahj's soldiers outnumbered
by the mass of people who had waited,
barefoot, white-robed, since dawn.

In desert heat, King Xau dismounted:
too thin, too pale, thirsty, sandy,
his tunic travel-stained.

No one spoke in all the thousands
as Xau watered the horses,
as he pulled off his boots.

"Baraz," said Xau, the single word
carrying in the stillness, as he took
from a saddlebag a white marble urn.

A man walked out of the crowd,
bearded, stooped, his white robes immaculate.
Behind him, a woman wailed.

Xau gave the urn to the man,
who set it down,
who pressed Xau's hands in his,
who wept, tears drying to salt on his cheeks.
Xau stood, no more than that.
The man said, brokenly, "Baraz,"
lifted the urn and left.

"Jafir," said Xau
as he took from a saddlebag
a second white urn.

A man walked toward him,
heavy, balding, his white robes immaculate.
From the crowd, manyfold, sobbing.

Xau gave the urn to the man,
who set it down,
who kissed Xau's forehead, his cheeks.
Xau stood, no more than that.
He had watched this man's son, Jafir,
kill one of his guards,
could not set that death down,
held it,
sharp,
with the others,
back and back and back
to his father,
whose death Xau had warded by anger
for so long.
Jafir's father lifted the urn
with his son's ashes.

"Nahr," said Xau and took out a third urn.

A man walked over,
tall, beak-nosed, gulping noisily,
white robes crumpled.

Nahr's father set the urn down,
folded Xau in his arms,
Xau whom his son had poisoned,
Xau who had slain his son,
but had let that death slip,
lightly,
a thing of no weight,

no guilt, no cost,
that he would do again
if it would bring back
one of his guards.
Xau shivered, despite the heat,
as Nahr's father held him,
as he lifted the death
he had let slip,
heavy as granite.
Salt on Xau's face.

Sunlight on the burnished splendor
of King Tahj's thousand soldiers.
Of King Tahj himself, no sign.

Xau helped Nahr's father lift the urn,
fastened the saddlebags,
put his boots back on.

"King Xau!" called out a woman
as he mounted his horse,
as the crowd knelt.

INTERLUDE

Two hours into the forest
its timelessness entered Heng,
as if he had always been riding
behind King Xau, beneath the ribs
of oak and pine, the oak leaves
on the cusp of crisping brown.

The spare horses followed the king
without lead rope, without halter,
as if they had always done so.
The three guards rode to left,
right, front of the king
as if they always would.

Almost out of sight, their escort:
one hundred and twenty of Tahj's cavalry
who had met them in the mountains
thirteen days or a century ago,
the horses' hoofbeats softened
by distance and leaf-mulched dirt.

The rhythm of Heng's horse unhurried;
the parched air resinous.
The gap between Heng and Xau narrowed
until they rode beside each other,
the king humming to himself
a tune Heng half-remembered.

An ease between them
that had not been there
on the outward journey;
an ease in the king
that had not been there
before he gave back the ashes.

Five hours, six hours,
the slow onset of dusk;
unsaddling the horses,
sharing dried meat and pickles;
Atun, one of the guards,
laughing like a boy.

Heng careful not to ask for more,
not to look beyond this day.

FIRE

Shouts, Li's hand on his shoulder:
King Xau comes awake before he understands
that the smoke is not dream.

In the distance, fire:
a lithe, live light leaping tree to tree.

Li saddles a horse,
helps Heng mount,
hoists Xau up onto Narson,
who is unsaddled and snorting,
but quiets to Xau's touch.

Xau looks to the fire: a mile away?
In the dark, he cannot gauge distance,
but Tahj's soldiers, Tahj's horses
between him and the fire,
and Tahj's horses will panic—

No. He calls his own horses over to Atun,
whom they trust.

"Ride for the river," Xau tells Atun.
"Wait for us across the bridge.
Leong, Heng, follow Atun."

Atun tries to turn his horse back,
but Xau wills the horses gone
and they run from him,
would race their hearts out
but that Xau calms them,
knowing the river miles ahead,
further than they can gallop.

Li, ahorse beside Xau,
shouts, "Follow Atun!"

Xau shouts back, "No! Tahj's soldiers!"

Xau and Li ride toward fire.

Xau sights Tahj's horses,
close ahead,
bright-lit by crackling trees,
the horses snorting and rearing,
tethered, frantic;
Tahj's soldiers, equally frantic,
try to saddle the rearing horses.

Xau gallops over,
takes a slow breath,
pictures the river—
deep and cold and quenching—
the horses shudder to a halt,
quieting,
looking to Xau,
then sidelong into flame,
then back to Xau,
who holds the river
inside him,
deep and cool.

Heat on Xau's forehead,
cheeks, hands, throat.
He drops from Narson,
takes his dagger
and starts cutting horses free,
Li at his side.
Two soldiers shout and run at Xau,

374 · Mary Soon Lee

but others—
seeing the horses stilled, silent—
step between the oncoming men and Li
(who is bristling with sword in one hand,
dagger in the other)
and help cut more horses free.

Men scramble on horses,
and Xau lets each horse
head for the river (deep, cold, quenching)
as soon as it has a rider,
but the horses' fear
is hot and quick as fire,
and it is hard to hold separate
the horses that may leave
from those that must stay;
hard to slow those that leave
from headlong gallop;
hard to maintain
the image of the river;
hard and harder to breathe.
He doubles over,
coughing,
his eyes tearing, smoke-filled.

Li helps him upright.

Only ten or twenty men
left unmounted,
but many horses still tethered.
More horses than men, of course,
Xau thinks slowly, painstakingly:
spare mounts, packhorses.

Golden firelight flickers
on Li's black hair,
on the stand of trees
just beyond them.
Xau works to cut more horses free,
the air scorching,
his skin hotter than fever,
his fingers trembling,
the image of the river
trembling.

Xau tries to ask Li
if all the soldiers are mounted,

but he can't speak for coughing,
can't see any man left but Li
who has one hand on Narson's mane.

A treetop bursts into flame.
Acrid smoke pours down.
Xau stumbles,
falls flat onto dirt,
cooler,
air clearer,
his thoughts clearer,
enough to know
they have no more time.

He stands up, unsteady, dizzy,
and Li is there,
always there,
on Narson.

Li hauls Xau up in front of him,
the wall of fire
right beside them
as Narson turns
and gallops away.

Xau gulps cool air
as they outrun the fire;
he strokes Narson's neck
until the horse slows;
he looks back over Li's shoulder
and sees the fire retreat
into a darkness
that enfolds him.

CYRUS

As the last riders crossed the bridge,
Prince Cyrus, commander of Tahj's cavalry,
stood, peering into darkness:
dirt road, trees, night sky.
Of King Xau, no sign.

King Xau who had—how?—
calmed the horses
despite the leaping flames,
so that Cyrus's men could mount them

and outride the fire,
Xau who must have stayed too long
and burnt—
which might, after all, be best,
the peace between their countries tenuous
and Xau a formidable opponent.

Cyrus spat into the river
to turn that thought aside.

His brother, King Tahj, despised Xau,
had only ordered Cyrus to protect Xau
because honor required it.
But over the past two weeks,
Cyrus had come to disagree
with his brother,
Xau's death a grief
that held him in place,
peering into dark.

None of Cyrus's own soldiers lost—
he had tallied them on the ride to the river.
Horses, yes, twenty or thirty missing,
together with supplies, weapons.

A blackness moved
in the distant trees:
a horse, no, several horses.

Cyrus was on horseback
before he thought it through,
riding ahead of his men,
so that he was the first
to count the six riderless horses
pressed round a horse in their midst,
double-mounted,
King Xau a shadowed limpness
in the arms of his guard.

One dark moment
when Cyrus wondered
if Xau were dead after all,
then Cyrus was up by the horses,
close enough to see
the king breathing.

Cyrus turned his horse

back to the bridge,
shouting for the surgeon,
for every soldier
to set their weapons
on the ground,
so that there could be no mischance,
no zealot's dagger in Xau's back.

Cyrus's exertions
unlikely to earn him
thanks from Tahj,
but when Cyrus helped ease Xau
down from the horse,
when Xau opened his eyes and stood,
in that moment,
Cyrus didn't give a damn
what Tahj wanted.

DAWN

Li's hand on his shoulder:
King Xau came awake before he understood
that Li was not on fire,
no skeleton of branching bone, indigo flame.
The demon long dead.

Dawn. The sky red but not with fire,
Cyrus's men watching as Xau got to his feet.
Xau looked a question at Li.

"You screamed," said Li.

Demon fire in his dreams,
but it wasn't the demon,
but Xau himself
who had led Li into fire,
a few hours ago:
choking smoke, panicked horses,
the wall of flame—

"Are you well?" asked Li.

"Well enough," said Xau,
pushing away exhaustion,
pushing away the thought
that Li could have died.

Prince Cyrus walked over.

Xau set his hand briefly on Li's arm,
then bowed to Cyrus,
lifted the weight of the day.

A WARNING

Punctuated by pauses
for Xau's translator,
Cyrus, Prince of Sumbral,
commander of Tahj's cavalry,
said to Xau, King of Meqing:

"The fire was set deliberately.
I guessed as much—
no lightning to spark it,
too close,
too sudden—
my scouts found large urns
upwind of the camp.
Probably filled with oil.
Probably you were the target."

Cyrus glanced at King Xau,
who rode alongside him,
attentive but silent,
no obvious reaction
to Cyrus's disclosure.

"Probably guessed you were
encamped with my soldiers.
Whether it was the work
of one man or several,
I can't tell,
but we should put distance
between us and them,
ride all day,
if you can manage it."

Another glance at Xau
who merely nodded.

"Of course, there might
be zealots anywhere.
Ahead as well as behind.

So I'm taking you back to Meqing
by a different route than you came.
It'll take longer,
but hopefully avoid
another surprise.
By the way, I told my men
to say nothing about
how you saved us—
which guarantees all Sumbral
will know within two weeks."

As he said this,
Cyrus wondered if Xau might be
the sole commander in the known world
whose soldiers would all
hold silence
if he asked it.

"For now, everyone's amazed
that you brought the fire bones.
Probably explains
why no one else has attacked you—
no honor in attacking
a man who comes
for such a purpose."

A protracted pause,
before Cyrus added,
in a sudden outburst:

"Don't come back.
If you come back
for any lesser reason,
they'll kill you."

Xau raised his eyebrows, said,
"We will bear that in mind."

The captain of Xau's guards—
the man who'd followed Xau into fire
and brought the king back out in his arms—
said something,
and Xau laughed,
his whole face lightening.

The translator looked to Xau
for permission before saying,

"Li said that if Xau
does decide to come back,
he will kill him himself."

Cyrus stared from Li to the king,
trying to understand what lay between them,
why the king didn't reprimand Li,
why Li would follow Xau
into fire.

AGAIN

Li's hand on his shoulder:
King Xau awake before he understood
that his horse wasn't on fire,
the fire three days ago.

Overhead, the moon,
shifted across the sky
by about an hour's distance
since he last woke.

Li and Atun both watching him,
but Heng and Leong still asleep,
and Cyrus's men sleeping beyond them,
save for the sentries.

An effort to nod to Atun and Li,
to close his eyes,
so that his guards
could stop fretting.

Xau so tired that the ground
beneath him rolled like the sea,
but if he slept
the horses would burn again.

A long time then,
lying as if asleep
but fighting sleep,
balancing on the brink of dream.

Until the horses burnt.

REASONS

Many reasons why Xau
might have been delayed—
bad weather,
a lamed horse,
a bridge out along the route,
one of his guards down with dysentery,
Xau down with dysentery—
but Donal's duty to dwell on one:
that Tahj had killed Xau.

If that proved true, Donal would lead
the joint armies of Innis and Meqing
against King Tahj.

Donal tested the edge of a dagger,
set it down, lifted a flail.
Spent the next half hour squinting at blades,
bowstrings, bolts, handles, spikes,
before he found an axe
with a loose wedge
at the top of its haft.
He slammed the axe down,
and the master armorer, a gray-haired man
with hardly a tooth left in his mouth,
backed up against the wall
as if afraid Donal would knock out
his remaining teeth.

"You've done well," said Donal,
forcing himself to speak softly.
Not the armorer's fault
that Xau might be dead.

He tilted the axe head,
showed the armorer the loose wedge.
"You did well. But check them all again."

The armorer nodded vigorously.

Donal strode out,
followed by his guards.
When he was younger,
they had called him red-handed in war,
but what he'd done then would be as nothing

to what he would do to Tahj
if Xau were dead.

A messenger ran up.
"Queen Hana's come, Xau's queen.
She asked to see you."

"Where is she?"

"In the stables."

       *

In the stables, Hana:
tall, assured, full-breasted,
her black hair beaded, braided
in the style of the horse lords,
a bow on her back, knife at her belt.

"I'm King Donal. Why have you come?"

"To greet Xau, if he returns.
To avenge him, if he does not."

Donal looked her over a second time.
From the little Xau had told him,
he knew that she could use that bow.
But even if she was the best fucking archer
in Meqing, she couldn't go to war.
"You're more use back at the palace
having supper with ambassadors."

"Maybe if I knew what to say to them.
I don't. Let me go with you. Please."
She didn't look as if *please*
was a word she often used.

"A woman would be a distraction—"

"I'd hardly be the only woman with the army!"

"But the whores don't ride into battle."

She lifted her chin at that. Glared.
"Then let me sit in a tent
and mend your bows."

Many reasons to refuse—
that she didn't know what war was like,

that Xau wanted her safe,
that she might die,
that her presence might lead to others dying.
Which last reason was unanswerable.

"No," said Donal.
"You can stay here if you choose.
I won't order you back to the palace.
But you cannot ride to war."

Defeat in her eyes,
yet still she held her head up
and looked at him levelly.
"When do you set out?"

"If there's no news,
two days from now."

"Let me help until then.
I can work with your bowyers."

"Fine."

"Thank you." Hana bowed
so deeply her beaded braids
brushed the floor.

Donal bowed back,
tasked Fergus, chief of his guards,
with taking Hana to the bowyers,
left to talk to his generals.

Many reasons Xau might have been delayed.
Many.

THE BORDER

Prince Cyrus rode into cloud,
King Xau riding on his right,
the high air hinting at snow.

"Not much further," said Cyrus,
echoed by the translator.
"My scouts said your army
crossed the border into Sumbral,
and we're near the border now,
only a few miles from the top
of the mountain pass."

King Xau nodded.

"Another month or two," said Cyrus,
"and there'll be snow up here.
I came once in late autumn,
a few years back. On foot.
Properly equipped.
With two men who knew
the mountains.
Still almost got stranded."

Xau nodded, but said nothing.

"You'll be glad to be back,"
said Cyrus. "Sleep under a roof,
good food, clean clothes.
By the third day of a trip,
I'd pay well for hot water
to soak my feet, pay more
for a mattress, fresh sheets."

Cyrus glanced at Xau,
riding beside him
in soot-stained clothes.
No bed rolls, no tents,
not even enough saddles
since the fire—
two of Xau's guards
and twenty of Cyrus's men
riding bareback—
at least they'd been able
to buy horse feed and rice.
None of them hungry,
Cyrus's soldiers griping anyhow,
but no complaint from Xau.

"Speaking of which," said Cyrus,
"thank you for offering hospitality,
but my men and I will turn round
once we reach your army.
Head straight back."

"Are you certain?"
Xau looked at Cyrus.

"I'm certain," said Cyrus.
"We're running four days

behind schedule, not likely
to make up much of that
on the return trip.
My brother, King Tahj,
will be expecting me
to make all haste."

Tahj would be furious
about what had happened,
even though it had not been
Cyrus's doing.

A pause, before Cyrus added
in a sudden outburst,
aware that what he said
would be repeated to Tahj,
saying it anyhow:
"I owe you my life,
and the life of my men.
I won't forget it.
I can't repay you.
But I swear beneath
the eye of the sun
that I will never bear arms
against you, nor command
others to do so."

Cyrus took a deep breath,
added more quietly,
"Had I been in your position,
I wouldn't have done what you did.
Riding into fire.
Thank you."

Xau turned to look at him,
his gaze level, intent.
"We would do it again."

Cyrus silent as Xau then,
the cloudy dampness beading his hair
as they crossed the snow line.

And then the serried ranks
of the combined armies
of Innis and Meqing:
cavalry, archers, pikemen,

spearmen, scouts, siege units,
sword and shield and spear,
bow, catapult, lance, axe.
Silent. Still. Only their eyes
shifting to track Xau.
Their massed might a message
meant for Tahj, not Cyrus.
One that Tahj would take
as both threat and tribute,
a measure of respect.

Cyrus halted his horse,
his soldiers stopping behind him.
He bowed to Xau.

Xau bowed back, more deeply
than Cyrus's rank merited.

Cyrus turned his horse round,
headed down the mountain
toward his brother's anger,
which seemed to him
a smaller matter
than it ever had.

HEAT

King Donal, his armor burnished bright,
his horse caparisoned in green and gold,
rode from the still and serried ranks
of the combined armies of Innis and Meqing
to come alongside King Xau—

   Xau, four days late returning:
   grimy, even his horse grimy—

   Xau who looked after his horses
   better than he looked after himself—

   but both man and horse alike
   filthy, reeking of smoke—

   Xau looked at Donal. "Thank you.
   For the show of force."

"What happened?
Did Tahj set a dragon on you?"

"One of his supporters
started a forest fire."

"And you decided to ride into it,
rather than retreat?" Donal joked.

Xau silent.
No trace of a smile.

Only the jerk of his shoulders
as he straightened up—

Xau not just filthy, but exhausted,
barely holding himself upright—

"You fucking did. You rode into the fire."

"Tahj's horses were panicking.
His men would have burnt."

Heat rose in Donal like flame.
"You could have died. And for what?
They're the enemy, or as close
as makes no fucking difference."

A matching heat in Xau's voice.
"We would not abandon
even our enemies to burn.
As you should know."

The ranked soldiers watched
from the side of the road.
Donal swallowed what he wanted to say:
that Xau was a fool,
had been a fool six years ago,
risking himself—"Were you injured?"

"No. We're well. Just tired."

Then both of them silent
for the last mile back to the fort.

HER

Tired,
a gray tiredness,
scarcely able to sit his horse,

to reach the fort, dismount,
the horse taken from him
as he mumbles instructions
for its care;
his generals assembling,
his advisors pressing for attention.
He thanks the four men
who accompanied him, bows deep,
dismisses them to wash and eat and sleep,
though Li, captain of his guards,
refuses to leave,
remains at his side, a bulwark, a shield.
The short walk to the meeting room
lengthened by weariness,
the gray, remorseless spool of duties
unwinding before him.
Within: table, maps, a tray with tea,
a woman standing,
her back to him,
staring out the window:
Hana.
His wife, his queen.

He is afraid to breathe.

She turns to him.

He is afraid to breathe,
afraid she is a figment
of his longing.

She cannot, should not be here;
he cannot, should not be glad
that she left the palace,
her duty, his children.

He is afraid to breathe,
wide awake,
nervous as a boy,
all else displaced
but her.

HIM

Hana hardly knows him,
this man, King Xau, her husband,

returned to her in glory,
another deed notched
in his legend.

(This sleeping man pressed against her
in the narrow soldier's bed
in the mountain fort.)

She hardly knows him.
One day together before he left,
then the waiting, the rumors of war,
learning about him
by the shadows he cast:

> Tian, his elderly cleaning woman,
> rubbing oil into the wood
> of his desk, the soft fierce sound
> of the cloth wiping and wiping,
> as if that act would hold Xau safe.

> Donal, King of Innis,
> red-haired and red-handed in war,
> strong, brash, dauntless:
> the deference in his voice
> when he spoke of Xau.

Xau starts awake beside her.
Dark, not yet morning.
He strokes her hair, her arm,
dismisses the guard
stationed in their room.

She pushes him onto his back,
neither of them gentle.
Afterward, he maps her body by touch,
his hands scarred, a roughness.

He calls the guard back,
pulls on warm clothes.
She dresses as quickly,
follows Xau and two guards
to the stables.

That smell of horse, of hay, of leather
as Xau checks on his horses,
his guards' horses,
her horses.

The horses turn
to inhale his breath,
nicker when he scratches their withers,
but there is nothing to sing about,
no leaping flame, no clash of battle.

Only this man whom she hardly knows.

MONSTER: OASIS

Six-eyed, six-mouthed, within his caves,
the monster schemed to gain more slaves.

Every scheme must have a basis,
he began with an oasis:

A desert haven and the clan
who dwelt there (perfect for his plan).

His touch a trap that linked his mind
to man or beast of any kind.

By this foul means he claimed the clan,
adult and babe, woman and man.

The monster's link a ghastly chain
that bound his pleasure to their pain.

Each one a puppet to his whims,
his mind the master of their limbs.

From caravans, he plundered more,
travelers, traders by the score.

Soon whip and blade and burning brand
equipped his lair below the sand.

Then how pleasing proved his toys,
their hurts the tastiest of joys.

THE HORSE WOMAN

A problem indeed,
a problem that formed no part
of Jun Xi's duties as Finance Minister—

Matters of revenue, expenditure,

diversification of trade,
annual production of silk, tea, spices,
those issues familiar, quantifiable,
far easier than the current matter,
the matter sitting impatiently
across from him—

"Your Highness," began Jun Xi,
"given the circumstances,
the court overlooked the hastiness
of your marriage to King Xau,
but there is no justification
for omitting the wedding banquet,
a tradition as old as Meqing itself."

Her Highness snorted.
"They just want to gawk at me."

Jun Xi endeavored not to gawk,
though there was much to gawk at:
Queen Hana dressed in trousers (trousers!),
her hair beaded and braided
like a... like a barbarian horse woman,
which, regrettably, she was.

Jun Xi cleared his throat,
adjusted the position
of the red sash of his office.
"Your Highness, unless you attend
the principal court functions,
you will be a liability to King Xau
rather than an asset."

She lifted her chin.
"I chose to marry Xau.
I will support him as best I can,
but a banquet is a mistake.
I would only embarrass him."

Quite.
Jun Xi looked down
to hide his agreement.
This task of speaking to the queen
the sole personal favor King Xau
had ever asked of him.

And though Jun Xi had clashed

with the king initially,
their hostility had ended
the day that the king,
then barely more than a boy,
had first met Jun Xi's wife,
his beloved, much-missed wife.
Had met her,
and had neither
looked aside in horror
nor stared at Sim's scarred face.
Had, instead, attended to all she said,
then led them to the greenhouses
(Sim being a chrysanthemum enthusiast),
where Sim had opened like a flower
to the young king's questions.

Jun Xi unable to repay that debt,
yet he would do what he could.
He bowed to Queen Hana.
"The wedding banquet is highly ceremonial
with rigid rules of behavior.
With your permission,
perhaps I could tutor you."

*

At the wedding banquet,
the new queen sat at the king's side,
gowned in silk, jeweled,
powdered, painted, perfumed, poised,
her head held high.

Jun Xi fretted from start to finish,
but the queen comported herself well,
the sole breach of protocol
coming from King Xau,
who kissed his new wife
in full view of the court
no fewer than three times.

NEGOTIATION

The acclimatization of the Meqingese court
to King Xau's new queen
proved a protracted process

of negotiation, compromise,
and occasional capitulation:

That Queen Hana would attend
the principal court functions.
That she would attend them
dressed decorously.
And unarmed.

That in private she could dress
according to the traditions
of the horse tribes,
even down to the trousers
and the knife at her belt.

That, regardless of Hana's ability
to outshoot her guards,
she might carry
neither bow nor arrows
anywhere within the palace.

That she might ride
whenever and wherever she chose,
provided two guards accompanied her.
That she could take Princess Ying
with her when she rode.

But that she must never again
instruct the eight-year-old in archery.
Moreover, Hana must explain to the princess
why archery was neither a necessary
nor desirable skill in a princess.

That it was... argumentative... of King Xau
to observe that the Ulixian princesses
hunted tigers with the Ulixian court,
and that such customs had no bearing
on court life *in Meqing*.

That nonetheless the court deferred,
in this as in all else,
to the king's wishes.
The archery lessons might resume.
Discretion would be appreciated.

STEPMOTHER

Princess,
what are you doing?
Riding beside the new queen,
applauding the arrows
that fly from her bow?
Remember the rules:
mistrust her.
Oh, she's a huntress, all right,
captured your father's heart,
or rather his groin.
A man's prick,
even a king's prick,
hasty not wise.

Woman,
what are you doing?
Wasting your time on a girl
who threatens your grip
on the throne?
Remember the rules:
the brat's not your own,
it's your duty
to hate and despise her.
So honey your tongue
with false promises,
and go plot the princess's
comeuppance.

Both of you,
stop this at once!
Remember the rules:
you are rivals.
Don't look to each other
for friendship,
just look to the men
who define you.
Claim your prince!
Claim your king!
For females divided are weaker
and that's reason enough
for the rules.

KING'S GUARD ˒

Past midnight,
unable to sleep,
Atun sat on the floor of the armory
fletching arrows with Captain Li.

Both men on edge
after the New Year's banquet:
too many guests,
too many potential threats,
alerting to every raised voice,
every sudden movement.

In the lamplit quiet of the armory,
working side by side,
Atun finally asked a question
he'd long wondered about.
"Captain, why did you pick me
as a king's guard?"

Years since Atun had ridden to Lipoh,
young and proud and ignorant,
thinking to serve King Xau,
not realizing that tradition
fixed the king's personal guards
at eight men,
that there would no place
for a barbarian horse warrior.

Li, who'd broken tradition,
who'd spoken to the king
on Atun's behalf,
didn't answer at first.

The captain finished the arrow
he was working on, said,
"Who would you pick
as a replacement guard,
if we needed one now?"

"Feng," said Atun at once.

"Why not Zuo?"
The captain's gaze on him,
steady, intent.

"Zuo would be a fine choice.
He's better with a sword
and at hand-to-hand than Feng."

"So why Feng?"

"Because of the fire drill."

Among the many men
serving as palace sentries,
only a dozen whom the captain
entrusted to stand watch
outside the king's bedroom.
Feng and Zuo the two on duty
the night of the drill.

—Atun had been stationed
in the king's bedroom itself,
had heard King Xau scream,
seen him hurtle out of bed
as Feng and Zuo ran in
yelling "Fire!"

—No matter that Li had forewarned
the king of the drill,
for those first few moments
Xau had thought himself
back in the forest flames,
back in Sumbral.

"Zuo did everything he was meant to,
got the king and queen outdoors.
Feng... did more."

—Outside, in the courtyard,
the king composed, controlled.
Feng the one who'd noticed
Xau scanning the doors, the windows,
who'd said, quietly,
"The captain's fine, Your Majesty.
He's running the drill from inside."

—Feng who had guessed
that the king was still
halfway back in the forest fire,
picturing Li trapped in flame.

"After the drill,
the king couldn't sleep.
We spent hours walking
round the palace.
Feng told him stories."

Li's eyebrows rose. "Feng?"

Atun nodded.
Feng was usually reserved
to the point of reticence,
yet he'd spun long rambling stories,
each one ending in a bad pun,
had done so until the king
relaxed enough to groan
at the puns.

"I think," said Atun slowly,
"that both Feng and Zuo
would shield the king in battle,
but Feng the one
who would follow him
into fire."

Atun looked over at his captain,
his captain who had done exactly that,
that night in the forest.

"As would you," said Li,
"which is why I chose you
as a king's guard."

VETO

"Stop! Do not mount that horse!"
Hana's husband, King Xau,
who never shouted,
stood at the stable entrance.
Shouting. "Do not ride!"

"What's wrong? Is she hurt?"
Hana looked to Gerel, her mare—
the horse fine as far as Hana could tell.

Xau ran over, followed by his guards.
"Don't ride!"

"Why not?" Hana calm, reasonable.
Xau—what?—panicked? angry?

"You are not to ride
while you are pregnant."

A moment to absorb what he'd said,
longer to realize he meant it,
to quash the first three things
she thought of yelling at him,
to say, instead,
calmly, reasonably,
"I feel fine. I am fine.
And I choose to ride."

"We forbid it."

"You *forbid* it?!"

"We forbid it." Xau took Gerel,
led the horse back to her stall.
"The horse's movement could hurt you.
Or you could fall."

"I could have fallen yesterday!
I could fall while walking
down the palace stairs—
Do you think my mother stopped riding
when she was pregnant with me? Xau!"

He made no answer.
He unbridled her horse.
He lifted the saddle off.

"Xau! Say something!"

He leaned his forehead against
the wooden stall partition, said,
quiet now, barely audible,
"Shazia died in childbirth.
We would keep you safe."

Her anger emptied.
In its place,
something more complicated,
uncomfortable, that held her still,
watching this man, King Xau, her husband,
this king they sang about,

who'd killed a demon with his sword
then saved its servants with his touch;
who had risked his own life,
over and over,
in battle and earthquake and fire;
who had saved strangers,
enemies,
but had not been able
to save his first wife.

"You cannot keep me safe,"
she said, "but this risk is small,
and I will be careful."

She went to him then,
while his guards and her guards
and the stablehands
watched the pair of them,
and her horse, Gerel,
munched a mouthful of hay.

Hana put her arms about Xau,
and he turned to hug her.

After a time,
he stepped back,
tacked up her horse for her,
and let her ride.

Horse
Country

EXTRACTS FROM THE RECOLLECTIONS OF ARTOCH,
SENIOR ADVISOR TO KING XAU

The worst advice I ever gave King Xau?
Judged by what measure?
Had Xau heeded my advice
when he was sixteen,
he'd never have walked off
into the hills with that horse lord:
not one weapon between them,
not one soldier to protect them.
The rash foolishness of a boy
fed up with listening to old men.

Yet he returned, unhurt,
with eighteen hundred wild horses
and, equally significant,
with the unshakable loyalty
of the horse lords.

Was my advice therefore poor?
No. As Zhang told Xau,
good outcomes are not proof
of good decisions—

Zhang had been Xau's tutor,
he knew the boy better
than the rest of us.

Zhang was, Zhang was—
I'm sorry—what was your question?

The boy? Xau?
Where is he? Where did the boy go?
Tell Tsung I need to see Xau—

   [Archivist's note: at this point Artoch became
   increasingly confused. I returned the following
   morning.]

The worst advice I ever gave Xau?
The question is ill-posed,
but if you will pour me a bowl of tea,

I will tell you of the time
I deliberately gave him
poor advice.

Thank you.
Xau was thirty years old,
widowed, remarried,
had spent the winter
attempting to reconcile his second wife,
Queen Hana, to life at court,
while simultaneously attempting
to reconcile his court
to life with his new queen.

A difficult few months.

Then that spring the king caught a cold
which settled in his lungs.
Three weeks in bed.
He was back on his feet,
almost himself again,
when he came to me to review
his appointments—
everything askew because of his illness:
meetings canceled,
certain trade negotiations stalled.

And I recommended that he take his family
and spend the entire summer
with the horse lords.

I believed his absence from court
would disadvantage Meqing,
yet I disregarded that,
laid out spurious justifications—
that Xau should inspect the eastern borders,
that he could discuss strategy
with the horse lords,
that Queen Hana might accept
court life more readily
after a hiatus—

Why? Because I wished him to be happy.

He had spent his youth in service to Meqing,
and I, I had come to care for him
as though he were my son.

I gave him the same poor advice
each year after that.
And I'm glad—write that down—
glad that I did so,
glad that he went.

ENTOURAGE

"We had thought,"
King Xau said deferentially, respectfully,
"of taking one of the younger amahs.
We will be sleeping in tents,
riding for hours at a stretch—"

"Despite my advanced age," said Gek,
the inestimable gray-haired woman
who served as senior amah
to the king's children,
"I still remember how to ride.
And I have no intention
of abandoning the children
for the entire summer."

"Thank you."
Xau bowed very deeply.
"We are both grateful and relieved.
May we assist you in any way?"

"Tell me," said Gek,
"do they drink tea
in the horse country?"

*

Accompanying King Xau when he set out:
his wife, his children, their guards,
packhorses, mounts, spare mounts,
and a single solitary servant,
the inestimable Gek.

No valets, no aides, no advisors,
but two saddlebags filled
with cakes of the finest tea,
carefully wrapped tea bowls,
tea tongs, brazier, ewer.

Early each morning King Xau himself
went to the children's tent
and dismissed his children
to run around outdoors
while he brewed tea for Gek.

BETWEEN

Behind, ahead,
the dawn, the dusk,
the undimming and the dimming
of the bounded, measured world;
time's unremitting tread.

But that morning as Xau set out,
his horse beneath him,
his men about him,
his wife beside him,
leaving court and capital
for the windblown grass
of the horse country,
day warming round them,
hooves sounding on the road—
that morning on the cusp of summer,
time paused.
Held still.
No cloud could mar Xau's mood,
brimming and overbrimming
as he shared his horse with Suyin,
his youngest,
four years old, going on five,
her hair fresh-washed,
the smell of it,
her laugh.

Behind, ahead,
his crown, his duty,
the large and lesser loads:
the battle's dead,
a child unheld.

THE WILD HORSES CAME HASTENING

On the rain-blown steppe
the wild horses came hastening,
hooves denting the mud.

Warm but wet, that first night
in the horse country,
rain trickling down his neck
as Wen Xun stood sentry duty.

He heard the horses
before he saw them,
unshod hooves sounding
softly on sodden grass.

Eight horses, riderless,
halted on the low hill crest
overlooking the king's camp
by the Guang Yun river.

> *Asleep in his tent,*
> *how could the king summon them?*
> *What call did they hear?*

Wen Xun went into the king's tent,
woke Captain Li, who woke the king.
Through darkness and rain,
the three men walked up the hill.

King Xau signaled the guards to halt,
went, alone, from horse to horse,
speaking to them,
laying his hands on them.

Wen Xun knew every verse of the song
about wild horses coming to the king.
Witnessing such a thing himself
scared him so much he shook.

> *Unbroken, untamed,*
> *nothing they claimed from him, save*
> *the touch of his hand.*

Wen Xun was still trembling
when the king came over,
set his hand on Wen Xun's shoulder—
"I'm sorry," said Wen Xun, mortified.

"It's all right. Come with us."
And the king steered him forward
until they stood amid the smell,
heat, breath of the wild horses.

And there, his king beside him,
Wen Xun's fear lifted clear,
and he trembled not at all
though more horses galloped up.

> *Their promise they gave:*
> *to come if he needed them,*
> *no matter how far.*

At dawn, the horses left.
The three men went down the hill.
Silent. The rain had stopped.
The king's face was streaked wet.

They hung their coats to dry.
Princess Suyin, already awake,
ran out to join them.
Wen Xun heated breakfast.

The night behind them, unspoken,
as it would have remained unspoken
except that the horses returned,
a dozen times in as many weeks.

> *By hill and by stream,*
> *the wild horses came hastening.*
> *What call did they hear?*

FEALTY

Word of his coming
swept across the wide grasslands
like fire on the wind:
Xau had come, Xau the Horse King,
Xau had come to the horse lords!

With bows and with blades
rode a hundred horse archers,
men stalwart and strong.
Yet reaching the king, they knelt
at his feet, eager as boys.

Oaths they did offer,
pledged their blood to protect him,
to serve as his guards.
Xau knelt in his turn, but took
only friendship, plighted the same.

SHEEP

In the fourteenth year of his reign,
burnished with legends,
weary of fame,
King Xau quit palace and city,
servant and ceremony.

In place of his retinue:
his wife at his side,
his children, their amah,
and nine guards to shield him,
closer than brothers.

No crown on his head,
no attendants to dress him.
He slept in a tent,
spent hours in the saddle
herding mutinous sheep.

The horses obeyed him,
went wheresoever he wished;
the sheep lacked respect.
Why then his gladness
watching those foolish creatures
cropping the grass?

The sheep on the surface,
woolly-headed and loud.
Beneath them,
the hills and the horses;
his guards at their ease;
his children half-wild,
scab-kneed and grubby;

and, inmost of all,
Hana, his queen,
her heart unhurt.

THE EIGHTH SON OF GANBATAAR

Once, when I was a boy of seventeen,
there came into the horse country
a scarred king
whose destiny was ordained
by dragons.

When King Xau first arrived
to summer with our tribe,
I saw his scarred hands
and pictured the two of us
battling demons side by side.

Instead the king herded sheep. Badly.
Worse, girls kept riding over to meet him,
sparing not a single glance on me,
the eighth son
of the horse lord Ganbataar.

Then, ten days into King Xau's visit,
my younger sister Sarnai went missing.
Every man and every woman of our tribe,
plus seven of the king's guards
and the king's wife
rode out at dusk to look for her.

King Xau stayed behind.

As did I,
left to help with the children
and guard the camp,
a decision I stridently protested,
careless of the trust
my father had placed in me.

The king sat cross-legged on the grass,
not even seeing to his own children,
leaving that to their amah.

I heated stew.
The amah and I fed the children.

Dark. The king still sitting
on the grass,
a strain on his face
which I took for guilt.
His two remaining guards
standing either side of him,
his guards who might have
joined the search
if only Xau had let them—
miles upon miles
of windblown hills
where Sarnai might be lying,
Sarnai, my little sister,
fearless but reckless.

Most of the riders had returned
when the king at last stood up,
unsteady on his feet,
his captain supporting him
as if he were ill.

Out of darkness,
a horse came to the king,
unsaddled, unbridled,
a wild horse,
and the king laid his scarred hands
on its withers.

Then noise, lamplight,
people pressing about the king,
his guards tacking up fresh horses.

Just before they set out,
the king and his guards
and my father Ganbataar,
the king spoke:
"Let her brother come too."

He dipped his head to me,
and I, I did not know what to think.
Hard to let go of anger,
but I mounted a horse
and rode.

And the wild horse led the king
through darkness to Sarnai,
her ankle broken,
her horse dead beside her
(she having slit its throat
after it stumbled and broke a leg).

Small beside King Xau's other deeds,
finding one reckless girl,
but she was my sister,
and all the long ride back to camp
I rode double with her,
holding her safe in my arms.

ANCHOR

The wild horse diminished,
dark brushed on dark,
became no more than movement
inked on night.

King Xau stared after it.
The girl was safe,
her ankle broken,
but Leong said she would be fine.

Lantern-light behind him,
the girl, her brother, her father,
Leong setting the girl's ankle.
A blur of voices.

"King Xau—Your Majesty—"

The girl's father. Kneeling.
"Your Majesty, thank you
for summoning the wild horses,
for finding my daughter."

Nearby, loud, a cricket chirped.
Xau set his hand under the man's arm,
raised him up. Words slower to come.
"We are glad we succeeded."

Xau hadn't known whether
the horses would hear him.
Far to reach, to ask their help,

hard to hold that thought clear.

How many horses had heard him?
Enough. The girl safe.
The horses' trust bright as gold,
heavy. He closed his eyes.

"Xau. Time to head back."

He jolted awake. The sky paling.
Sitting cross-legged on the grass.
Li's hand on his shoulder,
Li, captain of his guards.

Who helped him onto a horse.
The wrong horse, Li's horse.
Li swung up behind him,
reached his arms round Xau.

"What?" said Xau, sleep-muddled.

"You're riding with me," said Li.
"Don't argue. Don't fall asleep.
I can't hold you on the horse
all the way back to camp."

Too tired to protest,
Xau swayed and drooped
in rhythm with the horse's trot.
Something he wanted to say.

Had wanted to say, years ago,
riding double with Li
under worse circumstances.
A man dead, no girl saved.

"Li," said Xau. Stopped.
Too tired to say this well,
how much he valued Li,
and surely Li already knew.

Worse never to say it at all.
"We, I, depend on you.
You are an anchor,
always there when I need you."

"An anchor? Weighing you down?"
Amusement in Li's voice.

Then, matter-of-factly,
"Nowhere I would rather be."

KHIDYR

"Gan, wrestle with me."
Leong pulled off his tunic,
threw it on the grass. "Hurry."

Gan, sitting cross-legged
beside King Xau's tent,
shook his head. "I'm resting.
I stood guard last night."

"You've rested enough."
Leong looked over at Khidyr,
the woman standing beside King Xau,
the latest—
and to Leong's mind the finest—
of the many horse women
who'd approached King Xau:
Khidyr plumper (pleasingly so)
and a few years older than most,
offering the king
not a night in her tent
but her expertise as a midwife.

Leong, who served double duty
as both guard and field surgeon,
had watched Khidyr examine the queen
(now six months into her pregnancy),
had admired her dry humor,
the deftness of her hands.

Khidyr bowed to King Xau—
was she leaving already?—
"Gan, come on. One bout.
And if you let me win,
I'll stand your next night duty."

"Done." Gan took off his boots.
"Is this about the woman?"

"The woman?" Leong feigned nonchalance.

Gan looked pointedly

at Leong's discarded tunic.
"You don't usually strip down
to your pants for fights."

Leong flushed as they bowed to each other.

He closed on Gan,
grappled with him,
Gan a giant of a man,
his biceps like iron.
Leong slid his left foot forward,
a mistake—his base unstable,
but instead of attacking,
Gan released him,
presenting a possible opening.
Leong seized him by knee and wrist—
a move Gan himself had taught Leong,
along with two ways to block it—
and threw Gan.

Gan hit the grass,
groaned theatrically...
which would have been perfect,
except that Captain Li
was standing ten feet away.

"Gan." Li's voice ice.
"You're a king's guard.
Your poor performance,
your intentionally poor performance,
disgraces the king. Get up.
Put your boots on."

Gan got up,
pulled on his boots,
while Li turned on Leong:
"As for you, if you are determined
to make a spectacle of yourself,
then spar with me instead."

Not good.
Not good at all.
Leong, already halfway
to being thoroughly ashamed,
bowed to Li.
They circled briefly.

Leong saw Li's weight shift,
backed up,
went for a left heel kick—
Li pivoted,
the captain's hands a blur
as he hurled Leong hard
to the ground.

Leong lay there. Winded.
In no state to appreciate
Li's skill, the minimal exertion,
maximal precision with which the captain
had converted Leong's momentum
to his downfall.

Li gave the merest dip of his head to Leong,
withdrew to stand by the king.

Leong managed a sitting position,
looked up at Gan, muttered,
"Sorry."

Gan shrugged, helped him to his feet.
"You were thinking with your balls.
I should have known better."

"You both should have known better."
The woman—right there—
her eyes on a level with Leong's—
"Next time I'll bring
ankle bones so you two can play
like the other little boys."

"Ankle bones?" echoed Gan
as Khidyr walked over to her horses.

Next time, thought Leong,
watching the sway of her ample hips.
There was going to be a next time.

PROPOSITION

Leong arrayed his many weapons
on a scarlet cloth near the king's tent,
pulled off his tunic
to display his muscled chest,

picked up his sword,
thinking to clean and oil it
where Khidyr would see him.
No. Not the sword.
Khidyr was from the horse tribes,
she would value bows over swords.
He took his second-best bow from its case.

And then the object of Leong's calculations,
the marvelous, magnificent Khidyr,
midwife and horse archer,
emerged from the tent.

Khidyr strode past him—
her beaded braids swinging,
her ample hips swaying—
to where Captain Li and King Xau
were training with weights.

Khidyr said something.
King Xau's eyebrows shot upward.
The captain nodded.

Khidyr strode back over to Leong:
"Captain Li tells me you are off duty.
If this exhibition is aimed at me—"
she gestured at Leong's naked chest,
at the weapons laid out below her—
"I presume you wish to have sex?"

"Here?! Now?"

"Well, I imagined we'd choose
a less conspicuous location."

             *

He didn't ask her why.
Of course not.
Too overexcited and distracted
even to stow his weapons
without help,
his fellow-guard Gan
taking pity on him.

If Leong *had* asked,
Khidyr would have told him

she wanted a lover who offered
no complications,
a man who would be gone
at summer's end.

That a part of the truth,
not the whole of it.
She wanted a child.

Twenty-nine years old,
ready to nurse her own baby,
not help other women birth theirs.
And with no wish to become
the second or third wife
of a horse lord.

       *

Both of them bared
to the sun's heat,
braced one atop the other
on an old felt blanket,
amid the smell of wild thyme
and a profusion of blue irises
so thick they seemed a second sky,
Khidyr the Horse Woman
rode Leong first at a gallop,
and then, Leong as eager
but less hasty,
at a walk.

Afterward,
Leong lay on his side,
curved round Khidyr's curves,
watching a tiny beetle
negotiate its way
between grass stems.

A long unmeasured contentment,
Leong holding the woman
he knew he loved,
all their promises
still unspoken.

       *

Before he voiced it,
before the afternoon ended,

Khidyr knew he loved her,
a complication as unanticipated
as his tenderness,
a tenderness that entangled her,
drew her to the man
she'd thought to discard.

So that she kept to herself,
then and always,
that she'd come to him
only to get a child.

Kept also the blanket
they'd lain on,
kept it long after the smell
of wild thyme had faded,
after it was worn through with holes,
when it held nothing
but a memory of blue irises
and his arms enfolded
around her.

PAIRED

In steady rain, late afternoon,
Hana's husband, King Xau,
stood on a hillside. Wet.
Surrounded by horses.
His horses, their guards' horses,
Ganbataar's horses.

Hana beside him, relatively dry
inside an oiled cape
though her braids dripped.
Xau not much to look at:
thin, beardless, plainly dressed,
stroking one horse then another,
breathing horse breath.

"Three days left," said Xau,
glancing at Hana and away again.
And then, in a rush, "We are sorry.
We know you are happier here
than at the palace."

"Xau." She touched his wet cheek.

"I chose you, hardly knowing you,
because of what Vihaz did,
and because you stayed
to fight beside your guards."

Swift, the first shift
from respecting Xau to liking him.
Slower, only in these past weeks,
that her liking for Xau
had set down roots. Grown.

Xau's eyes on hers, intent,
as she said, her voice firm,
"Now, knowing you,
I would choose you again
even if I had to stay indoors
every day of my life.
I choose you."

An easing in Xau's stance
as he took in her words.

The horses watched, sidelong,
as Xau kissed her in the rain,
water dripping from his hair,
his chin, his ears.

And then a dun mare
with a black-striped back
lay down and rolled vigorously
in a mud patch,
and once she was done
Narson, Xau's black gelding,
rolled in the same spot,
and Xau put his arm around Hana
and together they watched
as one after another
all the horses rolled
in the rain and the mud,
foolish as foals.

SUMMER'S END

They lay on the felt blanket
in the grasslands of the horse country,
the day warming to heat around them,

Leong stroking Khidyr's ample curves,
summer coming to an end.

"I love you," said Leong helplessly
for the fifth time that morning.
He was forty-one years old,
but less wise than a lovesick boy.
He loved her, but he was leaving.

"Ask me," said Khidyr.

"Ask you what?"

Khidyr pushed him away, sat up.
"Of all the clever men I've known,
you are by far the most stupid.
Ask me to come with you,
ask me to marry you."

Hope flooded Leong.
And as quickly abandoned him.
Khidyr didn't understand.
"I work long hours.
I have no home of my own—"

"I live in my sister's tent. Ask me."

"Will you marry me? Please."

"All right," said Khidyr.
She lay back down beside him
on the blanket on the grass,
and Leong hugged her tight,
his heart leaping like a boy's.

HOMECOMING

The day the king was due home,
Huang woke long before dawn.
He lay in bed a while,
searching for sleep,
his thoughts turning on King Xau,
shifting from one memory to another,
all the way back to when Xau
was but the least and youngest
of four princes,

how the boy would sneak
into the stables
any chance he could, and Huang,
not yet promoted to stablemaster,
would teach him to clean a horse's hooves
or mend a broken halter.

Still dark when Huang gave up on sleep.
He surprised the overnight stableboy
by arriving hours early;
checked on every horse,
every stall, every piece of tack;
went out to the pastures,
checked the horses there,
the fencing, water troughs,
the state of the shade trees;
went back and rechecked the stables.

Heard King Xau's party
before he saw them—
the clatter of hooves on stone,
the clinking of bridles—
ran to the stables' main entrance
without thought for the dignity
appropriate to his age—
two of the king's guards riding ahead
to secure the stables—
Huang nodded to them,
but his eyes on King Xau
in the distance, riding Micha,
both of them looking well,
and then the king spotted him,
grinned, waved.

Huang came up to him
as the king dismounted.
A moment when both men
attended to the mare:
the king loosening her girth,
Huang rubbing her withers
by way of a greeting.

That done,
Huang bowed very deeply,
his old eyes watering a little,
straightened up to find himself
being hugged by King Xau,

held tight and holding tight
for two full breaths.
All that Huang had most needed
to tell the king expressed
before they spoke a word.

SATISFACTORY

The accommodations adequate.
The paper window banishes
the impertinent breeze,
lets the light fall on the carpet,
the silk soft beneath her,
now that she has clawed it
into submission.

Permissible that the king pauses,
pushes away paper and brush,
bends down to stroke
behind her ears.

Later, she will inspect his desk.
Items may need to be rearranged.

The situation satisfactory,
and yet, frankly,
so much more is possible.

The king's guards should bow to her
whenever she approaches.
Each day at noon, a bell should ring,
announcing a trifold offering
of pigeon, mouse,
bowl with goldfish.

Jade would be acceptable,
for her statue.

TIAN

Two of the king's guards came in
to check his rooms
while Tian—
King Xau's elderly cleaning woman—
was changing the bed.

Tian distracted
until the king followed his guards,
his baby son in his arms,
until Tian had seen for herself
that the king looked well.

"Tian, we've chosen a name."
Xau brought the baby over to her.
"Khyert, this is Tian."

Unheard of for a king to entrust
the name of his child
to a menial servant like Tian
a month before the naming ceremony.

She cleared her throat,
said brusquely,
not wanting the guards to see
how much his trust meant to her:
"After that stableboy
who died years back?"

Xau nodded.

"A good choice," said Tian.
She touched the king's hand.
"Thank you for telling me."

The baby squirmed in Xau's arms,
and the king started softly singing
one of those foreign lullabies
his first wife had taught him.

Tian finished up with the bed.
She tidied. She dusted.

She set out fresh water,
the pickled cucumber
that Xau favored;
folded a paper horse,
placed it by the cucumber;
lingered a little while,
listening to Xau sing.

MONSTER: SISTER

Six-eyed, six-mouthed, within his caves
the monster sported with his slaves.

Like puppets dancing on a string,
their limbs obeyed the monster king.

His mind to theirs, he forged a chain
that bound his pleasure to their pain.

The knife, the whip, the red-hot brand
equipped his lair below the sand.

No prison bars, no guards, no rope,
his mind the leash that deadened hope.

Far from the caves he sent his spies
to be his soldiers and his eyes.

And thus he learned of one like him
with servants dancing to her whim.

(An elder sister of his breed
corrupted merely by her greed.)

He might have seen her as a friend,
beseeched her help his ways to mend.

But he grasped a hidden danger:
she knew more than any stranger.

His sister's death the only cure
his future safety to ensure.

DRAGON MOUNTAIN

Then to the dragon mountain
rode the scarred king
with nine guards to shield him,
closer than brothers.

"What is this? Meat?"
Li, captain of King Xau's guards,
chewed on a hardened lump
from the way-fort
where they'd changed horses.

"Diseased pig," said Leong.

"Old dog," said Atun.

"Dog food," said Gan.

"Lunch," said King Xau.

And so they rode.
Sixteen, seventeen hours a day,
setting out before dawn,
eating in the saddle;
Captain Li careful to keep
at least two guards
riding ahead of the king,
two behind, two flanking him;
every traveler, every tree
measured for threat.

Yet, dried dog food or not,
the journey itself a joy to Li,
to ride at Xau's side
past farmers tilling fields,
a scattering of sheep.

On the fourth day
an undulation on the horizon,
a hazy blue-gray unevenness
that formed into foothills,
a ridge of rock and ice and snow,
the dragon mountain itself,
where kings were chosen,
where Xau's brothers' bones lay,

where Xau, then only a boy,
had claimed a throne.

Li's third time at the mountain,
his first to accompany the king
to the heights.

Leaving the others behind
at the mountain fastness,
Li and Xau set off
in the middle afternoon.
No weapons. No armor. No horses.

Li looked up at the mass
of sharp-edged rock and ice,
holding back questions.

Three miles. Four miles.
The way steepened.
Dusk,
the mountain fastness
lost in shadow below.
A black speck descended,
growing, hinged wings beating.

Li placed himself
between the dragon
and his king.

Wind, a reek of smoke
as the dragon landed a man's length from Li,
its golden eyes, dark-flecked,
staring right at him,
steam issuing from the black holes
of its nostrils.

"Step aside, Captain,"
said the dragon, her breath ash.
"I could burn your king to cinders
whether you stand in front of him
or not."

Li held his ground.

"Hah!" said the dragon. "You defy me.
Good. Shield your king at all costs."

Xau moved alongside him,
set his hand on Li's shoulder.
"It's all right, Li. We trust her."

"Do not! Do not trust anyone!
The Hidden Queen died three hours ago.
Murdered. Poisoned. A gasping death,
eight days from start to finish."

(How could the dragon know that?
No pigeon, no messenger so swift.)

She turned her head away, flamed hugely.
The thin snow cover vaporized,
the air where they stood flaring hot
as a blast from a blacksmith's forge.

Li weighed his options
if the dragon should attack—
to try for her eye sockets, barehanded,
perhaps gain enough time for Xau to run—

"We are sorry." Xau's voice soft.
"We met her once. We liked her."

"Liked her? She was manipulative,
gluttonous and devious."
The dragon lowered her neck,
laid her head flat.
"I will miss her greatly.
We spoke to each other often,
she in her underground squalor,
I on my mountain."

(They'd spoken—
with hundreds of miles between them—
Li careful not to react.)

"Are you in danger also?" asked Xau.
"Can we help you?"

"Me?!" An explosive snort.
"I summoned you to warn you.
The Hidden Queen's death
will be ruled an accident. It was not.
I have tasted a malevolence in my dreams,
a foul force that I believe
lies behind the queen's death."

Li caught the slight shift
in the king's stance,
that bracing,
but Xau's voice calm, level:
"A force like the demon?"

"Neither demon, nor human.
Concealed. Corrupt. Cruel.
Slowly, slowly, its power grows.
Strengthen your alliances.
Ready your army for war."

"How long do we have?" asked Xau.

"Years, not months, I think."
The dragon's eyes darker,
her nostrils smoking.
She lifted her head, looked at Li.
"Captain, you must be ready now.
They may try to eliminate Xau
well before they move to open war."

"Thank you for the warning."
Bleak the thought of how many ways
a king, his king, might be killed.

His king who stepped past him,
sat down by the dragon,
leaning his back against her
as if it were a normal thing to do,
a thing he had done before.

Then the king and the dragon talked,
and Li stood, watching them,
as dusk deepened to night.
The sky hung bright with stars
when Xau at last settled himself
against the dragon's bulk,
slept.

The dragon sighed. Closed her eyes.

The slow-wheeling stars marked another hour
while Li stood guard, his back chilled,
the heat of the dragon's body
warming his face, his chest,
the front of his legs.

The world below him charcoal on charcoal.
Remote. Unreal.

The dragon opened one eye,
a faint golden glow.
"Do you plan," she asked Li,
"on staying awake all night?"

"I do."

That eye considered him.
"Good. He chose his captain well."
The eye closed.

Li stood,
watching over his king,
as the stars swept out the hours.

ALLIES

*Then to the horse country
rode Donal the Red King,
ruler of Innis,
to meet with the man
once his enemy, now his ally,
who had slain a demon
and saved both their kingdoms.*

King Donal was still thirty miles from Xau
when the scouts announced themselves,
requested, politely enough,
that Donal and his men
accompany them.

Thirty miles later,
in a valley so green
it might have been stitched
on a princess's tapestry,
Donal found King Xau herding sheep.
Or trying to herd them:
half the sheep scattered
at Donal's approach.

"I thought," said Donal,
"you were training more cavalry,
not minding sheep."

"General Qiang is training our cavalry."

"Why Qiang? Why not you?"
Xau the one with horse magic,
the one that the horses were besotted by—

"We worked with Qiang for one day."

"One day? That's all?"

"Yes." Xau's tone flat.

Li, captain of Xau's guards,
looked to his king for permission
before saying, "When King Xau was there,
the horses did whatever he wished.
It served no purpose
except to accustom the riders
to their mounts maneuvering
at the king's will."

"Best that our cavalry learn
to operate without us," said Xau.

Donal heard what Xau didn't say,
that he was planning for a time
when he was wounded,
or dead.

"So," said Donal,
"you still think war's coming?
None of my spies think so."

"Our source was persuasive."

"Persuasive? They didn't even name the enemy!"

"Someone who profited
from the Hidden Queen's death."

"Which could be anyone or no one.
It's fucking little to go on."

"It's all we have," said Xau.
"And based on that knowledge,
we will double our cavalry
over the next year,
and increase our foot soldiers
by one quarter."

"And bankrupt your treasury."

Xau raised his eyebrows, then nodded.
"There has been... lively debate
among our ministers."

"Fuck."
If Xau had been any other man,
Donal might have offered
several observations about his judgment,
then ridden back to Innis.
If Xau had been any other man,
Donal wouldn't have come
in the first place.
Shadow and darkness behind them
and a debt Donal couldn't repay.
He took a breath,
said with considerable restraint,
"All right. You wanted me.
I came. What next?"

"Tonight you meet the horse lords.
Tomorrow we discuss tactics."

"And until tonight? Do we mind the sheep?"

"If you like. It's harder than it looks."

"It's not hard at all.
This is a perfectly good valley.
Let the sheep go where they want."

Xau gazed ruefully
after the scattered sheep.
"We need to get them back
to camp for milking."

"The horse lords milk *sheep*?"

The remainder of that afternoon
not in any of the tales
about Donal or Xau,
an afternoon of no consequence,
of shared mishaps and recalcitrant sheep,
both men larking around like boys.

KHAN

King Xau sat on a low chair
to the right of the Khan's throne
in a tent so large a hundred people
might have slept in it:
the assembled horse lords
armed with bows, swords, daggers,
their long hair immaculately braided;
King Donal loomed on the Khan's left;
Subetei—the Khan—
atop his silver throne,
gold armbands twisting
from his elbows to his wrists,
his yellow pants edged with fur.

Xau the one who'd summoned them.
Five days planning for a war
of which there was as yet no sign
beyond the dragon's warning.
Yet Xau so certain war would come
that he had bent his will,
his army, his allies
to brace for it.

Much accomplished,
the hardest part left for last.
Only Li, captain of his guards,
standing stern beside him,
knew what Xau intended.

Subetei Khan straightened in his throne
as he came to the end of his summation.
"Half will join King Xau's army now,
half next spring."
Subetei looked at Xau. "Anything else?"

Xau nodded.
"If we ourself are absent,
or incapacitated,
we ask you to give command
of the joint armies to King Donal."

"No. I will yield command
to you and only to you."

If Xau had held any hope
of persuading Subetei,
he would have spoken to him,
alone, two nights ago.

He had none.

A risk to be taken instead,
a risk he had weighed
and accepted.

"Then," said Xau, standing up,
"we challenge you for the Khanship."

Chaos.
The lesser horse lords in uproar.
Horror on Subetei's face,
Subetei who revered Xau,
who had pledged his men to fight
at Xau's command.

Slowly Subetei stood up.
"If I must fight you,
then let it be to first blood,
no more."

Xau bowed deeply to him.
Men backed away from them,
cleared space for the fight.

They drew their swords. Bowed.

"Now," said Subetei,
advancing as he spoke,
Xau forced back,
blocking that first thrust,
then watching the line of Subetei's body
as the Khan swiped for Xau's off arm—
Xau stepped sideways,
no thought to it,
air from the sword's motion
sliding cold past his arm.
No thought to it
as Xau turned to thrust
at Subetei's abdomen.

Stopped himself.
Mid-thrust.

Stumbled backward—
he'd nearly skewered Subetei—
a valid move
but Xau determined
neither to cripple nor kill the Khan.
Off-balance, Xau parried.
The clashing weight of metal
jarred the length of his sword arm—
Subetei stronger than him—
Xau's breath too fast,
sweat running down his body—
thousands of hours practicing
with his guards,
learning to inflict maximum damage
at minimum risk—
trying now, today, to render
the least damage he could—
Subetei feinted, tried for a downward cut—
Xau countered, barely in time,
fighting his reflexes—
Subetei lunged for Xau's groin—
left an opening—
Xau parried, pivoted,
sword low but rising—
sliced Subetei's yellow pants,
the flesh of the Khan's thigh.

Red bloomed on the yellow fabric.
Subetei looked down as if puzzled.
"I yield."

Xau took one gasping breath—
not quite over—
he had to restore as much authority
as he could to Subetei.
Bracing himself,
he ran his forearm
along his sword blade,
deeper than he had meant,
held his bleeding arm up.

"Our blood to your blood," said Xau.
He pressed his arm to Subetei's thigh.
"As a brother you will be to us."

Not a sound from the watching men

as Subetei knelt heavily,
red running down his leg.
"My khan, my king, my brother,
the throne is yours."

Subetei's words unstinted,
but a bewildered sound to his voice,
like a man who has lost his bearings.

"We wish you to keep the throne," said Xau.
"You are a strong and just leader,
but if we ourself are absent,
or incapacitated,
we ask you to give command
of the armies to King Donal."

"I swear it," said Subetei.

Done then. Over.
All that Xau could have hoped.

An effort to help Subetei up,
to steer him back to the throne,
to wait while one of Subetei's men
bandaged the Khan's thigh,
to still his own face
while Li bound his arm.

An effort to bow to the horse lords
as they came up to him,
to say a few words to each one,
to listen to what they told him.

That last hour hardest of all,
the race run,
and only Xau's will
holding him upright,
but he smiled,
he listened,
he bowed.

LOYALTY

King Donal and Captain Li
flanked Xau as he walked,
Li looking so forbidding,

Donal so ferocious
that the dozen horse warriors
who approached as if to talk to Xau
all veered away.

Both men aware from Xau's silence,
the rigid precision of his stride
that Xau was spent;
both holding back their objections
to the risk Xau had run.
Time enough to harangue him tomorrow,
for now they would shield him.

TARGET

Scene: The horse country.
King Donal and King Xau are riding
at some distance from their guards.

DONAL
What's wrong?

XAU
Nothing.

DONAL
Nothing?
Did Subetei anger you?
Did he call you a weakling?
Did he insult Hana?

XAU
No.

DONAL
Then why the fuck did you challenge him?
He could have killed you—

XAU
A necessary risk.

DONAL
Horse shit.
Unless you're looking to be killed
that wasn't a risk worth taking.

XAU
Not looking for it, but anticipating it.

DONAL
You think you'll be killed.

XAU
We think the Hidden Queen was killed.
We were warned we might be next.

DONAL
Then double your guards.
Use a food taster.
Sleep in your armor.
All right. Let's begin again:
what's wrong?

XAU
War's coming.
We're expecting the enemy
to try to eliminate us.

DONAL
Fuck. You're an obvious target.
No cavalry can withstand you.

XAU
If the enemy kills us, we expect you
to defend both our kingdoms.

DONAL
If they kill you, I'll tear them apart, I'll—
Fuck.
I'll defend our kingdoms.

XAU
Thank you.

OATH

Once,
there came into the horse country
a scarred king
whose destiny was ordained
by dragons.

Their horses stood in the river,

seeking relief from the heat,
from the clouds of insects,
as the horse lords knelt
to the scarred king,
and the sunlight caught
on their gold armbands
as they placed their bows
at his feet:

"Our bows, our blood,
our men at your command,
wherever and whenever
you have need of us."

A thousand years and more
the horse lords had held
the eastern border of Meqing,
yet never before sworn to fight
beyond the horse country,
and the sunlight caught
on the hilt of King Xau's sword
as he stood by the river,
bitten alive by midge and mosquito,
and laid his hand
on each man's forehead.

Later,
when the time came,
the horse lords kept their oath.

RECRUITS

On the night of the half moon,
the scarred king went
to King Donal's tent
and, waking him from sleep,
led him to the hillside
where waited the wild horses.

Hundreds of horses,
the light of the waxing moon
glinting in their sideward glance;
the smell, heat, breath of them.
Donal a veteran of many battles,
blooded, bold, brave,

yet an emptiness to his stomach
as if he were falling.

He stood by King Xau
as a stocky, large-headed horse
came right up to them,
inhaled Xau's scent,
lowered its large head
at Xau's touch.

"Will you help us?"
Xau asked the horse.
"Will you follow King Donal?
Will you carry his soldiers?"

The horse swung its head round
to sniff Donal's breath,
nickered once.

And one after another
the horses came up
and Xau spoke to them
and laid his scarred hands on them,
and all the while Donal's heart pounded
as if he had run for miles.

When the last horse moved away,
the two men stood, side by side,
the hill below them
covered in horses.

Donal turned to Xau,
the younger king trembling now,
though he had shown no sign
of cold or strain earlier.
"Are you all right?"

A pause before Xau said, "Yes,"
and then, haltingly,
"Do not spend their lives lightly."

Donal nodded,
and in that singular night,
one more strangeness:
a sudden disconcerting impression
that Xau was receding further
and further from him—

he reached for Xau's shoulder,
reassuringly solid,
let go again.
Knelt.

> *And Donal the Red King*
> *pledged then his sword,*
> *his blood, his men*
> *to the scarred king;*
> *shadow and darkness behind them,*
> *shadow and darkness ahead.*

BRIDGE

Night after night, in dream,
King Xau stood at the midpoint
of a narrow span of green jade
high over a rocky gorge.

Behind him: drum rolls, trumpets,
battle cries, screams, groans.
He tried to turn. Couldn't.
Couldn't draw his sword.

Woke soaked in sweat,
gripped by the dragon's warning.
Then spent his days, his strength,
readying for war.

A war that did not come.
Days gave way to weeks,
weeks to months,
and though Xau knew
this respite would not last,
he set the thought of war aside
for whole hours at a time—

> Balanced the Khan's eagle
> on his gloved arm,
> that weight,
> the clench of talons.

> Took Ying, his daughter, shooting;
> her gaze steady, measured,
> as she drew the bow;
> her laugh as the arrow flew—

At night, in dream, the bridge.
The narrow span of green jade
the only color in a world
of rock and air and cloud.

From far below, the sound
of the river rushing over stone.
And then, behind him,
the din of battle.

WAY-FORT

Well past midnight,
Yang Du mucked out horse stalls
and pondered the quirks of fate.

He'd spent the past month
bemoaning his assignment
to a minor way-fort
on the edge of nowhere.
And yet, six hours ago,
the king himself had arrived
to stay for the night,
the king and his family
and their guards,
all returning from the horse country.

Yang Du had attended
to the half dozen spare mounts
while King Xau and his men
cared for their own horses.
Yang Du's commander had run in
halfway through,
then hovered over the king,
offering him tea, food, hay for his horse,
gazing about the stables in dismay
as if wishing he had thought
to fit the stalls with carpets.

That a tale Yang Du's grandma
would love to hear.
Of course, now the king
was sleeping in silk sheets
while Yang Du shoveled horse shit.

Noises sounded outside

in the courtyard—
a courier traveling through the night?—
no, not hooves on stone,
but hurried footsteps—

Yang Du opened the stable doors:
the king and three of his guards.
"Your Majesty?"

"The four of us are leaving,"
said the king.

Leaving? In the middle of the night?
Yang Du swallowed his curiosity,
asked only, "Which horses?"

"Please ready Fenfei.
We'll see to the others."
The king nodded to Fenfei's stall,
then turned to one of his guards.
"Leong, sit down, rest."

The guard, a man maybe forty years old,
a few white hairs among the black,
sank heavily onto a stool.
"Be quick. I'm dying."

Yang Du stared at the guard.
He'd never seen a dying man.
Not that the guard looked ill.
Yang Du bowed to him.
"Shall I call the surgeon for you?"

"I'm a surgeon," said the guard.
"Spoke to yours. Need to see the man
southwest of here. My only hope."

"Don't be alarmed," said the king,
accepting a hoof pick
and brushes from Yang Du.
"Leong will be fine. It's just his tooth—"

"Just my tooth! Abscessed at the least,
possible bone infection."

Yang Du went into Fenfei's stall,
began grooming the mare.

He heard Leong mutter,
"Just a tooth! I like that tooth.
Or at least, I liked it before
it attacked me."

"You mean"—the king's voice—
"before you tried cracking
walnuts with it."

"Don't remind me!"

Yang Du cleaned Fenfei's hooves,
brushed her, combed her,
tacked her up,
listening as Leong grumbled,
as the king filled in the spaces
in the conversation,
Yang Du slowly working out
that the king was trying
to distract Leong.

When the horses were ready,
Yang Du led Fenfei into the courtyard.

The king helped Leong mount.
"Let us know if the pain gets worse,
if you need to ride double."

"Worse! Impossible!"

The king turned to bow to Yang Du.
"Thank you for your help."

Then the king mounted up,
the four men rode away,
and Yang Du went inside
to shovel more horse shit
and rehearse the story
he would one day tell his grandma.

BOWL

The woman who worked willow and water
in bold black brushstrokes
on the bowl's thin shell
never went more than a day's walk

from the terraced hills
where she was born.

The cook whose night-duty wages paid
the doctor's fees for his son
layered noodles in the bowl,
added chopped spring onion,
fragrant slices of ginger duck,
a spoon of sesame sauce.

Hana, who'd left the wide grasslands
for a walled palace in a walled city,
placed the painted porcelain bowl
beside the inkstone on the desk.
King Xau, her husband, turned,
laid his hand gently on hers.

Xau set aside grain-tax reports,
the stack of unanswered letters
to share supper's tangy sweetness
with Hana and his guard;
managed, after repeated attempts,
to make the two of them laugh.

Next morning, scrubbing dishes,
one of the kitchen staff paused,
lifted the bowl to the light,
looked at line and leaf,
how the willow was drawn
in air as much as brushstroke.

LANTERN FESTIVAL

Bustle, noise, the last night
of the New Year celebrations,
the streets of Lipoh crowded
with revelers, dragon dancers,
people selling sweet dumplings,
children running every which way,
a sea of scarlet lanterns—
small, large, plain, decorated,
riddles painted on their sides.

Prince Keng, thirteen,
followed his father, King Xau,
up the steep stairs of the city wall,

Keng double-checking his pockets
for the little red envelopes
as he climbed.

This the first time
that his father had asked Keng
to join him Walking-the-Wall,
a ceremony his father had added
fifteen years ago today.

Only their guards with them
as they climbed up and up,
the noise and the crowds dropping away,
the lanterns merging into a red carpet.

At the top,
Keng glanced down the far side
at the shiny dark of the moat,
the full moon trembling
in the water.

No lanterns up here,
but men lining the stone ramparts.

King Xau bowed very deeply
to the first man,
a man who leaned on a stick,
whose eyes shone in the moonlight
as Keng's father bowed.

Keng bowed in turn,
gave the man a red envelope.

His father bowed to the second man,
an old man, nearly bald,
with a beard that straggled down
to his thin waist.

Keng bowed, gave him an envelope,
followed his father to the next man.

He knew the men were veterans,
and at first it was fun,
handing them the envelopes
with money tucked inside,
feeling pleased with himself,
he, the young prince,
bringing them gifts.

But some men had missing ears,
or eyes, or a hand.
Some had no legs,
sat propped against the parapet.
Some of them smelt bad.
Some reached to touch his father
and his father stopped
and held their hands.
Some spoke to his father
and his father answered,
patiently, quietly,
and some, who'd said nothing,
his father spoke to anyhow.

Some of them looked at Keng
the way they looked at his father,
as if Keng were a hero,
and the more that happened,
the more uncomfortable Keng felt.

He bowed.
He gave out envelopes.
His feet hurt.
The moon moved across the sky.
The crowds below thinned.

One man reached not for his father
but for Keng,
reached with a wrinkled claw-hand
that lacked two fingers—

—Keng backed away, revolted.

The man pressed his fingers
to his forehead,
made the abject bow of a servant
who has displeased his master.

Keng stood, staring at the man,
thinking of war.
Not the way he had before,
not like a story.
Thought of men ending up
with no legs or no arms
because they'd fought for him.

One gulping breath,

thinking on that,
then Keng stepped forward,
took the man's claw-hand
between his own hands,
a cold bony dryness.

"I'm sorry," said Keng.
"Thank you for fighting for Meqing."
He couldn't think what else to say.

The man nodded to him,
not a bow this time, just a nod,
as if to a friend.

Keng nodded back,
followed after his father
who had turned to watch him.
His father said nothing,
only hugged Keng,
briefly,
there on the wall
above the city of Lipoh.

Then, together,
they walked the wall.

COAST

Salt wind whipped Hana's hair,
she and Xau steadying each other
as they clambered over wet stones.
A fuming fury crashed onto rock.
Black-headed gulls rode the air
above the unwalled ocean.

No gold, no jewels,
no herd of horses
equal to this gift.

MONSTER: OPENING GAMBIT

The monster, neither brave nor bold,
had bided months and spent much gold.
Seven horses brought to his caves
where he transformed them into slaves.

His touch a trap that linked his mind
to any creature he would bind.
Those seven horses then resold;
the monster's mark, his lair, untold.

And now, at last, the time drew near
to kill the king whom men held dear.
One horse of rare and precious breed
picked yesterday as King Xau's steed.

That horse equipped with hidden sting,
for when the monster pulled its string
the horse would rear and throw the king,
trample the man into a thing.

      *

Atun, king's guard, beamed
as he led Kuan, the new horse,
out of the stables to King Xau,
the chestnut stallion the fastest horse
either of them had ever seen.

Xau took the reins from Atun,
laid his free hand on Kuan's withers—
and gave a curious choking gasp—
Xau's eyes wide—
hand clamped white on the horse—
the horse snorting—
Atun reaching for the king
as the king screamed, "Kuan! Kuan!"

      *

A word, a name thrown like a spear,
hurled by the king whom men held dear,
the monster stricken in his cave
as King Xau fought to loose a slave.

Linked to the horse, its ears, its eyes,
the monster saw and heard Xau's cries.
Grappled, struggled, then darkness fell;
broken the bond, undone his spell.

The horse cut clear, its freedom won,
the monster's precious plans unspun;
his prey escaped beyond his grasp,
the strings unfastened from his clasp.

*

Atun caught the king
as Xau's knees buckled,
hoisted him in his arms—
only the other guards in sight—
no hint as to what had befallen Xau—
"Wen Xun, fetch Leong and the captain.
Shuen, take the horse away."

"Cruel. Not here. Not the horse," said Xau,
mumbling, making no sense.

"Easy there," said Atun,
willing reassurance into his voice,
a reassurance that was a lie.
Atun unmoored.
An enemy he could have fought,
but this? A seizure? A madness?
Helpless, he held his king.

"Like the demon," said Xau,
"but more human. Cruel."
The king met Atun's gaze.
"Set us down. We are not crazed."

Atun lowered the king,
and Xau, too pale,
leaned on him heavily.

"The horse. Kuan," said Xau.
"Kuan was... haunted?
Perhaps the first move
by our enemy."

Darkness then in the king's eyes,
shadows of what he'd faced
before Atun joined his service.
Demons, dragons, the risen dead.

Atun knew in that moment
the gripping terror
of a child's nightmares,
but he stood his ground,
steadied his king,
his king whom he would shield
at any cost.

SPY

Enlai busied himself with his harp,
checking the pitch of each string.
His performance had, predictably,
been a triumph—
the palace staff lapping up
every paean praising King Xau,
though the king himself had pointedly
declined to attend.

So why had Xau requested
a private audience?

The hall's great doors swung open
and the king entered,
flanked by three guards
and his senior advisor.

"Your Majesty."
Enlai bowed with an elaborate flourish
he'd copied from the Ulixians.

"Master Enlai."
Xau bowed hastily.
"You speak Sumbrese?"

"Yes, Your Majesty.
I spent a year in Sumbral
studying zither and setar."

"We would like you to return there."

Enlai frowned before he caught himself. "Why?"

"We would appreciate your assessment
of the country, especially anything
that appears out of the ordinary."

"You wish me to spy for you?"

"No—" said Artoch, the king's advisor.

"Yes—" said Xau.

Artoch continued smoothly,
"The term 'spy' has negative connotations.

456 · Mary Soon Lee

There is no need for secrecy,
a minstrel may hear rumors
merely in the course of his travels."

Enlai looked from Artoch to Xau.
"Though honored,
I confess I am surprised
that you would pick me."

"You are not the only person
we are asking," said Xau.

"Oh." Enlai sniffed.
"And what type of rumors
would I be fishing for?"

"War preparations."
The king's gaze on him,
straightforward, direct.
"If we're correct,
it may be dangerous."

Well then, danger, war,
no doubt discomfort too,
and Enlai very attached
to his own well-being.
Balanced against the risks,
the chance to earn the king's favor.

Enlai weighed it up,
considered requesting concessions
in return for his consent
(perhaps a royal commission
for a major song-suite).

Tempting, but Enlai,
perceptive when he cared to be,
judged that he would receive more
from a man like Xau
if he demanded less.

"Very well," said Enlai. "I'll go."

Xau bowed to him deeply. "Thank you."

The king looked at him again,
an approval in that look

that unsettled Enlai,
that almost made him wish
to be worthy of it.

LOTUS MOON

Over hill, over river,
across the wide steppe
far came the wild horses,
unbroken, untamed,
to meet the scarred king.

On the sixth night
of their return to the horse country,
Atun, king's guard,
followed King Xau onto the hill
where the wild horses waited.

A hundred horses or more,
among them a thin gray mare
who came right up to Atun,
just as she had done
during his last night duty.

And Atun wondered then
if the gray mare had chosen him,
but said nothing, his guess lying
too close to his heart's wish
for him to trust it.

Next night, the mare sought Atun
and he spoke to her softly,
and he marked, too, how a black horse
went over to Shuen and nickered.
So Atun told the king his thoughts.

On the eighth night,
the night when the Lotus Moon
rode round and full in the summer sky,
all nine guards accompanied
King Xau to the wild horses.

And the gray mare went to Atun
and breathed warm in his ear,
and the black horse went to Shuen,

and a horse to each other guard,
and a colt with a white blaze to the king.

And King Xau looked at his guards
and his guards looked at him,
and each man set his hands
on the horse that had come to him
and jumped up onto its back.

> *Rode then the scarred king*
> *and the nine guards*
> *who shielded him,*
> *closer than brothers,*
> *raced through the grass—*

> *Raced reckless and giddy,*
> *grinning like boys,*
> *the wind on their bare arms,*
> *the horses beneath them*
> *stretched into a gallop.*

FIVE ARROWS

Amid the smell of wild thyme,
on a hilltop in the horse country,
sheep cropping the grass below him,
King Xau sat on an old felt rug
listening to his children
tell him stories.

"My turn!" said Suyin,
Xau's youngest daughter.
"Two sisters and three brothers
met a huge fierce tiger.
The sisters wanted to fight it,
but their big brother wanted to hide,
and the other two brothers
wanted to run away—
I need six arrows for the next bit."

Xau's guard Atun,
one of the three guards on duty,
bowed very gravely to Suyin,
took six arrows from his quiver,
handed them to her.

"The sisters and brothers quarreled,
and the tiger ate them all up."
Suyin gave Xau one arrow.
"Break it, Papa."

Xau snapped the arrow in two,
remembering the one other time
he'd heard this story:
how startled Suyin had been
when Queen Hana gave her an arrow—
a real arrow—
to break.

"Yes!" said Suyin. "Like that!
The tiger ate them up, like that!
Then the tiger met five more
sisters and brothers,
only they didn't quarrel.
They fought side by side
and killed the tiger!"

Suyin used her sash to tie
the other five arrows into a bundle.
"Break them, Papa."

Xau took the five arrows
and tried—not too vigorously—
to break them.

"Papa, may I try?" said Ying.
She took the bundle of arrows
and strained and strained
without success.

"Let me," said Keng, Xau's eldest.
Keng stood up,
placed his boot on one end
of the bundle of arrows,
yanked the other end up,
snapped two arrows.

"No! Keng! Stop!" yelled Suyin.
"The sisters and brothers
are stronger together!"

"I'm sorry," said Keng,
looking more smug than sorry.

Suyin gave Keng a ferocious scowl
before scrambling into Xau's lap.
"Papa, what did you think?"

"It's a very fine story," said Xau,
his arms around her, his heart full.
"But if you keep telling it,
Atun will run out of arrows."

Suyin giggled.

Amid the smell of wild thyme,
far from the palace where his hours
were measured in meetings,
the king with his children.

KINGSHIP

Before King Xau slew a demon,
before the wild horses came to him,
before he was crowned,
before his sword was forged,
before the palace foundations were laid,
before his kingdom had a name,
before the dragon who ordained his destiny
hatched from out her shell,
before those things:
this tree,
this silver apricot tree
whose autumn leaves
Xau helps his youngest heap
into a pile of gold.

GAN

Stroke and counterstroke,
the clink of practice blades
echoed across the palace courtyard.
No heat to it, closer to a dance.

The king sparred with his guard
on a cold fall evening,
the courtyard lit by lanterns,
Captain Li watching them.

King Xau's sword pressed
the sleeve of Gan's jacket;
Gan's sword touched
the king's left thigh.

Both men careful to a fault
not to hurt the other.
Stroke and counterstroke.
Protracted. Pensive.

Until king and guard
looked full at each other
and sheathed their swords.
No victory gained or sought.

Tomorrow, Gan would assume
the position of armsmaster
to the young princes. An honor,
but not the equal of this.

This honor of being a king's guard
that Gan now renounced,
his strength, his speed
not what they once were.

They bowed to each other.
King Xau thanked Gan
for his long service,
gripped Gan's shoulder.

No words to thank him back.
Gan beset by a memory of the king,
then a boy, offering him water,
fifteen, sixteen years ago.

A small thing, but the boy's father
had never done so;
Gan's first inkling that Xau
might outmatch his father.

Gan took off his jacket,
the jacket of a king's guard.
Handed it to Captain Li.
Gan's guard duty done.

COUNTER GAMBIT

One moment Xau was upside down,
hurtling through the air,
then he hit grass,
shoulder-first,
rolled over onto his feet.

He bowed to Shuen,
the guard who had thrown him:
a curious way to spend
a perfect spring morning,
being assaulted by his guards.

Captain Li held up a hand. "Wait."

A palace sentry crossed the courtyard.
"Your Majesty, one of the people
on your list just arrived,
it's Master Enlai, the minstrel.
He's waiting to speak to you."

"He didn't ask to see to his horse first?"
One of the few things Xau liked
about Enlai was that the minstrel
took good care of Shira.

"He left his horse to the hostler."

Xau raised his eyebrows. "Fetch him."
He accepted a towel from Li,
rubbed his arms dry
as Enlai came over.

"Your Majesty."
Enlai bowed, a plain bow,
devoid of the flourishes
the minstrel usually favored,
a second, though minor, oddity.

"Master Enlai. Are you well?
How is Shira?"

"Shira?" A blankness in Enlai's face
that changed to blandness.
"Fine. Thank you."

That more than a minor oddity.
Xau made the warning finger-signal
to his guards, considered Enlai.
"What did you learn in Sumbral?"

"I'd like to go over my notes with you."
The minstrel pulled a roll of paper
from a pocket, stepped to Xau—

—Li sprang between them, knocked Enlai over.
Who fell. Badly. Thumped down hard.
Li on top of him, pinning him.

"What—" began Xau. Stared.
In Enlai's grip, a thin blade,
viscous yellow along its double edge.
"Li. Careful. Poison."

Shuen stepped onto Enlai's arm,
used a towel as he freed the blade,
three of Xau's other guards
now helping Li to pin Enlai.

"Li, did he cut you?" asked Xau.

"No."

"Leong, make sure."
Xau ignored everything else
until Leong had stripped Li down,
inspected every square inch of his skin.

"He's fine."
Leong moved over to examine the knife.
"But that does look like poison."

"Search Enlai," said Xau. "Then bind him."

He tried to think,
tried to think past the fact
that Li might have died.
Xau would never have taken Enlai
for an assassin,
the man entirely self-interested.
What profit to Enlai from this?

"Why?" asked Xau.

"Because you're an unmatched threat."
Enlai laughed,
a hollow, malevolent sound,
nothing like his normal laugh.

Instinct, impulse, half-formed thoughts
as Xau said, "Hold him still,"
laid his hand on Enlai's forehead.

Malice whipped him,
bared every hurt he'd ever borne,
broken bones, burnt flesh,
battle and flame and demon,
his hands red with Tsung's blood.
Underneath the furied flood, faint,
a wounded creature cried for help—

Xau staggered as Li pulled him loose.
"No. We must do this." Xau touched Enlai—

A skeleton of fire,
a horse slaughtered by his own hand,
blue-lipped children dead of cold,
Shazia dying as he held her,
as he fought to free the wounded creature,
fought to free Enlai—

Then the courtyard on a spring morning.
Enlai held fast in the guards' grip.
Xau breathless, dizzy, queasy,
Li supporting half his weight.
Xau gulped for breath. "Master Enlai?"

"Myself again. In your debt.
There's a monster in the desert—"

"One moment," said Xau,
his stomach churning violently.
He had time to growl,
"Don't ever make a song about this,"
before he doubled over
and vomited his breakfast
over his shoes.

VENEER

In the dry cool of the royal library,
two hours after the attempted
assassination of King Xau,
an orderly, rational, purposeful discussion:
the king, his advisors, his guards
careful, contained, controlled.

(King Xau's only outward discomposure
how often he glanced at Li,
captain of his guards,
Li, who could have died
two hours ago.)

The facts arrayed, assessed:
that a creature akin
to the Hidden Queen
lurked somewhere in the Sumbrese desert;
a creature with the power to possess
man or woman,
to control their very bodies;
a creature sadistic, deadly, depraved.

Actions agreed.
The palace sentries to be doubled.
Access to the king curtailed.
A letter dispatched to Tahj, King of Sumbral,
warning him of the foul creature,
offering aid to find and destroy it.

The library door opened,
the sentries admitted Queen Hana,
the queen composed, collected.
Only her muddied riding attire
hinted her haste.

Xau stood—"We are well. Unhurt."

"Good." She held his gaze.
"Suyin's in the hall.
She was with me when I heard."

He left the room.
His second-youngest stood
back flattened to the wall.

Too straight, too quiet.

He knelt upon the floor.
He hugged her close
and could not make himself
let go.

YUNXU

The king's dressing room was Yunxu's domain,
a domain defined by brocades, embroidery,
button knots, shoes, sashes, sleeve-weights.

Yunxu had worked for many men,
but King Xau the only one
who'd spoken to him
of anything beyond the joint business
of robes and ornaments—
the king more likely to mention
a song he'd heard
or to ask after Yunxu's pet larks.

Yunxu's hands unsteady
as he smoothed the silk he'd selected—
turquoise embroidered with cranes,
cranes the symbol of long life—
the king's life nearly cut short
that morning by an assassin—
tonight's inauguration of a High Judge
to proceed despite that—

The door opened
and the king entered
with four of his guards.

"Your Majesty." Yunxu bowed.

Captain Li handed Yunxu
an iron lamellar cuirass
fit for a battlefield:
"The king will wear this
beneath his robe tonight."

Yunxu bowed again.
He undressed the king,
armored him,

robed him,
groomed his hair.

No words, no small talk.

Only as Yunxu finished
did the king return
from whatever far road
his thoughts had traveled.
Xau dipped his head to Yunxu.
"Your family? Are they well?"

"Yes, Your Majesty. Thank you."
Yunxu bowed and the king left.

Yunxu distracted as he tidied up,
his own thoughts following
after the king.

CONCLUSIONS

Over the next three weeks,
aware now that a creature akin
to the Hidden Queen
conspired against them,
King Xau and his advisors
drew the following conclusions:

Firstly that,
unlike the Hidden Queen,
the creature was as malevolent
as it was powerful,
manipulating men, women, beasts
like puppets on a string.

Secondly,
that since Xau could unmask
the creature's minions,
the king should examine
as many people as possible.

(Every member of the palace staff,
every one of the palace soldiers,
every government minister,
every diplomat, every official
was duly brought to Xau's presence—

three more of the creature's minions
thus revealed, freed by the king.)

Thirdly,
that in order to possess
its victims in the first place,
the creature must fetch them to its lair
and touch them, skin to skin.

(This conclusion reached
after extensive questioning of Enlai
and of several former servants
of the Hidden Queen.)

Fourthly,
that the creature's lair
lay somewhere in the Sumbrese desert.

Letters dispatched in haste
to every city in Meqing,
every border fort, every ally,
alerting them to search for spies
among any who had traveled
to Sumbral.

The creature's foothold
in Meqing stamped out.

Within Sumbral itself, another story.

SINCE SUMBRAL

A quarter mile walk from his guest room,
a quarter mile promising himself
to neither beg nor weep,
then the entrance to King Xau's study
where the king's guards
searched him from head to toe.

The king rose from his desk,
bowed to Enlai,
who bowed back three times:
"Your Majesty. I'm sorry.
I'll leave by noon—"

"Master Enlai."

King Xau's voice gentle.
"We are not asking you to leave."

"You're not? I thought,
I assumed, you'd dismiss me
because of last night."

Last night a disaster.
Enlai's first performance
since the—since Sumbral—
singing for servants,
for greasy kitchen staff.

Entirely predictable
what would please such a crowd,
his own heroic ballads about their king.
But by the first chorus, Enlai in tears,
the words he'd cynically composed
unraveling him.

(A bawling, blubbering debacle,
the cooks and pot-washers baffled.)

Mortifying to realize
he now believed his own verses
like a lowly laborer;
believed the king a hero.

"Master Enlai."
That gentleness again.
"We had thought you would like
to perform, but it is not a condition
of your stay here. You are our guest."

A moment before Enlai managed,
"Thank you. I'm in your debt."

"No. We sent you to Sumbral."
Shadows in the king's eyes.
"The fault is ours.
The debt is ours."

Enlai bowed, not trusting his voice.

A long pause before the king asked,
"Is there anything we can do to help?"

"No. Thank you. Since Sumbral—"
He stopped.
Maybe he would have continued
had he been haunted by memories
of the monster's other victims.

(Men, women, boys, girls,
infants barely old enough to walk,
tormented, tortured, trapped.)

Except it wasn't their misery
that woke Enlai at night,
rather fear—terror—for himself.
That he would be recaptured.
Possessed. Persecuted. Punished.

The king did not force an answer.
Instead, Xau sent for tea
and they talked of small things,
Xau's children's lessons,
a new design of beehive.

Enlai grateful for every word,
the commonplace comfort
of tea and conversation.

FURTHER EXTRACTS FROM THE RECOLLECTIONS OF ARTOCH,

SENIOR ADVISOR TO KING XAU

Correct. King Xau returned
to the horse country that summer.
If you require a target to blame,
blame me. I argued him into it.

Had Xau stayed in Lipoh
he could have coordinated more easily
with his generals,
but to what purpose?
He had warned Tahj of the monster,
had offered his help,
help that Tahj had declined.

Even in hindsight, I believe

it was the correct decision—
the correct military decision—
for Xau to leave Lipoh.
If you pour me a bowl of tea,
I will elaborate.

Thank you.

Xau's alliances were strong,
his main army readied.
Whereas the horse lords,
though willing,
had never fought alongside others,
and would not have heeded
advice from anyone other
than King Xau himself.

May I remind you of the magnitude
of the Khan's concessions—
Three thousand of the Khan's warriors
incorporated into Xau's cavalry.
Every other horse warrior,
every single horse lord
sworn to fight at Xau's command,
a fealty never offered before or since
in the history of the horse tribes.
A fealty due solely
to their devotion, their love,
for Xau himself.

Even so I had great difficulty
convincing the king to leave.

He never did master detachment:
knowing that the monster lived,
knowing it preyed on others' pain,
he held himself at fault,
hadn't slept through the night
in nearly two months.

Compounding that,
Heng had not returned.

Heng? A translator whom Xau
had dispatched to Sumbral
to watch for war preparations.

Whether for the particular or the general,
Xau took responsibility.
The one man he'd sent into danger,
and the monster's uncounted victims
whom he had never met,
who were not from his country.

One man.

> [Archivist's note: at this point Artoch fell
> silent. I assumed he had become confused, as
> he was prone to do, and left for the day. But
> when I returned next morning, Artoch returned
> immediately, though briefly, to Heng.]

Heng. Set this down—
Heng, a translator in King Xau's service,
never returned from Sumbral.
Although his body wasn't identified,
he was likely our first casualty
in the Imperial War.

MONSTER: TAHJ

Six-eyed, six-mouthed, within his caves
the monster sported with his slaves.
With whip and blade and burning brand
he played his games beneath the sand.

Alas, how fragile proved his toys,
their deaths the costliest of joys.
The more he killed, the more he craved,
his tastes destructive and depraved.

His hellish harvest hard to hide
from soldiers searching far and wide
(sent by King Tahj who ruled the land
from forests green to desert sand).

So the monster spun a story
of golden tombs, desert glory,
an ancient crown with the power
its bearer's rivals to devour.

*

Lusting for greatness, King Tahj came.

In place of fame, found fear and shame.
Like puppets dancing on a string,
his subjects served the monster king.

Tahj watched his own guard kiss a girl
then flay her skin in one long curl.
He watched a mother blind her son
and bow to Tahj when she was done.

Briefly released, the poor souls crept
into fouled corners. How they wept.
His duty clear: to give his life
to try to free them from such strife.

And yet, alone, what chance had he?
So Tahj went down upon one knee,
offered a rather garbled plea
at least to set the children free.

The monster laughed and promised him
one life for his, a choice most grim.
Tahj wavered... the trade lopsided...
sacrifice would be misguided.

*

Instead they made a secret pact,
a contract simple but exact.
Together they would seek to rule
an empire vast as it was cruel.

The monster linked them mind to mind,
their thoughts invisibly entwined,
but swore he would not pull the string
with which he bound and held the king.

There in that cave the pair agreed
that Tahj would feed the monster's need,
supply a steady stream of toys,
both men and women, girls and boys.

But should Tahj falter or betray,
why then his family would pay,
and Tahj himself would wield the knives
that slew his sons, his seven wives.

BOYHOOD

Riding with the horse lords that summer,
the summer he turned fifteen,
Prince Keng couldn't settle,
couldn't relax, heart pounding
as if he'd been in a fight.

Back home, he rode better
than any other boy he knew.
Here, he was outridden by everyone,
even a six-year-old
who giggled as she stood—
stood!—
on her horse's back.

The same hills, same horses
as other summers;
the horse lords just as pleased
as they had been the other times
that King Xau, Keng's father,
had brought his family.

Everything the same
except Keng himself:
frustrated, humiliated.

But then a wedge of geese
would fly overhead, honking raucously,
or the riders would halt to watch
a herd of antelope swim a river,
and Keng's mood would lift.

One morning, restless,
he woke early, tacked up his horse,
his guards following
though he didn't want them.

Two miles' gallop from camp,
Keng stopped,
loosed his feet from the stirrups,
half-knelt on the horse's back.

"Keng." A guard's voice, level.
"Sit back down. Slowly."

Keng ignored him,
pushed himself upright—
stood!—
his shadow outstretched
on the grass below.

His horse took one step, tail swishing.

Keng lurched,
arms wheeling for balance,
and the horse reared.

Keng toppled.
Hit ground, hand first.
A shattering pain.
He tried to get up,
passed out.

Woke. Mouth dry. Hot.
Forced his eyelids open:
the roof of a tent,
his father leaning over him.
He shifted sideways.
Pain shot from wrist to shoulder,
a grinding scraping
that grayed out the tent.

Three weeks before they let him ride again
(his arm in a sling, his horse at a walk).

Three weeks.
First, lying on a blanket,
staring up at the tent's smoke hole,
at his father's face.
Then, lying on grass,
wind-shunted clouds overhead,
as his father's voice
stitched the hours together.
Days before Keng could walk, haltingly,
the length of the row of tents.

Each morning Keng told his father
he'd be fine, to leave him,
to go riding, hunting, shooting.

Each morning King Xau stayed.
And sometimes a sullenness

thickened in Keng's belly
until he wanted to yell at his father,
wanted his father to yell back,
to blame him, to punish him.

But his father neither yelled,
nor scolded him, only told Keng
that he should apologize to his guards,
then left Keng alone to do so.
A hard thing.

Other than that,
his father barely left him,
and at times Xau's gentleness—
helping Keng into clean clothes,
checking his shoulder,
replacing the dressings on his hand—
stirred in Keng a longing
for his father to hug him.

Most afternoons,
one or other of the horse lords
returned early to talk to King Xau,
and Keng, however surly his mood,
sat quietly by his father,
shifting only to ease the ache
in his shoulder.

Xau spoke to the horse lords for hours,
loose conversations covering
weather, horses, pastures, sheep;
their wives, sons, brothers;
the number of men in their tribe;
the position and condition
of wells, rivers, iron workings;
tales of raiders from across the border.

A while before Keng understood
that all the conversations
spiraled around war.

Toward the end of the third week,
walking outside with his father,
Keng said, "I'm sorry,
I know this isn't what you planned,
nursemaiding me.

You came here to gain
the horse lords' support."

King Xau shook his head.
"No. That is not why we came.
We gained their support years ago."

His father hesitated,
played with the buckle of his belt.
He was not a man who fidgeted,
not a man whom Keng had ever seen
struggle for words.
"We are sorry as well,
sorry war may be upon us
before you are ready."

Unspoken, the risk of death,
his father's death.
What that would mean for Keng.

Nothing Keng could think to say.
He turned away, saw a huge bird,
an eagle, flying over the hills: "Look."

Xau laid his hand on Keng's good shoulder.
Together, they watched the eagle
ride the wind.

JOY

A day of gold,
a day as faultless
as the clear blue sky,
a day that Atun rode beside his king
out of the sunstruck heat of the grasslands
into the shade of birch and larch
to hunt with Subetei Khan.

Not the season to hunt
deer or wolf or lynx or boar,
but the Khan minded to prove the prowess
of his oathsworn warriors,
so they rode to the forest
in search of squirrels.
And Atun outshot the king,
outshot Captain Li,

outshot the king's other guards,
outshot the Khan and his oathsworn:
each man allowed to loose a dozen arrows,
Atun managing to kill eight squirrels.

Subetei Khan dipped his head to him.
"I remember you, Atun, son of Anikha.
I see your arrows still fly as true
as they did before you left
the horse country."

Atun bowed deeply,
his braided hair swinging.
He wore the plain black
of a king's guard now,
but he had kept the silver armbands,
the braided hair of a horse warrior.

The Khan thumped Atun on the shoulder,
went off to congratulate the man
who'd done second-best.

King Xau, who had downed
only a single squirrel,
grinned at Atun.
"Don't let our gardeners learn
of your squirrel-slaughtering skills
or they'll try to hire you
away from us."

"Hmmm," said Atun.
"The work would be easier."

Captain Li shook his head.
"Don't worry, Your Majesty.
I couldn't get rid of him
even if I put him on night duty
for a month and stopped his pay."

"We know," said Xau softly,
his eyes on Atun.

Then two hours gentle riding
through the forest,
the resinous scent of larch needles,
the calls of the birds.

Back out onto the open grassland,
the shadows lengthening,
Atun guarding his king,
a day of gold.

MANEUVERS

"Show us," said Subetei Khan,
leader of the horse tribes,
"that we may be ready
if war comes."

Weighing the worth of that
against his reluctance
to ask it of the horses,
King Xau agreed.

And at summer's close
on a day of sunbaked heat
Subetei Khan's horse warriors
and one quarter of King Xau's infantry
jointly rehearsed for battle.

No blood, no broken bones,
no groans, no screams;
only the rhythm of drums,
the thrum of hoofbeats;
a river of horses following Xau,
answering his will,
maneuvering before their riders
even gave commands;
parting into streams
that arced across the grassland,
each separate stream in perfect order
as if the horses were a thousand shadows
of a single faultless form;
sweeping down upon the infantry,
scattering men like sheep.

When they were done,
Xau dismounted, sweaty and spent,
and Subetei Khan knelt to him
on the downtrodden grass,
but no words came to the Khan
for what he had witnessed.

ADDENDUM

"It will not be like that,"
said King Xau, walking his horse
to cool him down.
"If their infantry use pikes,
if they hold formation—"

"I know," said Subetei.
"Men and horses will die."

Xau silent, walking his horse,
his guards ringed round him.

"And yet," said Subetei,
"whatever you ask of them,
the horses will do
without signal or word.
An unrivaled advantage."

Xau silent.
Li, captain of his guards, silent.
Both men thinking of Enlai,
of how the enemy had tried
to end that advantage.

REUNION

Enlai could smell the audience
gathering in the Khan's tent:
the horse warriors didn't appear
to approve of bathing.

Months since he'd played in public,
his last performance a disaster,
but nervousness unnecessary.
He was ready, surely he was ready.

He rubbed at a speck on his harp,
allowed himself to anticipate
both his impending triumph
and the Khan's promised payment.

The audience fell silent and stood.
Enlai bowed with flamboyant flair

as Subetei Khan entered
amidst his wives, his brothers—

And—no, please no—King Xau—
King Xau looked over at Enlai,
the horror on Xau's face
mirroring Enlai's.

"Subetei Khan," blurted Enlai,
"I thought, didn't you say
I'd be performing my new work
just for your family?"

"You are."
Subetei Khan gripped Xau's arm.
"King Xau is my brother,
my blood brother."

The king regained his composure
before Enlai, whose hands trembled
as he positioned his harp.
Enlai took two deep breaths, sang:

In deepest night, a leaping light
set trees ablaze, a direful sight.
To save his foes, King Xau he chose
to ride into the fire.

Enlai's voice a trifle unsteady,
the harp rescuing him,
the notes flowing from his fingers,
pure and bright and clear.

Intoxicating, that first moment
he knew the audience was his,
following every word, every note,
Subetei nodding in time.

His men would burn, Prince Cyrus feared.
The flames neared, his horses reared.
Then through the smoke, the king appeared,
his captain at his side.

Uncanny skill and strength of will
let King Xau hold the horses still.
Onto their backs the men they leapt,
through the woods the fire swept.

The audience Enlai's, except for the king.
Xau too still, too stiffly straight,
his smile a polite pretense.
Xau hated being cast as a hero.

Once Enlai would have delighted
in the king's disguised discomfort.
Now, since Sumbral, it dismayed him.
He set his misgivings aside. Sang.

His foes all saved from danger dire,
the king fell down amid the fire.
The captain rushed to aid his sire,
and bore him from the flame.

Subetei and his brothers and his wives
and his cousins and his children
stamped and roared their approval,
leaned forward for the next song.

Enlai sang himself hoarse,
sang five ballads in praise of Xau,
three in praise of the horse lords,
two love songs, four comic chanties.

When it was all over,
when he was putting his harp away,
the king approached him.
"Your Majesty. I, I'm sorry—"

"Don't be." Xau bowed to him.
"This is what you were born to do.
We are glad you are better.
How is Shira?"

They chatted briefly,
nothing of great consequence.
Curious how deflated Enlai felt
when the Khan reclaimed Xau.

Beast

THE IMPERIUM

In the fifth year of his reign,
Tahj, King of Sumbral,
proclaimed himself Emperor Absolute,
ruler of every man, every woman
beneath the eye of the sun.

(Behind Tahj, hidden, a beast
who preyed on others' pain;
a beast whose touch
bound men like puppets.)

As the days shortened,
five kingdoms fell
without a single battle fought,
fell to the Imperium,
fell to evil.

One king yielded
out of avarice and ambition,
pledged slaves and soldiers
for private gain and public power,
a princeship second to the emperor.

Two kings yielded out of fear,
burying shame beneath Tahj's banner.

Two spurned Tahj's overtures.
Both speedily assassinated.
Their heirs complicit and corrupt,
in secret league with the beast,
linked to his thoughts
yet acting on their own.

At year's end,
Tahj and the beast
bent their attention
back to King Xau.

BENEATH THE BLADE

On the brink of war, courtesy abandoned.
Prince Cyrus strip-searched
before they let him enter King Xau's palace,

yet that insult trivial
beside the debt he owed to Xau,
a debt he had not forgotten,
a debt he could not repay.

Cyrus's doom decreed two months ago,
but that doom drawn out, delayed.
As if his head were bent
beneath a blade,
and his brother, the executioner,
savoring his torment.

His brother Tahj,
the Emperor Absolute,
whom Cyrus had idolized
when they were both boys,
that devotion moderating
to respect as they grew up,
respect turning late to doubt,
and doubt, at last, to dread.

Two months beneath the blade,
his family forfeit—
Cyrus's wives, his children
hostage to his brother.

Two months,
during which Cyrus met the monstrous beast
that had corrupted his brother—
its den drenched in blood,
its touch a trap
that linked its mind
to any creature it would bind—
a hundred horrors
Cyrus had witnessed in that place
and known that his sons, his daughters
would feed the beast's depravity
if he defied Tahj.

(Out of those hundred horrors,
one with him every night:
a little boy,
hands controlled by the monster,
mouth left free to scream
in the slow red hour
while the boy castrated himself

with a blunt knife.)

A hundred horrors,
yet Cyrus unscathed,
his mind his own
so that King Xau, touching him,
would sense no monster
steering his hand,
would trust him.

A trust misplaced.
Tahj's commands clear:
Cyrus must deliver either
Xau's surrender or his death.

Outside King Xau's audience chamber
guards searched Cyrus again,
probed his flesh from scalp to toe.
Two months beneath the blade.
Time now run out.

EQUINOX

1. Xau.

Dusk on the spring equinox,
light and dark in balance.

In the audience chamber
of the palace at Lipoh,
King Xau set his hand
on Prince Cyrus's forehead,
reaching for darkness,
for the taint of the beast
that preyed on pain.

Not there, the prince himself.
Xau drew back his hand, bowed,
his heart in that moment
light as a boy's.

A moment only, the friendship
they might have shared
shadowed by Tahj,
Cyrus's brother.

2. Li.

Li, captain of Xau's guards,
released his hold on Cyrus
at Xau's signal,
saw the king's gladness
spill into his smile.

The king quick to trust.
One of many reasons
Li valued him
at more than his crown,
but it made it harder
to shield him.

He stayed within sword's reach
of Prince Cyrus,
watching the language
of Cyrus's muscles.

3. Siak.

With practiced precision
Siak translated,
preserving nuance and tone—
King Xau's open warmth,
Prince Cyrus's hesitance.

Opening pleasantries
and then, laid bare,
the price of peace
as Cyrus presented
his brother's demands:

King Xau to acknowledge
Emperor Tahj's supremacy,
to render monthly tribute
of slaves and silver and silk
in such and such amounts,
on such and such dates.

Harder than usual for Siak
to banish his own thoughts.
Half his friends Sumbrese,
an attachment sustained
across years and miles
by a string of letters

in a language not his own,
a language he loved.

4. Artoch.

Artoch, Xau's senior advisor,
had anticipated Tahj's demands
in essence if not in detail,
had arrayed options for Xau,
predicted likely consequences.

None of which had swayed the king
from his initial position.
Xau usually moderate, measured,
but in this matter adamant.

Xau heard Cyrus out.
Declined Tahj's demands.
Added the words that shifted war
from likelihood to near certainty:
"We require Tahj to kill the beast."

Peace not always the correct path.

5. Keng.

Eager and curious,
Keng came at his father's summons
to meet Prince Cyrus,
his uncle—

A heaviness in the air
of the audience chamber
as if thunder approached—

Keng bowed to Cyrus,
welcomed him in Sumbrese,
Keng's mother's language,
his mother whom he alone
of her four children
remembered clearly.

6. Cyrus.

The boy, Xau's eldest son,
had Shazia's eyes,
the lilt of her voice.

Cyrus startled enough to say
without weighing it:
"I hadn't thought your father
would let you learn Sumbrese."

"Mama taught me,
and a tutor since then.
We're studying Sumbrese poetry,
which I like, and Sumbrese history,
which is difficult."

Their remarks translated
for King Xau's benefit,
Xau who laid his hand
on Keng's shoulder, said softly,
"We do not wish him to forget
his mother's language."

Neither Xau's words,
nor the boy's eagerness,
nor the boy's likeness to Shazia
should have mattered.

Cyrus's resolve set a month ago
in the cave where the beast
tortured its victims.
His own sons, his own family
forfeit if he failed Tahj.
Therefore he must not fail.

He looked at the boy
and his resolve faltered.
He fought himself,
fought the words out,
"Tell your father I was sent
to kill him—"

—Guards seized Cyrus at Siak's shout—

Cyrus kept talking,
his eyes on the boy:
"Tell him I will not hurt him,
that I remember how he rode
into fire
to save me and my men."

The spring equinox,

light and dark in balance,
history hinging
not on battle but on a boy,
a boy who stood awkwardly
as his uncle wept.

LOGIC

The audience chamber sealed.
Inside: King Xau. His nine guards. His eldest son.
His senior advisor. A translator. Cyrus.
A table arrayed with tea, bowls, water;
the bowls untouched, the water cooling.
Time short, their options poor.

Fact: Tahj had sent his brother Cyrus
to obtain King Xau's surrender.
Or Xau's death.

Fact: Xau would not surrender to Tahj.

Fact: Cyrus's family held hostage by Tahj.

Fact: Cyrus had betrayed Tahj,
had confessed to Xau.

The problem: to decide Cyrus's fate.

Cyrus, past helping them,
hunched over in a chair,
head buried in his arms,
a guard on either side.

If Tahj thought Cyrus had betrayed him,
then Cyrus's wives and children
would be tortured to death.

If Tahj believed Cyrus
had attempted to kill Xau,
then Tahj might, in brotherly mercy,
merely execute Cyrus's family.
This clearly the better option.

The boy, Xau's eldest son,
battled not to show his horror.
Failed.

Too late for Xau to shield his son,
but he stood beside him,
his hand on the boy's shoulder.

So Cyrus must appear to attack Xau.
If Tahj thought that Cyrus
had survived this attack
he would suspect a trick.

Therefore they must fake Cyrus's death
at the hands of Xau's guards.
Hiding Cyrus afterward
would be the easier part.
Producing persuasive proof
of his death near impossible.

A grim discussion followed.
Artoch the one to propose
cutting off Cyrus's hands
to send to Tahj.

That the only time
Cyrus raised his head.
He looked at Xau, said,
"No. Kill me."

Xau said nothing, only bowed,
and Xau's guards
and Artoch and Siak
bowed after him.

The details still to be decided.
Cyrus weaponless;
his clothes, his person
searched five times over.
Xau known to be well guarded—
lacking all credibility
for Cyrus to choke him
or to disarm a guard.

(If desperate,
if no better opportunity
had presented itself,
Cyrus might have tried
to break Xau's neck barehanded
or to shove him down a staircase,
but such possibilities hard to stage

without risking Xau in truth.)

One point in their favor:
Tahj would not expect them
either to sacrifice Cyrus
or to injure Xau.
The cost high, but perhaps
sufficient to trick Tahj.

In the end,
they settled on simplicity.
They would break a tea bowl,
stage an attack with a sharp shard.

> *They broke the bowl.*
> *They bade the boy*
> *turn his back,*
> *that he did not have to watch*
> *what happened next.*

BLOODSHED

To kill a man who might
have been his friend—

King Xau took Li's sword. Gripped it.
The bloodshed would be named to Li,
but Xau would not let Li
carry its weight.
The fault Xau's.
Who should have found
some better way.

Xau bowed to Cyrus.
Took a breath. Thrust.

   *

To injure the king
who was also his friend—

Leong lifted the sharp shard,
considered the anatomy of the neck.
The bloodshed to be named to Cyrus,
Cyrus who lay dead by Xau's hand,
Xau who looked at him,
said, "Make it convincing."

Leong took a breath.
Willed his hand steady.

WOUNDED

Less than his legend,
the king beside her in the bed.
Pale. In pain. Silent.

> Nothing he could say,
> neither what he'd done, nor why.
> His fault, his failure.

His deeds bright-burnished.
The man himself mortal, frangible,
reeking of ointment, of injury.

> No reassurance to offer her.
> He might not return.
> Might not win.

She reached for him,
said the words she hadn't said
last time he left for war.

> Those words as gold to him,
> her love the strength
> that girded him.

DAUNTED

Cold. Wet. Worn out.
King Xau floundered after Li,
the snow waist-high in places,
the wound on his neck
itching furiously,
a sign (so Leong said) of healing.

Discomfort unimportant.
His deficiencies disastrous.
The monstrous beast unslain, unchecked,
still preying on others' pain.

Clouds parted.
Sunlight woke snow to blue dazzle.
Xau squinted against the glare,

floundered on,
had been floundering
well before he set foot
on the dragon mountain,
since killing Cyrus,
a man who might have been his friend.

In a rush of heated air,
dropping out of cloud, the dragon—

Li, captain of Xau's guards,
stepped between Xau
and the dragon's black bulk.

Xau saw Li brace himself, weaponless,
willing to fight that immensity
barehanded,
a willingness that pierced Xau.
He didn't deserve such loyalty.
Had erred. Had fallen short.

The dragon fixed her golden eyes on Li,
steam issuing from the black holes
of her nostrils.
"Your king is hurt.
I told you to shield him."

"I failed."

The dragon snorted explosively,
shaking snow from both men's hair.
"At least you don't offer
sniveling excuses."

Xau moved to Li's side.
"It was our fault, not Li's."

All of it his fault.
The monster. Tahj. Cyrus.
To have found no better way.

"*Your* fault?"
A darker gold in the dragon's eyes.
"That you stand against Tahj and the beast?
That you forged an alliance opposing them?
That they would kill you for it?"

Xau set aside the sodden cold,
the fiery sting of his wound.
Shouldered what he'd done.
"Our fault. We killed a man
who did not merit death."

"I've killed many. So?
Tell me what you did and why."

The telling hard,
Xau shivering when he finished.

"Stop wallowing in guilt."
She turned her head away, flamed,
snow vaporizing in a plume of steam,
the air round Xau flaring hot.

She swung her head back,
stared long at him.
"You did well enough.
You have a war to win. Men die.
Let's get to work."

She hunkered down,
wings hinging to her haunches.
"I and my sister dragons hold the mountains.
Any forces Tahj brings within our reach,
we will destroy. Beyond the mountains,
you fight without us."

"Why?" asked Li.
"Why not fly to the monster's lair?
How could they stop you?"

"My power is in these mountains."
Her scales gleamed like glass,
like polished granite
in the slanting sunlight.
"Iron and ice, coal and fire.
I will not leave."

Five hours then debating strategy
with one who'd hatched
fourteen hundred years ago,
wise, inhuman, ruthless.
Even she unable to offer more
than thin chances, contingencies.

At dusk, discussion done,
Xau bowed to the dragon.
"One thing more. Our eldest son. Keng."

"Don't beg for his life.
That I will not promise, even to you."
Her breath ash.
"If you die,
if I deem him inadequate to be king,
I will kill him quickly."

"We ask you to teach him—"

"*Teach* him?"

"Yes. Ready him to be king.
He is neither arrogant, nor grasping,
nor cruel, nor cowardly.
He is merely young."

"Hah!" She laughed, a sound
like an anvil dropped on rock.
"He would not like my lessons."

"He doesn't have to like them,
only to profit from them."

"You overstep yourself.
I am no nursemaid."
She rose.
Belched smoke.
Bared yellow teeth long as daggers.
Brought her head, those jaws,
within an inch of Xau.

Who stood his ground. Firm.

Until Li yanked him back,
placed himself once more
between Xau and the dragon.

Her head prodded Li. Hard.
"I like you, Captain.
Keep shielding your king.
He undervalues himself."

She leaned her head round to Xau.
"I see you have your balls back.

Very well. Send Keng.
If he's a poor pupil,
I can eat him."

Xau bowed again.

With Li at his side,
he set off down the mountain.
Exhausted. Damp. Neck stinging.
Better.

THE IMPERIAL WAR: ONSET

King Xau's declaration of war
sped by pigeon and courier:
a day to signal his border posts,
two days to alert his nearest ally,
three days to notify his enemy.

That enemy, the Emperor Tahj,
feasting on figs soaked in syrup,
bespoke the beast who shared
his thoughts; the beast bespoke
their aides, spies, puppets.

Before Tahj finished his dessert,
before he licked his fingers
and lounged back on his throne,
his orders made known
across two thousand miles.

BOATMAN

Special cargo, the lieutenant told Shu. Top speed, don't dock at towns. Ten
men who can help you out on the barge. And twenty horses. Shu knew better
than to tell the lieutenant the river was running rough, glutted with spring
rain, horse-spooking. The horses came aboard nice and easy enough, and the
ten men worked hard and willing. Didn't give their names. Dressed like stablehands, except they carried swords and Shu saw bow-cases in their baggage.
Their leader a quiet man, lean, alert, surefooted. Took Shu a couple of days to
notice how the quiet man watched after an even quieter man, mute or silent,
blue scarf wrapped round his neck day and night, who did most of the grunt-
work with the horses. Took the storm for Shu to finish putting it together.
Bolts of lightning, rain in sheets, thunder fit to break his eardrums. Men
and horses belowdecks, the man with the scarf going from horse to horse,

laying his hands on them, his scarred hands, patient, and the horses watching him, still, calm. Unnatural. Only it didn't feel unnatural, it felt right. Like a shepherd calming a lambing ewe. Or the king, Shu's king, on his way to war, looking after his horses.

IMPOSTOR

"Tack up your horse. Now."
Gan kept his face neutral,
but didn't bother disguising
the disgust in his voice.

"I'm the king. You do it."

Gan glanced at the man.
"Stay in character. Act like him—"

"*We* are the king,
tack up our horse for us, guard."
A sneer on the man's face,
on his freshly-shaven face
slimmed down by diet,
his physical resemblance
to King Xau as remarkable
as his manner was repellent.

"Either you tack up your horse,"
said Gan, "or I'll set up the tent,
take you inside where no one can see us,
and beat your newly-scrawny arse."

The man gave his horse a hasty check-over,
hoisted the saddle blanket.

Gan grunted.
Three hours with the man so far,
a whole weary week ahead.
The technical challenge hard enough:
playing a pair of traveling traders,
letting slip sufficient clues
that they were king and king's guard.

Harder still not to punch out
the man's teeth.

An hour on horseback

before Gan simmered down.
The rhythm of the horse,
the dense honeyed smell
of the fields of flowering rapeseed
worked him past anger to anxiety.

He kept glancing up at the sky:
a pair of vultures paced their progress.
Spies? Sent by the Sumbrese beast?
Was that possible?

Somewhere,
Gan hadn't been told where,
the real King Xau was at risk,
traveling in secret,
traveling to war.

King Xau had been only a boy
when Gan had first guarded him
in truth not pretense,
a raw, puny, earnest boy
who'd treated Gan
as an equal, as a friend.

The king's safety now dependent
on Gan and an idiot
too lazy to saddle a horse.

FIRST LESSON

Scene: Prince Keng sitting on a rock.
The dragon enters, flying down.

DRAGON
Good morning, Princeling. Have you come to
admire my magnificence?

KENG
My father sent me. He said you would teach me
to be king.

DRAGON
Your father? Your father is your greatest
threat aside from me.

The dragon menaces the boy, who holds his place.

DRAGON
Good. You're brave. You'll make a fine king.
Now go away.

KENG
That's all? Don't you have advice for me?
I thought....

DRAGON
An excellent habit for a king, thinking.
You should try it more often.

KENG
[Kneeling] Please. Teach me what a king
should know.

DRAGON
A king should know that he cannot know
all he should know. Men's lives are
too short.

KENG
Then teach me what I most need to know.

DRAGON
I tried to do so. Perhaps you weren't
paying attention.

KENG
You said men's lives are short. That my
father is my greatest threat—why? Why is
he a threat?

DRAGON
Because men will measure you against him,
and find you lacking. No matter how hard
you try, his reputation will outmatch you
as the tiger outmatches the rabbit.

KENG
That would be true of anybody you chose as
king. No one can equal him.

DRAGON
No one? As for you, if you ever take the
throne, I advise you to begin badly.
Quickly quash people's hopes. Then any

mistakes you make will be no more than they expect, and any successes will appear the greater.

KENG
No.

DRAGON
No?

KENG
If I am king, I will do the best I can. From the beginning.

DRAGON
Good.

KENG
But you just said I should begin badly—

DRAGON
Indeed. And I may argue the merits of that at a later date. What pleased me is that you didn't blindly agree. However wise his advisors, a king should weigh their words for himself. And so ends your first lesson. You may come back tomorrow.

Keng bows, turns to leave, turns back.

KENG
What would you have done if I'd left when you first told me to go?

DRAGON
Eaten you.

THE IMPERIAL WAR: SECOND BATTLE

On a cool clear morning
in a meadow moist with dew,
two armies faced each other.

Memnor, King of Ritany,
gray-haired and great-hearted,

sat astride his warhorse,
his army outnumbered three to one,
his foot soldiers ranked nervously
behind the remnants of his cavalry—

Three quarters of his cavalry
lost in the first battle,
shielding the retreat
of his foot soldiers—

Due to that defeat,
the enemy now eighty miles
inside Memnor's borders.
Memnor's plan, his one chance,
a gambit hinging
on his ally, King Xau.

Opposite Memnor,
the marshaled might
of Tahj's Imperial army.
Sunlight glinted from spear and javelin,
sword and shield and axe,
from Tahj's cavalry, thousands-strong,
their armor burnished bright.

(The Emperor Tahj himself far away,
a girl-child oiling his shoulders
as he gloated, spying the battlefield
via the beast's borrowed visions.)

Behind Memnor's main army,
six hundred townsmen and farmers,
untrained, unready,
armed with pitchforks and scythes
or swords they'd never used.

Tam, a silversmith,
gripped his grandfather's sword,
stared at death, at Tahj's soldiers.
Those same soldiers
had overrun Tam's town.
He thought of his wife,
her bloodied body.
Held his place.

Standing on Tam's left,
hooded, hidden like his guards

among the farmers and townsmen,
King Xau waited.

Trumpets blared.
Tahj's cavalry charged.

King Memnor shouted,
"Attack! With me! For Ritany!"
He charged with his cavalry—
drums, trumpets, a thunder of hooves—

King Xau's guards stepped close,
ringing him with their bodies.
Xau pushed his hood back,
stared at the oncoming horses—

Tahj's cavalry veered,
horses scattering, rearing,
galloping off into the tall grass
away from Memnor's men.
Tahj's riders swore, kicked their mounts,
the horses wild,
rearing and bucking,
throwing their riders one after another,
then trotting, slower, riderless,
behind Memnor's lines.
Where they stood. Quiet.
Watching Xau.

(In his distant palace, Tahj shouted,
knocked the girl-child aside—
"No! Xau!"—
it must be Xau—
but Xau couldn't be there—
Xau had been riding to Donal, to Innis—)

King Xau swayed,
leaned on Li, captain of his guards,
looked round at Tahj's horses.
There. Where he'd willed them.
Xau weary as if he'd ridden
three days without halt.
Yet he mounted with Li's help,
rode with his guards
into battle.

Drums. Trumpets.

Metal clashing metal.
Memnor's cavalry, aided by Xau,
were precise, deadly,
yet too few.
Rider after rider fell
to spear and arrow and axe.

Foot soldiers fought in fury
or despair or desperation,
fought as they bled,
fought over and round
other men who lay dying
in a stench of piss
and blood and horse-shit.

Shot in the neck,
King Memnor slumped in his saddle.
Woke to a surgeon
working the arrow from his neck,
the sound of men cheering.

The battle turned,
Tahj's army in retreat.

Not yet noon.

HOW THE BATTLE TURNED

"How?" asked Memnor.

King Xau said nothing,
stared at Memnor,
but didn't see him,
saw Atun's horse falling,
Atun falling underneath,
the horse rolling—

Xau took a breath.
Came back to the tent
where King Memnor lay,
his neck red-bandaged.
Havnar, Memnor's army commander,
sat on a stool by the bed,
holding Memnor's hand.

"Atun fell," said Xau.

"One of our guards."

No more words in him.

"Xau dismounted," said Havnar.
"Stood guard over Atun,
sword drawn
as if to fight off
Tahj's army single-handed.
And then the horses came,
Tahj's horses,
thundering toward us,
three thousand riderless horses."

Standing over Atun's body—
trying to see whether he was breathing—
blood running from Atun's ear
down into his braided hair—

"I remember Atun. From the flood."
Memnor's voice gentle. "He's dead then?"

Xau nodded.
A pause.
Memnor and Havnar both watching him.

After a time, Havnar said,
"Tahj's men broke. A rout."

"An inspired move," said Memnor,
"using Tahj's horses."

Xau took a breath, looked at him.
"We didn't plan it."

Didn't plan it,
didn't ask the horses to charge,
a charge that might have trampled
Memnor's soldiers as easily as Tahj's,
save that the horses had swerved
to avoid the men—
Had Xau willed that?—

He didn't remember—
only the horse rolling—
Atun underneath—

Xau took a breath.

Came back to the tent.
To what he had to do next.

"Excuse us." Xau bowed. Left the tent.

Atun had written to his sisters
twice a year.
They'd ridden to the city
for his letters,
paid someone to read them aloud.

Xau's turn to write,
to send a letter to accompany
Atun's sword, his silver armbands.

COLLABORATION

Orderly, disciplined, efficient,
the running of the Imperium.

People, property, livestock, land
tabulated, tracked, taxed.

The Emperor Tahj the public face
of a private partnership.

His power augmented by muttered rumors
of the beast behind his throne.

Any dissenters dispatched
to feed that beast's nefarious needs.

(Remains returned on request,
damage doubling as deterrent.)

Tahj's rule expedited and enforced
by the Imperial Envoys—

government ministers, officials,
army commanders, Tahj's bodyguards—

bound to the beast's thoughts,
yet acting on their own.

One hundred and fourteen men.
No women. Complicit, corrupt.

JOURNAL

Survived.
When the horses charged
I thought they'd kill me.

Earlier, I lost my spear,
stuck it in a horse's flank,
horse ran off
and I nearly trod on a man
with a spear through his belly.
Took him for dead,
yanked the spear out and he fucking yelled.
Something I couldn't understand.
A curse?
Asking for water?

Darien's dead.

New orders from His Imperial Envoy:
we're not to talk about who's dead, how many.
He's as fucking scared
as the rest of us. I saw him run.
Mislaid his pretty-boy in the retreat.
Good.
The boy was younger than Cas.
Never spoke.

Thought about Cas
when I was running from the horses.
How we'd climb the olive trees
and our maid would scream at us.

Thought battle would be easier,
second time round. Wrong.

The fucking horses charging.
That fucking man, looking right at me,
yelling,
bowels hanging out of him
like a giant worm.

GUL

Left behind by Tahj's retreating army:

tents, blankets, pots;
sacks of wheat, rice, barley;
wood, waterskins, their wounded;
Gul, a boy of ten, bound by the beast.

Gul surfaced,
the monster claiming his limbs,
sitting him upright.
Men. Soldiers. Unfamiliar.
His mouth held shut by the monster,
his eyes moving where the monster chose.
Faces, armor, muddied boots.
Gul retreated, went inward
to summer, nighttime,
lying on the flat roof with his mother,
a waxing moon, warm wind,
the smell of the date palms,
his mother telling him a story
about a three-legged guard dog.

Shouts, men's shouts,
startled Gul from his mother
into the triple grip
of rope, men, the monster's yoke.
Gul's gaze fixed by the monster
on a man who reached
for his forehead,
the man's hand scarred as if burnt—

burnt—
the red-hot brand.
The monster's malice flayed Gul,
conjured a memory of its lair,
his mother with a branding iron,
mouth open, screaming,
as she set the brand
to Gul's stomach.

Interrupted. The lair,
his mother's screams faded,
the monster's attention shifted.
Gul surfaced, saw the man,
the man with the scarred hand—

hand—
the Envoy's hand.

The monster conjured
the Imperial Envoy's tent,
the pallet where Gul lay
pinned in place by the monster,
the Envoy's hand squeezing his balls,
the monster forcing
Gul's mouth open.

Interrupted.
Something, someone, interceded
between Gul and the monster,
holding back hurt.
A tenderness, a gentleness,
certain as daybreak,
sure as an anchor,
calling Gul home.

Sore, thirsty.
The monster gone. *Gone.*

Gul blinked, saw the man,
his scarred hand lifting away,
saw the man trembling, gasping,
saw him double over and vomit.
The man who had saved him.

PYRE

Smoke rose toward the stars
as all who could stand—
veteran or king or raw recruit,
cook or whore or smith—
each took their turn
to beat the drums.

Heaped one atop another,
the battle dead mixed up
with legs and arms fresh
from the surgeons' saws.

TENTH LESSON

"Now sing."
The dragon's head tilted sideways,
one golden eye fixed on Prince Keng

as he wobbled precariously on a rock,
left leg lifted high.

"Sing?!" Keng stared at the dragon.
"What's today's topic?"

"Marriage and sex."

Keng tumbled over.

The dragon laughed,
a sound like an anvil dropped on granite.
"Sit down, princeling.
Balancing wasn't part of the lesson.
It just amused me.
Now, marriage and sex.
Marriage is the third means
to manipulate foreign relations.
And sex is something you should seek soon."

Keng gaped at her like a fish.

The dragon burped, her breath ash.
"Were you to become king tomorrow,
I'd recommend postponing marriage
while other countries compete
for your favor.
Being young,
you're unlikely to postpone sex.
Have you had sex?"

Keng flushed. "Not exactly."

"Not exactly—Hah!"
She laughed again,
a booming that went on and on and on.
"Well, when having sex with *other* people,
don't let them gain power over you.
To that end, I advise multiple partners.
Preferably men, to prevent pregnancies.
Do you like men?"

"Not... that way."
Keng's cheeks on fire.
He wasn't looking forward
to the rest of the lesson.

BETWEEN BATTLES

A gentle waking,
the patter of rain on the tent,
six of his guards asleep
around him in the darkness,
King Xau's thoughts rising
from a dream of Shazia,
his first wife.

One quiet moment
holding Shazia's memory
before Xau sat up,
before Feng, standing guard,
signed that it was almost dawn.

Xau washed, dressed,
chewed a stick of dried meat,
settled with Li, captain of his guards,
that each guard, Li included,
would get three hours' rest during the day,
all of them tired, grieving.

Out into the rain,
sentries bowing to him
as he walked to the pastureland
beyond the camp,
the horses dark shapes
against the dark wet grass.

(An effort to push back
the thought of Atun,
Atun, whom Xau would have placed
in charge of the horses.)

One of the warhorses,
a huge black gelding,
trotted over to Xau, nickering,
stood by him, head lowered,
while the other horses approached,
not too close, leaving Xau space,
watching him, patient, trusting.
Xau sent for the chief farrier
and the horse-doctor,
reviewed the condition of the horses.

From the pasture over to the barns
where he checked on horse tack,
horse armor, sacks of feed.

Two hours past dawn,
still raining,
when Xau joined Havnar—
Memnor's army commander—
to hear reports from the scouts
who'd returned overnight:
Tahj's army retreated to a ridgeline
thirty miles to the west.

On to King Memnor's tent,
Memnor wounded, bedridden,
more cautious than Xau
had ever known him,
as if each day in bed
sapped more of his courage.
Havnar anxious to advance,
to attack along the ridgeline.
Memnor hesitant, unsure.

Xau stared at a map
without seeing it,
saw Atun's horse falling,
Atun falling underneath,
the horse rolling—

Xau took a breath,
brought his attention
back to Memnor, to Havnar,
considered the scouts' reports,
the mood of both armies.
Memnor's men outnumbered,
yet buoyed by victory;
Tahj's men unsettled.

Not Xau's country, not Xau's army,
but he added his weight to Havnar,
thinking what might happen
if enemy reinforcements arrived,
if enemy morale improved.

From Memnor to the surgeons' tents,
the soldiers used to his visits by now,

their jokes bawdier, their stories wilder
each time Xau came.
He spent longer than he had to spare
with a boy of seventeen
who panted for breath
as he asked about the food in Meqing,
a rotten fetid smell coming
from his bandaged chest.
Xau sat on the ground by the boy,
told him about chopsticks
and rice gruel and dumplings,
sesame balls and ginger duck.

Outside the surgeons' tents
the rain had finally slowed.
Xau drilled with five hundred farmers,
few of whom had ever handled a sword,
but who were quick with axe and scythe,
Havnar too short of men
to refuse volunteers.

An hour's planning
with Havnar and his officers;
then three hours practicing maneuvers
with the remnants of Memnor's cavalry,
dusk darkening to night
before they finished.

A report from another scout;
a late supper with Memnor;
then out to the pasture again,
the horses coming to him,
crescent moon hung in a clear sky;
then an hour in his own tent,
letting his guards fuss over him
while he wrote to Artoch,
Donal, Subetei, Hana.

Xau too restless to sleep.
Back to the surgeons' tents.
A gap where the boy
who'd asked about food had been,
a gap that halted Xau.

The boy. Atun.
New griefs layered
over old ones.

He took a breath.
Went over to the men
who were still awake,
listened to their wild stories.

WHEN KING XAU WAS GONE

Hana did not rend her hair,
nor neglect her duties,
nor number the days of his absence.

She did not listen to ballads
lauding his fabled deeds,
nor pause pensively by his portrait.

She did not picture him in battle,
heroic, valiant, leading his men,
his horse charging, his flesh torn—

Rather she imagined him
lounging in his tent, unshaven,
his hair greasy, his clothes grubby.

She took his daughters hunting,
taught them to fletch an arrow,
to shoot and skin a deer.

But at night,
heedless of the guard watching over her,
she laid Xau's letters on her pillow,
her hair on the brushstrokes
his hand had made.

TAUNTING FATE

Not yet full dark,
the lamps lit, brimful of oil,
a butter-yellow rug on the tent floor.

King Donal bent
over a blank breadth of paper,
barren of words, cup of wine untouched.

Rose, his woman,
patient, playing both sides
of a board game, humming to herself.

Humming to herself
as if they were safe home,
as if no enemy had breached their border.

Donal looked up,
long enough to let her see
how she pleased him. Seventeen years.

Never his queen,
never the only one he bedded,
but the one he'd befriended, his Rose.

Donal turned back
to the paper's bare breadth,
Xau, his ally, at the far battlefront.

Xau, wrote Donal.
Hundreds of miles between them.
Xau might be days dead before Donal heard.

Writing to Xau
taunted fate, presumed.
Failing to write a worse omen.

Fucking fish stew
with fucking parsnips. Again.
Tahj's forces have crossed the Muir river.

Donal filled the page,
began another, as if his words
could slow an arrow or carry Xau home.

THE IMPERIAL WAR:

THIRD BATTLE

An afternoon in late spring,
the valley sun-warmed,
cooler up on the ridgeline
where men fought, back and forth,
to the beat of drums
and the calls of carrion birds.

King Memnor's men outnumbered
but gaining ground,
the foot soldiers supported
by the remnants of Memnor's cavalry,

the horses turning and wheeling
over the rough terrain
in faultless form,
arrows speeding in glinting arcs,
the horses following the will
of one man, Memnor's ally, King Xau,
who rode at the front, lightly armored,
with seven men who guarded him,
closer than brothers.

Yard by slow yard,
the enemy soldiers gave way.

Xau's guard Wen Xun
swayed in his saddle,
bow slipping from his hand,
blood coursing from his opened arm—

Xau alongside Wen Xun,
Li on the far side,
the other guards ringed round them—

The horses in perfect step
as they held Wen Xun upright,
rode him to safety,
set him down,
galloped to rejoin the cavalry—

Further, faster,
the enemy soldiers gave way,
came to a crease in the ridge
where the land dipped behind them.
Braced there. A body of men brandishing
spear and pike and axe and javelin.
A curious many-throated wail
rose from the crease below.
Movement, men carrying forward: what?
Wooden shields? Sections of fence?
Taller than a man—

The pieces of wood pivoted.
Tied one to each section,
naked women,
breasts hacked off,
red ribboning down—

Memnor's men blundered to a stop.

Retched or screamed or looked away.
Havnar, commander of Memnor's army,
yelled at them to advance,
advanced himself,
but few went with him—

Enemy archers shot through gaps
between the wooden sections,
between the wailing women.
One volley, then another—

Twenty of Memnor's men downed—

King Xau and his guards
and the remnants of Memnor's cavalry
rode through that hail of arrows,
horses and men hit,
an arrow wedged in Xau's forearm,
another in his calf—

Xau and his guards dismounted,
ran to the nearest women,
cut the ropes,
hoisted the women onto their horses,
Memnor's cavalrymen following
their example.

In the time it took
to free the women,
one hundred and seventeen
of Memnor's riders killed or disabled,
forty-three horses dead.

*

Sunset.
Cold up on the ridgeline
where men had fought that afternoon.

No victory, a standoff,
both armies withdrawn,
carrion birds scouring the ground.

DOUBLE DUTY

Leong entered King Xau's tent. Bowed.
The king lifted his head

from where he lay on a blanket,
said only, "Leong,"
dropped his head back.

"How is he?" demanded Captain Li
before Leong, who served double duty
as both guard and field surgeon,
had laid one finger on the king.

"Exhausted. In pain."
No need to examine Xau
to know that much.
The king drove himself too hard,
had taken Atun's death badly,
had been struck by two arrows
in yesterday's battle.

The other guards watched
like suspicious old women
as Leong took Xau's twelve pulses,
unbandaged his leg,
probed the calf wound,
noted how Xau's breath hitched—
that arrow had been lodged in bone—
a protracted, difficult extraction.

"How is he?" asked Li. Again.

"His strength is spent. He needs rest."
Leong looked at the others.
"All of you should rest
except Li and Shuen,
who are fine—"

"My toe is broken!" said Shuen.

"A simple closed fracture—"

"It hurts! Every time I stand!"

Wen Xun, assigned to the king's cot
because he'd hemorrhaged heavily
after an arrow tore through his arm,
said, "You grumbled more than Shuen
when you had toothache, Leong."

"That tooth was abscessed,

my restraint remarkable."
Leong finished bandaging Xau.

"Thank you, Leong."
Xau started to sit up,
but Leong laid a hand on his chest,
said gently, "Rest."

Moved over to examine Wen Xun.

INSIDE THE TENT

Seven men in King Xau's tent
on the morning after the battle,
the king and five of his guards
injured, resting, the king mostly quiet,
lying on a blanket on the ground
while his guards chatted.

The seventh man, Li,
captain of King Xau's guards,
checked bowstrings, oiled swords,
cleaned armor, his thoughts jumping
from one difficulty to another.
That Xau was hurt.
That Li had only himself
and two other guards
well enough to stand watch outside.
That one of those two, Leong,
was busy in the surgeons' tents—

Footsteps approached.
Li on his feet between Xau
and the tent's entrance
when Shuen announced Havnar,
the commander of King Memnor's army.

Xau pushed himself to a sitting position.
Li didn't speak Ritan,
didn't understand what the two men said,
heard Havnar's urgency,
the careful evenness of Xau's voice,
the king in pain, measuring out his words.

Havnar left.
Li went to Xau:
"What did Havnar want?"

"Our help. Tahj's army is breaking camp.
Three nearby towns they might take."
Xau lay back down, his breathing ragged.

Li said quietly, "You cannot fight.
You cannot even sit a horse.
You can barely sit."

Xau half-smiled.
"It's all right, Li.
We promise to stay here.
In the tent."

Li stared,
touched Xau's forehead (unfevered),
Xau's compliance more alarming
than if the king had stood up
and attempted to put on his armor.
"Do you feel worse? Should I call Leong?"

"No. We are not dying."
Xau shifted where he lay,
reaching to clutch at his leg.
"We have an idea.
We will try to call Tahj's horses to us."

"Tahj's horses?" asked Wen Xun.
"You took his horses already,
three thousand horses—
are there reinforcements?"

"Not his warhorses. The others.
Packhorses. Cart horses.
Mules. If they will come."

*

Li sat cross-legged on the ground,
watching over the king,
the king's eyes shut.

The other guards quiet, still.
The rough catch of the king's breath
the only sound from within the tent.
Outside, a barrel rolled over stones,
one man laughed, another swore.

Twice Xau opened his eyes,

an easing in his face
when he saw Li beside him.

Li sat, silent.
A long road to this tent,
Li's father a fisherman.
From boats and nets and bait
and the run of the water
to sword and bow and shield,
the capital, the palace,
this man.

The king shivered, looked for Li again.
Li wrapped a blanket round him,
laid a hand on the king's arm.
Sat.

Outside,
in the sunlit day,
a sudden clamor, men shouting,
running, cheering, horses neighing.
Tahj's horses had come.

Later, Li would hear the story:
how the horses turned about
in their tracks;
how they headed for Xau
laden with panniers, dragging carts;
how aging draft horses galloped like foals
in their eagerness;
how Tahj's officers ordered the horses killed;
how the archers shot in fear of Tahj,
yet also in defiance;
shot too high, or too low,
or to left or right,
swore after that they had tried their best—

That came later.

In the tent,
Xau looked at Li,
tried to sit up, could not,
said, "We would see the horses."

Li lifted him in his arms
and carried him out
into the day.

QUIET

A rush of whispers then a rare hush
in the surgeons' tent.

Leong's grasp of Ritan
insufficient to decipher the whispers.
His puzzlement must have showed,
because his patient touched his arm,
pointed to the neighboring tent,
whispered: "Xau."

Leong ran—

Five heartbeats to reach the other tent.
Five heartbeats in which he pictured
the king poisoned, burnt,
impaled by pikes—

Inside:
King Xau sprawled supine,
eyes shut.

Li, captain of Xau's guards,
stopped Leong's onrush with one hand,
signed *asleep* with the other.

Two heartbeats to shift from relief
clear through to anger—
Leong had ordered Xau to rest—
the king wounded, worn out—
in no condition to pay courtesy calls
on the injured—

Slowly, the tent's quiet penetrated.

In silence,
a surgeon sutured a silent patient.
No other movement.
From ten-year veterans to beardless boys,
scarred, fevered, no matter,
a softness, a tenderness
as they watched the king,
all of them holding quiet
so that Xau might sleep.

SEVENTEENTH LESSON

Sunlight scattered like fire
from the dragon's wings
as she landed beside Prince Keng
in a rush of air and smoke,
snow melting beneath her belly,
beneath her clawed feet.

Keng bowed to her,
willed his face calm.
Two and a half weeks of lessons—
he should be used to her—
shouldn't keep thinking
she was about to eat him—

She grinned at him,
baring teeth long as daggers,
her breath ash, her eyes gold.
"Good morning, Princeling.
Today we will discuss
your father's failings."

Indignation braced Keng:
"A short lesson then.
My father is brave, honest,
honorable, always puts
the kingdom before himself,
always does what's right."

She snorted. "For a start,
excessive honesty is a failing
not a strength in a ruler.
Better to break your word
than lose your kingdom.
Name two more of Xau's flaws."

"If you fault him
for being honest,
then maybe you also fault him
for being weaker than you—
though that's unfair—
he's a great warrior."

"Perhaps not great,
but certainly proficient,

a skill he acquired
through hard work
not natural aptitude.
Try again."

Keng sat down on a rock,
scuffed his boot in the snow,
thought about his father,
whom he had been trying
not to think about,
not to worry about.

He said, not looking at her,
remembering his father
taking him riding, "Sometimes,
when he's not meeting people,
he looks... ordinary,
not like a king."

"Good," said the dragon.
"A king's power derives
from people acknowledging
him as a king. Wiser not
to give them cause to doubt it.
Name one more failing."

Keng hesitated,
not wanting to say it,
as if to say it was a betrayal,
shouted it in the end:
"Hana! There was no advantage
to the kingdom from marrying Hana!"

"Not quite, but close.
Xau's mistake was in seeking
to marry Hana in the first place.
Once that mistake was made,
it would have been still worse
to back down to Vihaz."

The dragon turned aside,
flamed hugely, vaporizing snow.
"Difficulties Xau might have avoided
by separating sex from marriage.
Better to bed her than wed her,
whoring expected of a king."

"He loved her!"

"A weakness."
Darker gold in the dragon's eyes.
"Love, friendship, affection,
all three are weaknesses.
Yet she who lacks all three
is worthless."

The dragon's eyes nearly black now.
"No other human I have ever
liked so well as your father."
She stared at Keng,
laid her head flat on the snow.
"He is hurt, Princeling."

"Hurt?"

"For the past three days,
he has been in pain.
I cannot tell the cause."

A thickness in Keng's throat.
"If you knew—three days?
Why didn't you tell me?"

"I hoped he would recover.
He has not yet done so,
and you are very young.
You will need time
to prepare yourself, if he dies,
if I name you king."

Keng shook his head,
as if that would push
her words away.
"I don't want to be king."

"Nor did he."

The lesson forgotten.
Both of them silent.

THE IMPERIAL WAR:

FOURTH BATTLE

A spring storm threatened,
the wind rising, moist, ominous
as the combined armies of Innis and Meqing
met the massed might of the Imperium.

The wind bent the grasses,
flattened the spring flowers,
flapped the bright silk banners.

The Emperor Tahj,
expecting the Horse King, Xau,
had sent no cavalry,
his fifty thousand soldiers
braced in broad ranks
behind a shield wall.
In front of the soldiers,
an angled line of iron-tipped stakes
anchored in earth.

Opposing them,
sixteen thousand foot soldiers,
seven thousand mounted horse lords,
plus six thousand of Xau's own cavalry,
but Xau himself
nine hundred miles away
on the war's far battlefront,
the army commanded instead
by Xau's ally, King Donal.

(The Emperor Tahj himself also far away,
sprawled at his ease in his palace,
spying the field of battle
via the beast's borrowed visions.)

King Donal raised his sword,
yelled "For Xau!"
charged at the forefront
of the cavalry.

The Imperial pikemen braced
behind their double bulwark
of shield wall and stakes;
the Imperial archers shot.

Riders and horses fell.
The cavalry wavered—

The Imperial archers shot again,
King Donal and the cavalry
neared the line of iron-tipped stakes,
faltered under a volley of arrows.
The horses balked—

Again, the Imperial archers shot,
and the cavalry scattered,
a chaotic mass of mounted men
turning, falling back—

(In his distant palace, Tahj smirked,
used the beast to relay his orders:
Tahj's soldiers to rush
the retreating riders,
complete the rout.)

Tahj's soldiers uprooted
the line of stakes,
sprinted forward with pike and spear—

The cavalry slowed,
halted their false retreat,
reformed in front of Donal's infantry,
Xau's six thousand cavalry
head-on to Tahj's forces
while the horse lords
wheeled to either side,
fell on the enemy's open flanks.

An early harvest reaped then,
heaped raw and red
on the grass,
the spring flowers.

Subetei, Khan of the Horse Lords,
shot eight men with his bow,
killed fourteen more up close,
his sword running red.

Few warriors then or since
to equal the horse lords in their wrath
as they honored their oath
to the Horse King.

King Donal one of those few,
cleaving men in two with his longsword Raid
as he fought for the man he'd once fought,
the man he now held as dear
as the brother he'd lost,
Xau whom Tahj had thrice tried
to assassinate.

Tahj would have spent his soldiers
down to the last man,
but the beast,
seven of his nine minion commanders
dead or dying,
called a late retreat.

When the rain broke
and washed the ground clean,
half Tahj's army had been slaughtered.

CONVERGENCE

The war halted.

Tahj's Imperial Army withdrew
from Innis, Meqing, Ritany.
Three separate delegations headed
toward a mountain border fort
for peace negotiations.

Donal, the Red King,
and Subetei, Khan of the Horse Lords,
rode from the Innish camp,
triumphant in battle:
bold, brash, brave, both unhurt,
both bringing a woman with them,
eight soldiers apiece,
no servants.

Memnor, King of Ritany,
gray-haired and great-hearted,
and Xau, the Horse King,
rode from the Ritan camp,
both men troubled, both men weary,
neither yet recovered
from their wounds:
rode with two translators,

Memnor's surgeon, Memnor's army commander,
a dozen of Memnor's cavalry,
seven of Xau's nine guards.

(One of Xau's guards killed in battle,
another—arrow wound festering—
too sick to sit a horse.)

From the perfumed halls
of the Imperial Palace
where he'd waged war remotely,
the Emperor Tahj emerged
with a retinue of over a hundred:
attendants, aides, advisors, lackeys,
cooks, scribes, scouts, officers,
grooms, guards, tailors, translators,
three junior wives.

As spring warmed to summer,
the three contingents
converged.

JUDGMENT

King Xau rode,
wounded, worn out, harrowed,
from war toward peace negotiations,
rode with his ally King Memnor,
likewise wounded, weary,
the two kings managing
thirty or forty miles
before their surgeons ordered
a halt for the day.

Swifter by far,
riding to intercept Xau,
rode Hana, his queen.
Rode from dawn to dusk,
a hundred and ten miles a day,
changing mounts at every way-fort,
her guards struggling
to match her endurance.
Rode armed with bow and knife
and the knowledge
that Xau would prize
each hour she gained with him.

Later,
no historian would note Hana's ride,
judging it incidental,
inconsequential.

Xau,
seeing the riders' rapid approach,
not allowing himself
to believe Hana had come
until he could make out her features—
his heart speeding
as he sped his horse toward her—
dismounting awkwardly,
leg stabbing with pain, unsteady,
holding onto his horse one-handed,
reaching for her with the other—
judged differently.

ENOUGH

After King Xau reached the fort,
after he'd spoken to Subetei Khan
and to the fort's commander
and to the stablemaster,
then, in the fort's inmost courtyard,
one hour alone with King Donal.

Or almost alone:
two of Xau's guards stood watch
and a vulture circled high overhead,
likely a spy for the beast.

Donal, blunt, asked,
"Is that limp permanent?"

"Too soon to say."
Xau continued his slow progress
around the courtyard,
leaning on a stick.

"Can you ride normally?"

Xau nodded;
it hurt, but he could ride.

"Good," said Donal.
"I heard you thwarted Tahj

even when you were lying
half-dead in your tent,
but it's easier to fight
from horseback."

"I heard," said Xau,
"that you impressed Subetei."

"He impressed me.
He's ferocious in battle,
almost unstoppable."

Working his way round the yard,
Xau said, "Thank you,
for taking the northern command,
for defeating Tahj's forces."

Donal said nothing,
only touched his hand to his heart,
offered it palm-up to Xau
in the old sign of allegiance.

Across the courtyard,
the guards were changing shift.
Xau limped over,
thanked them,
limped back to Donal,
who started in on a tall tale
of how he'd tried to outdrink Subetei,
woken up with a hangover
and his hair braided
like a horse warrior's.

Xau caught himself laughing,
and, doing so, realized
he hadn't laughed properly
in—how long?—
before Atun died.

"You all right?" asked Donal.

Xau took a breath. "Near enough."

Donal here, Hana close by,
Tahj still two days away.
Near enough.

PEACE TERMS

No sunlight penetrated
the stark, cold, windowless room
deep inside the mountain border fort.

Two small tables,
scribes seated at each table.
Lamps high on the stone walls.
Lining the walls, armored, armed,
half the fort's soldiers.

The Imperial delegation
at one end of the room,
Emperor Tahj in embroidered golden silks;
on Tahj's head: a golden winged crown
set with diamonds and rubies;
on Tahj's face: fury—
the captain of King Xau's guards
had taken Tahj's sword, his jeweled dagger,
searched every inch of him
before allowing him entrance.

King Xau and his allies
at the other end of the room,
Subetei Khan and King Donal
standing in full battle gear,
Donal's hand on the hilt
of his longsword;
King Xau and King Memnor seated,
Memnor robed in blue, sapphires on his crown,
Xau in black, his crown silver.

An elderly eunuch proclaimed Tahj's titles,
a prolonged procedure protracted
by its triple-translation
into Meqingese, Ritan, Innish.

Honorifics dealt with, the eunuch went on,
"His Imperial Majesty is willing,
in his most merciful munificence,
to withdraw his request for tribute
just as he has magnanimously
withdrawn his armies—"

Donal swore in Innish,

a remark that went untranslated.

"—Furthermore, His Imperial Majesty
will grant independent jurisdiction
to Meqing, Innis, and Ritany
subject to the following conditions:
firstly, your acknowledgement
of His Imperial Majesty's supremacy;
secondly, that you reduce
the size of your combined armies
to three thousand soldiers;
thirdly, that you accept
His Imperial Majesty's invitation
to host your eldest sons
at the Imperial Palace."

Memnor looked not to Tahj
but to Xau, said,
"I yield to King Xau.
I will abide by his decision."

Xau bowed his head to Memnor.

Subetei, Khan of the Horse Lords, said,
"Xau is my khan, my king, my brother.
I will do as he asks."

Again, Xau bowed his head,
this time to Subetei.

Donal unbuckled his longsword,
went to one knee beside Xau,
offered his sword to Xau.
"My sword, my blood, my men
at your command. Now and always."

Xau set his hand under Donal's arm,
held his gaze, raised him up.

Xau looked at Tahj, said,
no trace of anger in his voice,
only a gentleness,
"If you are bound by the beast,
if you will let us help you,
we would try to release you."

Tahj shivered.

An odd look, nearer despair than dislike,
passed over his face
before it hardened again.
"What do you take me for? A fool?!
Don't try your tricks on me—
Do you accept my terms or not?"

Xau took a breath,
let go what hope he'd held
that this would end well.

He knew what he must do now,
yet the doing of it hard.
To spend more lives
in the effort to end a distant evil
with what small chance of success?

Many already dead.
Atun, the horse rolling—

In pain, in grief,
masking both,
Xau said,
"We reject your terms.
These are ours.
You will kill the beast.
You will abdicate your throne."

"Never." Tahj spat on the floor.
"These talks are over.
Will you keep your word
and allow us safe departure?"

Xau nodded.
He sat, silent,
as Tahj and his entourage left,
followed by the remaining scribes
and translators and soldiers,
then Subetei and Memnor
and, last, Donal.

Only his guards with him
as Xau stayed on in the cold room,
shouldering the weight
of all that would follow.

PARTING

Hana fell asleep in Xau's embrace,
her head on his bare chest,
amid the mingled smells
of soap, ointment, Xau himself.

Woke in the hour after dawn
to find him still holding her,
that quiet tenderness
before he left for war.

SUPPLEMENTAL EXTRACTS
FROM THE RECOLLECTIONS OF ARTOCH, SENIOR ADVISOR TO KING XAU

The decision to invade Sumbral?
Which aspect? Tactical? Political?

My private reaction?
I worried about King Xau,
worried whether he could tolerate
the rigors of a war campaign.

The field surgeon's reports as revealing
as Xau's own correspondence was evasive:
the second arrow had been wedged in bone,
its extraction challenging,
the king still in pain a month later,
unlikely he would ever walk without a limp.

Had I known Xau's full plans,
I would have worried far more.

No, I did not attend
the peace negotiations.
I was seventy-five years old,
an age at which you, too,
may find travel an imposition.
Furthermore, King Xau had vested
civil authority in me.
In essence, I remained in Lipoh
to head the government.

Returning to the invasion,

it was apparent from the outset
that even if the Imperial capital fell,
even if Tahj himself were killed,
we could not hold Sumbral
without popular consent.

Such consent not unthinkable.

Tahj ruled through fear rather than acclaim,
whereas King Xau's reputation
had acquired near-mythic proportions
in Sumbral despite Tahj's efforts.
The tale of King Xau returning the ashes
of his would-be assassins
to their fathers
was eclipsed only by the tale
of how he rode into fire
to save Prince Cyrus's men—

Cyrus's men.
We didn't find out until much later.
Forty men—
Xau would have, the king would have,
would have....

    [Archivist's note: Tahj had tortured
    to death forty of Cyrus's soldiers
    for refusing to denounce King Xau.
    Recalling this, Artoch became confused.
    I came back the following day.]

The decision to invade Sumbral?

Indeed. It took five weeks
from the failure of the negotiations
to assemble the combined armies
of Meqing, Innis, and Ritany
near the Sumbrese border.

On the thirty-fifth day,
the army advanced into Sumbral.

MARCH

Break camp, march, make camp,
eat, sleep, break camp, march.

The baggage wagons rolled,
the foot soldiers marched,
King Donal and King Memnor
rode with their cavalry,
Subetei and his horse warriors
scouted the countryside.

King Xau went on foot
as much as he could,
working to strengthen his leg,
the soldiers around him
laden with packs and weapons,
Xau limping along with a stick.

After three weeks
Xau could walk an hour,
ride an hour, walk another hour,
alternating until the army
halted for the night.

Gradually the foot soldiers
relaxed from respectful diffidence
to open fondness,
offered him hoarded treats
of honey, nuts, dried fruit;
shared every wholesome joke they knew
and a few obscene ones.

High overhead,
higher than any arrow's flight,
tracking their progress: vultures,
the prying eyes of the enemy,
the birds bound by the beast.

Break camp, march, make camp,
eat, sleep, break camp,
march the river road
to the Imperial capital.

(Not the shortest route,
but the easiest for resupply,
the army seizing each riverside stronghold,
little skirmishing beyond that.)

By day, Xau's mood
boosted by the soldiers,
by Donal, by his guards.

Harder at camp.
Xau stared at maps
that yielded no answers,
or walked the wooden circuit
of the camp's palisade.

He slept poorly,
troubled by his leg,
by doubts he did not share,
would wake before light
into a dimness brimmed with memory,
the old shadows and the new,
Atun, Dao, Shazia,
back and back to Tsung,
to Khyert, to his brothers.

Still dark when Xau
went out among the horses,
the smell, heat, breath of them.
His guards stayed by his side
as the horses came up to him,
two or three at a time,
inhaling his scent,
heads lowering at his touch.
That wordless communion.

Then in the half-light
he trained with the guards,
Li solicitous, patient, teaching him
how a lame man could fight.

Break camp, march, make camp,
eat, sleep, break camp, march.

WORDS

Not a new sword,
nor armor, nor a horse;
not jade or silver,
nor any of the gifts
a prince might expect
from his father
on his sixteenth birthday.

Instead a letter.
Eleven pages.

No mention of the war.
Stories, often humorous,
of Keng's childhood.
Memories of the uncle
Keng was named after.

The final brushstrokes
faltered, uneven,
shaping words
Keng hadn't needed to be told,
that he already knew,
that he read and re-read
each night by lantern-light.

LAIR

Dusk. King Xau's tent.
The lamps lit.
A map spread out on the ground.

"How?! You don't know where it is—"

"We know roughly."

"Not fucking good enough."
King Donal stared down at the map:
the desert's yellow expanse,
the ring of black beads laid on top
that might—or might not—enclose,
somewhere within it, the beast's lair.
"It could take fucking weeks to find it."

"We will have Subetei's scouts with us."
Xau's voice quiet, even,
the king sitting on a stool,
one hand pressed to his left leg,
the way he did when it was hurting him.

"Even if you find it, what then?
You overpower the beast in its stronghold
with, what, forty scouts,
plus your seven guards?"

"We think its lair is lightly defended—"

"You *think*?!"

"Based on reports from those we freed,"
Xau said, quietly, evenly. "Most likely,
the beast only trusts its minions,
most likely there is a limit
to how many it can control."

"Fuck!" Donal thumped the map,
scattering black beads everywhere.
"You could die. Playing hero.
Send someone else.
Send Subetei.
Send me."

"And if the beast captures you? Subverts you?"
That same quietness as Xau looked at him.

"Worse if it captures you—"
Donal stopped. Thought it through.
If Xau were captured, he might resist the beast,
just as he'd once resisted the demon,
as he'd freed men, women, children
from the beast's bondage.

Xau might merely die,
not be turned into the beast's tool.

"Fuck."
Donal weighed Xau's plan again.
No chance of taking the beast by surprise:
the vultures—its prying spies—
always overhead, watching.
"The beast will know you're coming,
will move in more soldiers."

"We should reach the area
before any infantry reinforcements.
We will try to divert any horses."

"And if you can't divert the horses?
Or you guessed wrong,
and the beast has a thousand guards?"

Xau took a breath, said, quietly, evenly,
"This war, this evil will not end
unless the beast is killed.
It is worth the risk."

Donal grasped for denial,

for counterarguments, objections,
anything to dissuade Xau.
Failed.

He looked down at the map,
the scattered beads, the desert.
"At least take more men.
A hundred horse warriors,
not forty."

"Very well."

A silence then,
both men staring at each other.
Xau reached for Donal's arm,
gripped it briefly.
"Eat with us. Please."

They ate in the tent with Xau's guards.
Spoke of small things.

In the morning,
Xau rode for the beast's lair.

PERSPECTIVE

From high overhead,
higher than any arrow's flight,
vultures surveyed King Xau
and his guards and the horse warriors
as they rode for the desert.

The beast,
deep in his desert lair,
spied through the vultures' eyes,
men and horses clear but tiny:
miniature figures inching
across the landscape,
one hundred and eight men
with four horses apiece.

Three times the beast dispatched
squadrons of his cavalry
to kill them.

Three times the beast witnessed
his soldiers thrown from their horses,

watched the traitorous horses gallop
to his enemy,
saw the miniature figure
of the enemy king sway, unsteady,
on his horse.

Three times,
and after the third time
the small figure of the king
could not sit his horse
without one of his guards
riding double behind him
for the rest of the day,
and this the beast noted carefully.

The beast brooded then:
eight hundred of his cavalry left,
should he send them against Xau now,
perhaps disable the king?
Or order them into the desert
to garrison his lair?

In his agitation,
the beast used up half his toys
(men, women, children)
their torment balm to his doubts.

Only sixty soldiers at his lair—
trusted deputies,
double-bound both by his power
and their own dark inclinations—
sixty soldiers too few
to defeat Xau's horse warriors.

Thus the beast sent his cavalry
speeding toward his lair,
watched from the birds' high view
as the tiny figures of his enemies
advanced toward him.

DESERT

On the night of the half moon,
King Xau and his guards
and the horse warriors
reached the desert's edge.

Not the desert's sandy heart
but a stark plateau
of pebble and rock and stone
and stunted prickled plants.

They rode through the night,
startled small creatures—
lizard, snake, scorpion, beetle—
rode on into the dawning day.

Rode until the air scorched them,
retreated beneath white awnings,
sharing their shelter
with their horses.

For three days they rode
by night, by dawn, by dusk,
rode beneath a breadth of sky
that stretched unbroken.

The king sent his will
ahead of him as he rode,
reaching for the enemy's horses,
entreating them to leave the desert.

Rode without knowing
whether the horses heard him,
whether they heeded him,
whether they were even there.

On the fourth day, sand.
Ripples, waves, hills, mountains.
Sand in clothes, hair, nose,
mouth, eyes. Constant.

Day six, the spring on the map
dried up. Waterskins emptying.
Day seven, a second dry spring.
Waterskins empty.

On the eighth day,
a lake rimmed by date palms.
Every horse, every man
shoulder-deep in water.

WATER

"Better than getting drunk,"
said a horse warrior,
shoulder-deep in the lake,
a scarf draped over his head.

"Better than a horse race,"
said another, gulping water
from his cupped hands.

"Better than sleep,"
said a warrior who'd stood guard
last time they rested.

"Your turn," said Leong,
prodding King Xau,
who stood in the water
with the rest of them,
men and horses alike.

"Better than pickled cucumbers," said Xau.

"Pickled cucumbers?!" Leong snorted.
"That's the best you could come up with?
This water,
no doubt with an added infusion
of horse-piss,
is better than gold!"

"Better than a wrestling match,"
said a muscular horse warrior.

"Better than a woman," Leong sighed.

"Better than a man?"
asked the muscular horse warrior.
He submerged completely, stood,
water dripping from his braided hair,
eyeing Tai Seng, one of Xau's guards.

Tai Seng led him out of the water.

BESIEGED

The sun's first rays
glinted on the golden spires
of the Imperial Palace
where Tahj, Emperor Absolute,
stood on the highest balcony,
peering down upon his doom.

Beyond the city walls
burned the campfires
of Tahj's lesser enemies.
Donal. Memnor. Subetei.

Xau, chief of his foes, absent,
racing through the desert
to attack Tahj's ally,
but this siege Xau's doing:
Xau the Horse King,
Xau the Demon Slayer,
Xau the Undefeated.

Xau the Overrated, Xau the Doomed,
whispered the voice in his head,
Tahj's ally, the desert beast.

*Doomed? Do you think to stop him
with a mere sixty men?*
Tahj gulped,
tried to retract that thought,
to bury his bitterness
over the beast's failure—
its reinforcements in retreat,
the horses turned renegade
at Xau's behest.

Don't bother dissembling, the beast sneered.
*I don't need devotion, only obedience.
As for Xau, I will stop him
with four small, helpless children.*

The beast's laughter assaulted Tahj,
an avalanche of amusement.
Assured. Inhuman. Malevolent.
A laugh that shriveled Tahj's balls
as he looked down upon

his encircling enemies.

Too late to flee.
Too late to worry
that his ally was worse
than his enemy.

GAME

On their eleventh day in the desert,
near the beast's lair,
by a tiny spring-fed waterfall,
four children with daggers.

Li, captain of King Xau's guards,
held the king back by his arm,
certain it was a trap,
racing to work it out.

Four naked children,
three girls, one boy,
daggers held not to attack,
but point-first to their bellies.

Xau's guards grouped around him.
Behind them, the horse warriors,
half the men with their bows drawn.
The horses ranged behind the men.

"Greetings, King Xau,"
said the tallest girl,
maybe ten years old.
"Let's play a game together."

The girl laughed,
a hollow, malevolent sound:
the beast's laugh, not a child's.
"The children will come to you.

"One at a time. And you can try
to wrest them from my control.
If you don't play, the other children
will disembowel themselves. Ready?"

The girl set her dagger down,
walked slowly forward.
The king loosed his arm from Li.

"Xau," said Li. "They are hostages."

Xau was meant to walk away
in hostage situations.
He didn't. He looked at Li.
"We cannot leave them to die."

Li's options stark. To defy the king.
Or follow him into the beast's trap.
An instant's indecision
before Li dipped his head to Xau.

Xau reached for the girl's forehead,
Li holding her in place
so that the beast could not
use her to assault the king.

The girl jerked in Li's grip—
The horses squealed,
high-pitched, ear-piercing—
The king screamed—

Li stood. Held the girl—
Li forsworn, his oath broken—
His king unshielded,
snared in the beast's trap—

The king's screams stopped.
The girl sagged in Li's arms.
Freed. The king sank to his knees,
shivering, vomiting.

The girl said something. In Sumbrese?
Her face naked as her body,
flashing from fear to fragile hope
as she looked at the king.

Li pulled off his desert robes,
offered them to the girl,
crouched down beside Leong
who was examining the king.

"Xau," said Leong. "Stop. Now.
Your pulses are weak, uneven."
The king touched Leong's hand, said,
"We accept the risk. We must try."

The little boy dropped his dagger,

walked forward. "Such fun.
If you've finished retching,
let's play again."

The boy so short
Li knelt to hold him.
Xau knelt opposite Li,
laid his hand on the boy—

The boy jolted—
The horses squealed
as if they were dying—
The king screamed—

Then the boy trembled
like a scared puppy, freed.
The king doubled over,
gasping, pale, vomiting bile.

The boy started crying
and Xau's guard Shuen,
who had a son about that age,
lifted him in his arms.

A second girl came over.
"Had enough? We can end this game
if you order your men
to stay away from my lair."

"No."

"Then play again."

Longer. Worse. The king collapsed
when he finally freed the girl,
lay gasping for breath, ashen,
Leong trying to help him.

Li heard the beast's laughter,
looked round to see the last girl
plunge the dagger in her own belly.
"Three out of four. Well played."

She began dying noisily, messily.
Xau looked away, looked at Li.
"Li." Xau fought to speak.
"Help her. Please."

Li went to her, kissed her forehead,
drew his sword across her throat.
Returned to Xau. Bent down.
Tried to find words. None came.

Emptiness vast as the desert.
The king's eyes on his.

SHARDS

Bright even beneath the awning
stretched overhead.

Li, captain of King Xau's guards,
picked up a loose handful of sand,
warm, let it run through his fingers.
He sat beside his king,
the other guards at a distance
so Li could say what he must.

"Xau—" said Li, and stopped.
Weighed what he had done,
and what he had not done.
The girl he had killed.
The king he'd failed to protect.

King Xau waited, pale, patient,
propped up against a saddlebag,
breath labored.

"Xau—it's likely we will face
more hostage situations,
now that the beast knows
they are effective against you."

Xau said nothing, looked east
to where the children sat,
being fed by Shuen and Leong.

"Next time," said Li,
"you cannot cooperate.
Doing so yields control
to the beast, and endangers you."

"They would have died.
All four of them."

Li nodded.
"You are the king.
Your life is worth more.
That is the way of things."

"No," said Xau flatly,
only that one word. Final.

As if something broke inside Li then,
as if he took the splintered shards,
turned them on Xau.
"If not your own life,
surely your *kingdom* is worth more—"

Xau jolted as if he'd been struck.
"If it comes to that—
if there is no other way
to safeguard Meqing,
no other way to defeat the beast,
we will sacrifice hostages."

They sat, silent,
beneath the awning,
the day bright around them.

BREATH

In the desert darkness,
King Xau lay propped up
on a saddlebag,
his orders given,
Subetei's scouts ridden out
in search of the beast's lair.

Hillier here, sand swept
over limestone and sandstone.
No pain, except when his leg
reminded him he was lame,
but a breathlessness
that kept him from sleep.

He stared up at the patterned stars;
listened to the splashing
of the tiny waterfall
that fed the oasis,
the small sounds of the horses.

Xau tried to get his breath,
thought about the day ahead—
whether the scouts would find the beast—
whether he would be able to ride—
though the others would kill the beast
without him if necessary—
if they could—
if—

Enough—
nothing more he could do
until the scouts returned—

Xau shifted, looked at the moon,
three days past full,
thought back to the night
that Micha had foaled,
the moonlit pasture,
the wind-stirred leaves.

This year's foals would be
two months, maybe three months old,
still a little ungainly.
When he got home (if he got home),
he'd take his children
to inspect the foals with him,
spend a whole day over it.

Xau shifted again
to check on his guards,
Shuen standing watch,
the rest curled in their blankets.

Li, captain of his guards,
sat up beside him,
either woken by Xau's restlessness
or not asleep in the first place.

Li touched Xau's forehead,
offered him water.
Xau made the hand sign for all-well,
watched Li go over to Shuen,
watched him return
and sit down cross-legged at his side.

Easier to breathe with Li there,
a weight shared.

After a time
Xau said the words
that they both understood,
that he did not need to say aloud,
said them anyhow, his voice a breath,
"Li. Always there when I need you.
Thank you."

"Nowhere I would rather be."

Grief then,
thinking of Li,
Li the one he worried most about,
more even than his children,
their lives ahead of them, full of incident,
Li who might only look backward.

To the east the stars withdrew,
paleness spreading in the sky.

A little lizard,
no longer than Xau's thumb,
darted onto a rock near Xau's feet,
bobbed its head,
puffed its throat out hugely.

Over and over,
claiming its territory
or perhaps showing off for some female.

Together Xau and Li
watched the little lizard.

COMFORT

Neither King Xau's guards
nor the horse warriors
could calm the small boy
when he woke in tears.

The boy's thin body shook
with the force of his crying.
He clutched his blanket,
cowered when they approached.

Xau got to his feet carefully,
walked partway toward the boy,

sat down by a large rock,
working to catch his breath.

A moment's hesitation
before the boy bolted for Xau,
wrapped his arms around the king,
clung to him.

Xau held him
while the boy's gulping slowed,
eased him down onto his lap,
held him again.

Held him as the boy sniffled.
Thought of his own children,
how, if things went well,
he could be home by winter.

Held him as the guards
stretched an awning over them;
held him as Subetei's scouts
began returning.

By mid-morning all three children
were clustered round the king
as he folded a piece of paper
into crane and horse and sampan boat.

A pair of scouts came over.
Bowed deeply. Gave their report.
The beast's lair found.
Fourteen more hostages.

BEAST

1. Outside.

A stench of rotting meat
leaked from the entrance cavern
into the desert dusk
where King Xau waited
for his scouts to come out.

His guards and the horse warriors
had dismounted, ready to fight;
Xau still sat his horse,
conserving his strength.

2. Entrance cavern.

Dark. At the back,
blocking off an inner cave,
the beast's hostages:
a dozen women, two children,
each naked, each holding a dagger
to their own belly.

"Good morning, Horse King.
I offer you a trade,"
said the tallest woman,
the beast speaking through her.
"My playmates for your oath
to leave me in peace."

"No," said Xau.

"No? You would watch them die?"
Shadows shifted behind her.

"A trick!" yelled Li on Xau's left
as Xau caught the glint of metal.
The naked hostages turned,
ran into the inner cave
as from out that darkness
poured armored men.

Xau drew his sword
as the beast's men
rushed straight at him.
The horse warriors raced forward,
blocking Xau from the enemy,
his guards forming
an inner shield around him.

The battle brief but brutal.
All the beast's men killed,
along with thirteen horse warriors.

3. Descent.

Xau limped after his men
into the inner cave,
ten of the horse warriors
carrying torches.
The cave floor sloped steadily down
past bed rolls, food, chairs, pots.

Beyond a narrow gap
the stench of putrefaction grew so strong
Xau breathed through his mouth.
The torches flickered on corpses:
thousands upon thousands of corpses
heaped high on either side,
reaped by the beast.

Water dripped from the cavern roof
as the way descended
deeper and deeper.

4. Lair.

Into a cave lit with lanterns,
yellow light catching
on stained tools of torture;
on the glistening, tentacled,
six-eyed, six-mouthed beast;
on the naked hostages
ringed round the beast,
blades to their bellies.

Xau called a halt
beyond the beast's reach,
its touch a trap
that bound men to it.

"Will you trade now?"
the beast asked, speaking for itself
in a six-mouthed echoing.
"Their lives for mine."

"No."
Xau played his only gambit.
"Release them and we promise you
a quick death. If not,
we will seal you in this cave
and let you starve."

The beast laughed,
a hollow, sixfold malevolence.
"You're bluffing, Horse King.
You lack Tahj's flair for cruelty.
I have a better bargain.
Stay here with me, alone, unarmed,
and I will surrender one playmate

for each hour's entertainment."

Xau weighed it up, wary of trickery:
faster, surer to sacrifice the hostages,
to order his men to riddle
the beast with arrows.
End this now.

Expedient, effective, easy
to give that order.
That did not make it right.

The risk in accepting
the beast's bargain low—
nowhere left for the beast to hide—
none of its soldiers left—
no matter what happened to Xau himself,
his men could kill the beast.

The risk in accepting low.
The cost high.

Xau looked at the women, the children,
balanced their lives
against his,
nodded to the beast.
"If you free both children first,
then we will send our men away,
stay here alone with you—"

"No!" Li shouted,
stepped between Xau and the beast,
set his hands on Xau's shoulders,
a shield, an anchor.
"Xau—you cannot trust it.
The beast would torture you,
try to make you its puppet—"

"We know. We see no other way
to save the hostages."
Xau took a breath.
He knew what he must say next,
yet the saying of it hard.
"Li, afterward, if I am alive,
but not myself,
kill me."

Denial, desolation in Li's face,

Li's hands holding Xau back.
Xau reached for words,
for explanation, apology, solace.
Found none.

Slowly, Li let go of Xau,
bowed very low.

Xau bowed back, equally deep,
turned to the beast.
"Let the children go,
and we will stay with you.
At the end of each hour,
you will free one of the women.
If not, our soldiers will kill you."

That sixfold inhuman laugh. Callous. Cruel.
"You expect the children as a gift?
That isn't the deal I offered, Horse King.
But close enough.
Agreed."

5. *Torment.*

Three of the women stripped Xau,
tied him spread-eagled
to an iron frame.

The beast extended a suckered tentacle,
touched Xau. "Join me, Horse King."

The beast's thoughts tore into Xau,
bared every hurt he'd ever borne,
the girl plunging the dagger in her belly,
the horse rolling, Atun underneath,
Shazia dying, cradling their son—

Gloating, the beast flaunted its plan:
Xau would tell his soldiers he'd persuaded
the beast to mend its ways—
Xau's men would seize any justification
to have their king safe—
with Xau subverted,
the beast would be unstoppable—

"No!"
Xau battled,
beat back the beast's thoughts

as he'd fought to free its victims,
the three children, Gul,
back and back to Enlai and further,
fought as he had once defied a demon
though it borrowed his brother's voice—

The beast screamed then,
a cacophonous sixfold screech,
snatched its tentacle away,
retreated from his mind.

"Very well," hissed the beast.
"I will persuade you."

One of the women selected
a metal instrument,
inserted the tip
under Xau's left thumbnail,
pushed.

Xau stifled a scream
as the nail separated,
as the woman repeated the procedure
with his fingernails.

The woman inspected Xau's little finger,
prodded the bloodied tip,
placed a vise around the finger.
Tightened the vise slowly,
waited,
tightened it a fraction more,
waited, waited,
tightened it more—

Xau shouted as his finger broke,
begged when she moved the vise
to his next finger,
his voice a whimper, a child's plea.
"Stop, please stop."

"Are you ready to cooperate?"

"No."

The woman reached for the vise.

Xau tried to think of Hana:
how she rode as if she

and her horse were one;
the feel of her against him.
He told himself this would end,
that he might see her again.

Could not hold any thought
once the vise tightened.

The world shrank
to his body's breaking.
Whip, blade, brand, hammer,
the smell of burnt flesh,
his incremental emasculation.

Hour upon red hour.
Over and over the beast asked,
"Are you ready to cooperate?"

Over and over Xau refused.
Not bravely, not well.
He begged, sobbed, sniveled,
retched, pissed himself.
Yet he refused.

LAST WATCH

Li the first to reach the king—
Xau tied to an iron frame,
his body broken—
arms, legs, feet, fingers, ribs—
his groin a red ruin.

One breath to take it in
before Li bowed very deeply,
said, in case the king had not seen,
"The beast is dead."

"The hostages?"

"Safe."

Leong beside them then,
palpating Xau gently. Stopping.
"Xau." Leong's voice soft.
"You're dying. You cannot live
with wounds like these."

"We understand."

Leong bowed, stepped back,
left Li alone beside the king.
Li touched the king's forehead.
"If you wish, I will speed your death."

"No." The king's eyes on his.
"Take us outside. Please."

*

In the bright, dry, desert air,
Li laid Xau down gently, carefully,
sat down cross-legged beside him,
helped him drink,
wiped his face clean.

The king struggled for air,
struggled to speak.
"Not your fault. This.
Do not blame yourself later."

Li said nothing,
only set his hand on Xau's forehead,
held it lightly there.

A long time before Xau spoke again.
"Li. Stay. Until."

Li nodded.
A moment before he managed
to say the words he wished to say.
"Nowhere I would rather be."

He sat beside his king
beneath the wide clear sky.

RETURN

Set aside your crown, King Xau,
that crown of war, alliances, duty.
Your strength is spent,
your deeds are done.
Rest a while and remember.

Return to the horse country,

that third summer, that sea of grass;
return to Hana's people, moving, restless,
across the wide grasslands,
tents for their homes, horses for their wealth.

Return to the hills
where the wild horses waited under starlight
for you to come, night after night,
how you laid your hands on them,
breath mingling with theirs.

Return to the night of the Lotus Moon
when you rode bareback on the wild horses,
you and the nine men who shielded you,
closer than brothers;
you and the guards and the horses
racing, reckless,
through that sea of grass;
how the horse beneath you stretched into a gallop,
the wind on your bare arms,
the pounding of hooves.

MORTAL

No earthquake, no thunder
when King Xau died.
Only the weeping of the women
for whom he'd laid down his life;
the sobs of a small boy
who placed a paper boat
on the king's broken body;
the horse warriors loosing
their hair from its braids;
his guards kneeling to kiss
his cold forehead.

THE SIGN OF THE DRAGON

Keng knew before she told him,
knew when he saw her waiting,
stretched flat on the bare rock,
wings hinged tight to her sides.

"Your father is dead."
The dragon's breath ash,

her words ash in his heart,
his father never coming home.

He knelt to her then,
there on the high mountain,
hiding neither his grief nor his fear,
wondering if she would kill him.

"I name you king."
The gold gone from her eyes,
only the black of coal left.
"Go claim your throne."

Hard to think, to take it in.
His father dead. The kingship his.
How would the dragon furnish proof?
A crown? One of her scales?—"How?"

The dragon snorted.
"You expect a trophy?
I have named you king.
The steward will know. Go."

Keng got to his feet, bowed.
He did not feel like a king,
did not wish to be king.
"Thank you. For your lessons."

The dragon said nothing,
so Keng wiped his face dry
with his sleeve,
set off down the mountain.

EXECUTION

The combined armies
of three kingdoms
watched as Donal stood,
his longsword drawn.

On the dirt in front of Donal,
chained, shackled, terrified,
cowered Tahj.

Donal reached for rage—
thought of the war,
the reaping of lives,

the monster's machinations,
Xau's death.
Xau.

No anger answered,
only the well-worn wasteland
of desolation.
Donal raised his sword,
brought it down cleanly,
cleaved Tahj in two.

He wiped his sword.
He walked away.

ADDENDUM TO THE RECOLLECTIONS OF ARTOCH,

SENIOR ADVISOR TO KING XAU

A waste? Hardly.

You think a king
worth more than other men?
Xau did not,
despite my efforts
to correct his misconception.

In matters of state,
a king *is* worth more than other men.
And a king's death, too,
is worth more than other men's,
though I doubt Xau looked
beyond those fourteen people,
seeing them as sufficient cause
in themselves.

Xau's sacrifice—
the hours of torment endured
for those fourteen women and children—
turned him into a legend in Sumbral,
a mythic figure to match King Nariz.
The peace between our countries
is anchored in that act.

Hardly a waste!

And yet when Captain Li returned
with the king's body,
I shouted at him,
shouted that he'd abandoned Xau,
that he'd failed in his duty.

Perhaps the worst thing I ever did,
shouting at Li that day.
Yes, perhaps the worst.

BURIAL

They buried him at dusk,
he whose name was known
across half the world,
his body shrouded in white,
the mourners robed in white,
white candles in his children's hands.

His guards bore his litter
to the graveside,
lowered him into the earth.
One by one, silent,
the guards drew their swords,
placed them by his body.

The captain of the guards last.
He laid down his sword,
turned to bow to the new king.
Walked, weaponless, alone,
away from the graveside.
No speeches. No songs.

CORONATION

A court ceremony,
a piece of pageantry,
weeks late,
the power Keng's from the hour
that the dragon had named him king.

Bare-headed,
robed in crimson silk,
even his feet in soft red slippers,
Keng walked the marbled aisle

between two silken scarlet seas
of ministers, magistrates, ambassadors,
scholars, advisors, army commanders,
a rubied splendor broken only
by the black of his guards,
the white of his father's widow.

Keng knelt on the bottom step
of the massive dragon throne,
bent his bare head.

The assembly silent, still
as the steward set the crown
on Keng's head,
then a manyfold rustling
as people prostrated themselves:
every man, every woman
flattened to the floor.

Keng took a breath,
accepted the weight of that,
ascended his throne.

THE SIGN OF THE KING

Cold,
that first night in the horse country,
autumn on the way,
but Li didn't put up his tent.
He lay on the grass,
rolled in a blanket.
Stared up at the stars,
waiting in case the wild horses came,
sent, somehow, by King Xau.

Woke at dawn.
No wild horses.
His king, his friend, dead.

Li put the pack saddle and bags
onto Narson, mounted Kuan.
Rode on into the steppe,
pushing the thought of Xau away.
Nothing more that day
than wind-stirred grass,
the rhythm of the horse beneath him,

a hawk overhead.

On the second night he drank
a bottle of rice wine.
Found no comfort in it.
Woke up stiff, chilled.
Saddled the horses.
Rode, the grasslands extending
as if without limit.

At times,
the memory of Xau unstoppable.
The king's broken body,
the king struggling to speak,
telling Li not to blame himself,
but the fault Li's, the failure Li's,
Li who had been captain
of the king's guards.

Li shouted out as he rode,
shouted for forgiveness, for a sign,
for the wild horses to come.
Nothing.

On the fourth day
he saw smoke in the distance,
an encampment of horse warriors.
Li wanted no company,
turned his horses aside.

When it rained at night,
he set up the tent,
otherwise he slept on the ground.
He took care of the horses
and little else,
subsisted on dried meat and nuts,
his hair tangled, greasy,
his clothes grimy.

One night in his tent,
over the sound of rain,
a pounding of hooves.
Li bolted outside.

"Li, give me a hand, will you?"

Gan. Gan who had been a king's guard once.

Gan and two horses.
Only Gan.

Li unsaddled one of the horses,
carried Gan's bags into the tent.
Gan came in after him, dripping wet.
A long fumbling delay
while Gan lit a lamp.

Li blinked back brightness.

"You look rough," said Gan,
foraging in a saddlebag.
He pulled out a bruised pear,
gave it to Li. "Here. Eat something,
then I'll get you cleaned up."

The bruised pear in Li's hands.
He stared down at it.

"Eat, Captain," said Gan.

"I'm not captain anymore.
I stepped down."
Another way Li had failed Xau,
by refusing Keng, Xau's son.

"You'll always be Xau's captain," said Gan.
"And he wants you safe."

"Wanted," corrected Li.

"Wants," said Gan. "I didn't know
how I was going to find you,
but once I crossed the Guang Yun river
the horses led me straight to you."

The patter of rain, Gan watching him.
Li turned Gan's words over,
trying to find in them
the proof he needed.

Tears streamed down Li's face.
He took a bite of pear.

THE CAT'S EPILOGUE

Peace, war, treaties
mean nothing to her.
The new king in her rooms:
that is significant.

The new king is noisier, disruptive,
displaces her from the desk.
He offers her tidbits,
but they are the wrong tidbits.
Where is her egg yolk?
The pale chicken flesh?

She is too old for change,
too old to seek new territory.
Instead she withholds her favors,
declines to be touched,
retreats behind a cupboard.

The new king, contrite,
crouches on hands and knees,
proffers water, milk, crab meat.
He has not groomed recently,
yet his face is wet.

It is nothing to her.
She stays behind the cupboard,
resolute.

Comes then a softness,
a warmth that is not sunlight.
She neither sees nor smells him,
yet the old king is near,
his steady calmness,
his love.

She inches out,
rubs her head, briefly,
against the new king's legs.

A month before order
is fully restored,
the new king trained,
the egg yolk hers again.

TWO WEEKS

In the sixteenth year of Keng's reign,
at the start of summer,
two weeks with his twins.

Two weeks stolen from crown and court,
from ambassadors, ministers, merchants,
ceremonies, inspections, reviews,
the never-ending negotiations.
Incredible how a land at peace
demanded so much attention.

Two weeks camping by a lake,
the twins, seven years old,
learning to swim, to fish.
Nya, his daughter, solemnly teaching
her brother to fletch an arrow,
a skill her Aunt Ying had taught her.

Riding, running, skimming stones;
water battles in the warm lake.
Shan, his son, hair braided
like a miniature horse warrior,
forever asking questions:
"Who's the strongest guard?"
"How do horses sleep standing up?"
"Why don't rocks burn?"

Evenings round the fire.
Fresh fish, rice, dried plums,
the guards singing,
Nya and Shan crowding Keng's lap,
the smell of smoke caught in their hair.

On the last night,
Keng took the blankets from the tent,
laid them on a patch of grass.
He stretched out on his back
beneath the patterned stars,
a child on either side.
Spun stories about talking tigers
until Nya fell asleep.

Down near the water
a frog croaked.

Shan yawned, wriggled closer.
"What was Grandpapa Xau like?"

Keng took a breath, said,
"He liked horses,
and training with his guards,
and pickled cucumbers."

"Hmmm. I like pickled cucumbers."
Shan's voice was drowsy, sleep soft.

Keng waited,
but no more questions came,
only memories, worn with use.
That day in the boat,
his father wearing a bamboo hat
like a rice farmer.
Riding together through snow.
His father's hand on his shoulder
as they watched an eagle
ride the wind.

Years ago now,
years ago.

A NOTE ON THE TITLE

When I was a child, I was a frequent visitor to a bookstore called "At the Sign of the Dragon," drawn there not only by the array of science fiction and fantasy books, but by the kindness of the owners, Marion and Richard Van Der Voort. Xau's story is titled in honor of their bookstore.

AT THE SIGN OF THE DRAGON

In Memory of Marion Van Der Voort

Inside were dragons
of every color and size,
dragons who reasoned
and dealt in magic,
and interspersed among them:
a host of talking rabbits,
a blind space poet,
and all the true kings.

I found myself
inside the stories—
in the reading of them,
and in the friendship
of the couple
who owned the bookshop
(for it was a bookshop).

They led me, book by book,
through worlds I fell in love with.
So that when I lay outside,
reading on the grass
in the boundless summers
of my childhood,
I was not alone,
but part of their
fellowship of readers.

Inside were dragons.

ACKNOWLEDGMENTS

I am indebted to many people, but I would especially like to thank the following.

Timons Esaias for his invaluable critique of the whole manuscript and for his friendship over thirty years.

Lisa Rodgers, my agent, for championing the book and helping me improve it.

F. J. Bergmann and Joe Morey for publishing the first part of Xau's story, and for their unstinting support.

Chris Atkeson for Chinese meals, a place to stay, Star Trek enthusiasm, and many other kindnesses when I was starting out as a writer.

Roger Dutcher for the cards he sent even when I wasn't writing science fiction or fantasy, making me feel a part of the community.

Joe Coluccio for letting me read my poetry at PARSEC meetings.

Bernadette Harris for answering medical questions (it's my own fault that I sometimes disregarded her advice).

Adrian Simmons for letting me include poems that were forthcoming in *Heroic Fantasy Quarterly*, and for introducing me to the work of Gary McCluskey.

Gary McCluskey for turning my words into his extraordinary art.

Patrick Disselhorst and Joshua Bilmes at JABberwocky Literary Agency for making the pandemic-era edition of this book possible.

Lastly but most importantly, Andrew, William, and Lucy for letting Xau into our family, warning me that he was too perfect, and giving feedback on the poems as I was writing them.

Thank you all.

ABOUT THE AUTHOR

Mary Soon Lee was born and raised in London, but has lived in Pittsburgh for thirty years. She is a Grand Master of the Science Fiction & Fantasy Poetry Association, and a three-time winner of both the AnLab Readers' Award and the Rhysling Award. Her work has appeared in a wide range of publications including *American Scholar*, the *Magazine of Fantasy & Science Fiction*, the *Pittsburgh Post-Gazette*, and *Science*.

She is also the author of two collections of science poetry: *How to Navigate Our Universe* and *Elemental Haiku: Poems to honor the periodic table three lines at a time.*

Once upon a time, she earned a degree in mathematics from Cambridge University. She hides her online presence with a cryptically named website (marysoonlee.com).

For those looking for more personal information about her, she notes that her parents were both immigrants, her father from Malaysia, her mother from Ireland, and offers this short autobiographical poem:

HALF-CASTE

Privileged child of immigrant parents,
I jettisoned Malay, Hokkien, Gaelic,
the words they spoke before they met;

cribbed an accent from my schoolmates,
my London birth a guarantee
of passport, health care, cups of tea.

Poems from this collection first appeared in the following publications:

"Interregnum," *Star*Line* #36.4, Autumn 2013

"Guarded," *Crowned: The Sign of the Dragon, Book 1;* Dark Renaissance Books, 2015

"Training: Weights," *Crowned: The Sign of the Dragon, Book 1;* Dark Renaissance Books, 2015

"Succession," *Red Rock Review* #34, Fall 2014

"Grief," *Crowned: The Sign of the Dragon, Book 1;* Dark Renaissance Books, 2015

"Map," *Crowned: The Sign of the Dragon, Book 1;* Dark Renaissance Books, 2015

"Not So," *Crowned: The Sign of the Dragon, Book 1;* Dark Renaissance Books, 2015

"Training: Stances," *Crowned: The Sign of the Dragon, Book 1;* Dark Renaissance Books, 2015

"The Horse Lord," *Ideomancer,* Volume 13, Issue 3, September 2014

"Tutor," *Rune,* 2014

"Horses," *Crowned: The Sign of the Dragon, Book 1;* Dark Renaissance Books, 2015

"Training: Horse," *Mirror Dance,* Spring 2015

"Shazia," *Crowned: The Sign of the Dragon, Book 1;* Dark Renaissance Books, 2015

"Wedding Gifts," *Crowned: The Sign of the Dragon, Book 1;* Dark Renaissance Books, 2015

"Training: Sparring," *Crowned: The Sign of the Dragon, Book 1;* Dark Renaissance Books, 2015

"Wolf Moon," *Crowned: The Sign of the Dragon, Book 1;* Dark Renaissance Books, 2015

"Crossing," *Crowned: The Sign of the Dragon, Book 1;* Dark Renaissance Books, 2015

"Pigeon Six," *Uppagus* #11, April 2015

"Setting Out," *Crowned: The Sign of the Dragon, Book 1;* Dark Renaissance Books, 2015

"Thirty-Eighth War Between Innis and Meqing: First Battle," *Crowned: The Sign of the Dragon, Book 1;* Dark Renaissance Books, 2015

"Rose," *Crowned: The Sign of the Dragon, Book 1;* Dark Renaissance Books, 2015

"Khyert," *Crowned: The Sign of the Dragon, Book 1;* Dark Renaissance Books, 2015

"Moon Swan," *Star*Line* #38.1, Winter 2015

"Thirty-Eighth War Between Innis and Meqing: Second Battle," *Crowned: The Sign of the Dragon, Book 1;* Dark Renaissance Books, 2015

"Leong," *Crowned: The Sign of the Dragon, Book 1;* Dark Renaissance Books, 2015

"Midnight," *Crowned: The Sign of the Dragon, Book 1;* Dark Renaissance Books, 2015

"Thirty-Eighth War Between Innis and Meqing: Third Battle," *Crowned: The Sign of the Dragon, Book 1;* Dark Renaissance Books, 2015

"Tsung's Battle," *Crowned: The Sign of the Dragon, Book 1;* Dark Renaissance Books, 2015

"Down," *Crowned: The Sign of the Dragon, Book 1;* Dark Renaissance Books, 2015

"Donal," *Crowned: The Sign of the Dragon, Book 1;* Dark Renaissance Books, 2015

"Surgeon," *Crowned: The Sign of the Dragon, Book 1;* Dark Renaissance Books, 2015

"The Matter of the Horses," *Ideomancer,* Volume 13, Issue 4, December 2014

"Training: Running," *Crowned: The Sign of the Dragon, Book 1;* Dark Renaissance Books, 2015

"What Xau Ran From," *Crowned: The Sign of the Dragon, Book 1;* Dark Renaissance Books, 2015

"The Queen's War," *Crowned: The Sign of the Dragon, Book 1;* Dark Renaissance Books, 2015

"Night," *Ship of Fools* #72, Winter 2015

"Memorials," *Crowned: The Sign of the Dragon, Book 1;* Dark Renaissance Books, 2015

"Stables," *Songs of Eretz Poetry Review,* February 2015

"Training: Dark," *Crowned: The Sign of the Dragon, Book 1;* Dark Renaissance Books, 2015

"Dragonslayer," *Crowned: The Sign of the Dragon, Book 1;* Dark Renaissance Books, 2015

"Companionship," *Songs of Eretz Poetry Review,* March 2015

"Training: Carry," *Crowned: The Sign of the Dragon, Book 1;* Dark Renaissance Books, 2015

"Naming," *Crowned: The Sign of the Dragon, Book 1;* Dark Renaissance Books, 2015

"Decoration," *Crowned: The Sign of the Dragon, Book 1;* Dark Renaissance Books, 2015

"A Handful of Nights," *Crowned: The Sign of the Dragon, Book 1;* Dark Renaissance Books, 2015

"Artoch," *Crowned: The Sign of the Dragon, Book 1;* Dark Renaissance Books, 2015

"Afterward," *Crowned: The Sign of the Dragon, Book 1;* Dark Renaissance Books, 2015

"What Xau Remembered," *Uppagus* #8, October 2014

"One Week," *Crowned: The Sign of the Dragon, Book 1;* Dark Renaissance Books, 2015

"Bedtime," *Crowned: The Sign of the Dragon, Book 1;* Dark Renaissance Books, 2015

"Help," *Crowned: The Sign of the Dragon, Book 1;* Dark Renaissance Books, 2015

"What They Brought," *Crowned: The Sign of the Dragon, Book 1;* Dark Renaissance Books, 2015

"Route," *Crowned: The Sign of the Dragon, Book 1;* Dark Renaissance Books, 2015

"Camp," *Crowned: The Sign of the Dragon, Book 1;* Dark Renaissance Books, 2015

"Aftershock," *Crowned: The Sign of the Dragon, Book 1;* Dark Renaissance Books, 2015

"Scalpel," *Crowned: The Sign of the Dragon, Book 1;* Dark Renaissance Books, 2015

"Scared," *Crowned: The Sign of the Dragon, Book 1;* Dark Renaissance Books, 2015

"Girl," *Crowned: The Sign of the Dragon, Book 1;* Dark Renaissance Books, 2015

"Cure," *Star*Line* #38.2, Spring 2015

"In Honor of the King," *Crowned: The Sign of the Dragon, Book 1;* Dark Renaissance Books, 2015

"Micha," *Songs of Eretz Poetry Review,* April 2016

"Thirty-Ninth War Between Innis and Meqing: Commencement," first published in the 2020 ebook edition of *The Sign of the Dragon*; reprinted in *Heroic Fantasy Quarterly*

"Fault," *Songs of Eretz Poetry Review,* April 2016

"Messengers," *Grievous Angel,* October 2016

"Demon Fire," *Tales of the Talisman,* Volume X, Issue 3, Winter 2014/2015

"Necromancer," *HWA Poetry Showcase,* Volume II, 2015

"Angshan," *Rune,* 2017

"Midsummer's Day," *Songs of Eretz Poetry Review,* January 2016

"Training: Endurance," *Apex Magazine,* Issue 75, August 2015

"Dragon," *Dreams & Nightmares* #102, January 2016

"Daybreak," *Tales of the Talisman,* Volume X, Issue 3, Winter 2014/2015

"Numbers," *Star*Line* #37.2, Spring 2014

"Darkness," *Star*Line* #38.3, Summer 2015

"Tirron," *Mirror Dance,* Summer 2017

"Returning," *Open Mouse*, May 2016

"After," *Star*Line* #38.2, Spring 2015

"Demon Stain," *Dreams & Nightmares* #99, September 2014

"Dark Harvest," *Mirror Dance*, Winter 2017

"Brighid," *Apex Magazine*, Issue 61, June 2014

"Respect," *Polu Texni*, January 2017

"Second Sight," *Rune*, 2017

"Her Thousand Faces," forthcoming in *The Magazine of Speculative Poetry*

"Solstice," *Songs of Eretz Poetry Review*, September 2016

"Jumble," *Heroic Fantasy Quarterly* #43, February 2020

"Captain," *Songs of Eretz Poetry Review*, August 2016

"Bespeaking: Riddles," *Star*Line* #40.3, Summer 2017

"Li," *Songs of Eretz Poetry Review*, August 2016

"Widow," *Songs of Eretz Poetry Review*, July 2016

"Opus," *Star*Line* #38.3, Summer 2015

"Shade," *Silver Blade* #34, Spring 2017

"What Atun Learned," *Star*Line* #38.3, Summer 2015

"Traveling," *Ship of Fools* #76, Fall 2016

"Ford," first published in the 2020 ebook edition of *The Sign of the Dragon*; reprinted in
    Heroic Fantasy Quarterly

"Not Like This," *Apex Magazine*, Issue 87, August 2016

"Why the King Wept," *Uppagus* #17, April 2016

"Dread," *Mirror Dance*, Winter 2015

"Hero," *Star*Line* #39.2, Spring 2016

"Vengeance," *Star*Line* #38.4, Fall 2015

"Another Week," *Songs of Eretz Poetry Review*, May 2016

"Inheritance," *Heroic Fantasy Quarterly* #28, May 2016

"Keng," *Ligature Works*, Issue 1, 2016

"Stay," *Songs of Eretz Poetry Review*, February 2017

"Portraits," *Songs of Eretz Poetry Review*, April 2017

"Monster: Puppeteer," *Apex Magazine*, Issue 104, January 2018

"Eligible," *Ship of Fools* #77, Spring 2017

"Arrow," *Songs of Eretz Poetry Review*, October 2016

"The Ride," *Star*Line* #38.1, Winter 2015

"Unsaid," *Uppagus* #25, September 2017

"The Hundred Dragons of Sumbral," *Star*Line* #37.4, Fall 2014

"The Path to Peace," *The Magazine of Fantasy & Science Fiction*, May/June 2017

"A Gift," *Dreams & Nightmares* #101, July 2015

"Again," *Dreams & Nightmares* #108, January 2018

"Stepmother," *Eye to the Telescope* #21, July 2016

"Between," *Uppagus* #24, July 2017

"The Wild Horses Came Hastening," *Silver Blade* #28, Fall 2015

"Sheep," *Ship of Fools* #76, Fall 2016

"Homecoming," *Songs of Eretz Poetry Review*, June 2016

"Dragon Mountain," *Heroic Fantasy Quarterly* #35, February 2018

"Recruits," *Mirror Dance,* Winter 2016

"Bowl," *Ship of Fools* #75, Spring 2016

"Lotus Moon," *Mythic Delirium* #4.2, October-December 2017

"Five Arrows," *Songs of Eretz Poetry Review,* March 2017

"Kingship," *The Magazine of Fantasy & Science Fiction,* January/February 2017

"Further Extracts from the Recollections of Artoch, Senior Advisor to King Xau," *Mirror Dance,* Summer 2016

"Daunted," *Dreams & Nightmares* #105, January 2017

"The Imperial War: Onset," *Grievous Angel,* January 2017

"Boatman," *Mithila Review* #9, 2017

"First Lesson," *Silver Blade* #30, Spring 2016

"Between Battles," *Heroic Fantasy Quarterly* #38, November 2018

"When King Xau was Gone," *Uppagus* #23, May 2017

"Seventeenth Lesson," *Heroic Fantasy Quarterly* #31, February 2017

"Judgment," *Songs of Eretz Poetry Review,* December 2016

"Mortal," *Spillway* #25, Summer 2017

"The Sign of the King," *Strange Horizons,* April 2017

"At the Sign of the Dragon," *Uppagus* #20, October 2016

"Half-Caste," *Main Street Rag* Volume 17, Number 3, Summer 2012